PUSH NOT THE RIVER

PUSH NOT THE RIVER

JAMES CONROYD MARTIN

Thomas Dunne Books
St. Martin's Griffin ❧ New York

For my parents,
John and Bette Martin

THOMAS DUNNE BOOKS.
An imprint of St. Martin's Press.

www.stmartins.com

Design by Phil Mazzone

Maps by Ray Martin

Papercut illustrations by Frances Drwal

Eagle illustration by Kenneth Mitchell

Library of Congress Cataloging-in-Publication Data

Martin, James Conroyd.
    Push not the river / James Conroyd Martin.
        p. cm.
    ISBN 0-312-31150-8 (hc)
    EAN 978-0312-31150-6
    ISBN 0-312-31153-2 (pbk)
    EAN 978-0312-31153-7
    I. Title.
PS3613.A779P87 2003
813'.6–dc21   2003053158

10 9

Acknowledgments

I wish to thank John A. Stelnicki for the translation of the original diary. Exceptional editing kudos go to editors Mary Rita Mitchell and Sally Kim. The wycinanki (vih-chee-nahn-kee), or Polish folk papercuts, are the courtesy of artist Frances Drwal, and the maps of the Partition Periods are the work of Ray Martin. Poland's white eagle was drawn by Kenneth Mitchell. And agent Albert Zuckerman found a way when there seemed to be none.

I also wish to thank those who have given me, over the years, suggestions, guidance, and moral support. These include countless family members, friends, and colleagues. The few I would like to single out are Piers Anthony, Marilyn Bricks, Ken Brown, Basia Brzozowska, Lorron Farani, Mary Frances Fabianski, Judi Free, Julie Grignaschi-Baumann, Scott Hagensee, Gary Holtey, Waclaw J. Jedrzejczak, Donald Kaminski, Edward Kaminski, Patrick Keefe, Kevin Kelly, Sophie Hodorowicz Knab, Jan Lorys, Sr. Mary Paul McCaughey O.P., Mike McCaughey, Ken Mitchell, Marta Muszynska, Bill Poplar, Robert Perkins, Alicia Rockwell, George Worth, and Pam Sourelis and the members of the Green Door Studio, Chicago, 1998–99.

Author's Note

The cornerstone of this novel is the unpublished diary of Countess Anna Maria Berezowska, translated into English from the Polish by her descendant John A. Stelnicki. Countess Berezowska began keeping a diary when her personal world began to disintegrate and writing became for her, I suspect, a great therapy. She sometimes read and copied into her own diary the colorful entries from her cousin Zofia's diary. It was Zofia's often risqué content that most likely accounted for subsequent generations' withholding the document from the public. For some decades, it was even sealed in wax and hidden away. Amazingly, the years of the countess' personal crises coincided with some of the most important years in all of Polish history: the Third of May Constitution years. It is fortunate that such a remarkable private view—and a woman's view—of those perilous years has survived.

Pronunciation Key

Częstochowa = Chehn-staw-haẃ-vah
Dniestr = Dnyehstr
Jan = Yahn
Jósef = Yú-zef
Halicz = Haĺi-leech
kasza = kasha
kołacz = kaw-watch
Kołłątaj = Kaw-wohń-tīe
Kościuszko = Kawsh-cheẃ-shkaw
Kraków = Krah-kooff
Michał = Mee-how
Paweł = Pah-vel
Sochaczew = Saw-haĺi-cheff
Stanisław = Stan-neesś-wahf
szlachta = shlacĺi-ta
Wilanów = Vee-lahń-ooff
żur = zhoor

The Partioning of Poland

The dotted outline indicates the partioning extremes assumed by
Prussia, Austria, and Russia in 1772, 1793, and 1795.

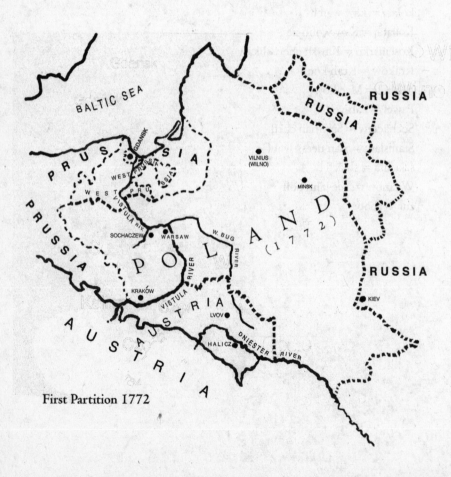

First Partition 1772

Second Partition 1793

Third Partition 1795

Prologue

Wherever you go,
you can never leave yourself behind.

–POLISH PROVERB

Sochaczew, 1779

Anna's eyelids fluttered briefly in the morning light, then flew back. The girl felt the pace of her heart increase. This was the day she had awaited, the twenty-sixth of July. Her name's day. She sat up immediately and looked to the table near the window. On it sat the package wrapped in red paper. She gave out a little sigh of relief.

She sprang spritelike from her bed, pulling at her nightdress. She washed and dressed quickly, donning the blue dress trimmed in lace and the glossy white leather shoes. These were worn only for special occasions. She worked overly hard at brushing her brown curls. She was too impatient, she knew, and when she drew the brush through a tangle, she saw herself wince in the mirror. It was a very grownup expression, one she had seen her mother use.

She brushed and brushed. A bad job would bring a light scolding from Luisa when it came time for braiding. Still, her mind was not on the task at hand. Time and again, her amber-flecked green eyes would shift in the mirror to where the red package sat in her line of sight. Tired as she had been the night before, she fought off sleep for as long as possible, fearing that the present might disappear somehow. But it had not. It was here and it was hers. She had only to look at it, red as a ripe apple and many times more inviting, to make certain.

3

Her morning rites finished in record time, Anna gingerly slid the package from the table into a tight, two-armed grasp. Taking special care with the opening and closing of her bedchamber door, she moved out into the hall and to the stairway. The aroma of coffee and breakfast sausages was familiar, but this was no usual day. She reached high for the banister and descended with the hesitating care of an old woman, stopping on each stair with a little jolt, until at last she came to the main floor of the country manor house.

Her mother was breakfasting in the dining room while the maid stood at her side pouring coffee into a china cup. Several pans steamed on the sideboard.

The dark-haired Countess Teresa Berezowska glanced up, smiled. "Good morning, Anna Maria. Happy name's day."

"Happy feast day, Anna," Luisa said in a cheerful tone. "How old is my little lady?"

Anna smiled, delighted at the attention. "Five!" she said. Her first instinct was to hold up the fingers of her right hand to underscore the fact, but she realized in the nick of time that doing so would cause her to drop the package. Her heart beat faster at the thought.

"A bowl of *kasza* with milk and a poached egg this morning," Luisa was saying, "and if you finish that off there will be some fluffy *babka* for this happy day."

Taking small, measured steps, she moved, as was her morning routine, to give her mother a kiss on the cheek. The countess leaned over to accommodate her daughter. Anna thought her mother the most beautiful woman she had ever seen. Her father's chair was empty, so she went directly to her own place. Carefully she positioned the package next to her plate. Freed of her treasure, she clambered up onto her chair.

Luisa placed Anna's breakfast before her, humming very prettily. Anna was determined to eat every bite, for she could smell the delicious iced *babka*. Where is it? she wondered. The light, sugary cake with its hidden raisins was her favorite.

Lifting the first spoonful of egg to her mouth, the girl noticed that her mother's violet-gray eyes were locked upon the red package—and that her smile had died away.

A little bell of alarm sounded in Anna's head. She put down her spoon. Her immediate thought was for support. "Where's Papa?"

"He's gone off on business," the countess replied. "Always some farm business."

Her mother's tone frightened the child. The countess' eyes moved from the package to her.

"Now what have we here, Anna Maria Berezowska? Is this your new doll?"

"No, Mama."

"I see. I thought not. The package seems neither the correct shape nor size. Where is it, then?"

Anna's lips were dry. "I . . . I didn't choose a doll."

The countess' mouth tightened. "But your father took you all the way to the capital yesterday for the express purpose of buying you a doll, one with a painted face, glass eyes, and real hair. Were there none to be found in all of Warsaw?"

"Oh, yes, there were many dolls, Mama, only—"

"Only what?"

"Only I chose this."

"You did, did you? You were quite deliberate, then, in going against my wishes. You were to have chosen a doll."

Anna didn't know what to say. Her mother did not raise her voice to her, never had. But Anna recognized the seriousness in her tone and steady gaze. Her little limbs trembled; she would not cry.

"Would you leave us now, Luisa?" the countess asked, smiling.

Anna's heart dropped. She had seen that smile before. She had learned that it wasn't a real smile. She longed to have old Luisa stay but knew to say nothing.

The maid curtsied, then crossed the room toward the kitchen door. She smiled at Anna, a smile that was a smile. The girl knew Luisa meant to give her courage, but it didn't help much.

"Open it up," the countess said, once the maid had vanished behind the swinging door. "Let's see what can be more amusing to a little girl than a new doll."

"Shouldn't we wait for Papa?"

"Open it, Anna Maria." The countess was not to be put off by the cleverness of a five-year-old.

Anna had been so caught up in the wonder of the gift that she had not thought about her mother's reaction. She started to tear clumsily at the well-wrapped package. Her hands were sweating.

It had been her first trip to the capital. Wide-eyed, she had sat on her father's lap as the carriage rattled along for what seemed hours and hours. They entered Warsaw at the western gate of the walled city, the coach vibrating and the wheels clacking along the cobbled streets. It was the most amazing thing, this city, like something from one of her books. "Oh, Father!" she cried. There passing before her was the Royal Castle. "Does the king live there? Truly?" Her father was smiling. "He does, indeed." They passed the Cathedral of Saint Jan, and the city mansions of the nobles—the *very* rich ones.

Magnates, her father called them. "Why aren't you a magnate?" she asked. "I have all the wealth I need," he laughed, hugging her to him. In the castle's outer courtyard the two craned their necks up at Zygmunt's Column. The bronze figure of the long-dead king held a cross in one hand, a sword in the other—like some warrior saint. He had been the one, her father told her, who moved the capital from Kraków to Warsaw. Years later she would remember the Royal Castle as merely massive and daunting, but the memory of her father's embrace—his strength, his warmth, and the faint scent of a shaving soap—she would carry with her always.

They continued then to the Market Square, a glittering honeycomb of shops and stalls. And Anna did see dolls that she liked, too, dolls of every description and recent style. Beautiful dolls. But once her eyes settled on that sparkling object she was now unwrapping, nothing else would do. "Is this what you truly wish, little Ania?" her father asked, using her diminutive. She looked up at him, realizing at once that her wish was his wish. "Oh, yes!" she cried. It was then—in the enchanting city of kings—that the notions of feast days and wishes and magic were sealed together in her mind, it seemed, forever.

The red paper was tearing away at one corner, then another. Something under it flashed and gleamed.

When the paper would not pull wholly free, the countess became impatient, moving swiftly to the girl's aid.

In moments it stood stripped of its wrappings. The translucent object seemed now to draw in the sun from every direction. It stood before the countess as if pulsing and glowing with warm life. The molding and cutting of the crystal were exquisite. Secured in a crystal base, the delicately carved legs seemed to thrust the body forward. The wings were extended as if for flight, the beak lifted in anticipation.

"What is *this?*" the countess cried.

Anna could not tell whether her mother was happily surprised, puzzled, or angry. Still, her fears momentarily disappeared at the sight of the marvel. "Oh, it's a bird, Mother. A crystal dove! Isn't it beautiful?"

"I can see for myself it's a bird, Anna Maria. But why should you or any little girl want such a thing? . . . And in place of the doll of your choice!"

"Because it's so pretty, Mama. You know I love birds. I've always wished for one, but Papa says they are meant to be free. This is a bird I can keep. See how it sparkles. And . . . it has magic!"

"Magic?"

"Oh, yes."

"What magic?"

"See how the light goes through it? It makes colors just like a rainbow."

"Much like a prism," the countess conceded.

"A what?"

"Never mind. Go on."

"Well, the merchant said that's a sign of magic. He said this bird will carry me anywhere I want to go. Even to the pot of gold at the end of the rainbow!"

"What a lot of bombast! The magic was not in the bird but on that wily merchant's tongue. I'll wager he wheedled a pretty price out of your father for this bit of nonsense!"

Anna felt her heart fluttering against her chest. She looked up into her mother's face, which seemed to have reddened slightly. "Oh, but Father . . ." Anna's words died away when the countess lifted a forefinger in a shushing motion.

"Anna Maria, darling, it was your *mother* who suggested the doll for your feast day, was it not? Don't you think your mother knows a bit more than you?"

Anna held back the tears. If only she could explain her love for the bird. She *had* tried, but her mother did not understand.

"You do get the strangest notions, dearest," her mother was saying, "and you just don't let go. Yes, you can look at the bird, but you can *play* with the doll."

Was there a softening to her tone? Anna dared to hope so.

Seizing the crystal bird, the countess carried it across the room and placed it on the uppermost shelf of the china cabinet, well out of Anna's reach. "It'll stay here until I decide what's to be done with it. If you don't want a doll—"

"But I have Buttons!"

The countess turned around. "An old rag doll!"

"I don't need another—"

"And so you won't have another, either. Perhaps you will just do without a present this year. Do you have any idea how you've upset your mother?"

Anna stared. Her mother's lips seemed to thin, then disappear.

"Do you?"

Anna couldn't speak.

"I see you do not. I'm going upstairs to lie down. Finish your break-fast." The countess left the dining room.

The girl did slowly finish her porridge and egg, cold as they were. As she ate, her wide, dry eyes never strayed from the cabinet that held the bird captive.

"Ah, Anna," Luisa chimed as she came in from the kitchen and bus-tled toward the sideboard, "I can see you're ready for your fluffy *babka*, my little feast-day girl!"

Anna, however, slipped quietly from the room before the maid turned around with the cake. She was halfway up the stairs when she heard Luisa calling her.

She did not turn back.

"What is it, little green eyes?" her father asked. He dismounted and stood tall before her. "Have you been crying? Why?"

Anna had been in the stable for over an hour awaiting his return. Bravely she had crept out of her room, down the servants' stairway, and through the kitchen to the back door. She crossed the yard and entered the stable. She waited nervously. When she was in such a state as this, she would thrust the extended fingers of both hands back through her long brown hair in a brushing movement, rudely simulating the soothing strokes the maid employed in brushing her hair. But today this oddly ner-vous motion of the hands agitated more than soothed. Even the presence there of the wonderfully majestic horses failed to divert her attention.

"Ania," her father pressed, lifting her up onto his empty saddle. "You've been pulling at your hair again . . . Tell me what the matter is."

She found herself looking down into her father's face. It was the first time she had sat on a horse, and she felt her heart racing. The great animal stirred slightly beneath her, like some mountain come alive. It was a thrilling moment, but she was not about to lose thought of the bird. She let the story spill from her, holding back tears. She had done all of her crying earlier in her room; she would not cry in front of anyone, not even in front of her father.

"This is serious," Count Berezowski announced at the end of the account.

"Must I give it up, Father? The crystal bird, must I?"

"Did your mother say you must?"

"No, she didn't *say* so."

"But you think she means as much?"

Anna nodded. She bit her lower lip. One hand moved unconsciously toward her hair.

"Well then, Anna," her father said, gently catching and restraining her hand, "we must not lose hope. I'll see what I can do."

"You'll talk to her?"

"Oh, I suspect she'll talk to me first," he said with a laugh. "But, yes, I'll talk to her."

"Oh, thank you, Papa!"

"Come along, now." He lifted her down from the horse, so that his mouth was close to her ear when he said, "Sometimes you must put yourself in the way of destiny."

Anna's arms tightened around her father's neck. He smelled of the fields, another scent to lock away in her memory.

"There, there, no promises. And if we are successful, Ania, it might mean you may have to do something to please your mother. Or give up something."

"Oh, anything, I'll do anything."

"I'll see what I can do."

Somehow her father met with success, for when Anna awoke the next morning, it was to the sight of the crystal dove gleaming on the table beside her bed. She picked it up gently, as if it were alive, mesmerized at the rainbow she thought she saw within. It would be years before she would find out what had been yielded for the sake of the glass bird; years also before her father's brief and enigmatic philosophy would find resonance in Anna's mind: *Sometimes you must put yourself in the way of destiny.*

Part One

There are three things that are
difficult to keep hidden:
a fire, a cold, and love.

—POLISH PROVERB

1

Halicz, 1791

S he stood motionless now, in a painter's tableau of flowers and grasses, a long distance from home, alone. It was only recent events—not the intervening years—that made Anna question her childhood attachment to the mythical. Today, in fact, the young girl who stood poised on the threshold of womanhood questioned the very world around her.

The afternoon was idyllic, the meadow at midday a canvas of color and warmth. A breeze stirred the wheat and barley fields nearby, coercing the spikes into graceful, rippling waves. Next year the meadow in which she stood would be made to produce also, but for now it was thickly green with overgrown grasses and rampant with late-summer wildflowers, birds, and butterflies.

To all of this Anna was coolly indifferent. She stood there, her black dress billowing in the breeze, vaguely aware of a bee that buzzed nearby. In time, though, her eyes found focus as she observed a few fallen leaves hurl themselves at the trunk of the solitary oak, whirl away, and come back again. In them—their detachment and their restless movement—she somehow felt a comradeship. She was as mindlessly driven as they. And from somewhere deep at her core, a keening rose up, piercing her, like a mournful siren from some unseen island.

How had it come to this? Only months before, upon the passing of the Constitution in May, Anna's universe had been complete and happy. The reform seemed to place her father in a good disposition. The Third of May Constitution did not threaten him, as it did some of the nobility. Count Samuel Berezowski was of the minor nobility, the *szlachta*, his great-great grandfather having been conferred the title of count when in 1683 he aided the legendary King Jan Sobieski and much of Christian Europe in keeping Vienna—and therefore Eastern Europe—from the Turks. The count managed his single estate himself and he already allowed his village of twelve peasant families liberal freedoms of thought and action. As was the custom, the peasants addressed him as Lord Berezowski.

It was a happy time for Anna's mother, too, because she was eight months with child. As a young girl, Countess Teresa Berezowska had gone against her parents' wishes, forgoing marriage into a magnate family for the dictates of the heart. This did not preclude, however, her own ambition to bring into the world children who would go on to make matches that would distinguish the family. Though her heart had been set on a first-born boy, she rejoiced with Samuel in the birth of their healthy, green-eyed girl, Anna Maria. She was confident that many childbearing years were left to her and that there would be a troop of boys to fill up the house. Instead, a succession of miscarriages ensued and her health grew frail, her beauty fragile. Still, the countess persisted against doctors' advice, until at last—nearly seventeen years after the birth of Anna—it seemed certain that she was to bring another child full term.

Anna's relationship with her mother improved after the incident with the crystal dove, but a certain distance between mother and daughter remained. Anna came to realize that while she was loved by both parents, her mother was much concerned with bringing boys into the world. While Anna's father gave his love freely, her mother inculcated in her—through the spoken and the unspoken—a sense of inadequacy that sent her into herself, into her own realm of imagination.

Alone in her books of fable and fairy tales and the myriad places they took her, Anna longed for a brother or sister to anchor her to the real world.

But it was not to be.

Feliks Paduch, one of Count Berezowski's peasants, had always been trouble. Since adolescence he had been involved in numerous thefts and brawls. At thirty, he was lazy, alcoholic, and spiteful, a man who questioned and resented his lot in life. Some peasants whispered, too, that he had been involved in the murder of a traveling Frenchman, but no one dared accuse him.

Countess Berezowska had encouraged her husband to evict Paduch, and he had nearly done so twice, but each time relented. A few days after the passing of the Third of May Constitution, Count Berezowski set out for the Paduch cottage in response to a local noble's complaint that Feliks had stolen several bags of grain. The *starosta* should settle the matter, the countess insisted, but the count, claiming he was ultimately responsible for his peasants, would not leave the matter to a magistrate.

It was on that day that life changed forever for the happy family. Anna was sitting in the window seat of her second-floor bedroom reading a French translation of *A Midsummer Night's Dream* when she heard the commotion below. She looked down to see eight or ten peasants accompanying a tumbril in which her father's body lay on a matting of straw.

Because of the sincere mutual respect between the count and his peasants, this time they seemed unafraid to name Feliks Paduch the murderer. It was Anna who had to tell her mother, and who—in her own bereavement—had to listen to the countess mourn her husband while in the same breath rail against him for playing estate manager and attending to most ignoble business well beneath his station, business like Feliks Paduch.

Countess Berezowska was devastated. Anna believed that it was the traumatic effects of her father's murder that precipitated the premature birth of the baby. The boy lived only two days. The countess never recovered from her husband's murder and the difficult birth—thirteen hours it had taken. After the baby's death, the countess stopped taking nourishment. A week later, in a delirium of grief, anger, and despair, she died.

And so it was that within a matter of days, Anna had lost everyone. The fabric of her peaceful life at Sochaczew had come undone, never to be made whole again. She stood alone in her garden that day, the day of her mother's death, somehow unable to cry. How her mother had loved the flowers grown there. In fact, Anna had taken to gardening, initially, to please the countess, who so loved to have flowers in the house. Her father had helped her start the garden that year, the year the five-year-old precocious child had brought home the crystal dove. She had been allowed to keep it and wanted so to please her mother by producing bushels and bushels of flowers.

The garden venture took no time at all to instill in Anna a passion for growing things. Her father gave her an array of bulbs, imports from Holland. She dutifully planted them in the fall, wondering to herself how such funny-looking things could ever produce something delicate and pretty. But in the spring the green feelers peeked out of the brown earth, and amid fine rains, reached brave, thickening arms upward. Anna had arranged them in neat rows, like soldiers, so that when the heads burst open with hues of reds, purples, oranges, and yellows she could scarcely contain her delight. It seemed a miracle. That first bouquet to her astonished mother was her proudest moment. In time she came to see in the flowers an almost symbolic difference between her parents: while her father loved the living, growing flowers still rooted to the earth and warmed by the sun, her mother preferred them cut, placed in cool water, and set out in shaded rooms to be admired.

Anna's lesson with the crystal dove so many years before had provided a defining moment for her relationship with her mother. Anna persisted in her love for her mother, but its foundation seemed to be one of fractures and fissures which, while they never fully broke away, seemed always to hold the threat of doing so. The difficult truth was that she questioned her mother's love for her. The countess' love was a cool kind of love, taking the form of a nod or a light pat on the head, a love given out sparingly, like formal candies in tiny wrappings, and on occasions few enough for Anna to store away in a half-filled memory box. Anna, in turn, grew up confident only in her father's unconditional love, a love that radiated like sunshine. She came to place herself fully in his guardianship, so much so that at his death she found that her reservoir of trust had been emptied. Even he, in dying, had failed her. If what he had done was place himself in the way of destiny, no good had come of it.

The Countess Berezowska's older sister, Countess Stella Gronska, arrived with her husband and daughter Zofia for one funeral and stayed for three. When they left Sochaczew to return home to Halicz in southern Poland, they insisted on taking Anna with them. The count and countess would provide guardianship for her until she reached eighteen.

At first, Anna was grateful. Her world shattered, she was happy to have someone deciding and doing for her. And her aunt and uncle were warm and loving people. Zofia, too, was welcoming. Anna found her cousin very different from herself, so outgoing and worldly-wise.

The Gronskis tried their best to be a family to her. But as the days at Halicz wore on, Anna came to miss her home and its familiar surroundings more and more. Sleep brought with it dark dreams of abandonment and isolation. At night she sometimes awoke to her own voice calling out for her father. Her aunt and uncle responded to her melancholy with genuine concern, but she would only pretend to be comforted. What she longed for was the cocoon of her father's library, where she had spent countless hours of her childhood transported to other times and places by the stories on the darkly varnished shelves. And, most of all, she missed the opportunity to mourn at her family's graves, to touch the earth that held them, when she could not.

Anna often wondered why it was that *she* survived. Had she *done* something to lose her whole world? Sometimes she found herself wishing she could join her family in the earth on that little hill where they and three other generations rested amid daisies, cornflowers, and poppies. What did living have to offer now?

Her life had taken on a tragic dimension that reminded her of the many tales and legends she knew. So often they, too, ended tragically. Why? In growing up, she would often read a tale only to the point when things went wrong. Then she would stop in order to provide her own, happier, ending. Her favorite story was of Jurata, Queen of the Baltic. If Anna could not quite identify with the mythical beauty of Jurata, she did acknowledge that they had in common their green eyes. What she admired most about the goddess was her passion. Oh, Anna wished for such passion in her own life.

Jurata lived in a palace of amber under the sea. One day a young fisherman broke one of her laws, but the kind Jurata forgave him. Falling in love with the fisherman, the goddess courageously defied custom and law, swimming to shore to meet him every evening. Anna thought the myth very romantic. It was at this point that she chose to amend the story. She had no taste for the unhappy ending that went on to depict the god of lightning and thunder, Piorun—who loved Jurata—flying into a rage because Jurata, too, broke a law: that magical beings marry only among themselves. Piorun destroyed the palace with his thunderbolts and Jurata was never seen again. The pieces of the broken palace, then, accounted for the bits of amber found in the Baltic area.

In Anna's ending, Jurata chipped away at her amber palace, breaking it down bit by bit, a mythical feat in itself. She then cleverly created among the gods and goddesses a great desire for the yellow stones. At last, she was able to assuage Piorun's anger by presenting him with the largest cache of amber in the world, thus making him more respected and powerful. Jurata's passion was so great that she assumed a human form, giving up her immortality for the love of her fisherman.

Now, transfixed in the meadow, Anna was aware of the sights and sounds about her only in a peculiar and distant way, as though she stood—an intruder—in some French bucolic painting. She wondered if this panorama were even real. Perhaps her very life was no more than a dream. Might she be *dreaming* her life? Strange as it was, the notion caught hold in her imagination. Was such a thing possible? Somehow, at that moment, it made sense. *If only recent events were illusions,* she thought. . . . *If only—*

Suddenly a voice shattered the trance: "You must be the Countess Anna!"

The deep voice jarred her into consciousness, and an instinctive, fearful cry escaped her lips before her mind could work. She wheeled about, shielding her face against the western sun, her eyes raised to take in the mounted rider.

Her skin felt the full heat of the afternoon sun. His visage was at first little more than a silhouette cut against the sunlight, like a black-on-yellow paper cutting. Still, she knew he was not from the Gronski estate.

"It is a fine day, is it not?" He was smiling at her, a smile she could not interpret.

"Who are you?" She hardly recognized the voice as her own. It sounded distant and tiny. Her heart beat rapidly against her chest, and for a moment she thought of running.

"I'm sorry if I startled you." The smile was fading. "I assumed you would have heard my horse."

"You did—and I had not." Anna swallowed hard. She fought for composure. She would not run. "You might have called out from a distance."

"Truly, I am sorry. Really, Countess Anna—it *is* Countess Anna?"

She mustered decorum now. "*Lady* Anna Maria. My parents didn't use their titles."

"Forgive me." He was maneuvering his horse around her now. "Around here you'll find that some of the *szlachta* do."

"Do you often go about sneaking up on people?" She lifted her head to him, feigning boldness. She found herself turning, too, in a half circle until it was no longer necessary for her to shade her eyes against the sun. She was certain that he had initiated that little dance for just that end.

He was laughing. "It's a habit I thought I had broken, Lady Anna Maria."

His cavalier attitude was disconcerting. Anna chose not to answer.

"And what," he pressed, "is it that brings you out here, milady?"

Anna conjured up one of her mother's smiles that wasn't a smile. "I might ask you the same question."

"Fair enough." It was he who was shading his eyes now, but he took his hand away long enough to point. "Your uncle's land ends there to the west with that wheat field. This meadow is mine."

"Oh." Anna felt her confidence go cold and drop within her, draining away like a mountain stream. How neatly he had put her in her place. "I am nothing more than an interloper then, is that it? I'll go back immediately."

He smiled. "You need do nothing of the kind, Lady Anna. There's no key to the woods and fields."

It was a saying she had heard her father use, one she had thought was his alone. Her gaze was held by the stranger. She answered: "It's just that I found the meadow so very peaceful, so conducive to thinking."

"Ah, so pretty—and thoughtful into the bargain!"

"Are they qualities so incompatible with each other?" The man was impossible, she decided, her spine stiffening.

"No, of course not. It was a stupid comment." The cobalt eyes flashed as he stared down at her.

She smiled now, her head lifting to meet his gaze. "At last we agree on something."

He laughed.

Anna sensed her little victory a hollow one. Was he laughing *at* her? She turned away. "It's well past time for me to return to the house, so if you'll excuse me—"

In one quick movement the stranger swung down from the black stallion.

Anna felt fear rise again. She took a cautious step backward.

"Oh, but we haven't met yet," he was saying. "Allow me to detain you but a moment longer. I am Jan Stelnicki of Uście Zielone." He bowed, stood erect, gazed down at Anna. The dark gray trousers tucked into high black boots, white silk shirt, and red sash around the waist made for an impeccable appearance. His costume was a mix of Western and Polish influence, but that he wore no hat was neither Western nor Polish.

Anna nodded, lifting her eyes to take in his considerable height. "Well, since you seem to already know my identity, there's little else to say." She persisted in her petulant tone even while her mind was seeking its own course. Despite the missing hat and familiar manner, his nobility was evident in his speech and bearing. Once he stood in the shade of the great oak, she took in the aristocratic and masculine features chiseled under a mane of wavy yellow-gold, the laughing smile above a dimpled chin, and those dark blue eyes. Some current at her core stirred: something profound and alien. *No man should be so beautiful.*

"Lady Anna," he was saying in a voice almost intimate, "may I offer my sincerest condolences? I was saddened to hear of your parents' deaths."

"Thank you, Lord Stelnicki."

The mourning which for months had consumed her life took on a strangely distant quality now. Her impatience with the stranger was giving way involuntarily to a dichotomous mix of caution and attraction. She watched the motion of his mouth, the porcelain flash of teeth. He wore no moustache. This, too, ran against the Polish mode of the day. There was a mesmerizing presence about him and a strength, not merely physical strength—though he possessed that, too—but a force that came from deep within and resonated in his gaze, in his voice.

"Will you be staying with the Gronski family long?" he asked.

Her immediate response was to tell him that it was of no concern to him, but she took just a moment too long to formulate the reply and her annoyance dissipated. She heard herself telling him that she would be staying with the Gronskis for some time and that, yes, they were treating her very well. While he turned to tether his horse to a wiry branch jutting from the thick tree trunk, he continued his questioning, asking why they had not previously met. Studying him at his task, Anna replied that she had been to visit her aunt and uncle twice several years before. He took studies at the university then, it seemed. When he turned to face her, Anna averted her eyes, politely asking where. In Kraków, he responded, then two years in Paris.

Anna feigned nonchalance. She had never been to Kraków, but she had been to Warsaw—not often, even though her home was so near Poland's capital. Paris, however, seemed worlds away. Paris was the City of Light: the quintessence of European culture. She longed to see it. Now, of course, the unrest there made it quite unsafe. . . . How old is he? she wondered. *Twenty-two? Twenty-three?*

"I am glad that you will be staying," he said now. "I trust that I will be allowed to show you the sights here at Halicz. Our Harvest Home will be concluding with much celebration. . . ."

Her mind a blur, Anna watched as the young man went on speaking of the local autumn customs. What emboldened him to speak to her as though he had known her all his life? She absently fingered the dark lace at her throat. The voice was so warm, so musical, the eyes inviting as a lake in August. Still, she wondered at his sincerity. Did sincerity and boldness coexist? "Lord Stelnicki," she managed when he took a breath, "I am afraid that such festivities are out of the question for me for some little while yet."

"Of course. Forgive me." He bowed from the waist. "But once you are out of mourning there will be many winter gatherings to which we shall look forward—parties, sleigh rides, and—"

Anna interrupted, smiling indulgently. "Oh, I'm afraid that in a few weeks my aunt and uncle will shut up the house. We are to winter in Warsaw."

"Of course. For the moment I forgot the Gronski custom. Why, were you staying, I would personally organize a *kulig*. Our joyrides are well-known around here and no Halicz manor home turns away a sleigh party!"

"At least," Anna laughed, "until the master's vodka reserve has been drained!"

"I expect so." Lord Stelnicki laughed, too. Then he let out a great sigh and his face fell with an exaggerated disappointment. "Ah, winter will not be such a happy prospect for me."

He was so glibly forward that Anna could only stare. *This* comment, certainly, was insincere.

But the mocking attitude vanished suddenly and he brightened. The blue eyes held Anna's. "Time is the world's landlord and he may be friend or foe. May he be our *friend,* Lady Anna Maria."

Anna had never heard this saying before, but she knew his meaning and she felt her face burn. His forwardness unnerved her. No man, and certainly no stranger, had ever behaved toward her with such familiarity. Her throat, already dry, tightened as she sought a diversionary tactic. "Do you not winter in the city, Lord Stelnicki?"

"You must call me Jan. Please."

She longed to extinguish that expectant smile. Did this man ever meet with resistance? Even as she thought this, she found herself nodding in acquiescence. Silently she promised herself to ignore the request.

He was satisfied, nonetheless, and told her that in years past he had spent December and January in Kraków—where his father lived now—but that he enjoyed the country far more. Yes, he assured her, even in winter, admitting himself to be an odd sort. His mother, it seemed, had died some years before and he assured Anna from experience that Time would help to heal the hurt.

Despite his forwardness and her own awkwardness, Anna was surprised by some interior part of her which sought to prolong the conversation, but having been reminded of her mourning, Duty, not Time, prompted her to insist that she return to the house.

"Very well, then," he said, "I'll lead my horse to the Gronski home, if you would care to ride."

"Oh, no!"

"You do ride?"

"Of course, but I did come out for the walk, you see. Otherwise, I would have ridden out myself. I look forward to walking back." The words had spilled out in a rush, but he seemed satisfied with her excuse.

"Well, Lady Anna Maria," he said, bowing, "I welcome you to Halicz and look forward to our next meeting. I hope that one day soon we will ride together. The countryside is breathtaking. When do you put off your mourning?"

"In three weeks' time." His deep voice was no longer alien and startling. It was somehow a lyrical voice she had not known but had held always within her, like some ancestral song, primal yet soothing. Is his interest as keen as it seems, she wondered, or am I too vulnerable in my grief? Or merely too easily snared by my own imagination? What stupid and easily caught bird was it that Polonius had compared Ophelia to? A woodcock, that was it. Is that what I am? Her heart was quickening nonetheless. He wanted to see her again. The thought was at once exciting and unnerving.

"Forgive me for disturbing you today," Lord Stelnicki was saying. "It was just that from the distance I took you for Zofia and so I rode over. I will make a point of calling on the Gronski family in exactly three weeks. What is it? Why, Lady Anna, I do believe that you're blushing!"

Anna inwardly cursed him for pointing out her embarrassment. She forced out a little laugh. "It is funny, I should think. I have never been mistaken for my beautiful cousin, I can assure you. I could only wish for such beauty."

"Why, Anna—it's only fair now that I address you so—you have little reason for such wishing." He mounted his black steed. The leather creaked as he settled into the saddle with the grace and ease of one who has ridden all of his life.

Once again Anna found herself staring up at him.

"Look!" he said, gesturing in a sweeping motion. "See the two meadow flowers, the yellow and the violet? One is as different from the other as day from night. Yet who will say that one is more beautiful? Oh, a fool might. But only a fool." The saddle groaned again as he leaned over, motioning her nearer, as if to impart some great secret. "But do you know what may determine the desirability of one over the other?" He spoke with a great earnestness.

The intense eyes held Anna's, and she could only shake her head in mute response.

"The fragrance!"

The playful, widening smile, set against a complexion colored by the sun, revealed the even white teeth. Suddenly, he drew up on the reins, and as the animal reared, he waved and turned the horse into the wind. Anna stood close enough that she felt the earth tremble when the horse's forelegs came down. She took a stumbling step backward, feeling a quick breeze made by the swish of the animal's tail.

As the horse thundered off, Jan Stelnicki called out his good-bye.

Her lips apart as if to speak, she stood and stared until the figure crested the hill and fell from sight.

Anna's legs quaked. She felt as one abandoned by the enemy on a battlefield. The man was incorrigible: insufferably confident, proud, strutting. He caused defenses within her to rise like drawbridges. And he was toying with her to the last. *Yellow and violet flowers, indeed. You are a scoundrel and a rogue, Jan Stelnicki!*

And yet she was drawn to him. For a short while, her life had been filled with something other than death and darkness and mourning. Anna sank now to the ground, the stiff satin skirt billowing up around her like a great black cushion.

The world went on as it had before he arrived. The leaves were continuing their circuitous movement. A butterfly fluttered among the meadow flowers. A tiny sparrow sat appraisingly upon a nearby branch.

The meeting with Jan Stelnicki played out again in her mind. She tried to make sense of her feelings. Of course, he is strikingly handsome, she conceded. There was something else about him, too, a special manly grace or energy that accounted for an immediate and deep attraction. A simple meeting, and yet Anna felt that somehow her life had changed. Was this to be the kind of mythical romance of which she read, dreamt, invented?

Doubt ran close behind and she scoffed at the notion: I will not be some easily snared woodcock. I am too old for such a wishful and girlish infatuation.

But her mind grasped and held to one thought, one memory. Anna's mother often had told her that she herself had known she would marry Anna's father from the very first meeting. And she *had,* despite the concerns of her parents and offers from other wealthier and higher-placed nobles.

She had known! It is possible. Anna's heart surged at the thought. *Might it be so with me?*

Her mind was not through playing devil's advocate, however, conjuring up myriad reservations and fears. Maybe Jan Stelnicki is less than sincere, she thought. Maybe he is merely taking advantage of his looks and charm. To what end? Perhaps he has long been skilled in the arts of seduction. Perhaps it is only his ego. . . .

But there was something deeper—some mysterious link—which attracted Anna and gave profound meaning to what seemed a happenstance encounter, a link that the blacksmith of the gods, Hephaestos himself, might have forged.

Anna sat, her eyes alert now, suddenly aware that the meadow about her teemed with color and movement and warmth and life. This experience of intense attraction she savored for the first time in her life. She drank it in like a fine French wine and it lifted both her body and her mind to a strangely ethereal plane.

Rainless clouds came and went. The sun slowly moved over her. Anna stood at last, and the movement stirred the little sparrow from its perch. With purposeful steps she set out in the direction of the Gronski home.

Perhaps she was to have a future, after all. If the endings of myths might be changed, why not the ending to *her* story?

A gusty wind began to blow, catching the folds of her black skirt as it might a sail, pushing her along.

Anna laughed to herself as she broke into a run. She was thinking about his expression that Time was the world's landlord. She would conscript Time as friend rather than foe. "After all," she said aloud, "it will take time to learn how to ride a horse!"

2

Here, at Hawthorn House, the Gronski manor home, no one would forbid her to ride. Not like at home. Anna went directly to her bedchamber on the second floor. After washing and changing for supper, she walked to the massive old dresser and tugged at the bottom drawer. She lifted from it a carved wooden box with delicate inlay, a work of art fashioned by the artisans of the Tatra Mountains. Carefully she placed it on the dresser top and lifted the lid.

Even away from the window, the translucent object shone brightly against the red velvet lining. Anna removed it from the box and placed it on the black marble. She turned it first this way, then that way, somehow dissatisfied. It was only just before her mother died that she had learned its secret. How strange that this beautiful but lifeless object kept her from riding horses. The sight of the dove had never failed to please her, yet the familiar serenity was absent today.

She had told Jan Stelnicki that she could ride. She had never lied before and found it unsettling. No good could come of it.

No matter, she resolved after some moments, Zofia will teach me how. And one day I *shall go* riding with Jan.

It was the first time she had thought of the stranger on a first-name basis. She looked up into the mirror to find her expression an odd combination of surprise and pleasure, as if in his absence some intimacy had been established between them.

She left the crystal dove on the dresser, certain that the maid would not dare touch it, and went downstairs to seek out Zofia.

Anna found her cousin sitting with her mother in the small parlor that led to the count and countess' antechamber and bedroom. Her buoyancy would not allow her to sit. Thoughtlessly and with a childlike abandon, she poured out the news of the meeting with Lord Jan Stelnicki. Zofia expressed the keener interest, and Anna forgot for the moment that Countess Stella Gronska was even present. When the story was told, however, Anna saw that her aunt's face had bled to white and the expressive brown eyes widened now in horror. "Do you mean, Anna, that you met Jan Stelnicki in some *field?* You were *alone?*"

"No," Zofia joked before Anna could reply, "Anna told you: Jan was there. Well, cousin, what do you think? Is he not handsome?"

"Oh, yes," Anna replied softly, "and charming."

"And one day," Zofia said, "he will be Count Jan Stelnicki."

"Count or not, his behavior is unheard of," the countess protested. "The boldness! There was no introduction and no chaperone. And he had not the decency to wear a hat."

"Oh, Mother," Zofia said, "don't excite yourself so. You'll bring on your heart palpitations. This is a new day."

"That I should live to see it!"

A maid appeared now to announce supper.

Anna had no appetite; she was suddenly as spiritless as a willow tree jilted by the breeze. At her heart's core, she herself had thought the meeting improper. Why had she not, then, anticipated her aunt's response? How stupidly impulsive to blurt out everything as she had! *What a little fool I am,* she thought. *I must learn to think before I speak.*

Walking to the countess' chair, Anna knelt and reached out to touch her hand. "Oh, please don't hold his forwardness against him, Aunt. He approached me only because from the distance he thought me to be Zofia."

"And where was I?" Zofia intoned. "If only I had known the fields were ripe with men!"

"Zofia!"

Zofia pulled a face. "You are too serious, Mother!"

"Not as serious as your father should he hear such scandalous talk." The countess took Anna's hand in hers and softened her tone. "Perhaps you do not realize the impropriety of such an occurrence, my child. In any event, your parents would not have approved, Anna. Jan Stelnicki, though a good friend and neighbor, is not a Catholic but an adherent of the Arian heresy."

"His *father* is an Arian, Mother," Zofia said. "Jan has little interest in religion."

The Countess Gronska's lips tightened like a purse drawn closed. "The difference between a heretic and a heathen is thin, Zofia, and one I will not argue." She stood abruptly, drawing Anna also to her feet. "We will go into supper now." Although she had to look up into Anna's face, there was no questioning the older woman's resolve. "Anna Maria, I must forbid you to venture beyond the outer buildings on your own. Be certain that not a word of this—this *meeting*—reaches your uncle's ears. He's called men out to duel over less. And understand me well, Anna: under no circumstances are you to see Jan Stelnicki again."

For all appearances, supper was cordial. Anna conversed with her aunt, uncle, and cousin, answering questions, smiling and even laughing a little. But her mind and emotions were working on a different level. She remembered a baby bird with a broken wing she had once found. Her father made for it a little splint, and Anna lovingly nursed it, anticipating the day it would experience its first flight. But one morning she discovered that despite their efforts and its own tiny will to live, it had died during the night.

By the time supper was finished, Anna was, as she had been so many years before, inconsolable.

3

Zofia sat at her white French vanity table with its painted design, absently running the hairbrush through her dark, lustrous hair. She had removed a mask of makeup, so that her expression was stark in its seriousness. She sighed deeply at her reflection. There was nothing to do but confront Anna and put an end to her childish infatuation.

But how to handle it? She continued to brush, staring, as if entranced by her own reflection. Her mind struck two options. She might douse Anna's interest by merely supporting her mother's opinion regarding Jan's religion, or lack of it. Anna was too simple and timid a soul to go against the whole family.

Or she could tell Anna the truth: that she had her own designs on Jan Stelnicki. Doing so, however, meant problems. She wondered if she should chance Anna's violating the confidence. If Zofia's parents found out, they would be furious with her. And her intentions would be put to a certain end.

The almond-shaped black eyes stared into the mirror, searching. She could not escape the question. Did *she* love Jan? She cocked her head, considering. He was certainly breathtakingly handsome and every sinew held charm. Their mutual attraction was undeniable. In the few months that he had been back from Paris, they had met secretly several times. But two weeks ago—at their last meeting before Zofia accompanied her parents to collect Anna at Sochaczew—she had made a serious miscalculation that put their romance in jeopardy. However, if she had nothing else, she had faith in herself and was certain that her beauty and finesse could—would!—win him back.

Her eyes peered into the mirror, as if into her soul. *Do I love him?* She asked herself this question now because, whether or not she did love him, she might very well have to tell Anna that she did. And if it were to be a lie . . . well, she would have to be prepared. She continued to stare, and, ultimately, she was honest with herself: no, she did not think she loved him. The truth was, he fit into her plans. He was going to be of invaluable service to her. His looks and charms were merely dividends.

She was not about to sign him over to Anna. It was too bad, but she would have to lie and scuttle from the start her cousin's hopes for romance with Jan. Zofia put her mind to work. She knew from experience that for lies to work effectively, every option, every possibility, must be considered in advance. She would be careful. There must be no blunder.

Still, she felt the pressure of the clock. At Christmas, she was expected to marry a man she had never met, someone to whom her parents had promised her when she was only an infant.

Zofia's blood rose at the thought.

The world was changing—but too late for her parents. They, especially her father, would not relent unless circumstances somehow forced them to do so. But she could be stubborn, too. And clever. She was not about to sacrifice her youth and vitality to a life of formality with some crushing bore.

I will not.

Jan was her ticket out of a life of narrow convention. Her plan was to tell her parents of their relationship once the affair was consummated. If they chose not to cancel the long-standing engagement, she would tell her betrothed herself. But what if he were some spineless creature who didn't care that she hadn't saved herself for the bridal chamber? It would be just her luck. What then? If necessary, she would go so far as to claim to be in a family way. As for marriage with Jan, perhaps she would agree to it in a few years. She doubted she could find a better match. Yes, she might love him one day. For now, she longed for freedom, not marriage. She took seriously the jest that one should live wildly for three years before marrying. She didn't want to play the age-old roles of wife, mother, grandmother—not before she had lived and enjoyed her life. These years were golden ducats to be spent on pleasure.

Her own parents were conspiring to rob her of her youth. She felt a fierce shiver course through her at the thought of having to live out the obligation. *I might as well be dead.*

Zofia's thoughts came back to her cousin. She sincerely regretted Anna's peculiar part in this. She liked Anna. It was just that her cousin had unwittingly stepped between two powers greater than herself. No doubt Jan was being his polite and ingratiating self, but he could harbor no real interest in the girl. It was ridiculous. In her innocence, Anna had misinterpreted his attention, pure and simple.

Oh, the braided, wide-eyed Anna was pretty in her own childlike way, but Zofia had long been aware of her own dark beauty and was unused to any serious competition. At gatherings in the country as well as in the city, she was always the sole focus of attention, attracting men like insects to a flame. Others much more beautiful than Anna had been unable to steal the light from Zofia. No, she decided, the girl posed no real threat.

Zofia was certain that for Anna's part, it was just a silly infatuation, no doubt her first. She would let her country cousin down as easily as possible. She will get over it, she mused, for there would be no choice in the matter.

A timid tapping came at the door. Zofia opened it to find the maid's daughter standing there, her face pale, her words garbled.

"What is it?" Zofia demanded. "Did he write? Did he give you a message? Speak up!"

The frightened thirteen-year-old Marcelina was but a mouse trapped by an owl.

Zofia grasped her by the wrist and pulled her into her room, shutting the door behind her. "Now tell me what happened!"

The girl's eyes were gray discs of fear. "He . . . he returned your letter, my lady." Her hand reached into her apron pocket.

"He didn't read it?"

She shook her head.

Zofia struck the girl hard across her mouth. "Answer me!"

"No, he would not read it, my lady," Marcelina wailed as she handed the sealed envelope to Zofia. The tears were coming now and blood trickled from the corner of her mouth. "He asked . . . he asked that you please . . . you please—"

"Yes?" Zofia demanded. She wanted to strike the girl again but held back. "*What* did he ask?"

The girl steeled herself. "That you not write to him again."

Zofia snatched the letter and stared dumbly at it while the shock passed over her in galvanizing waves.

Marcelina, expecting to be struck again, began to shake and sob.

It took Zofia a moment to recoup her presence of mind. "All right, all right, stop it, Marcelina. Stop it, I say! Take this kerchief and wipe your mouth and eyes. You can go now."

The girl turned to leave.

Zofia again locked onto the girl's wrist. "You know not to say anything about this, don't you? I swear, Marcelina, if you do I'll see that my father puts your whole family out. Without a day's notice. Do you understand?"

The girl stared in mute despair.

Zofia took her by the shoulders and shook her. "Do you understand?" she demanded. Her long nails cut into the girl's flesh.

Marcelina managed a nod and a whisper. "Oui, Mademoiselle."

"Good." Zofia composed herself now, even managing a smile. "Your accent is improving. Wait now, let me get you one of my ribbons for your hair. I know how you like them."

Zofia fumbled through her vanity drawer, but by the time she turned around with the red ribbon, the girl had fled.

Zofia sank into her chair. Was it possible that he had sent back her letter without even reading it? Jan Stelnicki had rejected her.

Rejection. The sensation was a new one for Zofia and one she didn't like. How can this be? she wondered. Her plans were collapsing before they could be implemented.

What was she to do? Her mind reeled as she searched for an answer.

Some minutes passed. At last, her hand closed into a fist and crumpled the letter, the long, polished nails coming together. Zofia was not one to send up the white flag on the first volley. She would *do* something. But what? She just needed a little more time to think out her next move. Things had been going well enough. She and Jan had been getting more and more intimate through their meetings in the forest. Although he played the gentleman, holding his passion in check, she was certain that he loved her.

She thought back to that last meeting. It had proven a disaster. She had lost patience with his reserve in making love. She was, she realized now, too anxious in securing this physical commitment. Her preoccupation with the timetable for marriage that her parents had set made her so . . . And his code of behavior was scarcely more modern than that of courtly love in the old French legends. He worried over her honor, he said.

If only he knew.

It was on this occasion that Zofia took the initiative in their too-innocent lovemaking, her mouth returning his kiss with undiluted intensity, her hands working at his sash. Jan was shocked by her aggressiveness, shocked and inexplicably angry. They argued. It was a major blunder on her part, of course. Her forwardness had served only to smother the desire she knew burned within him. Their parting, just before the Gronskis traveled to Sochaczew, was unresolved and unhappy. But she was certain that his reaction was an eruption of male pride, a pride of the moment that would settle in the ensuing weeks.

Evidently, it had not lessened. Zofia had sorely misjudged him. Her mind came back to the present, her eyes focusing on the sealed envelope. Why had he not even read her letter? Angrily she tore it into little pieces.

She sat quietly seething for several minutes. Might there be something more to his behavior? she wondered. Was it her planned marriage that put him off? He had known of her long-standing engagement although she had told him of her intention to refuse it at the proper time. Was he afraid of her father? Her fiancé? Or was it possible that he did not care enough for her?

She dismissed the last thought immediately. He *did* love her: she well knew when she made a conquest.

So what was this ploy of his? How would she manage to see him? She had learned that she could not be too assertive. But how could she *do* something while at the same time appear not to be taking the initiative?

Further, this now complicated what she would tell Anna.

Anna! Zofia suddenly sat forward in her chair. Of course! Her eyes widened at their own reflection. Why hadn't she seen it immediately? It was exactly what she would do were she in his place. It was so transparent!

Jan is using Anna to make me jealous!

What interest could he possibly have in a rustic *girl*? Anna with her green eyes, braided hair, enthusiasm, and naiveté! It was a silly ruse, nothing more.

She smiled at her reflection. Well, let him proceed with his plan—she had underrated him, after all. It will serve him right when it backfires, she thought.

Zofia determined her course of action: she would send no more letters, admit no interest. Her lack of initiative would now bring him back to her. Her confidence, a longtime companion, was restored. Jan would come begging.

And she would let him beg. She would relish every moment of it.

No, she would not tell Anna of her own involvement with Stelnicki. On the contrary, she would *encourage* her, just for fun. The girl's simplicity would be her undoing; why, once her mourning was over, she would probably revert to wearing her village costume. Jan's boredom with Anna would speed his steps back to Zofia. She laughed aloud, studying her reflection as it seemed to join her in her mirth.

She still had until December before her time would run out. At Christmas her parents were to execute their plan to marry her off. If the wedding were to take place, it would truly be, she darkly mused, her execution. *No, I will beat them at their game and Stelnicki at his, and if Anna steps in the way, well, God help her!*

Zofia knocked and entered Anna's room without waiting for permission. "Hello, dearest."

"Hello." Anna sat at a small French writing desk.

"Writing poetry?"

"No." Anna laughed. "I keep a journal sometimes."

"A diary? What a wonderful idea! *I* should keep one." Zofia smiled wickedly. "My guess is that you're writing of Jan Stelnicki?"

Anna blushed.

"I thought so!" Zofia put her hands on her hips.

"What?"

"Oh, don't be coy! Or is it shyness that I detect? Well, that will get you nowhere. Were you taken by him, or not? Just try to deny it, I dare you."

"You can be cruel, Zofia," Anna said, feigning disinterest. "What difference can it make anyway? I'm not likely to see him again."

"You mean Mother's interdict?" Zofia walked mincingly into the room. "I wouldn't let that worry you."

"What do you mean?"

"I mean that a resourceful girl like yourself can certainly manage a little flirtation on the quiet."

"I should not like to go against your mother."

"She needn't know. Anna, dearest, a year from now you will be of age and managing your own estate. What will it matter then? You are only young once."

"How old is Jan?"

"Too old for you!"

"Really? Do you think so?"

"Really?" Zofia mimicked, turning to her cousin with an exaggerated expression. "Do you think so?"

"Zofia, please!"

"He's twenty-five." Her mouth curled upward as she studied Anna, then broke into a broad, knowing smile. "Why, you *are* smitten! Aren't you? He must've been in a very charming mood, indeed. He can be most irresistible when he chooses. Be careful, my darling. His moods are as changeable as the weather. But today I can see that he was a Don Juan!"

Color and excitement pulsed in Anna's cheeks. "I suppose that every girl must be entranced by him. Aren't you, Zofia?"

"Me? No!"

"Is it his age?"

"Hardly. I was joking about the age difference, you goose. Why, I've already had admirers older than Jan. He and I are but friends. Oh, I admit him to be the handsomest of men, but my taste runs, shall we say, wider." Zofia's laugh was sharp and naughty. She was enjoying shocking her cousin. "Why settle for a rose when all the flowers in the garden are yours for the picking?"

"You're so beautiful, Zofia. I imagine that you must have many suitors."

"Too few here in the country, let me tell you. Ah! But in Warsaw! Well, you would be surprised, I expect. As would my parents. Oh, they are a problem!"

Zofia began to pace. "Secrecy is impossible in the country, but in the city . . . well, there are ways. Sooner or later, though, I must confront them. Oh, Anna, they expect me to marry some baron's son whom I've never met. It is a union promised by the families years ago, when I was a child. Can you imagine? And he doesn't even receive his title and property until the old baron is cold in his grave." Zofia turned back to Anna and let out a great sigh. "The old ways are dead, but do my parents know it?"

"Perhaps you'll find that you can love him. He may be handsome and noble."

"Like your Don Juan?" she scoffed. "You're a hopeless optimist, Anna. I don't know how we shall ever get along." Zofia's eyes focused now on the glass bird, and she moved immediately to it. "Why, Anna, what is this figurine? It's a dove! Is it crystal?"

"Yes. I received it for my fifth feast day." Anna stood now, clearly afraid for the safety of the glass treasure. "Papa took me to Warsaw to pick out a doll with glass eyes and real hair, but I fell in love with the crystal bird. Mama had a fit when she saw it."

In a flash Zofia scooped it off the dresser and held it to the candle-light, turning it this way and that. "Why it's lovely, the way the light plays through it." She sensed Anna hovering behind her. "Don't worry, dearest, I shan't drop it."

"I found out only recently that in return for my keeping the dove Mama made Papa promise never to teach me how to ride."

Zofia turned to face her cousin. "Why would she do that?"

"Because I was the only child, she was forever worried about my health. If any of the other expectancies had gone to term, I don't think she would have been quite so protective."

"I dare say you'll come out of your shell soon enough. And you can start with Jan Stelnicki!"

"Zofia!" Anna gasped.

"Oh, don't play the tepid heroine of one of your books."

"You don't mean to say I should go against your parents?"

"Of course! As long as you do it secretly." She carefully returned the dove to the dresser top. "I'm off to bed, darling."

"Zofia?"

She turned again to Anna. "Yes?"

Anna advanced a few steps. "Will you teach me to ride?"

Zofia's eyes narrowed in laughing appraisal. "Why, Ania, you are as transparent as your glass bird! You want to go riding with Jan, of course. Oh, don't fret, I shall teach you." She hugged her cousin. "I love it! This may be your first romance."

"I . . . I don't know how I shall manage it."

Zofia suddenly held Anna at arm's length. "Do you mean to tell me that you never once tried to outwit your parents? You *never* rode a horse?

"Oh, I thought about it. When words wouldn't work on them . . . well, on Mother mostly . . . I planned a hundred schemes. I even bribed a villager to teach me."

"And?"

Anna dropped her eyes. "I couldn't go through with it."

"Oh, Anna! Out of fear—or integrity?"

"I don't know. Perhaps it was a mix of the two."

Zofia released her cousin. "You may have grown up sheltered, Anna Maria Berezowska, but it is I who would wish to be in your shoes today. You have your title already, and in less than a year you will be in sole control of your life. And I? I'm likely to be an old married woman with the best part of my life behind me."

"Oh, Zofia, you exaggerate. Somehow I can't help but feel that however it turns out, you'll have your way in the matter."

Zofia was caught for a moment by the sincerity in Anna's green eyes. Then she threw her head back and laughed. "Why, my dear cousin, I shouldn't be a bit surprised."

4

Jan remained in Anna's thoughts. His laughing smile and piercing blue eyes haunted her like an angelic specter. Zofia's words of encouragement dallied in her ears, too, prompting in Anna a boldness that made her dare to think she *should* see him again. Didn't the goddess Jurata defy custom and law to meet with her fisherman?

Anna realized, however, that Aunt Stella was no minor problem. She had been adamant. And she was for the time being, after all, her guardian.

But for now Anna was secretly elated by Zofia's assurance that *she* herself had no interest in Jan Stelnicki. Anna would find some way to deal with her aunt, but if Zofia had expressed an interest in Jan, Anna would have been crushed. She would have stepped aside silently, not only out of a sense of honor, but also out of the belief that Zofia could not help but win any man she chose.

Only weeks before when the Gronski family had come for her at her parents' estate in Sochaczew, Anna had been astounded by her cousin's metamorphosis. She remembered Zofia as a boyish, gangling girl whose constant complaint was that her older brother would not include her in his outdoor activities. She was spoiled even then and, invariably, Walter was made to look after and entertain his sister. Zofia had a certain inexplicable talent for dealing with her parents that Anna held in awe. Clever enough to realize that tantrums would not move the stalwart Gronskis, Zofia had honed to a fine perfection a honeyed diplomacy that seldom failed.

Just five years later, Anna found her cousin a raven-haired, black-eyed woman of sophisticated beauty and bearing. No more did she allow anyone to call her by her diminutive, "Zosia." As the carriage lurched and trundled on in the direction of Halicz, Anna's gaze was kept involuntarily glued to Zofia. Anna marveled at—and envied, too—her cousin's great blossoming. Was it possible that Zofia was but eighteen, one year older than she?

Anna had never considered herself beautiful and certainly not the stunning creature that Zofia had become, but she thought that at times she could appear attractive. Her mother had told her that beauty is a beacon that emanates from within. And Anna would try to believe it, though sometimes failing to see past the irony that her mother was a great natural beauty.

Anna had grown to be as tall as most men, and her frame was at once sturdy and slender. "Your curves are still in evolution," her mother told her when Anna came to her with concern over her slenderness. "Be patient. You are now half-woman, half-child, Anna Maria. In a very short time you will attract your share of men."

Anna thought her hair her best feature. It had darkened slightly to a chestnut brown that in certain lights came alive with a reddish fire. At home she had worn it in the village fashion: in two thick braids that extended almost to her waist, but during this period of mourning she had taken to winding a single braid about her head. It was her emerald eyes, however, that most people commented upon, deeply set as they were and strikingly flecked with amber.

Anna now recognized in her cousin Zofia the same great dark beauty of her own mother. Zofia was perhaps even more striking. She sighed with relief: If Zofia *had been* attracted to Jan Stelnicki, she feared, all would have been lost.

For several days Anna stayed within the boundaries that her aunt had set, becoming acquainted with what the servants called "the great house," which rested majestically on a bluff above the River Dniestr. Like her own home at Sochaczew and countless manor homes of the minor nobility that were the very soul of Poland, it was fronted by a covered porch with two sturdy columns of whitewashed stone, a porch that promised Polish hospitality. The many rooms and niceties of the limestone home impressed Anna, but it was that it had a third floor replete with hooded windows jutting from the evergreen-shingled roof that made her think it as elegant as any city mansion. Outside, she took winding paths as she investigated flower gardens, orchards, a pond, the farm manager's cottage, and countless outer buildings.

The majority of Count Leo Gronski's multiple tracts of land were let to peasant families Anna never met, but she did come to know the extended family that ran the Gronski farm and household. One day she came upon Katarzyna and Marcelina, daughters of the farm manager, hard at work in the vegetable garden. She gave greeting and they curtsied nicely, but eyed her strangely as she made her way through rows of beetroot, peppers, cabbage, and onions.

At home Anna had enjoyed cultivating her own patch and so took an interest in one so large and varied. When she paused to comment on the variety of an onion, the girls stared, wide-eyed. It was unthinkable that a lady, a countess, should know about or concern herself with such things.

She could read it in their faces: Lady Zofia would never be found in a vegetable garden.

Anna was amused at their reaction but unashamed of her more rustic background. Her father had taught her to touch, to smell, to love and work the land. *"If a Pole holds nothing more than his own patch of land,"* he would say, *"he is a wealthy man."* Still, Anna realized that there would be talk, and not wishing to irritate the Countess Stella, she declined to associate with the girls in the following days, hoping that the whisperings did not reach her aunt's ears.

By the end of the week, Anna had fully explored the interior and exterior of the house. While she hoped that such activity would assuage the sadness of her parents' loss, she knew at her core that she was trying to counter the strange and powerful force that ran through her like a river. Her thoughts were drawn, almost unwillingly, toward the vague yet mighty notions of a girl's heart—and toward Jan Stelnicki.

Defying her aunt, she found herself in the meadow where she had met him. Aimlessly she moved among the wildflowers and tall grasses, lost deep within herself.

He wasn't there, of course. Not that she truly thought he would be. Yet, just as the compass needle points north, she was drawn to that spot.

She lost track of time. She hadn't been listening to the birds, or she would have noticed when they suddenly ceased their chatter. A storm was on the rise.

A clap of thunder shook her from her trance. The sky already loomed black with rain clouds. As Anna picked up her dark skirts to flee the meadow, large drops—cold and stinging—awoke in her a sense of foolishness for her girlish hopes.

She ran now against the wet wind. *The loss of my parents and my unsteady mind have done this,* she thought. *I am behaving like a fool, sneaking behind my aunt's back, allowing a single meeting with a man to control me so. Tonight at supper I will ask Aunt Stella if I may return home.*

Anna was soaked to her undershift when she noiselessly entered the house through a side door, breathless that she might be discovered.

A sharp voice startled her immediately: "And where have you been?"

It was Zofia.

Anna stood mute, a shiver rippling through her.

"You are quite a sight, Anna!"

"I . . . I was walking." She sniffled. "I got caught in the storm."

"Obviously. Mother was looking for you."

"She didn't go out to look, did she?" Anna tried to disguise the panic she felt welling up in her.

"No, she sent me—and I must say that I searched every inch of the *grounds.*"

"Oh." Anna chose now to face her humiliation. "Well, I might as well tell you that I was—"

"I told her, dearest cousin," Zofia interrupted, "that you were resting in your room, that you had a bit of a headache." She stared past her fine straight nose with knowing, laughing eyes. "Now, do go get yourself dried off, for if your headache leads to a death of pneumonia I shall be hard pressed to explain it."

Returning to her room, Anna collapsed onto her bed in a state of exhaustion. She felt as if her execution had been stayed, and in relief silently vowed to keep away from the meadow.

It was at supper, however, that the Countess Stella herself gave Anna's thoughts a second shaking. "You are so quiet tonight, my dear," her aunt said, peering solicitously at her over dessert. "Is it the headache?"

Anna felt her throat tighten. What was she to say? She was caught up in a lie and could only regret her disobedience.

"Anna's tired, Mother," Zofia said, coming to her rescue in a heart-beat. "And still so sad." She lifted a spoonful of her plum dumpling to full lips which smiled secretly at Anna.

Anna stared for the moment at her cousin's honeyed innocence, taking in the mischief that danced in the dark eyes, then she nervously turned her gaze to her own dessert, which sat untouched before her.

"You have taken the deaths so very hard, child," the countess said. "It is a shame that death must so affect the young. Well, mourning will soon be over. But you need to begin, even now, to focus your thoughts on other things. You are young and you must get back to the business of being young. My sister was especially fond of some stoical saying about the past. Do you remember it, Anna Maria?"

"Yes, Aunt Stella."

The musical voice of Anna's mother played vividly in her memory. "She would say that what is past, one cannot change, so each backward glance is a bit of the present slipping away."

"Yes," the countess exclaimed. "That is it precisely!"

Anna could only think how in the last days of her mother's life that saying was merely a saying. In the end, her mother had not been able to prevent herself from letting the past undo her.

For Anna, though, her mother's advice dovetailed now with her father's: *"Sometimes you must put yourself in the way of destiny."*

5

The walk in the meadow became for Anna a daily event. For several days, it was a solitary experience.

When she had begun to think that she would never meet him there again, that his very existence was a trick of her imagination, he appeared. This time she had seen him in the distance, and as he hastened his horse in her direction, she found her heart involuntarily quickening.

"Good afternoon, Lady Anna," he said, bringing his horse to a halt.

"Good afternoon, Lord Stelnicki," she replied, unable to attempt a smile as forward as his.

"Jan—remember?"

"Yes."

"Still deep in thought?"

"Not so very."

"Good!" He swung down gracefully from his horse.

To counter the increase of some foreign excitement that ran beneath her surface, Anna attempted conversation. "I thought that your harvesting would still be under way."

"Oh, it is."

"And yet you can go riding?"

"My men are hardworking and trustworthy." He tied his horse to a low-hanging branch.

"Is it your wheat?"

"Yes."

"What other crops do you cultivate . . . Jan?"

He smiled. "Barley and oats."

"The rotational grains."

His eyes widened beneath the raised brows, so blond as to be almost invisible.

"What is it?" she asked.

"You surprise me."

"That I should know about such things?" Anna laughed, tilting her head to the side. "Well, I expect you'd be quite astonished if I told you I had a knowledge of the planting, maintenance, and yield of numerous fruits and vegetables—as well as tobacco."

"Indeed!" His interest was piqued. "Traditionally our peasants have been left to farm the fruits and vegetables—their mainstays are beetroot and potatoes—so my knowledge is limited. And as for tobacco, I'm at a complete loss! How have you come by this?"

"I've learned about the land from my father. I have my own little garden, too." The memories called up were sudden and painful and Anna fought to keep the tears away. "In time I will return to see to the management of my estate."

Jan's soft tone bespoke his compassion. "It's near Warsaw, isn't it?"

"Just a morning's ride to the west."

"Anna, would you care to sit for a while in the shade of the oak? Even with your bonnet, you're likely to burn in this sun."

"I shouldn't be staying away from the house for very long."

"Not for long. But you could squander a few minutes on a rogue such as I." The blue pools that were his eyes seemed to plead.

Anna laughed. "A few, then." That he called himself a rogue, an appellation she had privately given him at their last meeting, gave depth to her laugh.

On the dry, overgrown grass, Jan spread out his coat and helped Anna to sit. She watched him as he moved effortlessly into a cross-legged position before her. Again, defying convention, he had worn no hat. His shirt was fine-woven cotton, loose-sleeved, with a ruff at the neck. His trousers were brown, a lighter shade than the coat. The calf-high, reddish brown boots were of an excellent leather, supple and shining.

"What is your family name, Anna? You must have thought me insolent in the manner I addressed you last week, but you see, I didn't know it. It's not Gronski, is it?"

"No. My mother and Aunt Stella were sisters, though my mother was the younger by many years. My father's name was Berezowski–Samuel Berezowski."

Jan alluded to the meaning of her surname's root–birch–telling her how beautiful the tree is, so tall and white, so graceful, strong, and healthy. It was, he said, a fitting name for her.

Anna blushed. "My father would say fitting because I was always deserving of a thrashing with a birch rod."

Jan's laughter was explosive. "He never did!"

"No," she laughed. "Not that he didn't want to thrash me on occasion."

"Lady Anna Maria Berezowska–it is a fine name."

"Thank you." Anna smiled, leaned forward, and nodded her head, giving from her seat a mock curtsy.

Jan's brow furrowed slightly now and Anna saw him serious for the first time. But she was unprepared for his next question.

"How is it that your parents died, Anna, one so close upon the other?"

Anna stared mutely for a moment, then averted her eyes.

"Forgive me," he said, "it was stupid of me to have brought up the subject."

Anna gave a slight wave. "There is no need to apologize."

"Oh, but there is. I am a colossal idiot."

"No, I'm silly, I suppose, but it's as if there were some part of me that would block it out . . . as if their deaths had never happened." Anna could not bring herself to face him. She continued: "Sometimes I find myself thinking that I am merely on holiday here at Halicz and that at the end of September I'll return to Sochaczew, to my home and parents. Then my heart remembers and I wonder: Is this the sign of a girl's stupidity . . . or a disordered mind?"

"It is neither. The attempt to put pain outside of the heart is only human, Anna." He leaned very close to her then, lifted his forefinger to her chin, and slowly turned her head so that her eyes could not escape his. His voice was as light as his touch, yet somehow firm and steadying. "But you must be careful not to delude yourself. To speak of their deaths is to accept. Only when there is this acceptance can the healing begin."

Other than her father, Anna had never heard a man speak with such gentleness. Somewhere deep within her she felt a dam crumbling and giving way. A current of affection for this man, not merely attraction, rushed through her.

"Jan," she said, calling on all of her reserve, "my father was murdered."

He blinked in surprise. "Murdered?"

Anna nodded. "He had only just turned forty." Tears started to bead in her eyes.

"There, Anna, you don't have to talk about it."

She managed to hold her tears in check. "I'm fine. You're right. Perhaps I *should* talk about it."

"You loved him very much."

"One couldn't help but love him. He was more at ease roaming the fields on his white stallion than in making idle conversation in the castles of the magnates. I think it was because he was so close to the land that he treated his peasants so well. He saw them as belonging more to the land than to himself. He often said it was merely fate and a little courage that prompted his great-great-grandfather to ride with King Jan Sobieski against the Turks a hundred years ago. That was when the family was declared noble and granted our estate on the River Vistula."

Anna paused, summoning the strength to continue. "Papa's peasants loved him. . . . Except for Feliks Paduch, a drunk and ne'er-do-well who stole anything left unattended for two ticks of the clock." She felt the taste of bitterness rising from her heart's center. "Had Papa evicted him years before as he so often threatened, he would still be alive."

"Paduch killed him?"

Anna nodded. "He was caught, too, but managed to escape the fool magistrate before he was sentenced. He has sworn to see my father's lineage end with me."

Jan's mouth dropped open slightly. "Is that why Count Gronski insisted you live with them for a year?"

"Partially, I suppose."

"And your mother?"

"As much as she loved my father, he remained an enigma to her to the last." Anna told him then of the circumstances preceding the deaths of her mother and infant brother.

"Oh, I am so sorry, Anna. My God, you've lost your entire family."

"Yes."

An awkward silence ensued. Neither wanted to protract the conversation. Anna watched as two birds flew from the branches overhead and circled out over the meadow.

It was Jan who broke the quiet. "More and more, men like this Feliks Paduch are taking such action, rising above their station. Such discontent can be traced, I suspect, to the peasants' revolt in France."

"Really?" Anna took the moment to surreptitiously push a tear from her eye. "You don't think such a thing could happen here, do you?"

"I would hope not. Our peasants are much better off than the wretched poor in France. They have some just grievances, to be certain, but our new constitution is a decided advancement for them, as well as for the middle classes." The blond brows came together as one now in an expression of deep concern. "However, should Poland succumb to anarchy, the blame must fall squarely on the nobility."

"On the nobility?"

Jan nodded. "Yes, there are a good many nobles, including some of the magnates, who are opposed to relinquishing any rights to the peasants and middle classes, and they swear that they will see the Third of May Constitution rescinded."

Anna's widening eyes reflected her bewilderment. "But it was passed only this year."

"Yes, and should we overthrow it, we would be asking for the same deserts that are even now being delivered up to the French nobility on the *guillotine*."

Anna sat quietly, stunned as much by what he was saying as by the intensity of his political thoughts. There were, she realized, several sides to the incorrigible cavalier of the first meeting. Now she ventured to ask of *his* family: "Where does your father stand?"

"Squarely behind the Constitution." A pride came into the musical voice. "He worked hard behind the scenes for it. But he is not a well man. I worry about him." He paused for a moment. "Anyway, this is to be a new life for you, Anna. It will be a fine one!"

"I hope so."

"You . . . you don't worry about the curse that Paduch fellow made?"

"No . . . no, I don't. I put that down to drunken swagger."

"I'm certain that that's all it was. Well, then, we must go riding soon—once your mourning is put off, of course. I would so enjoy showing you the countryside."

Though his enthusiasm held her, she felt her face flush hot with embarrassment. All her life she wished she could control the telltale reaction.

"What is it?" he asked, suddenly concerned.

Resigned, she inhaled, then blurted out the admission: "Lord Stelnicki, I cannot ride!"

It took a moment for realization to overcome puzzlement, but then he began to laugh, with great relish.

Anna's uncertain reaction now was to halfheartedly join in his mirth while trying to explain. "Papa had agreed to teach me, but Mama strictly forbade it. She worried over my safety. But Zofia has started to tutor me at riding! We go out mornings. It's an incredible feeling—like that of a bird soaring! I'm afraid I'm not very good at it, though. And I'm more than a little sore, too."

"I'll wager that you are!" Jan was trying, unsuccessfully, to control his laughter. "I'm sorry to laugh. Forgive me. Actually you gave me quite a fright when you became so serious. I thought for a moment that you were going to tell me you are already . . . betrothed."

"What? Oh no, no."

"Good. And don't worry. You'll win your horse over, I'm sure, as you must have done your cousin . . . I mean to get Zofia out and about in the *morning*."

He knew Zofia well enough, Anna thought. "Oh, it is *late* morning!"

The two fell to laughing again. Anna's amusement was genuine this time. Somehow she felt no guilt that it was at her cousin's expense.

"You'll be an expert before you know it." Jan placed his hand over Anna's. "And we shall take long, long rides." The texture of his voice thickened and he inclined his head toward hers.

Anna suddenly sobered, withdrawing her hand from his.

"What is it? What's wrong, Anna?"

"It's just that . . ." She paused, heart thumping. "Jan," she began again, "I am afraid that my aunt and uncle will not allow you to call."

He smiled as if in relief. "Of course, they will. We are the very best of neighbors."

"But . . . you see . . . you are not Catholic."

"Is that all?" He laughed.

His reaction stunned Anna. "You don't seem to understand what . . . what a great difference it *does* make . . . that you are not Catholic."

"Oh, it is true, I admit. My parents were of the Arian sect, though my father is more political now than religious. But I, myself, follow no religion."

"Lord Stelnicki," Anna said with an even preciseness, "that fact only serves to widen the chasm between us."

"Now, don't misunderstand me. I do believe in God. Look about us, Anna Maria. How could anyone with sight look and not believe? It's just that my God is with me here, in my heart, and all about us—in the meadow grass, in the fields of grain, in the flowers, in this old oak tree, and in the blue of the sky. Mine is a personal God. I haven't followed any of the religions of the churches, though I do not *disbelieve* their doctrines. Do you understand?"

"I . . . I think so." In truth, it was a puzzle to her—and disconcerting.

"I'll speak to your uncle," he was saying. "If we cannot agree, I shall become a Catholic."

Anna's mouth fell slack. "Jan! Please do not make light of this."

"Oh, I'll joke as often as the next fellow, but believe me when I say that I am quite in earnest."

"You can't be! A religion is not to be put on like a cloak or a hat."

"Just because I don't wear a hat doesn't mean that I *can't* wear one!"

Anna stared at him as if he had suddenly started speaking Serbian.

"Now let me finish, Lady Anna. I would not be simply bowing to the custom of your religion. I'm certain that my God can be found in your church. You see, I believe that He can be found in *all* of the churches."

Jan was becoming more and more enigmatic. Was he serious? Did he truly mean to become a Catholic for her sake? And why was it that she seemed always to be questioning his sincerity?

"If your aunt and uncle will permit," he was saying, "will you allow me to call on you?"

"Oh, yes." The words fell from her lips before the thought was processed. Discretion then reclaimed her. "I . . . I should return to the house now, Jan."

"Will you be walking tomorrow afternoon, Anna?"

Anna smiled. "I may."

"Good! Do you know you have dimples when you smile slyly like that?" Jan helped her to her feet, then mounted his horse. "I'll see you here, then . . . unless you would care to practice your horsemanship now?"

"Thank you, no. I'll walk. Oh, and Jan," she joked, "do be sure not to mistake me this time for Zofia."

His lips curled in a devilish smile. "Now it is I who have a confession to make, Anna. I have never seen Zofia dressed in black—why, if she were in mourning, I have no doubt that she would sidestep custom and appear in a delicious pink dress. So, you see, I knew full well who you were the other day—Lord Gronski had told me about your arrival."

He gave spur to his horse now and rode off.

Anna stood staring at the retreating figure, wondering what it was about this man that set her pulse running with the wind. But any doubts that this was the man whom she would love and wed dissipated like vapor at noon.

From her vantage point on the little hill above the meadow, Zofia had seen enough. Though she could not hear Jan and Anna, she was able to see the physical interactions and emotions play out on their faces as clearly as if they wore Greek masks.

She stood transfixed, her own emotions stirring a strange heat within her. Seeing was believing, but she could scarcely comprehend the tender scene she had just witnessed.

What was Jan up to? Anna had been correct: he *was* expressing his interest. And in no subtle way, either. Why? *Was* he interested in Anna? How deeply? Or was he trying, as Zofia suspected, to arouse her jealousy?

In frustration, Zofia struck her riding crop against the skirt of her dress. She knew her only course of action now was to let the little flirtation play out. It would come to nothing, she was certain. Still, she felt helpless, as if she were drowning. She didn't like it.

Zofia realized, with a jolt, that it was jealousy she felt. And she liked that less. *Did* she love Jan Stelnicki? Perhaps. Or perhaps she was reacting to the possibility of being the loser in this drama. A loser to a country innocent. She silently damned her cousin.

Zofia mounted her horse. Just for fun she had encouraged Anna in her attraction to Jan. Well, the game had turned dangerous, inciting the unforeseen, but Zofia became determined that any reversal of fortune not be hers. "Anna Maria Berezowska," she whispered, her teeth scarcely parting, "you will come to rue the day you came to Halicz."

6

Anna adapted to life at the Gronski manor house. She had not known what to expect, for according to the terms of the Partition of 1772, some twenty years earlier, the city and province of Halicz had fallen under the rule of Austria. However, she found Halicz essentially no different from her own town of Sochaczew, its citizens and their way of life no less Polish. The old culture survived and flourished under Austria's Leopold II.

But life's routine was very different for her now. At home she had assisted her mother and their servant Luisa in the management of the household, but here at Hawthorn House, the women sewed, read, and entertained, contributing relatively little to the real welfare of the home. For this, four servant women were designated to do all of the cooking and housework so that there were not the lightest of tasks for Countess Stella, Lady Zofia, or Anna.

She spent her mornings reading, and when Zofia arose—not much before noon—riding. Afternoons were spent with Jan. Countess Stella never questioned her whereabouts, and Anna suspected that Zofia made excuses on her behalf. She worried that she would be found out and that the rendezvous would be banned. How long could they be kept secret? Each day, too, Jan urged her to agree to a full day of riding.

The time spent with Jan was the highlight of her day. Whether walking in the meadow or sitting under the oak, the two seldom lacked a topic of conversation. As Anna spoke of her former life at Sochaczew, she realized she was coming to terms with her past. And as she listened to Jan talk of his thoughts and experiences, she was awed by his worldliness, intelligence, and humor.

At night, when Anna lay alone in her bed, her mind and heart were filled with thoughts of Jan Stelnicki. She came to hope that he loved her, a hope undermined at times with self-doubt. She was certain that his winning ways could bring him the woman of his choice: the richest, the most sophisticated, the most beautiful. Was it conceivable that he would one day propose to *her?*

On occasion, a certain intangible fear invaded her; later, she would put this dark foreboding down to the loss of everyone she had loved, but for now she fought it. Wasn't she deserving of some happiness? When a heart is in the full bloom of first love, destructive thought finds no welcome. And Anna was very much in love.

Anna saw Zofia waiting for her on the pillared porch.

"Walter is coming home, Anna!"

"How wonderful! It's been so many years that I wonder whether I'll recognize him. How old is he now?"

"Just twenty-two."

"And a soldier of fortune! You and your parents must be very proud and happy."

"I swear, you do have romantic notions, dearest. He's a mercenary in Catherine's military machine—an officer, true—but a mercenary just the same. He's as brash and incorrigible as ever, no doubt. We never did get along. Oh, don't look so puzzled."

Zofia hugged Anna to her. "If only I had had a sister like you, Ania. But his coming does at least mean some life in this dreary house, some entertaining, a party or two to while away these last dull days in the country. Oh! And then this fall I shall be able to show you Warsaw!"

"Zofia, I've been to the capital. Have you forgotten that Sochaczew is but a short distance away?"

"Ah! But have you been to the theater? To concerts? To the opera? Royal receptions?"

Anna could only shake her head.

"Well," Zofia scoffed, "then you have not been to Warsaw!"

"It all sounds so sophisticated and exciting."

"And, my dear, absolutely everything is done in the French fashion. It's that way on the entire continent."

"Is it? Well, in the meantime, I shall be glad to see my cousin. And you will be, too, though you may not admit to it. When does Walter arrive?"

"Wednesday. And now for the real surprise!"

"What? What is it?"

Zofia's dark eyes twinkled as she held Anna in suspense.

"Oh, Zofia, tell me!"

Zofia spoke slowly to heighten the effect. "Mother has agreed that you put off your mourning on that day."

"Really?" Anna gasped. "But that is so very soon."

"I know, and you can be certain it took some clever speeches on my part."

"But . . . do you think it proper?"

"It's every bit as proper as the way you spend your afternoons."

Anna was struck silent. Her face burnt with embarrassment.

"There, there. I only mean that it's wonderful, you little fool—nothing less. Walter was the perfect excuse. Oh, don't look like that! Now, I shall personally see to your apparel and *toilette* for the occasion. Come upstairs this minute and we shall select the dress!"

Anna hesitated. "Zofia?"

"Now you are not to feel guilty."

"No, it isn't that."

"What is it, then?"

"Today Jan made me promise to go riding on the very day after my mourning is finished. How can I keep that from your parents? I am not ready for a confrontation with them about Jan . . . not yet."

"Riding with Jan? The day after?" Zofia paused, her almond eyes narrowing into mere slits for a moment, then opening wide. "I know! What if I tell them I've arranged for a riding party, one that includes Walter and me?"

"Oh, that would be wonderful, really! In fact, I would prefer having the two of you along."

"It does sound like fun. Lutisha will pack a lunch basket. Let's set it for Thursday morning then."

"But do you think you can smooth it over with your parents . . . about Jan, I mean?"

Zofia shrugged. "What harm can there be in having him join our little riding party? It'll be perfectly innocent, darling."

"I hope so. I feel terrible about having disobeyed your mother."

"There is one thing, Anna."

"What?"

"I don't think you should tell Jan that Walter and I are to join you. At least not until Thursday morning."

"But why—"

"Just trust me, Ania. Now, come along. And don't fret so. I said that I would arrange it, didn't I?"

Countess Stella Gronska inspected the kitchen fireplace where a roast sizzled on the spit. "Is this being turned often enough?"

Old Lutisha rolled her eyes but answered in the French fashion in which all of the housemaids had been tutored. "Yes, Madame Gronska."

"And is it being basted enough?"

"Yes, Madame."

"Good. Everything must be perfection tonight." She walked quickly to the table near the great white ceramic stove used only for bread. "Marta, is this bread fresh? Not this morning's bread, that would never do."

Lutisha's daughter smiled indulgently. "It is still hot to the touch, Madame Gronska."

"So it is." The countess pulled a crust from a loaf of rye and tasted it. "Excellent! Without bread even meat has no flavor."

" 'Tis so," Lutisha said and laughed.

The countess finished her rounds of the kitchen. "Ah, I can see everything is in order, as I might have expected. I suppose I have only slowed the pace here, but it is over a year since my son has been home."

"A very long time," Lutisha said. "We are all glad to see Lord Walter again."

The countess checked the preparations in the dining room for the third time, then moved toward the west wing.

Walter had arrived in good spirits. He seemed happy. Proud of the work he was doing in Russia. The countess had her own thoughts about that, but what worried her now was how he would react to what she and Leo had to say concerning his future. He was hotheaded, as hotheaded as Leo. She would have to play peacemaker, no doubt, as in the old days.

The countess found her husband dressing for supper, buttoning his best shirt.

"How handsome you look, Leo!"

"For an old man, you mean?"

"I do not!"

"Damn, I'm all thumbs with these pearl buttons. Why must they make them so damn small?"

Moving to her husband, the countess assumed the task, as she had done a hundred times before. "You must take your complaint directly to the oysters," she laughed. "Tell them to make bigger pearls. Our children may be grown, Leo, but that doesn't make us old."

He grunted. "Nor does their growth mean that they are adults, Stella."

"You won't bring up at the table the subject of Walter's returning home, will you? Not at supper, not in front of Anna."

"No, I won't."

"And you won't drink too much?"

"No."

"And you won't encourage Walter to drink?"

"Walter doesn't need encouragement." The count laughed. "And you're nagging, my dear."

"I'm sorry. Leo, what will you do if Walter does not come back to Halicz?"

"We've spoken of that, Stella."

"You don't truly mean to say that you would disown him?"

"I sincerely hope it does not come to that."

"But if it even comes to making the threat, must you reveal . . . you know . . . that which we have kept from him?"

"I'm not so sure it was a wise thing not to have told him years ago. He will have to know someday."

"Be that as it may, I fear telling him now. I fear his reaction." The countess thought for a moment. "And there is Zofia, too—There, finished!"

The count turned to look in the mirror. "Thank you, my dear."

"You could do it, too, had you the patience." From behind, the countess stared at her husband's reflection. "Leo, sometimes I feel as if she knows our secret."

"Zofia? Nonsense, how could she know? As long I have you here, will you help me with my sash?"

"She can be very sly at times," the countess said, taking in hand the brown and purple silk of Turkish design. "She's my own daughter, but she has a touch of the devil in her." The countess pulled the sash tightly about her husband's waist and secured it. "You know, I never know what she's thinking. Not like a mother should."

"Is there any way she *could* know about Walter?"

"Perhaps. A few months ago I found my secretary unlocked. I never leave it unlocked, Leo. And I found some old papers and letters askew. I didn't want to make an issue of it. I didn't want to believe it."

"Well, let it be," the count said, turning to his wife, "unless she should say something about it. She's a wild one, Stella. Always has been. I dare say marriage will calm her down in a hurry."

"Don't you think we should tell her about the arrival of the Grawlinski family?"

"No! That's one secret I plan to *keep* from her. I don't want to put up with her arguments should she find out. They will arrive *unexpectedly*, the marriage will take place, and that will be that. Are we ready?"

Leaving their bedchamber, they passed through their anteroom. "Tell me, Stella, how have we managed to raise two children who so thoroughly reject our values? A man should leave behind more than land and money."

"They are just young, Leo. Young beer is frothy. You've said so yourself."

The answer seemed to quiet her husband, but as they came to the dining room, arm in arm, the countess could not empty herself of trepidation. Leo had patience in short supply.

Walter, too, was unpredictable.

Anna drew in her breath as Zofia helped her with the hooking of her dress.

"Black is for dead things, darling," Zofia hissed into her ear. "When a flower dies, it turns black with decay, as do animals and men. Who, then, ever decreed that the living be made to wear such a noncolor? Good riddance to your mourning! There. Now, turn around. Why, Anna, you look magnificent! Yellow isn't my color, but on you it looks divine."

"Really, Zofia?"

"Really, Zofia?" she mimicked, chuckling. "Believe me, it's a good thing that there is no suitor of mine downstairs for you to poach. Although there's to be a party on Saturday, and for that I think I shall have to lock you in your room."

Anna gazed into the long mirror. Zofia's gown did, indeed, seem to transform her.

"Have you seen Walter?" Anna asked.

"Yes." Zofia's voice was flat. "Now, let's see, you scarcely need any rouge on your cheeks." She smiled wickedly. "Those walks in the meadow have given you a lovely bloom."

Anna fell speechless with embarrassment. She felt blood rising to her head.

"Just a little touch of red to your lips and some powder—"

"Oh, I've never worn anything on my face."

Zofia cut short her cousin's concern with a flick of her hand. "There's a season for everything and everyone, Anna. Doesn't the Bible say something to that effect? This is *our* season, cousin."

Anna acquiesced and found herself impressed by the results.

When the two were ready to descend the stairs, Anna put her hand on her cousin's arm, detaining her. "Zofia, have you mentioned the riding party to your parents?"

Zofia stared opaquely. "No, dear," she said simply, starting down the stairs.

Anna raced after her. "But I've told Jan. He'll be here at seven to-morrow morning."

"Oh, I'll bring it up tonight. It will sound quite spontaneous. Leave it to me."

Anna had no time to worry further. Walter was waiting at the bottom of the stairs.

"Ah, the years can work wonders! Is it really you, Anna?" Walter kissed her on either cheek, in the French vogue.

"It is I."

"The same little urchin who fell out of the willow tree?"

"Oh, how memory can be manipulated," Anna said, laughing. "I seem to remember being pushed."

"You were," Zofia drolly intoned. "Chivalry was not one of Walter's strong suits as a boy. If indeed you had any, Walter. Or should I say *have* any?"

Walter bowed dramatically. "We all change, Zosia. I would hope that our dear cousin does not bear a grudge."

"You can be certain *I* will bear a grudge if you continue to call me Zosia. My name is Zofia."

"The stories!" Anna cried, hoping to avert an argument. "Do you remember, Zofia, how at night Walter would frighten us out of our wits with his stories of blood and gore?"

"I do."

"Good news, then," Walter said. "My experiences in the army have added significantly to my bank of bloody tales. And these new additions, ladies, are grounded in realism."

"I'm certain of it," Anna said with a laugh.

Walter and Anna chatted for a few minutes and were laughing as the three went in to supper. Zofia's usual effervescence was in short supply.

Anna and Zofia sat across from Walter. The count and countess, seated at either end of the great table, seemed delighted to have their little family reunited.

Anna thought Walter quite handsome in the gold-embellished red uniform of a lieutenant. It took little coaxing on her part to set him expounding on his adventures in the service of Empress Catherine. He claimed that because of his Polish background he was being groomed to do diplomatic work between the empress and King Stanisław. Anna was impressed. His parents listened, too, but Zofia sat quietly sipping her wine, uninterested in the conversation.

Lutisha began to serve an ambrosial meal of roast duck, dressing, and mushrooms. Anna glanced now across the table; her gaze was caught, and held, by Walter. She thought his hard, angular face somehow appropriate to that of a soldier. What was in those reddish brown eyes, deep-set under hair black as a starless night, that sent a cold tingling along her spine? It was a soldier's attitude, she decided, one that reflected a soldier's cumulative dark experiences.

As the supper continued and the wine flowed, she became aware of how his striking, yet brutish, face would turn in her direction when no one else was watching. However, by the time Anna's glass of wine was but half drained, she was immersed in private thoughts—of the riding party, and of Jan Stelnicki. . . .

Later, a change in the conversation's tone at the table reclaimed Anna's full attention. Walter's brusque words were directed at his father: "I can scarcely believe that you support the Third of May Constitution."

The Count Gronski's short, stout form shifted in his chair. "It is a great reform."

"For whom?"

"For everyone."

The wine had affected both father and son, and their volume rose as the debate escalated.

"Oh, it surely seems to contain something for everyone." Walter's tone was bitterly sarcastic. "Peasants are guaranteed human rights; indentured servants may purchase their own freedom; the middle classes are given political recognition; and full religious freedom is preserved for all. Now, tell me, how do *we* gain by it?"

"What do you mean?" the count asked.

"It would seem that everyone gains by it, Father, except the nobility."

"*I* can tell you what we've gained by it," Zofia said.

All eyes turned to her. Sitting smugly in her cinnamon-colored gown, she had suddenly come alive. Anna noticed that her second glass of wine stood empty.

"Walter," Zofia asked, "haven't you heard the mazurka that was specially written for the Constitution? Why, it's a splendid little tune complete with its own dance! I'll teach it to you, brother."

Count Gronski's fist came down on the table, rattling the plates, silver, and crystal and causing the candle flames on the candelabrums to flare and dance. "Your levity in this matter is not appreciated, young lady!"

Zofia had amused herself, though, and winked now at Anna.

"The Polish nobility," the count asserted, "will earn itself a high place in history for its declaration of rights to all people. If a fledgling country like the United States of America can succeed in a similar undertaking, by God, surely Poland, with its illustrious past, can attempt no less."

Walter shook his head. "To grant these concessions is to invite trouble. The rabble will only demand more and more from what they will construe as a weakened aristocracy, and with good reason."

Countess Gronska sat forward in her chair, her huge eyes reflecting concern that the harmony of her carefully orchestrated meal was threatened. "Leo, can't this discussion be postponed until after supper?"

The count seemed not to hear. "Can't you see, Walter," he persisted, "that if the middle classes and peasants are not allowed certain rights and privileges, we could take the same path that France is set upon?"

"Not if the aristocracy maintains a position of strength! I think that the *Sejm* that drew up this so-called constitution must have been made up of fools. As for King Stanisław's signing of it—it only confirms my image of him as a bumpkin and a weakling."

Count Gronski's face reddened with rage. "You dare speak that way of your king? Of your homeland? Where are your loyalties, Walter? Where?"

Walter shrugged.

"Please, please. Don't excite yourself so, dear," Countess Gronska begged. "There will be no more such political talk until after dinner when you two may discuss this matter privately. Whatever will Anna think?"

An awkward silence ensued. The count deferred to his wife's wishes, and his normal color returned.

Walter's eyes caught Anna's now. She thought something cold and calculating lurked in their brownish fire. Was this the way of soldiers?

Clearing her throat self-consciously, Anna asked, "How long will you be at home, Walter?"

"Less than a week, I'm afraid. The campaign against the Turks is being accelerated. I'm to go directly to the front."

"Oh, Walter!" his mother exclaimed, her hands raised to her face.

"Don't worry, Mother. We anticipate victory within a few months."

"You do promise to take care of yourself?"

"I do, Mother. Father, you must agree with me on this at least: that the whole of the continent will be a safer place once the Turks are duly trounced."

"More political talk," Zofia sighed. "I shall scream."

"I will admit," the count said, "that the barbarians deserve it. But the prowess of Catherine's generals will neither increase my liking for her, nor decrease my distrust. She may very well protect us by aborting some future invasion of the Turks, but who, for the love of the Almighty, is to protect us from *her?*"

"Did you know," Zofia whispered to Anna, "that Catherine was once mistress to our King Stanisław? They say she has been mistress to no fewer than–"

"Zofia!" the countess snapped. "I am not as deaf to your vulgar asides as you sometimes seem to think. The topic is not a fit one for the table–or a young lady. Do you understand me?"

"Yes, Mother. I'm sorry." She could not suppress a little laugh, however, and a softer comment murmured to Anna: "But it's far more amusing than anything else we've heard."

"Walter," the count was saying, "when the Turkish campaign is finished, I want you to resign your commission and come home."

Walter was momentarily startled, then piqued. "Father, I've written to you about that."

"Walter, dear," the countess pleaded, "we are getting no younger, your father and I. It is our wish . . . and it is time . . . that you take up your rightful duties here."

Walter seemed to have no wish to draw out the tears that welled in his mother's eyes. "Ah, look!" he exclaimed. "Lutisha has brought us dessert."

"Ouch!" the corpulent servant cried.

Walter had pinched her and one of the honey cakes fell from her platter. The strain was lifted for the moment and everyone laughed, even the befuddled, toothless servant, who retreated to the kitchen, her red apron held to her face.

Anna stared over the pages of the book she held, vacantly watching the small blaze in the reception room fireplace. The Countess Gronska had ordered it lighted to cut the chill of that mid-September evening. The countess absently took up her crewelwork. Zofia held a book but made no attempt to read it. All three were listening intently to the Count Gronski and Walter, who were raging at one another in the library.

The countess sighed sadly. "They agree on nothing, Anna. But they are cut from the same cloth. Each is willful; each has a terrible temper."

Zofia threw her book to the floor and jumped from her chair. "Listen!" she gasped, as if thrilled. "Father is taking Walter down to the cellar!"

Anna stared, noticing for the first time some dark facet of her cousin.

"Oh, don't look so puzzled, Anna darling," Zofia said. "Father would often punish Walter and me by taking us down to the wine cellar, sometimes leaving us there for the entire night. Until one time when we drank ourselves senseless." Zofia laughed at the memory. "I was clever enough, however, to escape the thrashing for that. Walter wasn't so lucky. Of course, we should be beyond that stage now. He must have said something terribly wicked for Father to become so enraged."

The countess was annoyed by her daughter's exultant attitude. "I expect your father merely wishes to spare Anna a scene. Zofia, perhaps you are not so old as to be beyond correction. Now keep to your own affairs."

"If only I had one to keep to," Zofia said in an aside to Anna.

"What?" the countess demanded.

"I said," Zofia lied, "that I'm now eighteen. Anna, don't you agree that family and society place too many restraints on young people, especially on our sex? Why, a woman must be forty before she can enjoy her freedom—and by that time, what does it matter?" She chuckled at her own comedy.

Anna was not about to be coaxed into a family quarrel. She felt intrusive and uncomfortable. "Good night, Aunt," she said, rising. She kissed the countess. "It's late and I'm tired."

She looked pointedly at Zofia. "I should like to go riding early tomorrow."

The hint seemed to elude her cousin.

Anna pressed the issue. "We should both be rested, Zofia."

"To bed! To bed! Oh, how I despise the dreary country. There are no weddings, no banquets, no opera, no balls—only the deathly fresh air. And the music—Oh! How I do miss the music!" Zofia flung her hands in the air now and began dancing the lively steps of the mazurka in front of the hearth, gaily humming its melody.

Anna started to leave the room, brooding that her cousin seemed bound to forget to mention the riding party to her parents.

Zofia halted her self-amusement. "Wait! Listen," she whispered sharply, "is it possible Father would use the whip on Walter?"

"Don't be absurd," Countess Stella said. Yet Anna could see that she was concerned.

Anna chose not to stay and listen. She gave her cousin a perfunctory kiss and went directly upstairs to her room.

For a long time Anna lay unable to sleep, unable to exorcise dark and vague premonitions. The evening had upset her. She felt uncomfortable, too, caught up as she was in a family squabble. Walter had not favorably impressed her; secretly she was glad that his stay would be short. Zofia, too, in her attitude toward her brother revealed a sinister side that had only been hinted at before. There must be real love there between brother and sister, but other issues seemed to keep it buried.

And why hadn't Zofia mentioned the riding party? Anna could not believe that she hadn't picked up on her hint. Her cousin was not so obtuse. She had deliberately put her off. Why?

Perhaps it was just as well, considering the humor the count and countess were in.

What was to happen now? She would almost surely have to send Jan away in the morning. Would he understand?

What was Zofia thinking of? Anna lay listening for the sound of her cousin passing her door so that she might speak to her. But the rich food and the wine lulled her into a deep drowsiness. With the strains of the mazurka still dallying in her head, sleep rose up to claim her.

7

Anna awoke just before seven, filled with tense anticipation. Shivering in the chilled room, she washed, quickly dressed, and hurried to her cousin's room.

"Wake up, Zofia," she whispered, gently shaking her. "Jan Stelnicki will be at the stable in only minutes. Perhaps he's already there. What are we to do?"

Zofia moaned and turned her face into the pillow.

"Zofia, please!"

She stirred. "Oh, is it truly morning?"

"It truly is. Now, what are we going to do about the outing? Surely we must cancel–"

"But why should we?"

"Your parents will–"

"I shall fix it," Zofia said, sitting up in bed.

"Oh, do you think you can? Did you speak to Walter about joining us?"

"Yes. Once everyone went to bed, I went down to the cellar to ask him. All I got for my effort is this headache."

"Zofia, you were drinking!"

"Oh, a little wine," she crooned as she wiped the sleep from her eyes. "We laughed over our childhood days. You know, you may be right, that I do hold some fondness for Walter."

"Of course you do. But he didn't wish to come with us?"

Zofia shook her head. "He seemed wholly disinterested. I suppose he's had enough riding of late. The three of us shall go."

"If you are certain . . ."

"I am. Why should your day be spoiled?"

"Do hurry out of bed, then."

"I must have time to get ready, Anna. You know how I am about my appearance."

"We'll wait for you at the stable. You must promise to hurry."

"What is this you've got on?"

"My silk blouse and green skirt."

"The skirt will never do, darling. It's so . . . rustic. Now that you're out of that horrid black, we must do something with you. In the wardrobe you'll find a russet riding skirt and matching jacket."

Anna suspected that it would be more expedient to comply with her cousin's wishes. She quickly found the outfit. "Why, it's stunning, Zofia!"

"You may keep it. Your blouse is fine; the creamy color will set off the russet nicely. Hurry and change!"

Zofia sat motionless, watching Anna slip into the outfit. "There! Now that's much better."

Anna moved to the bed. "Zofia, won't you please get up?"

"I've come up with an idea, darling," she announced. "Ride to that secret pond of ours in the forest. The stable master and I will take a shorter route I know of and perhaps be there even before you and Jan. That will give me time to get ready and Lutisha time to pack a lunch. I'm afraid I failed to mention the outing to her."

"Oh, no! I'll wait for you and the lunch. I'll send one of the servants out to tell Jan we've been detained."

"No, Anna, it's decided. You and Jan go ahead, I *insist*."

"But Aunt Stella," Anna breathed, "and your father, when they find out—"

"You are a worrywart, I swear. I'll take care of them, dearest."

Zofia took hold of Anna's hands and pulled her close, the dark eyes assessing her. "Janek is harmless, Ania, a tamed bear. I know. Moody sometimes, perhaps, but nothing to worry about. Now run along. Oh, and let my appearance at the pond be a surprise, all right?"

"Oh, Zofia," Anna whispered, realizing now that she was trembling. "I could not possibly—"

"Oh, yes, you can. And you will! Don't be a ninny, Anna. How can you ever hope to be cosmopolitan if you won't forget your country naiveté? Do you think a French girl would shy away from a handsome man? Never!"

Her heart racing, Anna hurried down the servants' stairs and through the house, praying that no one would catch sight of her. She was pondering something, too. Zofia had used Jan's diminutive, "Janek." Why? Was she on such familiar terms with Jan? Then she realized that Zofia and Jan must have been friends since childhood, and so such familiarity was only natural.

Outside, she pinned her riding hat to her head, and hastened through the damp morning air to the stable.

Her mind was a whirlwind. She knew that their going into the forest unchaperoned would be judged scandalous by most, but her pulse quickened at the thought of being alone with Jan for the first time since her mourning was put off. She was at once happy and fearful.

Zofia had been right: before meeting Jan, Anna had had no experience with men. And during the meetings with him in the meadow, her mourning had served as a kind of shield; without that, she was apprehensive about what she should say, how she should act. She wished that she had had the worldly-wise Zofia coach her in such things. There was never a lull in a conversation when her ebullient cousin was present. How will Jan act now? she wondered. What will he say? Might he say that he *loves* me?

Jan stood just inside the stable, smiling. His riding outfit was of deep blue, one that intensified the blue of his eyes. His shirt, open at the neck to reveal a matting of reddish blond chest hair, was very white against his tanned skin. He held the reins of his own black steed, as well as those of another horse, slightly smaller.

He nodded toward the snow-white mare. "This one is yours, Anna," he said, "if you want her."

"You don't mean . . ."

"I surely do." The smile widened.

Anna stood there fighting back a fountainhead of tears. Everything in her background suggested that she must refuse such a magnificent gift, but she could not bring herself to do it. Perhaps later, after she had a chance to consult her cousin. She had no wish to start off the day by hurting or even insulting Jan by refusing the gift.

The old stable master entered now.

"Look, Stanisław! Lord Stelnicki has given me my own horse. Isn't it a lovely creature?"

" 'Tis a beauty, milady."

"Do you think you can board another, Stanisław?" Jan asked.

"One more will be no bother, milord."

"Thank you, Jan," Anna said, "though it's too great a gift."

"Nonsense." The piercing eyes held Anna's for a moment.

Outside, Jan helped Anna to mount her horse. He then joked with the stable master, slipping some coins into his gnarled hand.

Anna yielded now to an impulse, thinking that she would show off her newly acquired riding skills. Without waiting for Jan to mount his horse, she slapped the riding crop against the milky flank.

Like a bolt of lightning, the highly muscled mare took off, her hooves pounding loudly upon the hardened ground.

Only the day before and on days previous, Anna had thoroughly relished her horseback outings with Zofia. As they made the progression from a tame canter to a lively gallop, new feelings of power and exhilaration surged within her. Her blood pulsed with a joy of life.

How very different were Anna's feelings today! Her animal ran so fast that Anna gasped for air and held on for dear life. She was too frightened to call out.

Somewhere behind her, she thought—prayed!—were the sounds of Jan's horse's hooves. She thought, too, that she could hear him calling to her.

The neatly tilled furrows of the farmland flew beneath her in a blinding fury as the wind cut into her face. The landscape about her was nothing more than a flashing blur of color.

Anna had learned to ride on a much smaller and more docile horse so that her efforts to slow the galloping mare were futile. She feared now that the horse would stumble and send her tumbling headlong to the hard ground, and she could not catch enough of a breath even to cry out.

At last, Jan caught up to Anna, the powerful shoulder of the stallion pressing into that of the mare. Reaching over, Jan took Anna's reins, and very near to where the furrowed acreage ended and the forest began, managed to bring her horse to a halt.

Anna panted for breath. She felt faint.

"Are you all right, Anna?" There was concern in Jan's voice, but Anna suspected an amusement, too.

"I think so. Only winded. And a bit humiliated. I dare say Angel is a more tranquil creature."

"I should have warned you that this one has spirit. Horses are like people, Anna, each with a different temperament. And as with people, you should get to know them before putting them to the test."

"Thank you for the advice, belated as it is." Anna managed a laugh, even if it were at her own expense. "Tell me, does this horse have a name?"

"We call her 'Pegasus.'"

"How appropriate! I think she does have wings, indeed!"

Jan laughed.

Anna spied then what she thought was a sparkle of impetuousness in his eyes.

Before them spread the great forest of giant oaks, cloaked now in hues that could only hint at the multicolored splendor to come. "Isn't it beautiful here?" Anna said, trying to appear composed.

"Let me help you down." His voice itself seemed a caress. "We'll rest here awhile."

"No," Anna replied. "I'm fine, really. Let's continue." ·

"You must keep tighter reins," he warned, handing them over to Anna. "She must be shown who is the master—or mistress." His hand lingered over Anna's for a few moments.

As their horses moved now, slowly, and the shadows of the high trees engulfed them, Anna's mind raced with as many thoughts as there were leaves. Why did I listen to Zofia? Why did I put my reputation at risk? And might there be an even greater risk? I've had no experience in the ways of courtship. How good of a judge of character can I be when I could not even anticipate a horse's temperament?

They were soon deep into the forest and had to pick their way delicately, as the old trail was largely covered by a thick undergrowth of sweet briar and bracken. Here and there, angling shafts of light squeezed through the treetops and fell in brilliant beams to the forest floor. The morning air was made visible by the rising mist. Saplings of oak leaned and stretched away from their own rooted earth in a life struggle for their share of a limited sunlight. The forest was cool and pleasant, the ride relaxing, and the anxiety within Anna began to lessen.

"Did you bring any coins, Anna?"

"Coins?" Her puzzlement lasted only a moment; then she, too, heard the eerie sound. Somewhere, far into the interior of the forest a cuckoo intoned its strange lament. "No, I have not."

"Nor I. Ah, well, what harm can befall us on such a magnificent day?"

Anna's love and respect for legends—more than superstition—made her regret that Jan had given his coins to Stanisław.

Anna's grandmother had told her the old folktale: A lovely maiden had made fun of Saint Anna, who was berry-picking in the woods; the offended saint transformed the girl into a cuckoo bird, destined forever to haunt the countryside bemoaning its fate. If, according to the tale, one jingles a few coins when the sound of the cuckoo is heard, all would be well.

Anna had always thought it a morbid story of revenge, one unworthy of a saint. She wondered at the precaution, too: could following superstition buy protection? And yet, her first reaction at not having coins was regret. Of course, Jan was right. What harm could befall them on such a day? She tried to shake her fears.

Jan halted and dismounted. Anna stopped, too, watching as he stooped down near a fallen tree. Laughing, he sprang up with an immense mushroom. "Would you look at this, Anna!" As large as his fist, it looked like a speckled beige flower.

"It may be poisonous," Anna said.

"No, it isn't, but you're right to be cautious. The forest does have its dangers, but it has its gifts, too." Jan took a knife and cut into the stalk. "See, Anna, it's pink as a baby's bottom. If it were white and oozing, then we'd worry. It's not especially good for eating, but fine for soups or stews. Lutisha will think it a fine gift."

Quartering it, he placed it in his saddlebag.

He stooped again.

"If they are all that size," Anna called, "we will not need many."

He stood now and approached Anna, his hand hidden behind his back, a hint of a smile playing on his lips.

"I do not presently have a taste for a mushroom," she joked.

"Hold out your hand."

Anna slowly put out her hand, and Jan placed in it a tiny red flower.

"Thank you, Jan."

He bent forward in a mock bow.

"Tell me," Anna asked, "does anyone ever call you Janek?"

"No, never. But you may do so if you wish."

Anna felt the heat rising to her face. She didn't know how to respond.

Jan was staring at her, his eyes narrowing, the smile deepening. At that moment, Anna felt that his mere glance could pierce through to her soul. Somehow, she was certain, he sensed what her feelings were and she dared to think she might know his. *Today, he will ask me to marry him.*

Anna made no effort to dismount, though she was certain that he wanted her to do so. In the cooling shadows, she watched appraisingly as he prepared to mount his horse. How manly he seemed; how handsome. Yet sensitive to others and to the fragile beauty of nature. The sweet wild vapors of the forest enraptured her, intoxicating her with what she knew was love for this man.

They rode leisurely through the lush woodland for nearly two hours. Anna's fears—intuitive and unnamable—blew over her from time to time like whiffs of stale air, but passed quickly.

They came to a tiny stream and paused to allow their horses to drink. Jan drew his horse very close to hers. "Anna," he said, leaning toward her. His arm moved to her waist and he brought her but a hair's breadth away from him.

Jan kissed Anna now for the first time, lightly. Anna did not return the pressure, but she did not pull away, either. She found his lips strangely supple and wonderful. The soft, yielding sigh that she heard now was her own. His grip at her waist tightened and her breasts pressed against his open coat while he kissed her mouth, then her neck. There was a kind of pain in his holding her so, but she was somehow numb to it. The horses moved restlessly beneath them, perhaps nervous at their own proximity. Jan was whispering something so low that she could not decipher it. When his mouth moved to her ear, she realized it was merely her name he was chanting, over and over.

"Let me help you down," he murmured now.

Anna pretended not to hear. His nearness, his kiss, had set off an alarm that sounded through her like the clang of an abbey's bell. She would not—could not—let this get out of hand. When he repeated himself in a voice too distinct for her to ignore, she withdrew from him.

"Jan, we have a long way to ride before we reach the pond I told you of." Anna sent Pegasus splashing into the narrow stream. She had lied: she knew that the pond was reasonably close.

Her fears returned in number. She should never have ventured into the forest alone with Jan. What had possessed her? Her mother had taught her to avoid temptation and risk. She was afraid, too, of certain intangible feelings that stirred and moved within her when Jan kissed her, when he touched her. Had she made the mistake Icarus had? Was she even now flying too near the sun? She could only pray that Zofia would be waiting at the pond for them.

The two followed the stream's course for some distance without speaking. Anna led the way and Jan followed, playing sweet music on his Jew's harp. Occasionally, he would stop his music and mimic the song of a nearby bird. Anna would laugh and turn her head to watch him, but his face seemed inscrutable. Had she angered him?

As they moved along, Anna became fascinated by thousands of

shimmering stones that lay in the shallow stream's bed. The small stones resembled shining rough garnets, emeralds, and amber. Or was it merely the sparkling interplay of water and light that made them appear so? Anna suppressed the desire to ask if some of them might actually be precious stones. She wished not to appear naive.

The stream sloped sharply now as it led them into a denser part of the forest.

Suddenly, Anna saw something odd beneath the waters. It was white, and the curved shape tapered to a jagged point at one end. She halted her horse. "Look, Jan!" she called. "There near to the shore!"

"What is it, Anna?"

"It looks like a tooth. Yes, it looks like a monstrous tooth!"

They approached the object. Jan dismounted at the very edge of the stream and stooped to pick it up with both hands.

"What do you suppose it is?" Anna asked.

"This *is* a kind of tooth, Anna, as big and heavy as it is!" He stared at the awesome object for a few moments, turning it over in his hands. "I would imagine that this is the tusk of a mastodon, an animal as tall and as long as that tree is high."

Anna felt a flicker of fear ignite in her stomach, but she chose to laugh. "Imagine, indeed. Do you mean a dragon?"

Jan indulged her with a smile. "Mastodons were animals that once roamed these lands. People believe the ancients killed all of them."

"Lucky for us," Anna said, with a laugh. "If only we could take it with us. I should like Zofia to see the tooth of a real dragon."

Agitation drew down the corners of Jan's mouth. "I'm serious, Anna. This is from no dragon but from a great beast that once roamed the countryside. Why, my peasants have found the bones of a whole such gigantic creature in my farm soil." When Anna's eyes challenged him further, he became distracted. "It's true!" he cried.

"I've heard of such beasts only in storybooks," Anna said. "You're teasing me."

As if in anger, Jan hurled the object out into the deepest part of the stream. Silently he mounted his horse.

Anna was stunned. Now he *was* angry with her. But why? Zofia was right: his moods *are* changeable.

They left the water now, picking their way through briar and brush, moving into the forest's dense heart.

"You're leading me through a maze of thicket!" he called from behind. "I trust you know the location of this hidden pond?"

"Oh, yes," Anna sang out, but a doubt did invade her private thoughts. Zofia had taken her to the secret place several times since her arrival. Anna believed that they were the only ones who knew of its existence. One could bathe and swim there in complete safety and privacy, but the insects, fish, and water plants inhibited Anna. Zofia was less restrained and splashed happily in the cool waters while Anna sat on the bank, envying her cousin's audacious spirit.

Now, as the horses led Anna and Jan through thick, overhanging willow branches, the pond came into view.

"Look there!" Anna said. She pointed to the small body of water that lay nestled in a circular corps of oaks and willows. Like a mighty sentry, one dead oak stood towering at the water's edge, its great twisted roots exposed at the sloping bank.

Anna's heart quickened. Her eyes scanned ahead, near to the water's edge, then all about. With the leisurely pace she had set and the stops they had made, she was certain that Zofia had had enough time to catch up. There was, however, no sign of her. Ah, Zofia, she thought, it would be a clever trick of you to leave me alone here with Jan Stelnicki.

Anna's knuckles whitened as her hands clenched and drew up reins. The horse came to a halt and Anna leaned forward.

"What are you looking for?" Jan asked, dismounting.

"Nothing." If he *were* angry with her, the storm had passed.

"Come, Anna, let me help you down." His voice was soft but insistent.

Jan's grip was tender as he effortlessly lifted her from the horse. He is so terribly strong, she thought. When her feet touched the ground, his arms went around her. He kissed her, harder than before, with firm lips that slid over and between hers.

The warmth of his mouth and the strength of his body made her feel as though she were being supported solely by him, and should he unfold his arms from her, she would fall to the ground.

Suddenly, she felt and tasted Jan's tongue and was stunned into an unwitting acknowledgment that this foreign kiss was the sweetest of sensations.

Though Anna tried to pull away, she was powerless in Jan's arms, and after a time her body sank with his into the dry, soft leaves beneath them.

Anna could only think that this must not happen. She struggled against Jan and against some interior part of her that wanted not to struggle. On the horse, she had felt an element of protection, an avenue of escape. On the ground, however, she felt suddenly vulnerable.

"Stop . . . please . . ."

The air near the earth smelled warm and heavy with the late summer dust of the leaves and flowers. The weight of the world pulled at her eyelids while Jan kissed her, again and again.

She forced open her eyes when she felt his silken blond hair beneath her chin, his warm mouth on her throat. She had left the top button of her blouse undone, and his lips moved down now, laying light, caressing kisses. Anna's feelings were new to her and undeniably blissful. But she knew their danger, too.

"Jan," she whispered, "please stop."

When he looked up, Anna saw only the fire of desire in his eyes, and she became afraid. He continued to watch her, to study her. Slowly the blue discs that were his eyes filled with a placid tenderness. Anna realized at once that where she thought there was danger, there was only safety, only strength.

"Marry me, Anna. I swear by the white eagle that I will love you always."

Some silent gasp escaped within Anna, but she was unable to speak. What she had dared to dream had come true, and her life would never be the same. Her loneliness would belong to the past. Once again she would be part of a family. And, like her parents, she would experience love and marriage.

She found breath, but words came with difficulty. "Jan, I . . . it is so soon after—"

"It is not! We were meant to find each other when we did. You've felt it all along, just as I have."

"It's just that—"

"I'll make you happy, I will! If we must wait a bit, so be it. We shall. Unhappily, perhaps, but willingly. Only say that you will marry me, Anna. I love you."

"Oh, Jan, I—"

"Anna! Jan!" Zofia's shrilly cheerful voice came from nearby.

Jan jumped to his feet, then aided Anna to hers.

"What is *she* doing here?" he whispered sharply. He had recognized the voice at once.

"She's brought a lunch. It was to be a surprise."

"Oh, it is that."

"Over here," Anna called weakly. She felt her face burning crimson. *What had she seen?*

"There you are!" Zofia cried, appearing from behind a tree. "Good afternoon, Anna . . . Jan." Her voice bubbled with life and innocence. She wore a rose riding outfit and a white lacy blouse. Her black hair fell in a free-flowing wavy mass.

"Good afternoon, Zofia," Jan said. He pretended to be busy tethering the already secured horses to a shrub.

"I began to think that you might not come." Anna was aware that her own voice and visage could not disguise her embarrassment. She could not say the truth: that she had begun to *wish* that her cousin would not appear at all.

"Oh, I *am* sorry to be late." Zofia hugged Anna.

Anna had come to realize that her cousin's apologies were but end-stops to a topic and required no reply.

Zofia helped Anna spread out a blanket on the ground, her perfume competing with the forest fragrances. Bending over, she whispered: "But I did it for you, dearest!" Then, in a louder voice: "I've brought the most delightful luncheon. Ah, what could be lovelier than an outing in the woods with my cousin and . . . my friend Janek?"

Anna looked to Jan, who was brushing down the horses. His annoyance at Zofia's presence was visible. Was he also annoyed she had used his diminutive? Or had he noticed?

"We might even bathe later, Anna," Zofia was saying. "That is, if Jan would be so good as to leave us alone for a while."

"I'd rather not, Zofia," Anna said. "You know how I am about the water."

Zofia sighed dramatically. "You do give the impression of being dainty and helpless, Anna. And I suppose there are men who find those characteristics attractive." Her dark eyes darted fleetingly to Jan, who seemed preoccupied with his task. "For me, though," she continued, "such a guise would require too much patience, a quality I readily admit I lack."

Anna thought for a moment that this last barb was directed at Jan, but she could not understand it. She was miffed by her cousin's teasing and chose to ignore it. "I have an idea," she said. "Let's pick some raspberries to eat with our meal. I had no breakfast, so I'm hungry as a bear. And I adore raspberries!"

"Well, it's not my idea of fun," Zofia said, "but I'll defer." She turned now, cupped her hands to her mouth, peasantlike, and shouted: "Stanisław!"

In a few moments the servant appeared, leading two horses. The three left him to unpack the small bundles that comprised their lunch and began walking through the dense greenery in search of a raspberry patch.

"Jan," Zofia asked, "will you walk ahead of us to make sure that the way is clear?"

Jan stepped a few paces ahead and began clearing the few obstructions. Anna thought he did so grudgingly.

Zofia pattered on casually, holding Anna back until Jan was out of earshot. "Well," she impatiently whispered, "what happened, darling?"

"What do you mean?" As they passed through a narrow clearing, Anna pretended to be concerned with her skirt and would not lift her eyes.

"Don't be coy!" Zofia hissed. "Tell me. Did he dare to kiss you?"

Anna looked up at Zofia and nodded.

"Honestly, Anna! Must I pry everything out of you?"

Anna drew in breath to blurt out her news. "He asked me to marry him."

"What?" Zofia's mouth dropped open. She appeared to be genuinely stunned. "Are you joking?"

"No."

Zofia let out a little gasp. "What . . . what did you tell him?"

"I put him off."

Zofia's blank look changed now as her tone and expression took on direction. "Oh, Anna, I'm so sorry to have done this to you. You don't hate me for it, do you? I thought that after your mourning you would enjoy a little dalliance with Jan. That's why I plotted for you to have this time alone with him. Who would have imagined that he would propose? He was serious?"

"Oh, yes."

"Now, don't worry, dearest. I'll fix things for you."

"Don't be silly, Zofia. I—" Anna stopped, realizing that Jan had waited for them to catch up.

"This way," Jan said. "I've found a decent patch."

While the three picked raspberries, Zofia babbled incessantly. Anna could not read her cousin's behavior. Did she think that her interest in Jan was only casual? If so, she could only bide her time until she could tell her differently.

Bored and perhaps irritated by Zofia's banter, Jan kept stealing impatient glances at Anna.

Finally, Anna became unnerved. "I'll let you two finish," she announced. "I'll go get the luncheon ready." She quickly moved off in the direction they had come.

"You were the one who wanted raspberries!" Zofia called.

Anna didn't know what she wanted. Her mind was as tangled as the briar and brambles she found herself encountering. Her feelings concerning Jan were strong and positive but tainted by some nameless sense of danger or inappropriateness. And her cousin's attitude was a mystery to her.

By the time Anna came to the clearing at the pond, she had made the decision to put an end to the outing. She ordered Stanisław to repack the bundles of food.

She walked down near to the water and paced, waiting for Jan and Zofia to return so that the day might end. Time and a clear head were needed. She was uncertain of marriage, though she knew she loved him, despite his changeable ways.

His advances and proposal *had* been impetuous. It was behavior very different from the custom of her parish. Tradition held that the suitor would arrive at his beloved's home with a flower-covered bottle of wine. The young lady would fetch the prescribed tiny wineglass, fill it, offer it to her suitor, then to her parents. When they had all sipped of the glass, she, too, would lift it to her lips, and the young man would know that his offer had met with a favorable response.

Anna felt guilt, too. Having had to hide her romance with Jan from her guardians, she could look forward only to objections.

She watched idly as Stanisław put the last of the bundles into the saddlebags. The servant then mounted his horse and spoke to it in a playful tone while he patiently waited.

A shadow passed overhead.

Looking up to the sky, Anna saw a huge eagle soaring majestically. She recalled how Jan had sworn by the white eagle that he would love her forever.

The bird circled now and fell into a sudden swoop, disappearing beyond the treetops.

"I reckon he's sighted his dinner," Stanisław called.

"I suppose he has," Anna heard herself say. Her mind, however, was recalling her father and remarks he had made numberless times. She could picture him at the supper table, knife and fork in hand but forgetting to eat so caught up was he in expounding on how strange it was that Poland should have as its symbol the eagle, a bird of prey; how Poland held no standing army and chose not to barter and threaten in the great throne rooms of Europe; how peaceful are the Polish citizens; how, in the past, it has been the countries bordering Poland—Prussia, Austria, and Russia—that have been the predators on Polish lands and peoples; how, only twenty years ago, these three partitioned Poland, taking spoils amounting to one-third of the land and one-half of the population.

It was peculiar, how her father's words carried so little weight at the time. It seemed a lifetime ago. How young she had been then . . . before things began to fall apart. How caught up she had been in frivolities of youth. Now, her father's words about his homeland echoed through the tunnel of her memory, ringing into the present with truth and portent.

Suddenly, Anna's attention was jarred from this tangent by the sound of Zofia's screaming. "Go back to the house, Stanisław!" she was crying. "Go back now!"

Anna turned around. "What is it, Zofia?" She could see only her cousin's back. "What is the matter?"

At Zofia's repeated command, the confused stable master gave spur to his horse and disappeared into the woods.

Zofia turned toward Anna now and dashed down the slope. "Jan did this to me!" she cried.

Anna stared in disbelief. The lace material covering Zofia's ample bosom was disheveled and torn.

Jan was in quick pursuit.

He ran to where the cousins stood and roughly turned Zofia to him. Beneath his blond hair his face was red with rage. "What did you say to Anna?" He held tightly to Zofia's arm. "Tell me!"

Zofia did not answer but only snarled at the brusque manner in which Jan treated her.

Jan cocked his head in Anna's direction. "What did this lying creature say to you, Anna?"

The scene unfolding before Anna seemed unreal. She became confused and terrorized as Jan continued to press for an answer and as Zofia cried, her free hand struggling for release, her high voice full of reproofs. Anna felt removed, as if this were happening to someone else.

Jan shoved the hysterical Zofia aside and moved toward Anna. "You need to know the truth about your cousin. . . ."

But panic surged within Anna, and she turned and ran.

In a flash Jan followed, barking out words of explanation that Anna's mind could no longer process.

Anna's feet padded along the dry and crusty shore of the pond. Her mind was in a ferment.

Where was she to go? Her breath came hard. Still, she increased the speed of her steps.

She could hear Jan's labored breathing close behind.

Anna raced up the incline of a little hill. She saw—too late—that it ended abruptly in a bluff of several feet.

She went tumbling headlong into a water-parched pocket below, coming to rest in an awkward sitting position. Her hat had fallen off and her braid, which had been wound about her head, had come loose.

Anna looked up to see Jan staring down at her from the little bluff. "Are you hurt, Anna?"

"Let me be!" she heard herself cry. Her foot burned with pain, but she said nothing of it.

Jan descended the bluff and came to where Anna sat. Kneeling in the dry earth, he clumsily held out his hand.

Anna averted her eyes, then covered her face. "Jan, please leave me. Please!"

After what seemed an eternity, she looked again. He was gone. She sat motionless and numb.

Should she call him back? Anna suddenly realized that she did not want him to leave.

But the sound now of a horse's hooves told her that it was too late. Hot, stinging tears brimmed in her eyes. What had she done?

She tried to stand but couldn't.

"Oh, Anna, you're hurt!" Zofia stood on the bluff now, gaping down at her.

Anna held the tears at bay. "My ankle feels like fire," she conceded, "but I don't think it's broken."

"Oh, it's your left ankle! We'll need Jan's help if you're to mount your horse. Don't try to move, darling. I'll catch up to him."

"Do be careful, Zofia," Anna called. Her cousin had already disappeared from view.

Using her elbows for support, she raised herself up onto a small mound from which she could see Zofia mounting her horse. As Zofia's horse galloped away, Pegasus, still tethered to a shrub, shied, unsuccessfully straining against her reins.

Anna knew that they would need a man's assistance. She prayed that her cousin would be able to overtake Jan and bring him back. And, perhaps more importantly, she wanted to give Jan a chance to explain himself. Only now did she process the genuine concern she had seen in his eyes. How could he have done what Zofia accused him of if Anna had won his heart?

She picked herself up on her hands and knees and struggled to a flat, shaded area at the edge of the pond. Removing her jacket, she lay down and, cupping her hands, brought cool water to her dry lips.

She fell back now, exhausted, eyes to a cloudless sky. Jan Stelnicki's appearance in her life had been the most exciting thing ever to happen to her. Perhaps, however, their meeting had occurred too soon. She was just seventeen. Anna dreamt of marriage, a home, children—yet life since she had come to live with the Gronski family seemed so grand and promising, especially by comparison with her more reserved and provincial background. She longed to shed her childlike innocence and acquire sophistication. She wanted to experience the splendid social and cultural life of Warsaw, of which Zofia spoke incessantly. In a year or two, she might grow tired of leisure and independence, but she hesitated to forfeit it now.

And there was, too, that vague fear of Jan's temperament. He appeared so impatient and impetuous. *Had* he attacked Zofia? It seemed inconceivable.

Would Zofia lie about such a serious thing? Why?

Anna worried over Zofia. Though she was a good horsewoman, the forest was rife with clawing undergrowth, fallen trees, low-hanging limbs. Anna looked about her, trying to concentrate only on the seemingly endless flow of drifting, autumnal leaves.

She felt alone and powerless. As time passed she struggled to stay alert.

It was a voice calling her name, Anna thought, that awakened her. She was instantly aware of a new pain. Hours had passed, it seemed, and the sun had shifted, burning her face. She felt as if the dry, pulsating skin had been drawn across her face like a mask.

"Oh, Anna," Zofia was calling, "Jan was furious!" She picked her way down the embankment and moved toward Anna. "Oh, darling, you're scorched. Your face is as red as a ripened strawberry!"

"He isn't coming back?"

"No, dearest."

Anna's heart dropped.

"I caught up to him a long ways from here. He hardly let me speak, though, he was so enraged. Oh, he's an impossible man!"

"What about Stanisław?"

"I tried to track him, that's what took me so long. But he had too great a head start."

"What are we to do, then?"

"Do you think that if we combined our efforts we could get you mounted?"

"Perhaps. We can try."

The cousins did make an effort of it; however, after half of an hour their attempt ended ingloriously when they found themselves both sitting upon the ground. "There's only one thing left to do," Zofia said. "I'll go back to the house for help."

"Must you? Can't we just wait? Surely the stable master—"

"No. I led Stanisław here." Zofia got to her feet. "I expect the old fool can find his way home, but I doubt that he could find the pond again on his own, and it will be dark before anyone will think to look for us. And they might *never* find us here. Walter and I discovered this place when we were but children and kept it secret from everyone."

Anna had to admit that Zofia's going back was the only logical plan.

"Don't fret," Zofia said. "I will hurry. Did Stanisław leave any of the food?"

"No, I had ordered him to repack it."

Zofia regarded Anna strangely at this but did not question her. She stood now. "I'll not be long in bringing help."

"Zofia?"

"Yes, dearest?"

"Is it true?"

"Is what true?"

"What you said . . . did Jan attack you?"

"I said that he did, didn't I? Do you question my word, Anna?"

"But I don't understand. Only a short time before he said that he loved me. He proposed *marriage* to me."

"And you believed him? Oh, Anna, you have so much to learn about life and about men! In the heat of romance a man will promise anything to gain satisfaction. He merely wanted his way with you, darling. Nothing else."

"I don't believe it! Jan is not like that!"

"It comes as a surprise to me, too, I must admit. Had I the slightest suspicion, I would never have allowed you to go with him. It's a good thing I came along when I did."

"Zofia, look at me. Is this the truth?" Anna's eyes searched her cousin's face for some sign of deceit. She prayed that it was a lie. She could not have so misjudged Jan. Anna pressed the issue: "You were not play-acting?"

Zofia's anger flared without warning. "You little fool!" she hissed. "You dare to call me liar? What makes you think that a man like Jan Stelnicki would want to marry a backwoods bog-trotter like you when he could have his pick of Warsaw's finest? He took you for an easy mark, that's all!"

Zofia turned now and left.

Stunned, Anna watched her leave with eyes that would not focus, parted lips that could not speak. A few minutes later, she realized that Zofia had not only taken her own horse, but she had taken Pegasus as well.

Anna removed her boots, first from the injured and swelling foot, then from the other.

Much later, sleep provided an escape.

Upon emerging from the woods on foot, the two horses in tow, Zofia paused and stared vacantly across a clearing.

She still seethed with anger. It had all gone so far wrong. Once again she had miscalculated. She had hoped that the outing would provide for Jan an opportunity to assess her and Anna side by side. Anna, with her rustic ways, would pale by contrast.

Her master plan had been thought out so carefully. In the months since Jan returned from school, Zofia had methodically, secretly, charmingly courted him. She was convinced that a relationship with Jan would help her escape the arranged marriage with Antoni Grawlinski.

Now, if she were forced to marry Grawlinski, it would be her witless cousin's fault. Anna had ruined her plans. Anna had ruined her life. *Damn her!*

Zofia blamed herself, too. She cursed the day she told Anna she had no interest in Stelnicki. How could she have known the outcome? And today in the raspberry patch, when she had set aside her pride and confronted Jan with her feelings, he dared to look into her eyes and say that he cared only for Anna.

To think that she had lost Jan Stelnicki to little Anna Maria from Sochaczew! What did he see in her? Was it possible her innocence was a pretense—that she was a little minx on the sly? Anna could not have arrived at Halicz at a worse time, for Zofia—or for herself. Zofia would never forgive her cousin for her interference.

She considered her options now. She knew that she could not reignite Jan's interest in her, at least not now. Oh, she was confident the day would come when she would pick up that challenge again. For now, though, she would have to find another way of escaping a marriage that was for her an execution.

Somehow, some way, she would engineer a reversal of fortune. Her first priority was clear: she must ruin Anna and Jan's romance. Anna must *never* have Jan. She would rather see them both dead.

Zofia did not mount her horse, as she had planned. What hurry was there? She would walk the remaining distance, walk and think. She would use her head. She would find a way out of her troubles. After all, she would not set sight on Grawlinski until Christmas.

And not even then if she played her hand correctly.

Leading her horse, Zofia started walking now, slowly but with direction. *The wheel of fortune will turn again, and with the next turn, or the turn after that, I will have my way.*

8

Anna awoke stretched out on an endless blanket of leaves, and though she had no appetite she was conscious of rumbling sounds in her empty stomach. Her ankle throbbed dully.

Night had fallen and with it a deathlike silence. A crescent moon and a scattering of stars cast a bluish filter of light. Each ripple in the pond caught the eerily diffused glow, providing the illusion that a thousand translucent eyes were watching her. The spiderlike roots of the dead oak appeared to move, slowly, grotesquely.

Anna's heart contracted. Too many hours had passed. What was keeping Zofia from returning with help?

Huddling so close to the pungent earth, Anna imagined herself the only human in the kingdom. She shivered with foreboding. To breathe the cold night vapors was to breathe fear itself. She would not allow herself to panic. Her mind struck then on the god Pan and how he enjoyed startling travelers through his woods by suddenly jumping out from behind a tree.

At that moment the silence was broken by the sound of crackling leaves. Anna's eyes became fixed, her body tense. Holding her breath, she slowly turned her head, fearful of what she might see. There, a few feet away at the water's edge, stood a doe and its fawn.

Anna's breath silently escaped as she relaxed. In moonlit pantomime the animals leisurely drank, and in the profound quiet their lapping was audible. The deer's presence somehow made her feel secure.

Anna lay flat and stared at the stars, experiencing now something very strange. She had the very real sensation of leaving her body and floating high above the earth and trees. She could peer down at the pond, at the deer, and at herself. It was as though her spirit had become too light for her body to hold.

After a time the sensation passed and she became sleepy again. She fought to stay awake, for certainly they would be arriving soon to take her to safety. But the fatigue was all-powerful.

A sharp noise jarred her awake. What was it? She tried to clear her head. Praying that help had come at last, Anna sat up, rubbed her eyes, and strained to look about her. She could see nothing. A dense cloud covering lay like a pall over the patch of forest, hiding the moon and stars. She listened, thinking that the noise might have been the wind, but there was not the slightest breeze to stir the trees. And she was certain the deer had long since vanished. The thought of wolves chilled her through to the bone. The long-toothed predators were known to prowl the neighboring forests in packs.

Time passed.

The noise had been a product of her imagination, Anna decided. She lay down again, where the earth and leaves provided a warm nest against the raw night.

There! Another sound.

Anna immediately sat erect and shook her head, trying to dispel her drowsiness.

A twig snapped. She had no doubt.

A footstep.

Another.

And another.

"Here!" she cried. "Near the water!"

The noises she heard then did not sound like any horse or man. From the brush, beyond the nearby bushes came heavy, shuffling footfalls and strange, grunting sounds. Her vapor-filled mind pictured one of the beasts Jan had told her about.

Her heart and mind raced. What was she to do?

A figure staggered out of the shrubbery. Its size made her seize on the notion that it was a bear, huge and menacing. Fear shot like lightning through her body. With the greatest effort she sprang up and began limping away. Her panic carried her through the thicket that surrounded the pond. She could hear its stumbling steps behind her. Terror numbed her injured ankle now as she ran, faster and faster, her arms flailing wildly against the dark of night.

A root caught her foot and sent her sprawling. Her face struck the rocky earth. White pain exploded within her head and traveled through her entire body.

A powerful grasp pulled at her blouse from behind, ripping it and exposing her back. Pulling at her, the creature moaned incoherently. Anna recognized the stale smell of liquor and knew that her attacker was no animal.

She turned to look up. The shirt he wore was white. His arms were reaching for her. *Who is it?*

Warm, stinging liquid ran into one eye and she reached up to wipe it away. It was blood, her own.

He grasped her now and she choked out a cry.

The response was a guttural laugh.

I must escape, she thought. *I must run!* Struggling to her knees first, then to her feet, she managed to twist away from his drunken grip.

Blindly she fled into the darkness, mindless to the briars pulling at her skirt, the willow branches lashing her face. She ran, stumbled and fell, picked herself up, ran again.

She halted a moment, her heart about to burst, breath coming fast. She could smell the pond nearby, the sharp sweetness of the water lilies unmistakable on the night air. She was situated, it seemed, on a little precipice above the water. She caught her breath: another step and she would have tumbled into it.

Anna turned around. Just twenty paces away the white shirt was moving forward like some nocturnal ghost.

Her heart dropped, for she was certain she was lost.

Then he paused. She knew he was listening for her.

Anna stood motionless, breathless.

Afraid that he might see the pale color of the torn blouse, she sidled toward a nearby tree for cover. Clinging to its trunk, she slowly inched her way around it, never for a moment taking her eyes from the white shirt.

As she moved, she dislodged some pebbles or bits of earth. These she heard slipping from the edge and falling into the pond with soft, distinct plops.

Damn, damn, damn. Anna's teeth bit hard into her lower lip. She felt and tasted the flow of blood.

Then, the white shirt moved in her direction.

Anna knew that she was trapped. Her head reeled. She had but one hope. Resolving to throw him into the pond, she stepped away from the tree, directly into his path.

He was nearly upon her with arms outstretched, reaching. When he was but a step from her, she deftly sidestepped him, closed her eyes in the effort, and pushed against his rock-hard form with every bit of strength she could summon.

He let out a little grunt of surprise and began to topple off the ledge. Anna felt a rush of relief and surprise at the strength that coursed through her. But he locked onto Anna's hand and held fast to it.

Anna crashed into the pond and cold water filled her ears, nose, mouth.

The impact broke her captor's hold. Pushing herself to the surface, she lifted her head above the turbulence of the waters. She found that she could stand and she immediately began to move away from him, making for the other side of the pond. Her clothing and the muddy bottom slowed her pace.

She gave no thought to her attacker, who splashed wildly nearby. He could drown for all she cared. She hoped he would drown! Her single instinct became survival.

After some minutes, she could smell the thick, sickeningly sweet water lilies she knew to be near the huge old oak—and a gently rising shore that would afford safety.

On impulse she fell forward on her stomach and forced her arms into the kind of stroking motions she had seen Zofia use. Miraculously her body moved. Despite the awkwardness of it, she found herself gliding along the surface of the water, and a sense of power and hope surged within her now, fueling her.

At last, Anna drew herself out of the mire-filled basin and collapsed. The dry bank was warm life under her wet and freezing body. She lay facedown, unable to move, her forehead on the stony earth. She could not focus her mind to any thought. Her back, legs, arms—every part of her that touched the night—seemed to draw into herself cold, cold air.

Suddenly, she felt the weight of the creature on her back.

Her bones snapped as he cruelly jerked her body toward himself, forcing her onto her back.

His breath, so close upon her, reeked of liquor. She thought that he said, "I've come for you, Anna."

"You drunken swine!" Anna cried. But the words made only slight, soundless movements on her broken lips.

Her upper torso was wrenched upward as he pulled and ripped at her blouse. His mouth moved roughly over her lips, neck, breasts.

At his touch, an energy fired by panic surged within her and she franticly thrashed about. She found her voice, too, and screamed.

But a hand quickly came down upon her mouth.

Anna's half-stifled screams turned from those of hatred and fear to those of excruciating pain as his full weight crushed against her.

9

Countess Stella Gronska was upset and angry with both her husband and son. At the afternoon meal Leo had confronted Walter, demanding that he resign his commission and return home to help manage the estate. Walter again indicated that he had no intention of obeying his parents' wishes.

The countess was relieved that Zofia and Anna were not there to hear the inflamed rhetoric; she assumed that they missed the meal because their daily riding lesson had started later than usual.

Father and son raged at one another, ignoring the countess' protests. Then the secret that she and Leo had withheld from Walter for so many years slipped out—along with Leo's resolution to disinherit Walter.

Walter was stunned, of course, and hurt. The countess saw through his false front in the moments before he stormed out of the house.

So the day was already a disaster when neither daughter nor niece appeared for supper. The mood darkened further when her husband found out from Stanisław that a riding party had taken place that day. The countess was livid that Zofia and Anna Maria, who had only just learned how to ride, would venture far—and in the company of Jan Stelnicki. The simple stable master provided a convoluted story of being ordered back to the house with the uneaten picnic lunch.

The countess didn't like it. Her spine ran cold with suspicion and fear: she knew something was wrong, very wrong.

At last, about twilight, Zofia appeared with the story of Anna's injured ankle. The countess insisted that she herself accompany her husband, Zofia, and the farm manager in the wagon.

The ride was long and tedious. When the unmarked trail became too narrow for the vehicle, the countess waited alone in the wagon while Zofia led Walek and Leo the rest of the way on foot.

When they returned with Anna in a kind of litter made of a quilt they had brought along, the countess' worst fears were realized. Beneath the cover, her niece's body was naked, bruised, and bloody.

The countess gasped. "Is she alive?"

Anna was shaken into consciousness when the wagon that was carrying her to safety came to an abrupt dip in the trail. She lay on her back, wrapped in a heavy, quilted cloth. Overhead passed vague outlines of the treetops. "May the Black Madonna keep her from death's door," her aunt was praying in a hushed tone. Anna could hear Zofia whimpering nearby, but she did not have the strength even to open her eyes.

Am I going to die? She thought about death, shivering at the thought of the worms in the earth. Why had the ancient Poles worshipped the creatures? Perhaps it was because no matter how hard one tried to kill the limbless beings, their indomitable hearts would pound on and on.

Her hands moved now over her body, slowly, achingly, and she felt her nakedness. She sensed that those taking her to safety had not undressed her. Her hands moved down, down to where the soreness was unbearable and blood still ran from the rupture. She attempted to grapple with the reality of what had happened.

Anna's mind's eye saw herself running with the other girls of Sochaczew, racing away from the river, up the weeded hillside, moving for the road. They were laughing and calling out to one another in mock terror. *"Run, Anna, run! You must not stumble! You must not fall! Be nimble or Marzanna will get you!"* Anna held her skirts high, her legs pumping, her heart ready to give out. She was nine that year and her father had allowed her to partake in the Lenten custom of drowning Marzanna in effigy. The local maidens had only just thrown the straw figure of the ancient goddess of death into the river, so that they ran with joy and abandon—but with wonder and fear, too.

The ceremony was to keep Marzanna away for the next year; any girl who fell on the way back to town would not live to see Christmas.

The girls slowed to a walk as they came into Sochaczew, tired but happy and ready for congratulations. They started to sing, over and over:

> Death is hanging around
> Looking for trouble.

Anna found herself running again, running from some unnamable force that moved toward her from behind. The field in which she ran erupted in fire now, flames flying all about her. Even the mythical Daedalus could not have conceived such a labyrinth, the walls of which threatened to scorch her, turn her to ash. She ran swiftly through the roaring heat. Dancing flames leaped onto her dress, climbing its folds and singeing her skin.

She forced open her eyes.

The fire was reduced at once to a single dancing flame. It belonged to a thick candle on her bedside table. The heat, however, did not dissipate. Her gaze moved down along the bed. There, standing motionless and staring, was Lutisha.

"I'm burning up," Anna whispered. She closed her eyes, trying to summon the strength to tell the woman to open the windows. Her cracked lips parted, but she could issue no sound.

"You are burning with fever, Mademoiselle Anna," the old woman said. "Lutisha will mend your health."

The bed was an insufferable furnace, the blankets coverings that entrapped and inflamed the pain within her.

"Please," Anna said, "take these covers from me."

"No!" Lutisha's voice was sharp. "The night vapors will kill you. You must stay warm, my lady."

Let go of me! Let me up! Anna struggled to push the covers from her, but she was no match for the powerful arms of the servant.

It started to rain during the night and the steady tapping and plashing against the windows gave Anna the blessed illusion of coolness. Before dawn her mind came into sharper focus and she could hear someone at her side praying. Then she felt her hand being taken and held.

The low whisper she heard was that of Countess Gronska: "If this is the work of Jan Stelnicki, as you said, my dear, he will pay handsomely for it."

By the time the meaning and gravity of the words pressed a chord within Anna, forcing open her eyes, her aunt was being relieved by Lutisha.

"Your fever is broken," the servant said. "God be praised! Marta will be bringing breakfast. Is the Countess thirsty?"

She could not believe it. Had *she* accused Jan?

"I want nothing."

After changing the dampened sheets, Lutisha lifted Anna into an upright position while she fluffed fresh pillows behind her. The activity provoked a painful paroxysm, but Anna had no energy to resist.

Lutisha was placing a cool wet towel to Anna's face and neck when the door opened. Anna lifted her heavy eyelids to see Marta enter and deposit a tray on the bedside table. Lutisha's daughter turned now, gawked blankly at the patient for several moments, curtsied, and left.

The woman's glance was enough to chill Anna's blood. *What must I look like?* Anna wondered. She became determined to make her way to the long mirror at the first opportunity, until she realized that its place on the wall stood vacant. Someone had removed it.

Her nostrils drew in the smell of food and her stomach recoiled. "I can't eat anything," she cried.

Lutisha removed the cover from the steaming plate. "Mashed duck livers," she announced.

"Oh, Lutisha, please take it away."

"If you do not eat, Lady Anna, you will die."

If I eat *that*, Anna thought, I will die. "I can't. Perhaps later."

Lutisha's finger forced itself through Anna's lips, and she was made to eat. After a dozen spoonfuls of the stewed meat and several swallows of milk, Anna's stomach tightened convulsively and she clenched her teeth, refusing another bite.

"Good enough, then. Would Mademoiselle wish some water? Your body has lost much fluid with your fever."

Anna drank a full glass and fell back into her goose-down pillows.

The rain continued outside. Despite the soothing pattering at the windows, she could not sleep. She remembered the horrific details of the attack only too well. The dark, the frigid pond, the pain, the smell of the creature . . . fear came over her in rushing waves of nausea. She fought hard to keep down the little meal.

Had she blamed Jan Stelnicki? What had made her do such a thing? It had been too dark, her fear too great. She had no recollection of a face, or even a voice.

She thought now. *Who* had attacked her?

She thought of Feliks Paduch, the man who had killed her father, the man who had vowed to end the Berezowski line. She had never taken that curse with any seriousness, but now she had to wonder. Would Paduch have been so motivated that he would follow her to Halicz, stalking her like some animal?

She felt her body stiffen, tightening with both pain and fear. Cold sweat beaded on her forehead. Perhaps he had done it and left her for dead. Her throat tightened. She reached for a glass of water and took a sip.

Her thoughts ran back to Jan. He was innocent. He *had* to be. He had sworn to love her. She believed him then. She believed him now. And she could not accept as true the allegation that he had attacked her cousin. But she *had* doubted his innocence in those few terrible moments that a hysterical Zofia leveled her accusations. Why had she lent Zofia's story any credence? And yet, who would suspect such deception of one's cousin? Whatever her reason, she could only have been lying about his ripping her blouse.

That aside, she realized that her own life had changed irrevocably. She had been raped. Her head reeled now and her stomach dropped as if it had gone into an unchecked fall.

What did such an attack mean? Would Jan still love her? Would he still respect her? Would she be able to return love? Was marriage to him, or to anyone, still possible?

And children, she thought, a shock ricocheting through her like a bullet. "Children," she whispered aloud. *What if I have conceived a child?*

She fought back the tears.

Anna remembered how Aunt Stella had taken her aside after the deaths of her parents and told her that as a young noblewoman she was not to worry about important matters, that they would be decided by her elders, that she need only maintain the graces of a lady. It was advice she wanted to follow in order to assuage her pain and confusion. But some chamber of her heart closed now to her aunt's advice, as if by the turning of a valve.

For twenty-four hours Anna would not acknowledge the visitors that came and went. She kept her eyes closed, pretending to be asleep. Depression held her captive.

The afternoon of the next day was strangely silent, except for the persistent pattering of the rain on the windows and sills.

Finally, Anna pulled herself out of bed. She could neither sleep nor deal with her dark thoughts. She pulled on a cotton wrap, noticing now that she was bruised over much of her body. Every part of her seemed raw and sore. Ignoring the pain in her foot and ankle, she made her way to the door and out into the hall.

She paused, listening, knowing how inexplicably strange was her own behavior. Yet she continued, moving toward the rear stairwell, the servants' passage. Here, the warm and thick kitchen aromas escaped to the second floor as through a chimney.

She descended the unlighted passage, listening to the sounds of the servants. She knew that few secrets were kept from the servants of a house and that from them she might learn something.

"You know that when a guest of the Gronski family is as ill as the

Countess Anna, there will be added chores for everyone. You too!" The crisp voice was Marta's.

"Yes, Mama."

Noiselessly Anna pushed the door ajar and peered into the large kitchen. Across the room the blond and bosomy Marta was ladling soup for her young son Tomasz.

The door to the outside opened now. Marta's husband entered, removed his rain-soaked sheepskin cloak and hat, and took his place at the oak table. Their two daughters must have been about their afternoon chores.

Walek tore at his dark bread, chewing with relish. He was a stocky man characterized by a great black moustache and a good disposition. Marta poured chicory into cups for her husband and herself. The servants were not allowed coffee, an expensive import.

She sat. "Walek, this morning Mama saw two magpies on the fence near the chicken coop." Her hand reached out to lightly touch her husband's in a gesture of concern. "The birds were facing *away* from the house. You know what that means."

Walek's dark eyes reflected concern.

"What does it mean?" piped eight-year-old Tomasz.

"Nothing," his mother said. "Have you finished?"

"Yes."

"Then you may see to the chickens."

The boy climbed down from his chair and raced across the kitchen. At the door, he turned. "May I feed the magpies, too?"

"Get out!" his father shouted.

The door slammed.

Despite their Catholicism, the peasants clung to old ways and superstitions much more so than did the nobles. They believed that a magpie that faces the house while sitting on a fence foretells of happy, welcome guests. If, however, it sits facing away from the house, it is to be taken as a warning of undesirable visitors.

"What is Lord Gronski up to?" Marta asked.

"Nothing. He's just waiting out the rain. I expect he'll go back to the pond and look for evidence."

"Evidence? What kind of evidence? Against whom?"

Walek shrugged.

"Walek, you know something. Tell me!"

"And you'll hound me if I don't," Walek said and sighed. "It seems that the madman at the pond was young Stelnicki."

"No!" Marta let out a gasp.

Anna's hand went to her mouth to muffle her own gasp. Even the servants knew of this false accusation!

"How is it you know that?" Marta asked.

"Because, my curious wife, I drove the wagon when the Gronski family fetched Lady Anna at the pond. She named her attacker."

"You heard her say it was Stelnicki?"

"Well, no, but Lady Zofia heard her."

Zofia! Anna became light-headed. It was impossible—there had to be some mistake, some terrible misunderstanding.

"Walek," Marta was saying, "you don't think that the master would be fool enough to attempt revenge on Stelnicki? At his age? By himself?"

"No!" he scoffed. "He'll turn the matter over to the *starosta* and the courts, as long as she can identify him as her attacker."

"And have the whole thing made public? I doubt that."

"When it concerns the nobility, things can be hushed." Walek paused, seeming to second-guess himself. "Although the count is a hard and stubborn man."

"He's an old man with a temper bigger than his strength! How can you be so calm about this?"

"Don't rile yourself, woman. It's a man's business."

"It's a *bad* business. And it's no man lying half dead upstairs."

The dining room door swung inward and Lutisha entered, balancing a tray of dirty dishes. "They've finished their noodle cakes and syrup," she announced. "Cook, serve, care for the sick. And now the Lady Gronska whispers that company is about to arrive. I tell you, there's not a moment's rest."

Marta and Walek exchanged meaningful looks at the news.

Anna's faintness increased. She leaned against the stone wall while the servants' talk droned on. What they had said about Uncle Leo chilled her to the marrow. Her mind raced.

Would he confront Jan? To what outcome? Perhaps after having witnessed Feliks Paduch escape the law, her uncle would not trust justice to the courts.

And why was Jan to be blamed? Because the half-conscious victim herself had raised the accusation. But Walek had not heard Anna: he had heard only *Zofia* make the charge!

Suddenly, Anna realized that Lutisha had crossed the room and was positioned but a very short distance away.

She held her breath.

Daring to peek back into the kitchen, she saw the old woman pick up a tray. "I'll take this up to the countess' room."

Before the servant could take the several steps to the stairwell entrance, Anna pulled her wrap to her, turned, and limped up the stairwell with surprising speed.

10

Anna had only just finished her lunch of broth and buttered bread when Zofia came fluttering into the room. "Oh, cousin, it's so good to find you awake! We thought you meant to sleep your life away. Our prayers must have turned the tide." Bending over, she kissed Anna lightly on the cheek. "How do you feel, darling?"

"A little better."

"You certainly appear very much improved."

"Really? I've no way of telling."

"What?" Zofia then caught Anna's meaning. "Oh, the mirror?" Her voice was unsteady only a moment before the lie came. "Well, you see, I'm having a new gown measured, and I needed the tall mirror. I'll see that it is returned soon."

Anna let the subject drop.

"Mother will be coming up to see you shortly."

Anna nodded.

Zofia drew up a chair and sat at the bedside. It was an awkward moment and neither spoke. Anna had not yet sorted out her feelings for her cousin.

The reason for Zofia's hesitation soon became apparent.

"When the rain stops, Father will be going out to the pond to

search for evidence." Zofia reached for her cousin's hand. The usual lu-
minous sparkle of her black eyes had been snuffed out. "I don't know
what he expects to discover. But whatever he finds or doesn't find, he
will then go to the magistrate."

"The magistrate?"

"Yes, dear. When you have recovered a bit more, you must answer
some questions and sign a paper."

"What paper?"

"A writ of accusation."

Anna only stared.

"Against Stelnicki, of course." Zofia's eyes narrowed. "Oh, Anna,
who would have thought it?"

"But, I don't remember—"

"It was Stelnicki who . . . who did this terrible thing to you."

"No, it was not Jan."

"Anna, when we came to collect you at the pond, you clearly cursed
Stelnicki."

"I have no memory of that, Zofia. I don't believe I could have said
such a thing."

"Then who was it?" Zofia demanded.

Anna lay back against the pillows, her eyes moving to the ceiling.
"It was too dark. I have no recollection of any face. Or voice, for that
matter. He mumbled only a few words, words that were distorted by his
drunkenness and my own fear. . . . It might have been Feliks Paduch."

"The man who killed your father? Ridiculous. It was Stelnicki."
Zofia unconsciously squeezed Anna's hand. "You know that it was.
Surely you don't mean to protect him . . . after *this?*"

Anna did not respond. There must be something about the man
she could recall, something that would exonerate Jan. Why couldn't she
remember?

Zofia's tone softened suddenly. "Perhaps because you cared for him
you're attempting to put all memory of the episode out of your mind."

"Zofia, I love him."

Zofia stiffened in her chair. "They say that a kind word must be
masked by a hard word, Anna. You cannot love him now! This is something unforgivable. He must be punished like any common criminal!"

Anna wanted to continue her defense of Jan, but she could not find the strength to answer or even move. She was undergoing a few minutes of protracted pain that raged and burned over the purple and black areas of her legs, stomach, and groin. Were she able, she would have called out in agony.

"Anna! What is it?" Zofia gasped. "You've turned as white as Marzanna herself. It was my fault! All mine. And I said such wicked things to you at the pond. You know I didn't mean them . . . really I didn't!" Zofia's voice shook as the tears spilled.

At last, Anna felt the paroxysm receding.

Zofia leaned over and kissed Anna, who could feel her cousin's wet cheek and the sweeping brush of her long eyelashes. "Please, Ania darling, you must get well. You *must*."

Anna then heard Zofia slip from the room.

Zofia hurried into her own room in an agitated disposition. Her tears were real. Things had gone too far. She would keep Anna from having Jan, but she didn't want her to *die*. Her cousin had a life to live, too. She would meet others. And as for Jan, well, he would pay for his fickleness in his affections. If he is not to be what keeps me from the wretched marriage my parents have planned, she thought, there will be another way. I am a woman of imagination.

She walked to the window. Outside, the rain splashed down in never-ending gray sheets. She doubted that her father would go to the pond today.

Zofia turned to the mantle and found herself staring at the sealed letter meant for Anna that she had taken from Katarzyna the morning after the incident at the pond. She was just leaving Anna's room as Katarzyna was coming to the top of the servants' stairwell with it. Zofia threatened death to the silly girl if she didn't keep quiet about its existence. The girl swore she alone was present when the Stelnicki messenger arrived at the kitchen door and that she wouldn't breathe a word.

The letter remained unopened. Zofia had been afraid to read it, afraid of what Jan felt for Anna, afraid to see it in writing.

She bent now to stoke the fire that had been lighted to counter the dampness in the room.

Standing erect, Zofia stared at the letter for a very long time, thinking that she should give it to Anna, that it would hasten her recovery. It was the right thing to do. Doing so would ease her own conscience, too. She could make that sacrifice.

She picked it up and started for the door. As she reached for the door handle, however, she recalled the moment she had come upon Jan and Anna lying in the leaves at the pond. Her blood surged anew at the image. What terrible fate had brought Anna to Halicz?

She turned back and moved to the fireplace. When a little orange flame ignited there, she took the letter and dropped it into the grate, watching with growing satisfaction as the flame greedily embraced the curling letter and molten red ran from the wax of the Stelnicki seal.

Zofia sighed now, thinking how the happenstance occurrence of intercepting the letter seemed to have brought her a seat higher on the wheel of fortune. She wasn't going to let Anna undo her plans.

After a few minutes she was pulled from her thoughts by the sound of carriage wheels turning on the gravel road in the front of the house.

How curious. She returned to the window. Approaching the house was the most elegant carriage she had ever seen. The wetness made its black leather shimmer and gleam. It was being drawn by four fine white horses and manned by a driver and two footmen . . . Who could this be?

A light knock came at her door.

"Come in," Zofia called, turning to see her mother enter.

The Countess Gronska seemed almost timid in her own daughter's bedchamber. Something about her mother's face immediately tied Zofia's tongue. "Zofia," the countess said, "we are receiving visitors today."

"Yes?" Her heart began to drop like a stone in a slow-moving dream. Suddenly, Zofia knew what her mother was going to say, and she felt as if an abyss opened up beneath her and at any moment the Furies would rise up to draw her in.

The countess drew a long breath, then said: "The Grawlinski family has arrived."

All through the afternoon hours, Anna heard the bustle of activity below. When Lutisha brought her supper, she told her that the Grawlinski family had come for a short stay.

Later, when Zofia came into the room, Anna was surprised that for once she could read Zofia's face so clearly. Distraught, her cousin crumpled into the chair next to Anna's bed.

"What is it?" Anna asked.

"Oh, Anna, I feel like a tiny fly entangled in a great spider's web." Clutching her cousin's hand, she held it to her breast. "I can't see a way out and all the spider has to do is pounce on me."

"What is it, Zofia? You're speaking in riddles." Anna suspected play-acting.

Her cousin drew a deep breath. "The Baron Grawlinski and his fat wife have come here with their son, Lord Antoni—on their way to their town house at Saint Petersburg from their estate at Opole—so that my parents may announce and set into motion our marriage. The fact that I'm meeting him for the first time means nothing. Our families have planned this since we were young children."

"I didn't know that guests were expected."

"Nor I! Mother and Father cleverly concealed their visit. Knowing my opposition, they used the element of surprise to entrap me. Oh, had I known, I would have gone to work and, I dare say, would have bent them to my wishes. But now . . . what am I to do, Anna?" She sobbed, though her eyes remained tearless. "Whatever am I to do?"

"You've met him?"

"Yes, we just finished supper."

"And?"

"Oh, he's not bad looking. Even a bit handsome in a way. But he's so priggishly proper. My life will be spent in boredom, unflinching, perpetual boredom!"

"Perhaps it's just the formality of the first meeting."

"Oh, no. He's of the old ways. It took little time to take measure of him. To his little mind a wife ranks no higher than a servant. Why, it's as if the three of them have come to bargain for some vase that will enhance their family mantle. I'm to be his *property!* And I have no doubt I'll be expected to produce children like Lutisha produces dumplings. Oh, I shall hate him. I do hate him!"

"Shush, Zofia, you'll be heard."

"I don't care. This is so ill-timed. I could always give a turn to Father's view on a subject, but now with Walter rebelling against 'home and homeland,' as Father says, he's not about to let me get away with anything."

"But Zofia, with Walter eventually inheriting the estate, you'll be doing well for yourself. You'll have a husband, estates in both Poland and Russia. You know men are quick to marry when they can advance themselves, but seldom when the woman—"

"It just may be that Walter will not inherit a thing, Anna."

"What?"

"Never mind. And you can be certain that Father has promised a healthy dowry." Zofia tilted her head upward. "*Baroness Zofia Grawlinska*— is there a ring to it? To me it rings dully of wifely chores, musty rooms, and lost opportunity. Yes, the baron is old and the estates will not be long in coming. But the baroness is scarcely fifty and possesses the vitality of a plow horse—and figure to match!—so she is likely to live to be ninety-five. And she'll sustain herself on the pleasure a dowager baroness derives from guiding and directing and browbeating a daughter-in-law who is not good enough for a son of hers." Zofia caught her breath here. "No, I'm confident enough in myself to know I can do better. And if I *never* marry, so what? Living my life only to please myself will be enough."

Anna found herself staring at her cousin. At last, she said, "Does Lord Antoni know of your reticence?"

"If he doesn't, he's a greater fool than I had imagined. I've done everything but send out criers."

"It doesn't affect him?"

"He ignores it. I've told you, Anna, it's as if they've come here to collect on some investment. My feelings are nothing to them. Father must have promised plenty."

"Don't you think you're seeing ghosts behind every stirring curtain? In many arranged marriages, the relationships have flourished afterward. Zofia, your own parents' marriage is just one such example."

"You, too, Anna? Why is everyone so willing to chop a fallen oak? Can you deny that you would rather have a marriage built on love, like *your* parents had?"

Anna felt her lips tighten. She could deny no such thing. And she could not help but wonder if her own chance at love was gone. Jan was being wrongly accused. It was so unfair. And yet he had not called and he had not written. What was there to do?

"And I've told you of his attitude toward women," Zofia was saying. "I couldn't bear to be his wife. Not in a thousand lifetimes!" The dark eyes narrowed with suspicion. "Why, Anna, I do believe you're playing the devil's advocate! Well, believe me when I say that before I marry Antoni Grawlinski, I would enter a convent!"

"You, Zofia?" Anna laughed. "A convent?"

"Well, at the very least, I would run off to France."

"Zofia, you are a count's daughter. That is hardly the best choice of climates. That is, if you wish to keep your head."

"But the *guillotine* would be an infinitely more merciful execution than the one my parents have in mind. My dear Anna, I can see you are improving when you're able to trade quips with me like this. Your lovely green eyes laugh at me. Oh, I know that I'm full of self-pity. There are certain advantages to the marriage, and who's to say that I couldn't indulge in a dalliance here and there? Such delicious evils are rampant in the city."

Zofia paused for a moment now, and her tone turned dark. "Ah, I'm being pressed more and more by the hour. If I'm to do anything . . ."

The half-sentence hung fire while her black eyes lost focus.

Anna wondered if some idea hadn't come into her cousin's head.

"But what *can* you do, Zofia?"

Emerging from her momentary trance, Zofia pressed Anna's hand and forced a laugh. "Oh, nothing, darling . . . but fall into the trap set for me so long ago. A trap from which I'll never escape."

"If you could only hear yourself, Zofia."

"Oh, I know how I must sound. Like Medea, I suppose, full of tragedy and angst. You think you know me, but you don't. I'll trouble you no more tonight." She stood and brushed her lips against Anna's cheek. "Your job, Ania, is to get well. Good night."

Anna watched her leave, thinking that somehow her cousin *had* thought of something, for Zofia appeared now to walk with some direction in her step. Inexplicably, Anna thought of an expression her mother had once applied to Feliks Paduch: *"A liar can go around the world, but can never come back."*

11

The rain stopped sometime during the night, and Count Gronski left for the pond before dawn.

By noon Countess Gronska's nerves were so on edge that she feared she might experience those palpitations that so terrified her. She wondered what he might find, if anything. What would Leo do if he did find something incriminating? Or if he didn't? Anna had insisted that the criminal was not Jan.

But Zofia had nearly convinced her father that Stelnicki was the guilty one. And Leo was as stubborn as a Lithuanian.

What if it were that Paduch fellow? What then? Might he some night murder all of them in their sleep? Such things were actually happening in France. Was Poland coming to such an end?

The countess hated conflict and she now found it all about her. She knew herself well enough to know that if she could, she would opt for the path of least resistance or outright denial, as she had done on numerous occasions when she overlooked the drinking and quarreling of both her husband and her son. But such a blind eye was impossible these days.

Since Walter had learned the truth, he appeared to care little about being dispossessed by his family. He seemed hell-bent on staying part of Catherine's machine. Once he left, the countess worried, would she ever see him again?

And Zofia. Where did she inherit her cheek? The countess was dumbstruck by her daughter's rudeness to the Grawlinski family. It would be a small miracle if the wedding were to go forward. Zofia seemed determined not to marry Lord Antoni. God only knows, the countess brooded, if Zofia had her choice, what kind she would make.

Countess Gronska smiled and singlehandedly tried to entertain her guests at the noon meal. Her own children had deserted her, it seemed, and she seethed inwardlly. To make things worse, the roast was overdone and the puddings were cold. She would have words for everyone later.

By midafternoon, however, her worry for her absent husband was her only concern. Zofia and Walter appeared at last. She would question and scold them later—or better, have Leo do it—for now she sent them off on fresh horses to search for their father.

The supper fare was improved, but the air was thick with tension and worry. The countess could no longer mask her concern. Hardly a word was spoken between hostess and guests, and she felt relieved when the meal came to end.

Anna had just finished her supper when her aunt came to visit. The countess brought her up-to-date on the whereabouts of her family, openly expressing her various concerns.

Anna, too, spoke her mind. "Are you certain, Aunt Stella, that there has been no word from Jan?"

"Absolutely."

"You would let me know, even if you don't approve of his attitude toward religion, and even if you suspect him of this terrible thing?"

"I would not deny his right to plead his innocence, Anna."

"May I write to him?"

"Certainly not!"

Anna retreated into silence. Why had she heard nothing from Jan? What news would Uncle Leo bring? Not knowing anything, she thought, must be more terrible than knowing the worst.

From below, to the rear of the house, came the sounds of horses and the cries of servants. The countess, jittery as a dragonfly, let out a fearful gasp. She excused herself and went directly to the servants' stairwell.

Anna climbed out of bed—doing so was getting easier of late. She pulled on her wrap. There had been a sense of immediacy in the voices of the servants that propelled her now to the window.

Twilight was fast giving way to night, but she could recognize her cousins Zofia and Walter in the violet shadows, both in the process of dismounting.

Draped unceremoniously across a third horse was a body.

Anna put her fist to her mouth to suppress a cry. For an instant she was back in Sochaczew sitting at her window seat, watching her father's body being brought home. A profound weakness came over her now. She closed her eyes momentarily as if to banish a bad dream. This could not be happening to her Uncle Leo, she thought, not again, not to Uncle Leo. It could not.

In seconds, the terrible, staccato screams of Countess Stella Gronska pierced the night.

Count Leo Gronski was waked in the reception room of Hawthorn House for the prescribed three days and three nights. A pine coffin without knots was ordered—out of tradition, Aunt Stella maintained, but some of the peasants still held to the folk belief that the number of knots foretold the number of children who would die that year, and should a knot fall out during the ceremonies, the deceased might peek out and take someone with him to eternity. Mourners arrived in shifts around the clock, telling stories, lamenting, singing, praying, and toasting with swigs of vodka the body in the open box.

Anna attended for a length of time each night, but Aunt Stella forbade her to go to the cemetery for the burial services. On the burial morning, she remained upstairs, sitting erect in her wickerwork chair, listening to the coffin being closed and nailed shut with wooden pegs, each strike of the hammer sending a shudder through her.

At last the hammering ceased and she heard the sounds of the men removing the coffin. They deliberately struck the front door frame with the box three times, for this was the way the deceased bade farewell to his home. Everything that could be opened—doors, windows, drawers, cabinets, and chests—was opened, so that should the count's soul be lingering in his home, it would find its way out.

Anna was left alone in the house. Lutisha offered to stay with her, but knowing that her uncle was much revered by the peasants, Anna said she had improved and insisted that the servant attend. It was true, too; the spasms of pain that had plagued her since the attack were becoming less frequent, less painful.

What plagued Anna now was her guilt. It consumed her. Were it not for her and the disobedience that led to tragedy, her uncle would not have fallen into the marshy area on his way to the pond. He would not have drowned in the quagmire.

Anna shivered. Aunt Stella was something of a fatalist and insisted Anna had no role in her husband's death. Neither of her cousins seemed to blame her, either. At least Zofia seemed not to hold it against her. As for Walter, he was not present in the reception room at those times Anna came down to join the mourners, so Anna had to accept Zofia's word that he did not hold her responsible. She had always been quick to forgive others: her father had told her once, "Forgive others easily, but don't be so quick to forgive yourself." In this, the matter of her uncle's death, the words rang true.

When everyone returned from the service, Countess Gronska came upstairs to visit Anna, who could not help but notice the toll her husband's death had taken. Her thin form seemed even slighter, her lined face more gaunt. Not only was her spirit gone, but she also seemed oddly distracted, peculiar.

Accompanying her aunt was Lord Antoni Grawlinski, whom Anna had met briefly during the mourning services. She had had no real opportunity to speak with him, however. "I'm pleased, indeed, to finally chat with you, Lady Anna Maria Berezowska," he said, "a bit more removed from the sad circumstances downstairs." He bent to kiss Anna's hand. "However, I must say that the Ladies Stella and Zofia have always been most generous in their speaking of you."

He is a charmer, Anna thought. Had they told him the nature of her "illness"? Of course, they had. She sensed it. It had been whispered of in some tactful way, no doubt, but he knew.

"Thank you, Lord Grawlinski. It's good to make your acquaintance." She would have to play the politician. "I have heard you spoken of, as well."

"I'm so glad to see that your health is improving," he said, smiling. "And I trust that we shall be more than mere acquaintances, Lady Anna."

What did he mean? Anna wondered whether Zofia had consented to the marriage, after all. Was he therefore to be her cousin? Now that the Gronska women were left without a man—Walter was leaving that day to rejoin his regiment—perhaps Aunt Stella had forced her daughter's hand, insisting on a prompt engagement and marriage.

The three made small talk for a time, idle and a bit strained. Anna watched Lord Antoni. He was very thin, but his considerable height, his black hair, and his refined features made for a handsomeness that belied Zofia's harsher commentary. He wore no moustache. The gray eyes seemed glazed—opaque—and this Anna put down to the sadness of the day. His disposition was certainly amiable.

At last, Countess Gronska said, "We should let Anna Maria get some rest now, Antoni."

"Of course." Lord Antoni rose and kissed Anna's hand again. "How dreadfully isolated you are up here, Lady Anna. If you would permit, may I visit again tomorrow?"

Anna smiled politely. "Yes, of course."

Later, Lutisha brought Anna her supper.

"Was the service at the cemetery nice, Lutisha?" Anna asked.

"Oh, yes, it was, Mademoiselle. I think all of Halicz must have turned out. The entire parish. And no one cried more than his peasants!"

"And Walter—I expect he will come up to say good-bye after supper—or has he decided to stay another day?"

"Walter, Mademoiselle?" Lutisha's eyes waxed full. "Oh, my lady, he left early in the afternoon with hardly a word to anyone!"

Lord Antoni Grawlinski visited Anna every day, often twice a day, for the next week, seeming to take a pointed interest in her progress. For the sake of propriety, Lutisha or Marta remained in the room during these times. Anna was feeling better, and as long as she could block out the death of her uncle and thoughts of Jan, she was in fair spirits.

Lord Antoni was no conversationalist, but he settled into a pattern of reading to Anna, a pastime that she came to enjoy. Marlowe and Shakespeare were frequent choices. Voltaire became a favorite.

Zofia, on the other hand, was suddenly as elusive as a butterfly. She would alight in Anna's doorway on occasion and ask how she was getting on, but she allowed no time for extended conversation before flitting away. Anna could only wonder if Zofia secretly blamed her for her father's death. She wondered, too, whether Zofia would accept Lord Antoni. That the Grawlinski family stayed on seemed proof that the hope for a marriage was still alive. Perhaps the families were allowing an interval of respect to pass following the count's funeral.

Anna dared not ask Lord Antoni himself. And as for Aunt Stella, she remained strangely morose and distant.

It was a Tuesday evening, and a fire in the grate warmed the bedchamber. Anna was still confined to her room. Although by now she spent much of her time in a comfortable wickerwork chair, she was already settled in her bed when her aunt and cousin appeared in her doorway.

"Are you awake, Anna Maria?"

"Yes, Aunt Stella. Do come in."

"We thought perhaps that you would like to say the rosary with us . . . for your Uncle Leo."

"Yes, of course."

Zofia followed her mother into the room, scarcely speaking. The two drew up chairs to Anna's bed.

Countess Gronska spoke her prayers clearly and fervently this night, even though since her husband's death there was some indefinable frailty about her.

It was Zofia who seemed a bit strange. Of course, she had never been one for prayers and she recited them absently now. From time to time Anna would catch her cousin looking at her with oddly analytical eyes. When Anna would return her gaze, she would immediately look away.

This is not the Zofia I know, Anna thought.

After prayers, the three sat for half an hour reminiscing about the count, each relating some touching or humorous anecdote. The shock was wearing off and acceptance seemed within reach.

Presently, the countess sobered and her rigid form leaned toward Anna, as if to impart some secret. "Now, Anna Maria, we wish to discuss something with you. . . ."

Zofia was suddenly on her feet.

Jan had been wrong, Anna thought, when he told her that Zofia would not defer to the custom of wearing black for mourning. Her cousin would wear black—and she was no less stunning in it.

"Excuse me, Mother—Anna, darling—but I've some things to attend to."

"What *things?*" her mother hissed in distraction.

Zofia deftly kissed her mother and Anna and glided quickly toward the door.

"Zofia!" the countess snapped. "I demand that you stay!"

Ignoring her mother, she turned in the doorway. "I'll look in on you later to say good night, Anna."

The door closed.

The countess clucked her tongue sadly. "She is every bit as incorrigible as her brother. Oh, where did Leo and I go wrong? It is a sad irony. I had always thought that my sister made a grave mistake in following her heart and marrying your father, but to look at you, Anna Maria, is to realize my own folly." She sighed. "Ah, Lord Antoni is fortunate not to be taking on the . . . the responsibilities . . . that would come with such a one as my Zofia."

"But I assumed . . . since the Grawlinski visit has been extended—"

"Anna, my dear child, you've been witness to so much tragedy within the course of a very short time. You must put it all behind you now. You must complete your recovery and look forward to a life bright with hope and promise." Her thin hands trembled as they took Anna's.

Anna could only stare in wonder. A dark, scarcely formed premonition took hold of her.

"Anna Maria, as I am your elder and guardian, it is my duty to serve as go-between."

What was she saying? Fingers of ice grasped at Anna's heart. "What do you mean?" She hardly recognized the voice as her own.

Distracted, Countess Gronska pressed Anna's hands so tightly as to cause pain. "Anna Maria Berezowska," she whispered gravely, "the Lord Antoni Grawlinski has asked for your hand in marriage." The countess continued to speak, but Anna's mind was erased of all thought and understanding.

Slowly this one incredible reality—that Lord Grawlinski wished to marry *her*, not Zofia—began to dawn on her. What a fool I have been, she thought. What a silly fool not to have seen behind Zofia's distance and Lord Antoni's attention! Yet, some part of her *had* seen, *had* known. But it was a thought she had not allowed to take root.

"The Grawlinski family," her aunt said, "is not related in any way to the Gronski or Berezowski houses, yet its history is a fine one, nonetheless." With a restrained voice, she related at length details as to the suitability of the young Grawlinski.

When the litany was finished, Anna smiled weakly. "I have no wish to marry, Aunt Stella."

"But, Anna Maria, here is the very thing that may turn your life onto the proper path. You should marry—and you should marry soon! The . . . accident . . . at the pond might have prevented *any* favorable match. And there is still the possibility that . . ." She broke off the sentence, embarrassed.

Leaving unsaid the possibility that Anna might have a child made it seem all the more ominous and terrible. And *possible*. Anna trembled at the thought.

"My dear niece, it may be a blessing in disguise that Zofia's engagement did not materialize and that young Antoni has taken a fancy to you."

"*Why* has he taken a fancy to me, Aunt Stella?"

"Why, he's found you beautiful and charming—'utterly charming,' he said."

"And he knows?"

Countess Gronska averted her eyes. "Yes, dear, he knows. And it doesn't matter to him." The huge brown eyes came back to Anna. "Doesn't that say something about his character?"

"His character will be considerably enhanced by my father's . . . by *my* fortune."

"Oh, Anna, how can you say that? He's a fine young man, and handsome, too. There are many girls who would consider themselves lucky to have him."

"Then let one of them have him! The man has bought a cage for Zofia and since she eludes him, he seeks another, tamer, bird."

"My dearest Anna, it hurts me deeply to say this, but can you afford to be so selective . . . after . . ."

"I know," Anna said, so that her aunt would not give voice to the thought.

The countess turned in her chair to stare blankly out the window into the dark sky.

Long, vacant moments passed.

Finally, the countess sighed heavily, saying, "I'm so alone now. My Leo! Why, people said we were as devoted as a pair of storks. He would not be dead were it not for his recklessness. He was always taking on too much without thinking. Once he dashed into the forest after some wild boar and didn't return for two days. Oh, if only this time he had just gone directly to the *starosta*. What a foolish, bull-headed man!"

Anna watched her aunt's back shaking now as she sobbed silently.

"And I am left with two children, Anna, neither of whom has the vaguest sense of responsibility. Zofia refuses a fine marriage that we've planned for so long, and Walter serves only himself and that wretched Empress Catherine. Leo pleaded with him to stay and help with our estate and yours. He flatly refused. I wonder that I'll ever see him again. I've been a failure in raising my children; they've thrust aside the old values."

Pitifully she wiped at her eyes. "We have no man to manage for us, Anna. Three women alone in this changing, hostile world. It is unheard of! What is to become of us? What is there left for me to do but to ask you, my child, to consent to the marriage? For the sake of all of us."

Anna knew that her aunt's face and gaze had turned once again toward her, but she had closed her own eyes.

"Anna?"

Anna could not bring herself to answer. She became aware of a pattering at the window: it was raining again.

The countess sat quietly, her lips whispering in prayer or absent thought.

After a time, she rose, brushed her wet cheek against Anna's, and wordlessly left.

It was no surprise that Anna's cousin did not look in to say good night. Anna lay staring vacantly at the window darkened by the night. Where in all of this was the hand of Zofia?

12

B y the time Jan Stelnicki had arrived at the family city residence in Kraków, his father had already died of a progressive cancer.

"He tried hard to hold on," Uncle Teodor told him. "He was determined to see you."

Jan was crushed. He had ridden the whole distance without sleep. He had known his father was ill, but never supposed it to be so serious.

"Did he say anything?" Jan asked.

"Only that you continue to fight on for him," Aunt Kasia said.

"The Patriotic Party?"

"Yes," Uncle Teodor said. "It was like his religion."

"It *was* his religion," Jan said.

The wake and burial of Piotr Stelnicki was concluded in the customary four days, but the legalities and mundane tasks associated with closing the city household took more than three weeks.

Jan had thought he was reasonably well informed politically, but in the days following his arrival in Kraków he absorbed volumes firsthand about Poland's internal and external struggles. And he learned from the very men who were shaping his country's future.

Through the innumerable visits with those who called to express condolences, he gained a knowledge that added substance and dimension to the cause that had possessed his father: a new and reformed Poland. He met Stanisław Staszic, a priest-turned-politician who, in his *Warning to Poland*, pleaded for an individual-based commonwealth in order for the nation to survive.

He met Hugo Kołłątaj, who had so influenced the four-year Great *Sejm*—of which Jan's father had been a part—with his vision of reform guaranteeing rights to all citizens.

Attending the funeral also were Ignacy Potocki and Stanisław Małachowski, who, along with Kołłątaj, had drawn up the Third of May Constitution.

King Stanisław Augustus himself sent a personal emissary bearing written condolences and words of the highest praise for Jan's father.

Jan was most impressed, however, by an old school fellow of his father's. He and his father had attended the new College of Chivalry, a state school for the training of military and administrative cadres. Tadeusz Kościuszko, now forty-five, had already made a name for himself by serving with George Washington and by fortifying West Point in the American drive for independence. He was back in Poland now, no less concerned about and energized by the Polish struggle for reform and independence from its longtime predators.

"I tried to enlist your father in the American pursuit," Kościuszko told young Jan, "but he would not leave his family. A fine man, Piotr was a patriot and a damn good friend. Truth is, he probably did as much here—for Poland—as he could have done there. Things will get bad here, my son, mark my words. The cause lost a good man. You should be proud."

Jan was buoyed by the outpouring of respect and sentiment for his father from the most prestigious and powerful men in the nation. He came to realize he had only partly understood his father, and at the funeral he unashamedly shed tears of both loss and regret.

Jan came to feel a deeper sense of the involvement of his father and, more notably, as the days of mourning wore on, a deeper sense of the importance of the cause.

The Third of May Constitution, the first of its kind in Europe, must be retained at all costs, he realized. It was a document dedicated to the rights of the peasantry and *szlachta* alike. The changes it effected were profound. The *Sejm* was to be the chief legislative and executive power, and only a strict majority was needed. The *liberum veto*—a longtime legal tool by which a single *Sejm* member could say "I oppose" and thus block any vote—was abolished. The *Sejm,* along with the King and his Royal Council, would effectively rule Poland. Everywhere Jan heard the slogan, "The King with the People, the People with the King." He found himself saying it, too.

Jan learned also of the growing opposition to the Constitution on the part of some of the nobility who wished to give up nothing to commoners and who were outraged at relinquishing their "golden freedom," the *liberum veto*. He prayed that, once enlightened, they would join the cause of democracy.

It was his aunt who inquired about his marriage plans. "You are twenty-five and so handsome," she pressed. "It is time."

Jan laughed. "Meaning that I'm at my zenith and starting to roll downhill toward antiquity?"

Aunt Kasia blushed. "No, I only wondered if you needed some help in meeting marriageable young ladies."

"Still and ever the matchmaker, Aunt Kasia? You'll not be able to enlist me. You'll be pleased to know that I have found my future wife."

His aunt blinked back her surprise. "Has she agreed?"

"Well, not yet . . . But she will."

"Who can deny a Stelnicki, is that it? Where is she?" Aunt Kasia's round face shone like the sun. "*Who* is she?"

"In Halicz. Her name is Anna Maria."

"What a lovely name . . . and so very Catholic."

"Yes, Aunt, she is Catholic."

Aunt Kasia smiled devilishly. "Well, I declare, it will be nice to have your side of the family back in the fold."

Jan smiled. "You are assuming I shall convert?"

"Oh, my, yes! If she is a Catholic worth her salt, you will."

Jan changed the subject then. He didn't tell his aunt about Anna's very sad and tragic past at Sochaczew. He didn't tell her that he had hoped that his marriage to Anna would provide a new life for her. The heat that pulsed in his cheeks reflected a terrible guilt. Jan had suffered deep pangs of regret for that day at the pond. He had been too quick to act on his emotions. Always had been, he knew. He would have to change that in himself. He had been too impatient with Anna. It was an irony: it was Anna's innocence that attracted him and it was her innocence that tried his patience. And it was Zofia's interference and lies that had—for the time being—come between them. But how could he have expected Anna to learn the truth about Zofia's character in so short a time when it had taken him quite a bit longer?

How could he have left her? She was as beautiful and fragile as a bird. He would have gone back to the pond that day had not the messenger been waiting at the house to tell him that his father was dying.

He hoped he had explained himself well enough in the letter. He was certain that she understood, that she would forgive. Within days now, there would be plenty of time to make it up to her in person.

Jan *would* make Anna his wife. How he longed for her! He had loved her from the first.

Part Two

Put in a good word for a bad girl;
for a good girl
you may say what you like.

—POLISH PROVERB

13

One week to the day after her conversation with Aunt Stella, Anna was married by a local priest of the parish to Lord Antoni Grawlinski. It was a Sunday, as tradition prescribed.

Lord Antoni was elegantly handsome in his full-dress attire. He stood stiffly, as if at attention, his right hand held to his purple sash of Turkish design.

Anna managed to stand during the ceremony in the reception room, holding to the back of a winged chair for support. She wore a pale silken robe and a simple cap. As custom dictated, her hair was unplaited and worn long and loose for the occasion, symbolizing her transition from girl to woman. But because of the nature of the attack at the pond, no joyous ceremony had been made of the unplaiting the night before. In a myriad of other ways, too, the events leading up to the marriage and the ceremony itself were significantly abridged.

There was to be a wedding bread, at least. Aunt Stella herself had taken charge of the baking of the *kołacz,* seeing to it that only the best wheat flour was used and that the dough was carefully prepared, for if the top of the braided wedding bread cracked, the marriage would not be a good one.

Anna's white-knuckled hands gripped the chair more and more tightly as the ceremony wore on, the priest's voice droning interminably. Her own wedding was becoming a torture, not the splendid celebration of her girlhood fantasies.

Anna looked past the priest to Baron Grawlinski, who stood near the window, a little apart from the women. Her father-in-law was very old, indeed. The only way Anna could detect that he was still alive was to catch sight of his laces beneath his loose-skinned neck as they stirred slightly under his breath. The baroness, a large and unattractive woman, stood stolidly, her hooded eyes set approvingly on her son.

Zofia, radiant in a rose gown, played at sniffling a little, but it was only Aunt Stella who cried.

Anna was beyond tears. She could not remember a specific point in those days after the proposal when she came to a conscious decision that she would accept. She had been beaten down, by her aunt, by Zofia, by herself. And disillusionment had set in when no word was forthcoming from Jan. Why? Had his attraction cooled? Was he the chameleon Zofia painted him to be? Was it something about *herself* that suddenly made him lose interest? Or had his interest been merely what Zofia called a "dalliance"? She regretted her extreme reaction to Zofia's accusation at the pond—turning on Jan as if in her confusion she trusted Zofia's word before his. But she felt certain that his anger, however justified, would have eased in time—*if* he cared for her.

What if he had heard about the attack? Would *that* have kept him away? She knew many men wanted only virgin brides. Or had the accusations against him on the part of the Gronski family held him at bay? Anna herself was convinced that he was not the guilty one. Yet, why had he disappeared?

As the ceremony drew to a merciful close, she tried to search within herself for some sense of assurance—or at least resignation—that fate now propelled them in different directions, that it was simply out of her hands.

Only the night before, Anna had peered out her window, vacantly watching the rain fill the driveway, walkways, and gullies below. Her father had once told her about the great reverence the Chinese held for water. It was a peaceful and humble entity, water, willing to seek the lowest level, willing to make way for the rock in its path. Always patient. Always surviving.

Anna looked to her husband, and she could not help brooding over her decision. She had for the moment become as meek and fluid as water. What would become of this marriage? She had followed neither her intuition nor her heart.

Outside the rain pattered on relentlessly. When the priest pronounced them married, Anna looked up at Lord Antoni and smiled. The Countess Gronska had told her: "No man, my dear, wants a reluctant bride."

Later, when Anna received her piece of the *kołacz,* she lifted the little decorative branch—symbol of fertility—only to see that, underneath it, the bread *had* cracked in the cooking.

Two days later, Anna was busy preparing for the journey to Warsaw, where she and Antoni would winter with the countess and Zofia. She was carefully wrapping a blanket around the box that held the crystal dove. Impulsively she unwrapped the box, opened it, and withdrew the bird. She moved a step or two to the window where the sunshine could pierce it with its warm life.

Once, the bird had seemed to be a happy omen of her future and that Warsaw shopkeeper of so many years before, a prophet from a Greek drama. He had told her the bird would carry her anywhere, that it would lead her to her dreams. She would hold it up to the light, as she did now, and imagine Iris, goddess of the rainbow, carrying her forward, ever forward, into the future.

There seemed no hint of Iris in the cold crystal now, no heat in the October sun. The bird was more a relic of the past. It had belonged to a child who had chosen an unlikely gift and who was singular in her passion to have and keep it. What had become of that child, that *passion?*

A commotion from below took her attention from the dove. Parting the lace curtains and looking down, she wondered if she could trust her eyes: Jan Stelnicki was just dismounting his horse.

She saw him as her memory had etched him, charismatic even in his movements. And beautiful. No man should be so beautiful, she had thought on that first day.

Anna was already at the stairhead when the knocker sounded, but she stopped suddenly. Zofia had been quick to see his approach, too, and she swept to the front of the house in a blur of movement, throwing open the huge oak door.

Anna could see only her cousin's back, but she could make out Jan's face and its serious expression. She hurried down the stairs to the midway landing so that she might hear what was said.

"Good morning, Zofia," Jan was saying, "I wish to offer my condolences. I've been to Kraków and only on my return yesterday did I hear of your father's death."

"You are not welcome here, Jan Stelnicki."

"Ah, straight to the point, as always, Zofia. Well, I've not come to speak to you, although allow me to congratulate you on your marriage."

"Oh," Zofia exulted, "your servants have gotten the news all wrong. It was not *I* who married Lord Grawlinski."

Zofia paused for effect.

Anna could see a quizzical look flash across Jan's face and with it a sharp pain pierced Anna's heart.

Zofia continued: "It is Anna who has earned your congratulations!"

Silence.

In the short time she had known him, Anna had never seen Jan at a loss for words, but he was stammering now, groping for some reply, his face screwed into a map of disbelief.

Anna held to the banister. She thought she would faint.

Zofia continued in her solicitous manner. "You wish my cousin well, of course. I shall relay your message. Now you are to leave this house." The curt voice was rising in volume. "And don't ever attempt to see Anna again!" Zofia slammed shut the heavy door.

The knocker sounded once more.

The Countess Gronska appeared now, dismissing Zofia and stepping out onto the pillared porch to talk to Jan.

As Zofia turned, she looked up to see Anna on the landing. Their eyes locked for a long moment.

Anna stared at her cousin in mute anger and despair. Zofia's expression reflected triumph, but as Anna watched, there did seem to come into the dark eyes a flicker of . . . what? Regret? Remorse? Anna could not decipher it.

Zofia then averted her gaze and wordlessly continued the business of closing the house. She seemed to be humming.

Anna went back to her room. Humiliation kept her from going down to see Jan. Humiliation and shame that she had not waited. She had not trusted in his love. There *had* been some reason why Jan had not come before this, she instinctively knew. And she had not waited. She had made the mistake of a lifetime and there would be no taking it back.

Still, she prayed that Jan would insist on seeing her. The countess could not stop him if he so decided.

In a few minutes, though, Anna heard the sound of his horse retreating. She could not bring herself to go to the window. Perhaps it is best this way, she thought. What was there to be said? What's been done cannot be undone. A priest of the Church had married her to a man she didn't love. She had pledged her love in a sacred vow.

She ceremoniously took the crystal dove now, holding it as if it were a dead thing, and laid it in the velvet of its finely crafted box.

Later, as the carriage trundled on toward Warsaw, away from Halicz, away from Jan, Anna recalled an exquisite vase her father once owned, a foot high and older than the collective lifetimes of fifty men. Against the azure background were the raised white figures of vines, birds, and an Egyptian woman. It was her father's most prized possession.

One winter day, her father himself accidentally jarred it from its pedestal. Anna watched that priceless treasure smash into pieces at her feet, pieces smaller than could ever be repaired. It was the only time she had seen her father cry. She had thought her heart would break then; only now did she know just what heartbreak was. And, like her father, she could only blame herself.

14

Countess Stella Gronska remained silent for most of the journey. Sometimes, in the days following Anna's attack, her son's disloyalty, and her husband's death, she felt as if she were moving into some dense, dark fog, as if her hold on reality were slipping away. Her strict and formal upbringing urged her to go forward, facing up to the demands of her title and station in life, no matter the setbacks. And so she tried to store her recent sorrows in some hidden compartment of her mind, in some locked place she willed herself to visit as little as possible. She needed to keep her wits about her. It was her sincere belief that in the coming days her judgment and moral authority would be needed by her niece, and especially by her daughter.

The countess prayed that life would resume some normalcy in Warsaw. Her diminished family had so much to put behind them. But she was a widow now, and there would be no denying or changing that.

Things had not stayed constant in the city, either. Soon after the enclosed carriage rumbled onto the cobbled streets of Praga, a Warsaw suburb on the east side of the River Vistula, the countess stared out an open window, shocked at the desperate situation of the poor.

Homeless peasants of every age and description evidently had crossed over from the capital, and they wearily carried themselves through the narrow streets, some begging, many more moving as if with no direction. She took in the blank faces, white masks of hopelessness.

The carriage slowed amid the foot traffic and some five or six ragged children ran alongside of it, crying out in thin voices for a coin or bit of food.

The countess, Zofia at her side, sat facing Antoni and Anna Maria. Her niece's sudden movements drew her attention. "Whatever are you doing, Anna?" she asked.

At the inn of the previous night's lodging, the travelers had purchased a luncheon basket, and Anna was rifling through its remains. "I am giving what might be left to these poor children."

"Are you insane?" Antoni intoned. "They are the brats of the city's worst elements."

"They are children and they are hungry."

"They certainly are *noisy* rapscallions," Zofia added.

"A peasant's mouth may be stopped with bread," Anna replied, dropping bread, a few sausages, and fruit from her window.

"Given the chance, those same little beggars would cut your throat." Antoni smiled tightly. "Isn't that right, Lady Gronska?"

"Perhaps it is unwise, Anna Maria." The countess was certain that had Antoni been alone with his wife, he would have restrained her.

Anna bristled. "That does not speak well for Warsaw, then. What kind of city can this be? Zofia, do you have any small coins? I have but three or four."

"To throw to the wind? No!"

"Zofia, please! Give me what you have."

The countess found it a curious thing how the cousins' eyes locked for a long moment. Then, as if suddenly deciding that she could afford acquiescence on this small issue, Zofia looked to her purse.

"Here. Father always said I have no concept of money, anyway." Her laughter tinkled like the coins she passed to Anna.

The countess said nothing as her niece tossed the combined coins out into the growing band of little beggars. She was coming to realize that sometimes Anna had a mind of her own. The countess felt a twinge of guilt as she recalled how she had pressured her niece into the marriage, ignoring her protests. She could only pray to the Black Madonna that she had done the right thing.

"Driver!" Antoni called out. "Put on some speed!"

Just then the countess noticed a particular child—a yellow-haired boy, the tiniest of the paupers—as he bent to pick up one of the coins. As the carriage sped away, he stood and triumphantly waved his tightly fisted little hand in the air. The countess caught but a glimpse of the gaunt and angular face, illuminated by a great childish grin. Her heart thumped. She suddenly regretted not having searched her own purse.

Countess Gronska had always been aware of the poor, but in recent years she recognized a greater chasm between the Polish peasantry and nobility. She saw, existing side by side, the lame hovels of the poor and the palatial mansions of the nobility and clergy. There were the homes and shops of the middle class, too—the tradesmen, artisans, and merchants—but these seemed lost in the contrast of rich and poor.

The texture of life for the nobles in Warsaw was thickening like a well-floured chowder of wealth, pomp, and pleasure. Often now, one could scarcely distinguish between the old moneyed families and the crass nouveaux riches. For this new mixture of nobility there was every manner of entertainment, everything of late organized according to Parisian customs and vogue. They rode in elaborate carriages drawn by teams of high-bred horses, they dressed in the most opulent styles, and both men and women wore great fashionable wigs. Foods and wines were delicious and delicacies like Russian caviar as commonplace on the table as salt. For the poor, the beggars with their colorless rags and crude foot coverings, there was only filth, hunger, and hopelessness.

The countess found herself explaining—matter-of-factly—to Anna Maria that such was the way of all cities. But, afterward, when the window shades had been drawn down by Antoni and only the clip-clopping of the horses' hooves on the cobblestones could be heard, she found herself questioning such a system.

The white, wooden Gronski town house was located in the wealthiest section of the suburb of Praga. The narrow, four-storied structure was one of a number situated on a bluff with a splendid view overlooking the River Vistula, the city walls, and Royal Castle. Though smaller than the country estate at Halicz, the Praga home struck Anna as even lovelier and more richly appointed.

Anna had agreed with Antoni and the countess that she should complete her recovery here. She and Antoni took up residence in the six rooms on the second floor while her aunt and cousin occupied the first level. The families took their meals together.

Anna had hoped for a peaceful marriage, one that—even if it remained loveless—would produce mutual respect and caring. However, it seemed that this simple hope had been dashed by Jan's appearance at Halicz. How could she ever be content with Antoni, knowing with certainty that she had lost the man she truly loved?

Antoni had made no effort to consummate the marriage on the wedding night or in the remaining days at Hawthorn House. It seemed an unspoken pact between them that she still needed time to convalesce.

Now, several weeks after their arrival in Warsaw, Antoni came into Anna's room. He was to leave the next day for Saint Petersburg. His mother had written that his father was gravely ill. Anna sat in bed, reading. She was quick to realize that an intent shone in his gray eyes, an intent that frightened her. She had known this moment would come but felt her stomach tighten, nonetheless.

Antoni sat upon the bed, took her book away, held her eyes with his, and kissed her softly.

Anna's entire body seemed to quake.

He was gentle. He was romantic. And he was her husband.

But she wanted no part of this. Nausea swept over her at his touch. She tried to turn her head. His lips searched for hers. She murmured something, asking him to stop.

He gripped her upper arms and held her rigid against the pillows while he kissed her again.

"No!" she cried, pushing him away.

He sat back and looked at her. "What is it?"

"I . . . I don't know. I'm not ready, Antoni."

"It's been weeks, Anna."

"I know."

"When will you be ready for us to be man and wife?"

"I don't know."

Antoni stood abruptly. He was flushed with anger. "I suggest you find an answer and find it soon, Anna Maria Grawlinska. I am patient only to a point. When I return from Saint Petersburg I expect it will be with my rightful title. You will be my baroness. And this marriage will *be* a marriage. Is that understood?"

She turned her head away from his pinched face. Hearing her married name sent cold shivers through her.

In a few moments, she heard the door close. *With my rightful title.* How coolly he anticipated his father's death. What she wouldn't give to have the briefest of moments with her own father.

Anna was struck by the irony of the situation. She remembered the advice she herself had given Zofia when her cousin complained about the marriage planned by her parents. She had said that Antoni might be handsome and noble, that Zofia might come to love him, that she might find happiness.

Little had Anna known then that she would fill Zofia's shoes. Little had she known the outcome of having to do so. She felt herself recoiling at her own stupidity. No woman should have to submit to an arranged marriage.

The waves of nausea returned and Anna broke out into a cold sweat. She pulled herself out of bed and hurried to the chamber pot. She vomited, violently, as if she wanted to force from her system every physical and nonphysical ill that plagued her.

Later, she lay sleepless, her eyes vacantly tracing little fissures in the ceiling. Antoni had given her a deadline. She must submit. Or else . . . what?

She dared to voice in her mind the thought that had been recurring for days: Was an annulment possible? Why not? The marriage had not been consummated. And while she had any strength, she vowed, it would never be consummated. Antoni was already disillusioned with her, even angry—why shouldn't he agree to be free of her?

Yes, it might work. It just might work. She didn't know how one went about getting an annulment, but under these circumstances, it must be possible.

Did she have the resolve to pursue it, however? No matter what? Did she have the resolve to take control of her own life? Anna imagined, if only for the moment, that she had that courage, and she fell asleep in the early morning hours, dreaming of a scene in which the Cardinal of Warsaw himself was assuring her of an annulment. She was content for the first time in weeks.

But Anna's new sense of ease did not outlast her dreams: she became ill again in the morning.

Lutisha attended her and must have spoken to the Countess Gronska after leaving Anna's room because the countess and Zofia entered soon afterward. The countess appraised the pale Anna, asking one question after another.

"What is it, Aunt Stella?" Anna asked after the litany was finished. She was becoming concerned by her aunt's grim expression and manner. "Am I terribly ill? Is it serious?"

"No, you're not ill. But, yes, it is serious."

"What do you mean?"

"It means, my dear, that you are with child."

Anna's heart dropped. She became dizzy with the news—even though she had denied her own suspicions for days.

Zofia gasped. "Anna, is this child—is it Antoni's?"

"No."

Aunt Stella's face bled to white. "Can you be so certain, Anna?"

"I can."

Zofia took her meaning immediately. "You mean to say that the marriage has not been consummated?"

"Zofia!" the countess cried.

"There, there, Aunt. I can speak of it. No," she said, shaking her head, "it has not."

In those first minutes, before all the other factors regarding having a child could complicate Anna's reaction, one thought rose to the surface: annulment was now impossible.

15

When Antoni Grawlinski returned from Saint Petersburg, his face and demeanor were dark, so Anna's first thought was that his father had died, that Antoni had come back a baron.

But, no, he told her abruptly, his father had astonished everyone by staging a recovery. And without further comment, he retired to his room.

On the day after Antoni's arrival, Countess Stella Gronska held what was, in essence, a family meeting after the evening meal. It was she who spoke first. "Anna Maria, I have told Antoni about your . . . condition. He understands, my dear."

Anna looked to her husband, who smiled weakly.

"And you will accept, Antoni?" Anna asked.

"Accept?" he asked.

"Yes. Does my aunt mean to say you will accept my child?"

Antoni cleared his throat. He was taken by surprise. "You mean as my own?"

Zofia spoke up now. "The child is not Antoni's, Anna, and as such will always—always—remain an impediment to your marriage."

"But Aunt Stella said that he understands. *Do* you understand, Antoni?"

"Yes, Anna, but I cannot recognize such a child as my own."

"I meant that Antoni would see you through your term," the countess said. "There are too many difficulties for him to adopt it, if that is your thought. Supposing the child is a boy . . . you could not expect Antoni to allow a child not his own to be his heir."

Anna felt her body go rigid. "Heir to *my* father's fortune and estate!"

"And to his own, dearest."

"Mother is right, Anna. Of course, no one needs to know that the child is not Antoni's, but from a legal point of view as well as from Antoni's, your baby could not inherit his title and estate. Listen, dearest, keeping the child will make things impossibly difficult for everyone concerned . . . including the child. You must think about that."

"I *have* thought about that," Anna said, her eyes making contact in turn with those of her aunt, her cousin, and her husband. "I had thought about the possibility of a child in those first days of recovery, but then I put it from my mind, or nearly so. God would not allow it, I thought. But now . . . it is strange . . . since I know there is life within me, my feelings have changed. Perhaps this life, like all life, is a gift from God. I want my baby."

"I do not mean to make light of the tragedies you've suffered," the countess said, "but only think if you had not married. My dear child! Your name has been saved. And can you question your good fortune in making a respectable match?"

While Antoni said little, the countess and Zofia continued to tap away at Anna's fragile shell of resistance. The child must be given up.

"What would become of my baby?" she asked at last.

"It would be offered to a good home in some other parish or city," the countess said. "We will say that you and Antoni lost your first child."

"The greatest secrecy will be taken with the matter," Zofia added. "Mother knows all about such matters, don't you, Mother?"

Countess Gronska's brown eyes flared with surprise and anger. Anna noticed some unspoken current pass between mother and daughter, but she was too concerned about her own child to care.

Anna respected and loved her aunt. And even though the countess seemed detached and distracted of late, her aunt's judgment was important to her. But Anna was not the same young girl who had come to live with the Gronski family only a few months before. She had loved and she had lost. She found herself locked in a loveless marriage, a marriage she was convinced had no future. In this matter, then, she vowed to follow her own mind and heart. She would not be the water making way for the rock; the rock would make way for her.

Anna stiffened in her chair, summoning her resolve. She realized that it would not be easy to defy everyone. "I intend to keep my child, Aunt Stella. It is the only reason for me to live."

Antoni's fist crashed onto the table. "Enough! I've listened to enough." He stood. "I'll leave it to you, Lady Gronska, to talk some sense into your niece. Good night."

The three women sat in silence for a long minute after Antoni's departure.

"Well," Zofia said, "I think that Anna's attitude is most admirable, Mother. Remember that she has many months to come to a decision."

Zofia is playing the solicitous diplomat, Anna thought. How confident she is that she will win me over.

"Mother, would you leave me alone with my cousin now?"

The countess seemed exhausted and had little argument left in her, so she deferred to her daughter, kissing them both and retiring to her room.

Zofia's black eyes assessed her cousin. "Now, Ania," she sighed, "you must be realistic."

"I want to keep my child, Zofia."

"What do you hope to gain by taking this stance?"

"I don't know what you mean."

"I think that you do."

"I have no hidden motive."

Zofia's smile seemed more a smirk. "I can see what you're up to."

Anna could only stare.

"You think if you insist on having this child that Antoni will have the marriage voided. Isn't that it? You still think that somehow you will have Jan one day!"

"I have no hope of that."

"In fact, you think—you know!—that this child is Jan's, don't you?"

"Zofia, I *know* that this child is not Jan's. Do you think that it is his?"

Zofia winced. "I don't really care." Her anger was on the rise.

Anna stood and moved toward the door.

"Anna, you will listen to me. If Antoni leaves you, you as a noblewoman cannot bear a child out of wedlock!"

"Zofia, it is unlike you to be so concerned with convention."

"Don't mock me! The sooner you realize that you will not have

Jan and that he is not worth having, the sooner you can get on with your life."

At the door Anna turned back to face her cousin. "I will keep my child, Zofia."

"Then don't expect help from me," Zofia hissed, "and don't expect Antoni to play Józef to your Virgin Mary!"

16

A few days went by without incident. Antoni began taking his meals out of the house. Anna, Zofia, and the countess settled into a peaceful existence, avoiding any subject that might cause conflict.

Anna had never thought about motherhood in any specific way; even as a child she had opted for a crystal dove instead of playing parent to a doll. But she was unable to avoid the subject these days and found herself changed somehow. It was strange to think that she carried life within her, a life for which she now felt wholly protective. Not for one moment had she wished that life away, no matter how much it complicated her own. She would welcome the baby into the world and treat it with the same love she would have given to a child of a man she loved. A child, she reasoned, does not pick its parents nor the circumstances of its birth.

A more immediate subject on Anna's mind was one of residence. Before her father-in-law's illness, she had expected that in the spring she and Antoni would go to live at her residence in Sochaczew. But now she feared that Antoni might want to be near his parents, should there be a change in his father's condition. Whether it was at the familial estate at Opole, in the south of Poland, or worse, at the Grawlinski city mansion in Saint Petersburg, Anna became unnerved. She wanted to be near her own estate. And she wanted to be near her aunt and in a place where there was warmth and love. She could not imagine love in the Grawlinski household. Antoni was a cold creature, as were his parents, cold as borsch.

One afternoon Anna was the lone diner at the noon meal. Lutisha told her that the countess and Zofia had gone out on some appointment. Anna wondered what common errand the two could possibly have.

She felt tiny, seated at the end of the long oak table, her back to the darkly ornate china cabinet that took up the full wall behind her, its shelves a treasury of pewter and silver rising to the high ceiling. She felt foolish, too, as three servants waited upon her and hovered near, like hummingbirds about a flower. They served her a mushroom soup and rump of deer in the Lithuanian style. That it was a bit dry indicated to her that Lutisha had larded it prior to cooking. Because the larding needle allowed too many juices to escape when it pierced the meat, Anna's mother had always strictly instructed their cook to prepare the roast by wrapping it in thin slices of pork fat. When it was nearly cooked, the fat would be removed and the meat coated with castor sugar that high heat transformed into a crisp caramel. This method produced generous juices that became the base of the delicious sauce. On occasion, Anna was allowed to partake in the sauce-making by folding in the heavy cream and squeezing the lemons. Her mouth watered at the thought. How much more delicious that recipe was. And how she longed for her mother and the old days at Sochaczew.

She had eaten and was preparing to go upstairs to her suite when there came a flashing brilliance, followed by a bone-snapping clap of thunder. Then came the sudden downpour.

It was an unusually warm fall day and the windows had been opened to air the house. Anna immediately began closing the dining room windows. There were four of them.

A flustered Lutisha rushed in from the rear of the house.

"Lutisha, if you'll hurry upstairs and see to the windows there, I think I can manage these downstairs."

"Yes, Madame," she replied, bustling toward the stairway.

Anna closed the windows in the library, the sewing room, the reception room, and the countess' bedchamber.

Zofia's room was the last. Anna had gone only a few feet into the chamber when she realized that the windows had not been opened. The air was stale and thick with perfume.

She was just about to leave when she spied a curious-looking book lying on the great feathered bed. Anna crossed the room, and picking up the object, turned it over in her hands. The gold-edged pages were bound by covers of red cloisonné enamel. "What a beautiful thing," she whispered to herself.

Anna opened to the first page then and gasped. It was a diary. Zofia's diary!

Another clap of thunder, deafening, and strong enough to make the house shudder.

Anna dropped the book and raced from the room. The hallway flared with light and shook with vibrating thunder as she went to check any windows she might have missed.

"They are all closed, Madame," Lutisha announced as she met Anna in the front hall. "I checked the third floor, too, and the attic. And not any too soon. The rain is heavy enough for an ark."

"Thank you, Lutisha."

The bulky servant made her slight curtsy. Anna had to suppress a smile at its comical execution.

Anna started for the stairs, then stopped and waited, watching the servant move toward the kitchen.

At Lutisha's disappearance, Anna bolted in the opposite direction, moving with the swiftness of a bird in flight.

In moments Anna found herself once again in Zofia's room. She closed the door behind her. Her brisk action precluded any extended battle with her conscience. *I will read it.*

Although she knew her action was an invasion of privacy, she was determined to crack Zofia's veneer and peer into the mind of her enigmatic cousin. She was convinced that Zofia had engineered her marriage to Antoni. The marriage had served several purposes. For Anna, it saved her from gossip, possible spinsterhood, and as it turned out, unwed motherhood; it saved the Gronskis, too, from gossip and it ended their responsibility for Anna; most of all, it saved Zofia from what she saw as a fate worse than death.

And Anna could not help but wonder what Zofia might have written about Jan. She opened the book.

Her cousin had titled her book *My Delights.* Anna began to read, pledging to herself that she would read only those passages that contained her own name. She was surprised to find it in the first paragraph.

I have more than once come upon my cousin Anna writing in her diary. Upon receiving this lovely book with its empty pages, I have decided to do some writing of my own. I expect Anna writes of dark and disappointing things. It will be my intention to write only of that which delights me.

Poor Anna! Married to a man like the would-be Baron Antoni. Unlike my cousin, I have had a relationship with a real baron, and I suspect that mine has been the more pleasurable.

It happened last year. We had been to a raucous party and we were sleepily intoxicated when we arrived at his rented city apartment shortly after midnight. The baron collapsed onto the bed and slept immediately.

While removing my clothing, I experienced ludicrous difficulty with my chemise. With giggling, drunken wrath I ripped the garment open to my knees and let it fall to the floor.

I looked to the baron who lay on his side, snoring. My drowsiness left me when I observed his muscular physique outlined in his tight breeches. How masculine he was!

A few kisses revived my suitor. He undressed quickly.

It was nothing less than blissful when Baron Driedruski laid himself upon me, and on that massive, feathered bed, our bodies melted into one dream of slow, constant pleasure. The baron was relentless. The night passed slowly, as in a dream.

Shedding perspiration, he was nearing the height of his passion when he suddenly spoke. "You must marry me, Zofia," he said with formality. "I do not want to leave you without the seed of my child."

I wanted to laugh! I had never had such an untimely proposal of marriage.—And did he think that a child would make me more completely his?

Suppressing my irreverent glee, I politely refused to marry him, but did agree to bear his child. Soon he had to return to his castle on the cliffs of the Carpathian Mountains. I would make certain that he leave me a sizable payment for a nurse, and if I were clever enough, he would continue to support the child.

I knew that it was unlikely that I would conceive at that time. Both nurse and child were but deft devices. The evening of pleasure would make it possible for me to stroke the rows of ermine on the most beautiful cape in the city.

The sorrowful baron did not answer me. For a man fifteen years older than I, he did not tire easily. His weight came to exhaust me, however. I was unenjoyably warm before I finished with him. But I would bear ten more such unenjoyable experiences for ten more such children as the one which now graces my wardrobe.

Anna suddenly became aware of the commotion outside of an arriving carriage. She flung the diary back onto Zofia's bed and quickly fled the room. She had just reached the front hall when the door swung open.

"Hello, Anna," Zofia said. "Is something wrong?"

Anna attempted a smile, trying to smother her stunned amazement. "Why, no."

"Well, you look like a woman with a secret," she sang.

Anna noticed the Countess Gronska now. While she had seemed distracted and unhealthy as of late, her face was quite ashen, the large brown eyes strangely wild. Whether the wetness of her face was rain or tears, Anna could not tell. The countess always had some cheerful greeting for Anna, but she whisked past her now without a word.

When Anna heard her aunt's door close, she turned to Zofia with questioning eyes.

"Oh, she's in a state, Anna!" Zofia clucked. "She received a bit of a shock today."

But *you* are positively buoyant, Anna thought. "What is it, Zofia? Where have you been? You don't seem so very shocked."

"Oh, but I am, darling! Only for me it is the happiest of shocks."

"Tell me."

Zofia motioned Anna into the reception room and closed the double doors.

"You will not believe it. We've just come from our attorney's."

"Zofia, do tell me."

"Anna . . . I've known for some time that Walter is not my brother by blood."

Anna's mouth dropped in surprise.

"When Mother and Father thought they would not have any children, they adopted Walter. Then a few years later along came a natural daughter. Isn't that just like me? I started my life surprising people. I suppose I shall end it that way."

"Walter knew?" Anna dropped into a winged armchair.

"Not until that last visit at Halicz. Father told him out of anger when he would not leave Catherine's service to come home." Zofia was standing in front of the ceramic stove, her face and hands full of animation. "Father told him also that he would disinherit him if he did not take up family duties. But Father was unable to follow through on it before his unexpected death. Of course, by law no title can go to an adopted child. I alone inherit a title. And darling, I have just put my claim against the entire estate."

"How could you do that?"

"It so happens I found the will Father had drawn up. It was an amazing stroke of luck! Mother didn't know I had it until we arrived at the attorney's. She was expecting to hear the will that had been drawn up years ago. Oh, you should have seen her face!"

"What about Walter?"

"What about him? Too bad for Walter! He wasn't about to follow Father's wishes. And he gambled that Father wouldn't disinherit him."

Anna didn't know what to say. Her worst fear was confirmed by her cousin's next words.

"So you see why Mother is so upset, darling. I am now in complete control. Of the estates, of the money, of the servants. Everything!"

Looking up at Zofia, Anna tried to put on a pleasant face. Underneath simmered only fear for the future of her aunt and cousins. She mumbled a few words of congratulations. "I think," Anna said, breaking into Zofia's rambling, "that I'll stop in a moment to see the countess."

"Correction, darling. The *dowager* countess. You are looking at

Countess Zofia Gronska. I have more than a dowry now, you can imagine. Perhaps I shall never marry! This Polish fixation with early marriages and fertility is absurd. Besides, if Russia's Catherine can manage a country alone, I think I can run the Gronski affairs. We're hardly a magnate family. But, then again, perhaps I'll marry into one."

Zofia leaned over and kissed Anna. "You go see Mother. I must find Lutisha and see that tonight at supper she serves some of that French sparkling wine that Father had stowed away. We will celebrate even if Mother will not."

"Zofia?"

"Yes?"

"Why would your father pass over your mother in such a way?"

Zofia stared at Anna a moment, then shrugged. "How should I know? Perhaps he thought she would be too sympathetic to Walter, that she would give him what my father meant to deny him." She turned heel and left.

Anna sat dazed. Even though she feared this news would put her aunt over the edge, she could not bring herself to go in to see her. Instead, she tried to sort through her own feelings. She had few thoughts about Walter's loss. Instead, she thought of her uncle who, she was certain, would not be dead, were it not for her. She thought of her aunt, who had lost her husband and—for all purposes—probably her son. What's more, the countess now had a daughter who would be impossible to control.

Oh, Zofia! Now in charge of the Gronski estate and finances and exultant over her brother's undoing. Anna suspected that some machinations of Zofia were at play here. Indeed, a subtle but telltale shadow had passed over her face when Anna questioned her as to why her father would do such a thing. Anna remembered Zofia herself telling how Count Gronski thought his daughter had not learned the value of money. Anna had heard it said that a dead man's will was a mirror to his life. She could not believe the truism applied to her uncle's will. It seemed so unlikely that he would leave his wife—whom he adored—at the mercy of Zofia for the very bread on the table. What would Zofia do with such power and money?

And freedom—such freedom her cousin had gained! Anna was stung with jealousy. Anna had been free but had allowed herself to become locked in a loveless marriage, one in which Antoni expected to make the decisions. Was this her future, or was there some way out?

Like the Empress Catherine, Zofia seemed obsessed with prestige, wealth, and freedom. Such power she had! And then there was the shocking sexual account in Zofia's diary. Anna realized for the first time that the words in that red book rang true. She shivered, then, as if in that well-heated room a cold draft had somehow overtaken her.

Where is my source of power, Anna brooded, *how will I summon it, and will it be enough to stand against all the forces in my path?*

The Countess Stella Gronska took supper in her room. Anna thought her absence at the table seemed almost an abdication to her daughter.

Anna could not help but notice that Zofia had seen to it that the table was exceedingly well set. Several of the large silver platters and dishes had been taken down from the high shelves of the china cabinet and placed in the center of the long table. The countess' best set of Saxon porcelain, from Meissen, was put to use as well, and the detailed design of blue, rose, and violet caught Anna's eye. Its beauty might have had a soothing effect were it not for the upsetting events of the day. She doubted that the countess was aware that the delicate set had been removed from the locked sideboard cupboards. Everything on the table, Anna realized, was to be used only on special occasions. While the crystal wine and water goblets were from Bohemia, Poland's own best silversmiths had fashioned the silverware, employing the insignia of the country's symbolic white eagle. Everything sparkled and shone in the light of a hundred candles.

Anna was amazed to find that the main course was a roast suckling pig, as if this were an Easter celebration.

Antoni, like his wife, spoke little. What went on behind those glass-gray eyes? Anna had resigned herself to the fact that he had married her for her estate and fortune, probably at Zofia's urging. For Anna, the single real benefit of the marriage was that it provided her child with the respectability of a father's name.

Anna studied her husband, who sat across from her. Now, with the revelation of Zofia's inheritance, was his mind moving in the direction she suspected? Had the long-arranged marriage gone forward, he would have gained a greater fortune, the Warsaw town house, the Halicz estate–and the beautiful Zofia.

How ironic. Instead he found himself saddled with a plainer and poorer woman who would bear another man's child. His once glittering bargain must have seemed to tarnish even as he watched.

It didn't take the augury of some ancient seer to tell her that the marriage was doomed. Still, she could not help but wonder just how the end would play out. Was her lifetime to be used up in the meanwhile?

If Zofia noticed that she was the only real celebrant at the table, she gave no such indication. After she called Lutisha over to fill her glass for the third time, Zofia lifted it to her smiling red lips. She was as effervescent as the wine.

17

In November, Jan Stelnicki rented a small town house in Warsaw proper. He had closed his family home in Kraków, Poland's one-time capital. He chose Warsaw because in the days following his father's death he had taken up the cause of the Patriotic Party, and Warsaw, of course, was now the center of all politics in Poland.

Those nobles, some of them magnates, who were disillusioned with the Constitution were becoming more and more vocal. And dangerous. There was a movement afoot, it was rumored, to ask the Russian Empress to intercede on behalf of them.

Such an action would mean war on a large scale, a kind of combined civil and foreign war: noble against noble; Pole against Russian. Consequently, Warsaw was a hive of activity with intrigue on many levels, from the back room of an inn to the throne room at the Royal Castle.

There were days, too, when Jan would admit to himself that he was in Warsaw for another reason.

These were the days he would wander down to the Queen's Head, an inn at the river's edge with an eclectic clientele. The weather had grown cold, so he sat indoors, sipping a coffee. Sometimes he overheard customers remark that he seemed utterly lost in thought or perhaps a bit simple. He was not staring into space, as they probably supposed. If they were to follow his gaze, they would find that it led out the filthy window, across the freezing river, to the white timbered town house on the bluff.

Once, he had dared to ride by the house in a closed cab. He caught a glimpse of Zofia at a window, but no sign of Anna.

He questioned his obsession with Anna, mocking himself for it. Why was he tortured by thoughts of a married woman? *Why* had she married? He had been so certain of her feelings for him.

He prayed for a glimpse of her, just one glimpse. But the great white house held her like a captive bird.

One day he ran into Zofia shopping at the Market Square. She was at once cool and coquettish. He was unable to read her.

They awkwardly exchanged greetings and trivial news. He asked about the Countess Gronska, but couldn't quite bring himself to ask about Anna. Zofia was full of a story about how she had inherited everything, Walter nothing. He wasn't interested and didn't quite follow its twists and turns. He thought only about Anna. When Zofia exhausted herself to little effect, they said good-bye.

Jan turned and started to walk away.

"Oh, Jan," Zofia called.

Jan turned around.

"Anna is quite happy. Did you know she is to have a baby?"

Jan felt the blood drain from his face.

Zofia was smiling strangely.

He said something, mumbled something he would not remember later, then fled.

That would end his obsession, he thought. He avoided the river after that, losing himself in his work, in the cause.

Within a month, though, he sat in the Queen's Head watching a curtain of snow fall onto the Vistula, a curtain that could not quite obscure the white house on the bluff.

18

O n Christmas Eve Anna did not feel well enough to attend Mass. She went to her husband's room to wish him a happy holiday. She was pleased to find that he was wearing a gift she had given him recently, an elegant blue velvet dressing gown. He stood in front of the mirror trimming his thin black moustache, a new addition. "Good morning, Antoni," Anna said, "I came to wish you—"

Then, out of the corner of her eye, she caught some slight movement and looked toward the bed.

There, lying on the satin quilt and turning a page to some small book of engravings was Minka, a young woman Antoni had hired to clean and care for the upstairs suite.

Anna could only stare.

With tiny eyes that dotted a round and chubby face, Minka stared back. "Hello, Madame."

Anna could not believe her bare-faced gall. She turned to her husband, only to witness a sly smile playing under the moustache. He is enjoying this, she realized.

Anna stood motionless, speechless, burning with embarrassment.

Suddenly, the Countess Gronska fluttered into the room. The door had stood open so that she had seen fit to enter after rapping lightly.

Anna's heart stopped as her aunt cordially greeted her and Antoni. She hoped that in her absentminded state, her aunt would not notice the servant.

"Mass was beautiful!" she declared. "I have brought a vial of holy water, my dear—" The countess stopped in midsentence to stare incredulously at Minka, who had resumed perusing the book.

Anna would have preferred death than have her aunt witness this scene. It was humiliating enough to endure herself.

Her eyes like two moons, the countess abruptly scurried from the room.

Anna was left to determine how she herself would respond to this affront. Antoni smiled and shrugged his shoulders, as if to comment on the Countess Gronska's eccentricities.

She wished Antoni a good night and turned to leave. It was all she would do. If he is taking some sadistic pleasure in my discomfort, she thought, I will not give him the satisfaction of enlarging it.

Anna was nearly run over at that moment by her aunt, who came rushing back into the room, moving faster than Anna could have imagined. The brown eyes flared wildly. The countess was brandishing a broom that was covered with filth from a commode!

"You brazen and wicked creature!" she shrieked as she dashed toward the horror-stricken Minka.

The chubby girl could not move quite fast enough. The countess thrashed the broom into Minka's elaborately plaited gold hair, again and again. "You fat, saucy witch!" she cried.

Minka became hysterical, shrieking vulgarities in an unintelligible dialect. Screaming and crying, she bolted from the room, the countess in quick pursuit.

Halfway down the stairs, the woman tripped on her skirts and tumbled headlong to the bottom. With injury only to her pride, she picked herself up and ran out the front door, into the night.

Lutisha, who had heard the commotion, held it open for her.

The countess, however, was not about to give up the chase and followed.

Enraged, Antoni pushed past Anna and stormed off to another part of the house.

Outside, Minka's screams pierced the serene holiday streets.

Anna returned to her own room. When she passed her mirror, she paused, caught by her own smile. She stared at herself some moments; then came the laughter, lilting at first, then unreserved. How long it had been since she laughed. "Merry Christmas, Minka!" she said aloud. "Merry Christmas, Antoni!"

The daughter of Jacob Szraber, the man who saw to the management of the Sochaczew estate, was being married and Anna attended the wedding. She did so against the will of her husband. Defying him was a small victory, but she relished it.

Antoni refused to attend the wedding of a commoner—and Jewess. Countess Gronska was upset that her niece was going unescorted, but Anna could still disguise her condition and knew that her presence would please her father's old friend and employee. Anna knew the mother of the bride well, too. Emma Szraber had been her governess for several years.

Anna did not have far to travel, for the wedding was held there in Praga, which over the years had welcomed many Jewish families. Anna found the Jewish ceremony charming, the youth handsome in his wide-brimmed black hat and suit, the bride resplendent in her white gown of homespun cotton. Observing the gaze that each held for the other there under the wedding canopy, Anna recognized immediately that here was a union of love. And she could not help but wince at the thought of her own blissless marriage.

All about her there was nothing but love and good wishes for the couple. She felt God present in the synagogue and she remembered Jan's saying that God, his God, could be found in *all* the churches. Now she thought she understood. God was in the people and in the love they had for one another.

The women on either side of her cried softly during the ceremony, and Anna felt a sense of guilt, knowing that her own tears were not wholly for the couple. They were selfish tears for a wedding that had been . . . and another that was never to be.

Anna would go to her grave loving only Jan Stelnicki. She wondered if he ever thought of her, and if he ever came to Warsaw. No, she decided, why would he? His family home is in Kraków. She recalled an old saying that the best things in Poland were liquor from Gdańsk, gingerbread from Toruń, shoes from Warsaw, and a maiden from Kraków. Her heart caught. Did women in Kraków possess such legendary beauty? Would Jan meet someone there? Perhaps he already had. He would attract almost any woman. She might as well resign herself to the fact that, sooner or later, he would meet someone. And he would marry.

Anna felt a tug at her sleeve. The woman next to her was offering her a handkerchief. Anna refused, blinking back her tears and the thoughts behind them.

The reception was held at the groom's familial home, a small brick dwelling, elegantly appointed and overflowing on this occasion with light and warmth and scores of people. Children were given their part in the celebration, too, and there were many of them, dressed in their finest and running all about. It was only right, Anna thought: marriage is all about children.

Putting aside thoughts of Jan, Anna came to feel exhilarated. After so many weeks of sickness and months of seclusion, she had almost forgotten what it was like to enjoy herself.

"Lady Anna Maria!" Jacob exclaimed. "I am delighted that you've honored me so. How well you look!"

"Thank you, Jacob," Anna said. If he only knew what has transpired in the past few months, she thought. "Your Judith is a beautiful bride. Congratulations!"

Jacob proudly introduced Anna to the newly married couple and to a score of friends and relatives. Then he begged his leave, saying, "I have a great many duties to attend to, but I must have a word with you later, before you leave. Now, you must say hello to your old tutor— where *is* my wife?" He laughed. "Don't dare tell her I called her old. Ah! there she is. And you must take some refreshment and fill a plate with this sumptuous food. The rump of deer is delicious, and I don't say that merely because I killed it myself. Emma will see that you get a plateful. Emma! The pike in gray sauce is good, too."

"Did you catch that, as well?"

"Yes," Jacob laughed, his dark eyes dancing. "Emma!"

"Anna!" Emma Szraber cried, hurrying forward and throwing her arms around her former charge. "Tell me," she asked after their kiss, "do you still play the piano?"

Anna felt herself flushing. Jacob had disappeared. "No, I'm afraid not, Madame Szraber. Oh, I play at it once in a while, but you must admit I had no real talent for it."

"Reading too many books to be bothered, I'll wager. *That* was always the case, I remember. And perhaps you needed a bit more confidence."

As Anna renewed her friendship with the woman who had taught her about literature, art, and languages, she could not help but wonder what news Jacob had. She was certain she had seen a momentary eclipse in his bright eyes.

When Anna had first observed that she was the only noble present, she became self-conscious, but as she watched the happy commoners display only love and warmth, she relaxed, coming to enjoy herself.

She soon found, however, that she wasn't the lone person of title. Standing in the doorway of the library that had been cleared of all furniture for dancing, she was watching the dancers' lively movements to the mazurka when a stranger spoke.

"It would seem that your tapping feet betray you, Lady Grawlinska. Would you care to dance?"

"Oh no, really." Anna swung around but did not recognize the face. "Have we met?"

"No. I confess Emma Szraber told me who you are and sent me over to dance with you."

"Oh?"

"I suspect we are their most highly placed guests and they thought it fitting we should amuse each other." He laughed. "I think that commoners sometimes think that all *szlachta* know one another and need no introductions."

Anna laughed, too.

"I am Michał Kolbi. I will merely whisper to you that I am a baron, for the Republic frowns on the excessive use of titles."

He was as garrulous as he was attractive. And a bit too bold in a frivolous sort of way, Anna thought at first.

About thirty, he was tall and muscular. His features were regular, but his curly brown hair and soft brown eyes lent him a striking handsomeness.

Anna countered his graceful phrases and entreaties to dance with the assertion that she was married.

"Jacob told me. Do women stop dancing when they marry? Even when a husband is foolish enough to allow her out of his sight?"

Anna felt warm blood rush to her face. She could not bring herself to tell a stranger she was expecting, especially when no one else present knew. As it was, it went against custom for her even to be out of the house. "Lord Kolbi, please accept my polite refusal. Another time."

He deferred for the moment, chatting with much élan, but he was not to be deterred. Anna came to enjoy his company and was soon coaxed into a waltz. She was certain it would do no harm to the child. She had misread him, she decided: while he *was* loquacious and forward, he was not shallow.

After the dance, Anna sipped on a cordial. "To a happy 1792!" she told the baron. "It is so good to see so many happy Polish faces."

"If only it could be so always."

"You don't think that it will be? Are you a pessimist, Lord Kolbi? I hardly would have thought so."

"I am a realist, my lady. This year will be a crucial one. Over the years our neighbors have stripped our country like a cabbage, leaf by leaf. I am a baron, but it is little more than an empty title. You see, our family lost its lands to the Russians with the Partition of 1772."

"Oh, I am sorry."

"I have long since adjusted. I was but a child at the time. I am fortunate enough to have a home here in the capital and the wherewithal to sustain myself. But I know that Catherine will not be satisfied until all of Poland has been partitioned, until she takes even Warsaw."

Anna felt a flicker of fear. While the flowering of her political knowledge had taken seed at the hands of her father, it was given further nourishment on innocent autumn afternoons in her uncle's meadow. She remembered those political conversations she had had with Jan. He, too, had been fearful of the future. "Tell me, are there still Polish nobles who are inviting Catherine's interest?"

"There are."

"What of our alliance with Prussia? Their king has sworn to protect us from any aggressor."

"While you are well-informed, Lady Grawlinska, you must not be so trusting."

"I am learning, Lord Kolbi. I am learning."

"Then place no confidence in Prussia. Frederick William is not to be trusted. He would drop our interest like a hot iron if he thought doing so would put a few ducats in his purse or provinces on his map."

"If only those nobles who would be so cozy with Catherine could see where it might lead."

"Where it *will* lead, my lady. Into the tangling web of a black widow spider. No, unlike you, they aren't thinking of Poland's interest, but only of their own petty grievances, their precious so-called Golden Freedom given up by the Constitution."

"How can they be so shortsighted?"

"You impress me with your interest. I have a host of friends who are of one mind in this matter. Perhaps one day you would like to meet them?"

"Yes, certainly!"

"Perhaps you might even join us?"

"Oh, Lord Kolbi, of what possible use could I be?"

"I sense in you a woman of strength, Lady Grawlinska, of mind and spirit. And you are of the nobility. Many of my friends are not. There is no telling but that one day you may be of invaluable service to us."

"And to Poland?" Anna chuckled.

"Perhaps. Do not laugh. Do not undervalue yourself, Anna. *May* I call you Anna?"

Anna nodded. "Well, I should like to meet your friends."

"Good!"

Jacob did take Anna aside before she left. "Lady Anna Maria," he stammered, "do you have plans for the farm that you may have . . . forgotten to tell me about?"

"Why, no, Jacob. Why?"

"Perhaps your husband is planning some changes?"

"Not that I'm aware of. Why do you ask?"

"I'm sure it is not my place—"

"My husband has been to the estate, is that it?"

"Yes."

"What did he have to say?"

"Very little. But he did ask many questions about the grain crops. And there were some men with him."

"Noblemen?"

"No. They seemed to be in your husband's employ. . . . They were discussing the logistics of something or other."

"What did you hear?"

"Oh, they spoke too quietly when I was within earshot."

"I see. You are not to worry. I'll question my husband. I'm certain there must be some reasonable explanation. Is everything else on the estate as it should be?"

"Yes."

Anna swallowed hard. "Has there ever been any sign of Feliks Paduch?"

His face darkened at the memory. He shook his head. "No, Lady Anna."

"I see. Well, Jacob, I must take my leave. I've had a lovely time. I will be in touch with you soon."

Jacob and Emma saw her to her carriage. "Godspeed!" they called as it pulled away. Anna waved and called out to them, attempting to smile despite the uneasy distraction she felt welling up within her.

As the carriage moved through the cobbled streets of Praga toward the Gronski home on the riverfront, she worried what it was that Antoni was about.

At home, Anna entered the sewing room where the countess, draped in her customary black, sat motionless, staring into a low fire that sent shadows playing about her. Her gray hair was unkempt.

On the floor were scattered several issues of the weekly *Monitor*, a digest that provided all the recent news of the kingdom, mostly political these days.

Anna wondered whether Aunt Stella would ever recover from the secret will that gave everything to Zofia. She had not yet even spoken to her daughter.

Anna tried to lift her aunt from her melancholy with lively descriptions of the reception: the Jewish customs, the food, the music, the dancing, the gaiety.

The countess nodded occasionally, disinterested, until Anna spoke of having met a charming man with a dour prediction.

"Oh? What was his prediction?"

"He believes that Poland, even Warsaw itself, is in danger."

Anna was tired and she realized—too late—that she should not have brought up such a grim topic.

Oddly enough, it was this subject that caused the countess to come to life. "*All* the countries of the civilized world are in danger, Anna

Maria! Look at the times we live in. The Russian whore-empress has liaisons with common soldiers. What scruples must she have? 'If gold
will rust, what then will iron do?' "

Anna recognized the biblical allusion. In *Canterbury Tales*, Chaucer
had made much of it, too, applying it to the Parson, one of the few
characters—out of an array of hypocrites—who stood as perfect examples
for others. Her aunt seemed possessed, and yet she spoke perfect sense.

"The great empire of France," Aunt Stella continued, "has fallen before the bloody pitchforks of the masses and its queen and king quake
in prison while the rioting pigs sharpen the edge of the *guillotine*. The few
French princesses that survive will be turned out into the streets to
marry cobblers or fish peddlers. The aristocracies of the world will
cease to exist."

Anna could only stare at her aunt.

"Poland," the countess went on, "must maintain its noble class even
if every other country about us collapses like houses made of sticks!"

Anna vowed to herself that in the future she would avoid speaking
of politics with her aunt.

The countess' voice softened, taking on a witchlike rhythm as she
continued. "The ruling powers of the future will be but poor imitations
of the true aristocracy, Anna Maria, deceivingly cut as the sparkling
Prussian glass." She sighed, her voice sputtering then to a close. "It is a
sad facsimile of a true diamond."

Anna could think of no words to answer her and she was afraid
that the wrong word would ignite her again, so she merely bade her
good night, kissing her lightly on the creased forehead.

Anna was startled to find Zofia in the hallway, seemingly eaves-
dropping. Her cousin had been out for the evening.

With a finger on her lips, Zofia motioned her into the kitchen. The
servants had retired. "She's not doing well, is she?" Zofia asked.

"She hasn't been herself lately."

"Oh, Anna, she's strange! All these peculiar political notions. I
think that it's her way of coping. Oh, she'll pass through this little period. Believe me, Anna, at her core, she's as sane as you or I. Now, do
tell me about the wedding."

Zofia, it seemed to Anna, had been trying for some time to secure a
closer relationship with her. While Anna questioned her sincerity, she
had no other friend or family member in whom she could confide, and

so sometimes found herself giving Zofia the benefit of her many doubts.

For the second time, Anna related the details of Judith Szraber's wedding and her meeting with Baron Kolbi.

While feigning interest in the account, Zofia took a bowl of thick yogurt over to a table, added a small amount of water to it, and whisked it thoroughly. "Well, I'm glad that you enjoyed yourself, darling. You haven't left the house in a very long time."

Anna watched with fascination as her cousin—making use of a mirror that hung above the table—dashed the paste of cool yogurt onto her face.

"This is absolutely splendid for the complexion, Anna." The mirror allowed for Zofia's eyes to hold Anna's. "Won't you try some? Half an hour will do you wonders."

Anna declined, watching Zofia take a seat at the kitchen table, her face a snow-white mask. She thought that her cousin possessed such beauty and vitality that God must have meant for her to live a hundred years, yogurt or no.

Where, she could not help but wonder, had Zofia spent *her* evening?

19

A week after her thrashing by Countess Gronska, Minka returned to the house to collect her things.

Anna met her on the upstairs landing. She was amused to see that the woman's beadlike eyes darted nervously about as if she expected at any moment to see the deranged countess fly at her, just as Marzanna, the Goddess Death, was thought to appear out of nowhere—dressed in her white gossamer gown and carrying a scythe—to escort a doomed soul to judgment.

Anna insisted that the chubby woman accept some coins as payment for the cleaning and plaiting of her hair. "But do be forewarned, Minka," Anna cautioned, "should you show your face here again, it will not be my aunt who lunges at you."

The woman's eyes reflected the sluggishness of her mind. It took a few moments for the surprise to register. Then an expression came into the woman's visage that Anna interpreted as surprise mingled with respect.

"Do you take my meaning?"

"Yes, Madame," she whispered.

In the days following Minka's episode with the Countess Gronska, Antoni's attitude toward Anna changed dramatically. He began to show a renewed concern for his wife, buying her little gifts and staying at home most evenings. Anna wondered at the change, but was appreciative of it.

On the morning after the Szraber wedding, Anna went to see her husband in the upstairs study. She was not certain how to broach the subject of his visit to her estate. She was not certain that she even had the nerve to do so.

"Good morning, Anna!" He was in a cheerful disposition. "Did you enjoy yourself yesterday?"

"Yes, I had a lovely time." Anna was taken aback, for he seemed to have forgotten his interdict against her going.

"Good! You should get out and about more. I was just about to come see you. There are some papers to be signed, legal matters from Lord Lubicki. It will take but a moment. Here, sit down, dear."

Anna seated herself at the desk that Antoni always kept so neat.

"Here are the papers. Your signature is needed next to mine in these three places." He pointed them out to Anna, then stood hovering over her.

Anna took in the seal of the Lubickis, the prestigious banking family her father had retained for many years. She remembered how before their marriage Antoni had been so impressed that the estate was worthy of their attention. The pages were filled with a multitude of numbers and legal terms.

Anna did not reach for the pen. "Antoni, what is the subject of these papers?"

"Oh, they are mere formalities." Antoni inked the quill and placed it in Anna's hand. "They express your willingness to have me share in your father's estate."

"But I signed that agreement at the time of our marriage. Antoni, I should like to read these before I sign them."

"Oh, Anna, there is no reason—"

"Then please tell me exactly what the content is."

"Very well." He sighed in defeat. "These papers will allow me to withdraw certain monies that Lubicki holds in trust."

"But haven't you had that power? How does this differ from the marriage agreement?"

"There is a clause in your father's will that supersedes the nuptial document. It states that your husband may, on his own signature, withdraw interests on the estate, but in order to withdraw any of the principal, your signature is needed as well."

"I see." Careless as he was in regard to his personal safety, her father had proven to be cautious in such matters as these. "It would seem that you need a large amount of money."

"Yes, rather . . . I have a number of expenses to see to, and as you know, my inheritance . . . well, I cannot be sure of when . . ."

"Would you be more specific as to where the money is going?"

Antoni bristled at what he clearly considered wifely impertinence. "No."

Anna put down the pen.

His tone softened immediately. "I only mean that it is a business venture of which I have been forbidden to speak."

Anna looked up, her eyes searching his face. "Antoni, do you plan to make changes at my farm?"

"What?" His mouth dropped slightly, almost imperceptibly.

"The farm at Sochaczew—do you intend to make some changes there? Is that why you need the money?"

Antoni's face reddened with anger. "That meddling Jew! What did he tell you?"

"Very little, actually." Anna looked down at the desk again. "Only that you seem to be making plans." She struggled to keep her voice from shaking. It was an unnerving thing to challenge her husband.

"Ah! It's true." His tone lightened deliberately. "I plan to renovate the house and a number of the outer buildings, as well as build a larger and more efficient barn. It will take a great deal of money." Displaying a facsimile of a smile beneath the perfectly trimmed moustache, he placed his hand lightly on her shoulder. "I had hoped to surprise you, Anna Maria, but now . . . well, Jacob has spoiled it."

"I see." Anna knew that they had reached an impasse. She also knew that he was lying.

Anna stood then so that she could face him. She prayed for the strength to hold her ground. What Jacob had told her at the wedding about Antoni and his murky intentions buoyed her now. Thoughts of her estate led inexorably to her father and the love of the land he had passed on to her. What were her husband's true intentions? The Szraber wedding had changed her in other ways, too; it had forged a new attitude. She had seen what a marriage, a real marriage, is about. It was time to see if there were any hope of having a marriage with Antoni. If there were, then she would adapt and strive to be content. If not . . . well, that was a precipice to which she had not quite come as yet. "Antoni, I wish to discuss another matter with you . . . about the child."

The smile faded. "Yes?"

"I haven't changed my mind." She steadied her eyes on him. "I still wish to keep my child."

"I see. If it is a girl, Anna, I will not interfere."

"And if it is a boy?"

"It is out of the question!"

"I have given that some thought." She could feel her heart beating rapidly. She could not retreat now. "It might be arranged that the child, if it is a boy, would inherit my estate. A second son, our son, would inherit yours."

"Are you mad?" The gray eyes glared in astonishment. "It is unthinkable! To divide the estates which our marriage has only just combined? One must strengthen one's family line and fortune, not weaken it. The legal entanglements would be endless. And what would people say?"

"I don't care what people will say."

"You will, my dear, when I do not recognize the child and it is put about that your son is a bastard." He smiled. "A child of yours without a father will be a commoner, and we both know commoners cannot own land."

Anna grew angry. He was very quick to play his highest card. Her anger gave her direction and voice. "That little device would turn on you, Antoni. Your pride is too great to allow any such ugly talk to get started. After all, what would people say of *you,* Antoni Grawlinski?" Anna managed her own smile now, the smile her mother had taught her. "They would call you a cuckold! That *is* the correct term, isn't it?"

Antoni was stunned into silence, his face empurpling with rage. He had not expected this from her.

Anna, too, was surprised at herself. She had gone from being un-nerved at this confrontation to feeling something akin to being invigo-rated by it. "Antoni, you married me for what I might bring to you and your family. Don't you think I know that? You also knew the circum-stances of my so-called *illness* and that—however slight the chance—I might bear a child."

"I did . . . but I did not expect that—"

"What? That I would dare go against the countess' advice or your wishes? I am telling you that I intend to keep my child at all costs. Per-haps you might wish an annulment. The grounds should be easily es-tablished. After all, the union has not been—"

"Stop this foolishness, Anna!" Antoni shouted. "There will be no annulment. Our estates have been joined and only a son we have to-gether will inherit them. You will listen to your husband and you will start by signing these papers now!"

"I will not!" Anna cried. Her rebellion had taken on a life of its own.

With the back of his hand, Antoni struck her hard across the face.

Anna wiped at her mouth, looked at the blood as if in amazement. Aside from the incident at the pond, no one had ever struck her.

She walked to the door.

"You will obey me, Anna Maria," Antoni said through clenched teeth. The door was open and he didn't want his voice to carry. "If you don't," he growled, "I'll . . ."

Anna turned around, her eyes taking him in. "You'll what, An-toni?" She smiled at her husband. "Kill me?"

Antoni could not respond. Something in his slate-colored eyes told Anna she had finished his sentence with precision.

Anna returned to her room. *That's what he gets for playing his high card too early,* she thought. *When he finds himself in a real bind, he resorts to a stupid, idle bluff.*

20

In mid-January Zofia employed for her personal use two French maids, Clarice and Babette. Anna thought the latter lovely but light-headed. Babette had two of the most beautiful children Anna had ever set eyes upon: a little boy and girl of fair coloring. The children occasionally performed light tasks or errands about the house. No mention was ever made of their father.

They seemed to have their share of toys and treats provided by the Countess Stella and Lutisha, but they were largely ignored by their mother and the rest of the household. Gifts and favors are poor replacements for love, Anna thought. She recognized their need for direction and genuine attention, and so did what she could to fill the void. She suspected that her condition and the maternal sensations she was experiencing made her feelings for them more poignant. She read to them on occasion, but more often astonished them with her bottomless store of myths and tales. For them, she always made certain to provide her own, happier, endings. They would know soon enough that happy endings occurred in literature more than in life.

Although Babette's performance as a mother was deficient, her execution of her duties was impeccable. She was meticulous in her care of Zofia's wigs and dresses. It was with the loyal assistance of Babette and Clarice that when a carriage stopped to collect Zofia, she left the house a stunning vision of color and beauty.

Anna gasped at Zofia's daring: she had taken to wearing the new high-waisted gowns that exhibited so much of her full breasts.

The Countess Gronska continued to ignore her daughter, but the will that established Zofia as the heiress was hardly the only reason. Anna came to suspect that Zofia was mistress to many men.

At night Anna stayed up late reading or lay awake thinking, yet she seldom noticed the hour when Zofia returned from her nighttime amusements. She was all but certain that some nights her cousin did not return until the following day.

Shortly before Zofia left for an evening, Clarice prepared for her a special raisin strudel swimming in thick rose syrup. When the tantalizing aroma of this food filled the house, Anna knew that Zofia's departure was imminent.

On several occasions, after Zofia had left the house, Anna secretly let herself into her cousin's room and, by the yellow light of a single taper, read from her diary. She despised her own behavior—there was no reconciling such deceit to everything she had learned—yet some dark power within her was not to be denied.

Of the raisin strudel ritual, she found this:

The rose syrup makes men hungry for my scented lips! Within a short time after I have eaten of the strudel, I could run from my home to the palace with energy to spare. But I cage this power so that I might release it at a time when it is most pleasurable for me.

I detest the raisins! But when this terrible food is fermented in a brew of adder's tongue, it takes on the most magical of powers. The strudel kindles within me the fire of life itself when I am with a man. All sensation seems to be elevated to glorious heights. Because of the strudel, all men are desirous of me, and I do not have to refuse any man who is desirable to me.

It makes me laugh to think that King Stanisław reminds me of a raisin! At court, the old king seldom passes me without thrusting his darting tongue into my mouth like some old and featherworn hummingbird.

The king is as wrinkled as—yet not as dry as—a raisin. My delight in the king is in making his flabby and withered flesh yield to that part of the raisin that is not yet dry. While others do not please him and dare not even look into his eyes, I have brought forth the age inhibited, yet living, part of his Royal Highness.

My greatest triumph is to see him shaking with the pain of age mingled with—then overpowered by—ecstasy!

Was there truth in this, Anna wondered. Had Zofia been bedded by the king?

Anna recalled now what the peasants in Sochaczew said about adder's tongue, the herb with a narrow spike thought to resemble the tongue of a snake. They held that it took a bold girl to seek it out in the forest—Satan's realm—but if she found it, boiled it, and drank of its brew, she would have great success with bachelors. Young girls at play would sing of it, too:

> Adder's tongue, I pluck you boldly
> Five fingers, the palm the sixth
> Let the men run after me
> Large, small, let them all pursue me.

The household simmered with uneasy relationships. Zofia and her mother, who was becoming more and more preoccupied, scarcely acknowledged one another. Anna and Antoni settled into a cool coexistence, but the question of the child always lay just beneath the surface.

The winter was proving to be the harshest in years. The house was drafty. Though Anna was starting to swell, her condition was not apparent to the unsuspecting. Over four months along now, Anna wondered when she would feel her child stirring within her body. She wanted this baby, her baby. What a miracle is life, she thought.

Her cousin Walter had been correct in his prediction months before— it seemed like *years* ago, that meal in the Gronski home at Halicz—that the Russian campaign against the Turks would take only a few months. Victory was now a realization and much of Warsaw was celebrating.

Anna had been corresponding with Baron Michał Kolbi since the Szraber wedding. At his urging, she decided to hold a reception that would celebrate the Russian triumph over the Turks, as well as bolster support for the February 14th general election that would accept or reject the Constitution the *Sejm* had passed the previous May.

Attending were some Russian acquaintances of the baron and those friends whom he had wished Anna to meet—members of the political pressure group he had asked her to join. Anna's own political philosophy, one influenced by her father, uncle, Michał, and Jan, was being forged into something with shape and strength. She even found herself reading her aunt's issues of the *Monitor*. Poland was coming to a crossroads the likes of which history had never seen, notwithstanding the treacherous crises the country had weathered to date, century after century.

Both the countess and Zofia agreed to allow Anna the use of the reception room and adjoining music room. Antoni had gone to his estate at Opole for a week and so had no say in the matter. Aunt Stella's protracted mourning relieved Anna of asking her to attend; she was certain that the number of commoners invited would upset her aunt. Anna invited Zofia merely as a courtesy, for she was routinely gone from the house at night, and it was unlikely she would make an appearance.

Anna studied the roomful of people. There were bankers, men of business, a priest, shopkeepers, and even a few country folk. No, neither her aunt nor her cousin would mix well with this group of patriots.

"The party is a success," Baron Kolbi said. "And you are radiant tonight, Anna Maria."

Anna felt a pulsing excitement. This was the first entertainment of any kind she had ever attempted and it was going beautifully. She wore a gown of silvery gray satin with lace trim at the shoulders. Babette had fashioned for her a coiffure that swept up all of her reddish brown hair high upon her head, holding it there with amber barrettes that Babette insisted amplified the amber flecks in Anna's green eyes.

The baron's group of friends was buoyant over Russia's victory. Anna thought they seemed such a diverse and convivial lot that it was odd to think an unseen and unsettling political thread bound them together.

Lutisha and Marta, dressed in their finest, served Anna's new acquaintances mulled wine, tiny meat pies, cheeses, and an assortment of delectable French desserts Babette and Clarice had engineered.

Anna was chatting with a banker and his wife when she became aware that the group of thirty or so was suddenly astir. She caught the banker's line of vision and turned around.

There, in the arched doorway, across the length of the reception room, stood Zofia, her dark eyes scanning the guests.

Anna suppressed a gasp.

Zofia glowed hotly in her gown of vivid red velvet, perilously low-cut. Black wiglets had been worked into her own hair and the high mound was set off by tiny red ribbons and diamond barrettes. Catching sight of Anna, she flashed a wide smile. "Anna, darling!"

As Zofia moved across the room, Anna held her breath in fear that the scant material covering her cousin's bosom would fall away.

Zofia walked with her back erect, her head poised, confident that every eye was upon her.

A hush fell over the room. The staring faces could be easily read: there were some who thought her beauty incredible; some who thought her appearance scandalous; and others who thought her both beautiful and scandalous.

Anna stepped forward to greet her.

"Anna!" she cried. "I could not leave without at least looking in on your little soirée. I had promised Charlotte ages ago that I would help hostess one of her affairs. Some two hundred people and she is a helpless soul. You will forgive me, won't you?"

Anna smiled, knowing a reply was not expected. She detected the scent of rose.

Zofia was surveying the group. "Oh my, I should say that I am a bit overdressed for your friends."

Anna chuckled. "Zofia, you are hardly that."

Zofia ignored the chiding. "Why, I don't know a soul here, darling. Who are these people? Are there no nobles present?"

Anna cringed. "There are a few here," she whispered, "but mostly they are commoners, friends of Lord Kolbi. . . . Don't you remember that when I told you of the reception I mentioned the baron and his little group of patriots?"

"No—oh, yes, something of the kind. But I had just come in after a long evening, and I'm afraid I didn't concentrate."

"Well, these good people are united in their common concern for Poland and the Third of May Constitution. They are artisans, men of business, a priest—even a few Russians."

"It looks to be a motley collection, indeed!" Zofia announced, making no effort to lower her voice.

Anna flushed.

"Now," Zofia intoned, the black eyes sparkling, "here is something of more immediate interest! I demand an introduction, Anna."

Anna turned to see the baron approaching. She introduced him to her cousin.

"Ah, Lord Kolbi," Zofia sang, "you are the one of whom Anna has been speaking so much! I am very pleased to meet you. I've listened to my cousin go on at great length about your little group. I find it fascinating."

Anna stared in amazement at her cousin.

The baron smiled. "Then you hold opinions similar to those of your cousin?"

"Opinions?"

"Yes, I take it you approve of our cause?"

"Your cause . . . of course." Zofia had been put off momentarily, but her recovery was quick. "Well, Lord Kolbi, it is my opinion that women are not political animals."

"Oh?"

"No. And further, I believe that *politics* is merely a polite term for the business of war."

"That is an interesting theory, Lady Gronska, and one not without its element of truth."

"Why, it is completely true!" Zofia's expression and voice took on a sultry forwardness. "Women are meant for other things–things much more interesting than politics."

"I see." The baron was not responding to her flirtation.

Zofia smiled, though her confidence was slightly rattled. Anna knew that her temperament demanded every man's attention.

"Had I the time, Lord Kolbi," Zofia said, "I'm certain that I could convince you of the difference between Ares and Aphrodite."

The baron smiled deprecatingly.

Zofia's black eyes iced over. She was not used to resistance. Her own smile was forced and liverish as she looked meaningfully from the baron to Anna.

Anna immediately realized that Zofia thought that the baron was interested in *her*.

"Anna, you are a sly one." She meant to vent her frustration. "You do know, Lord Kolbi, that my cousin is a married woman. And that she is very much in a family way. I would hope for your sake that she has not been keeping secrets." She smiled.

"I do, and she has not."

Anna tried to cover her surprise. She had *not* told him of her condition, yet he had not even blinked at the news.

"Well," Zofia said, "I should stay and discover just what *politics* are spoken here tonight. Perhaps I would be the one converted. But alas, I am already late in getting to the princess' party. I must fly, Anna. Good night, Lord Kolbi. I trust that we shall meet again."

"Good evening, Lady Gronska." The baron bowed but did not attempt to kiss her hand, a courtesy she clearly expected.

Zofia's face soured. She turned abruptly and whisked through the throng of people, many of whom were still enrapt with the vision in red.

Anna was mortified. For lack of something to say in Zofia's wake, she mentioned that her cousin was off to a party at the home of Charlotte Sic, a French princess.

Anna spied a flicker of recognition in the baron's eyes. "Do you know her, Michał?"

"I know *of* her." The softness of his brown hair and eyes could not offset a brooding quality. "The infection that brought to ruin the French nobility is even now at work here in the capital. And Princess Charlotte Sic is a carrier."

"I . . . I don't understand."

"Ah, never mind. I hope that you never need to. Enjoy yourself tonight, Anna." He brightened. "Besides, you already think me a terrible pessimist."

The two friends laughed.

But Anna considered his strange statement. She was certain that he had chosen not to pursue his indictment of the princess in order to spare Anna's feelings by steering clear of an indictment, by association, of her cousin Zofia.

After the small Russian delegation to the party left, an uncertain air settled over the Poles.

"Another toast to Catherine?" The voice was sarcastic.

"No, I will not drink to that whore!"

"Nor I!"

An old man with a grizzled beard spoke up. "It is all very well that she has squelched the threat of the barbarians, but where will she send her armies next? Her scythemen do not linger long before searching out new fields to mow."

"William is right!"

"But do we really have to worry?" the banker's wife asked. "Our King Stanisław has promised–"

The woman was interrupted by a chorus of tittering.

"Don't be naive," the priest said. "With all due respect to the king–"

"Ah!" cried the owner of a carpet shop, "why is it that when someone starts by saying 'With all due respect for the king' we know that the old man is being set up for a verbal drubbing?"

There was an eruption of concurring laughter.

"It is because the old man is hopeless," a woman answered. "Was he not one of Catherine's countless lovers? It was only through her machinations that he became king at all. He would think long before he'd step on her encroaching toes."

"Bunions is more like it," Baron Kolbi said, "but even so, we need the king and he needs us. We and thousands like us will provide the strength he lacks."

Before the night was over, a chorus went up: "The King with the People, the People with the King!"

The baron was the last to take his leave. "The reception was a fine success!" he told Anna. "We are most grateful to you. You see, already you have been of service to us."

"It is a small enough contribution."

"Anna, the cause is made up of little people and small contributions. That's how big things get done. I would hope you continue your association with us."

"I will. . . . Tell me, Michał, are all the stories of Catherine's . . . well, lustful disposition . . . true?"

The baron smiled.

Anna blushed. "What is so funny?"

"Oh, don't be embarrassed. Women seem to have a natural curiosity about her. Some of the stories are no doubt exaggerated, but it is true that her affairs have been numerous."

"I suppose you think curiosity in such matters is limited to women. Only tonight I observed a number of men take great relish in such gossip."

He laughed. "You're right, I'm sure." Then the brooding look overtook him again. "What worries me, Anna, is that Catherine's lust for men is matched only by her lust for land and holdings."

"Why is that, Michał? Russia is already so huge."

"Power, Anna."

"And her promiscuous behavior gives her power over men?"

"Yes, or at least the illusion of power."

Anna saw the baron to the door. "Michał," she said, "how did you know that I am expecting?"

He smiled. "I didn't."

Their eyes locked for a moment, and then they laughed. They parted happily.

Upon turning around, Anna paused, her eyes taking in the marble hallway with its fine rugs and glittering sconces, the graceful staircase, the priceless tapestries that represented years out of the lives of a hundred French nuns. All this was just a small part of what was now Zofia's. It was part of *her* power.

Anna thought that she had come to understand her cousin just a little bit better. It was all of this that Zofia was after, all of this—and more.

21

One day in the early afternoon, Anna sat reading in the reception room downstairs, where the many windows gave the best light. The countess was cloistered in her room, as she so often was of late. Zofia had gone off in a carriage earlier.

There came a forceful rapping at the door, and within a few minutes a flustered Lutisha stood before Anna. "Madame . . . there are three of the King's Guard at the door seeking admittance."

"The King's Guard?" Anna's heart raced with foreboding.

"Yes, Madame."

"For whom did they ask?"

"For Lady Zofia, Madame." The servant shifted her weight. "Shall I tell the Countess Stella?"

"No, Lutisha. I will handle it. Show them in."

A bearded officer and two guards entered and bowed formally. "Good afternoon, my lady," the officer said. He was dark and stout. The two younger, clean-shaven men didn't speak.

Anna started to rise from her chair. "Good afternoon. What may I do for you gentlemen?"

"No need to get up, my lady." The officer was cheerful. "We have brought royal favors which we are to install in the Countess Zofia Gronska's bedchamber."

Anna inhaled deeply. Would the king himself send gifts to Zofia? "I see," she said. It was all she could manage.

Her amazement was suddenly eclipsed by the thought of the diary and its entries dealing with the monarch. *Dear God!* It was almost certainly in plain sight. Zofia never made a point of hiding it because the servants could not read and she would not expect her mother or Anna to violate her privacy.

Anna thought that whether or not the officer read it, he might—out of service or hope of reward—confiscate it and present it to the king. Zofia's references to him would be viewed as nothing less than treasonous. And what if the guards' real reason for being there was to search the room? For what? The very idea that the King's Guard wanted access to her cousin's room seemed preposterous. But just as she knew that she could not deny them, she knew instinctively that the diary had to be protected at all costs.

Smiling, Anna struggled for composure. She had to think of something. "Gentlemen, won't you be seated?"

"No, thank you, my lady," the officer said. "We must be about our business."

"But you needn't rush so. I insist that you take some wine with me." Anna displayed what she hoped was a coquettish smile. "Why, I should be most offended if you decline. This is an occasion. It is not every day that we receive the King's Guard."

A smile threatened at the corners of the officer's mouth, but came to nothing.

Anna didn't give him a chance to reply. She turned to Lutisha, who stood at attendance in the doorway. "Bring some of our best wine for these very special guests."

Lutisha blinked back her surprise and disappeared. Anna tried to stay calm. She grasped now for a plan to get Zofia's diary out of harm's way.

"What are your names?" Anna asked. She knew that she was crossing the boundaries of class, but she had to do something to play for time.

"My name is Aleksy, my lady," the officer said, as if he were the only one there, the only one who mattered.

Anna chattered on, drawing out the minutes, speaking of the Russian campaign against the Turks.

The officer seemed to have no opinion. A queer smile, at first understated, then full and brash, unfurled itself beneath the officer's thick black moustache. He had moved closer to where she was sitting and stood eyeing her with a familiarity that raised goose flesh on her arms.

At last, Anna could think of nothing more to say. She felt weak, too. She leaned forward in her chair and put her hand to her head.

"The Countess is ill? May I do something?"

Kneeling, the officer brought his face near Anna's. The moustache had wilted at the corners, but Anna observed a gleam in his otherwise dull black eyes, a lurid light that seemed to denote some private humor.

"I'm feeling a bit faint."

"Here, my lady, lean forward a moment."

The officer placed his arm around Anna's shoulders, applying a light pressure. "Now, breathe deeply."

To Anna's surprise, he now ordered his men to wait in the hall. She looked up to catch odd, knowing glances pass between the two young guards.

"Now lean back in your chair," he said to Anna when the others were gone.

He lifted Anna's feet onto a footstool but did not withdraw his hands. As he knelt, his fingers moved caressingly over the ankles, then played dangerously higher along her calves. *You swine,* she silently cursed.

"I believe," he was saying, "that the feet and legs are the keys to true relaxation." The smile had returned, brasher than before.

Anna realized that the officer had interpreted her faintness as a device to encourage his advances. She longed to call him an insolent, stupid ass, but she held her tongue in check, knowing that an objection would prompt him to go directly to Zofia's room. What is keeping Lutisha? she brooded.

Anna wished now that her dress revealed her condition. She considered telling him that she was expecting. What would Zofia do?

Suddenly it came to her: He thinks that I *am* Zofia! Thought of the diary had made her forget to introduce herself.

That accounted for his boldness and his eagerness to believe that she would invite his attention. Anna caught her breath. Had Zofia's reputation spread so far as to the lower echelons of the King's Guard?

The officer's face was perilously close to Anna's. "Do you feel better?" His breath was sour.

Anna quickly stood. "Let me see what is taking the maid so long. Please wait here, Aleksy."

Anna hurried from the room, praying he wouldn't follow. She nodded to the two guards in the hall, realizing that she could not enter Zofia's room without their seeing her. She moved instead toward the swinging door that led to the kitchen.

Anna nearly collided with Lutisha, who was just about to leave the kitchen with a tray that held four crystal wineglasses. She saw that Lutisha's gray eyes were little mirrors to her feelings. "I know that you disapprove of my entertaining guards, Lutisha, but believe me when I say it's necessary. Here, I'll take the wine. I have a more serious task for you."

"But, Madame—"

"Listen to me," Anna hissed, "and do *exactly* as I say! All of our lives may depend upon it. Do you understand?"

Lutisha stared in bewilderment. Anna knew that this was a side of her the servant had never seen.

"Yes, Madame."

"Good! Now—somewhere in Zofia's room is a red book of writings. If it is not in plain sight, you must search it out. Find it and secrete it in your skirts. Then return to me and do not leave my side for a moment until those men are gone. Is that clear?"

Lutisha nodded. The gravity in Anna's voice had not escaped her. Her eyes narrowed now with determination.

Anna took wine to the two young guards, then went in to resume her charade with the smug officer. She prayed for Lutisha to hurry.

Anna did not sit but stood near the ceramic stove. She and the officer had only time for a sip before a nervous Lutisha came in and took
up her post near her.

Anna exulted. She could now steer the little game toward its conclusion. "Why, look at the hour!" she exclaimed, glancing at the freestanding clock. "I had not realized the time. My husband will soon be home."

"Your . . . husband?" The officer's smugness vanished.

Anna smiled. "Why, yes."

"You're teasing."

"But why should I tease you, Aleksy?" Anna was taking a perverse
enjoyment in her role.

"Well, I . . . I thought the Countess Gronska to be unmarried."

"Oh! The Countess Gronska *is* unmarried."

The officer stared.

Anna suppressed a laugh at his expression. "I am Anna Maria
Grawlinska, Countess of Sochaczew, and one day Baroness of Opole."
Anna smiled. "Countess Zofia Gronska is my cousin."

"Your cousin?"

"Why, yes. Oh! You took me to be Zofia? How amusing. We are
nothing alike!"

The officer did his best to conceal his surprise and anger, but the
moustache had wilted nonetheless.

Anna laughed. "Oh, it is good to laugh. They say that a woman
with child should sing and make merry so that her child will be lively
and jovial."

The officer stared, slowly registering her meaning. Setting down his
glass and squaring his shoulders then, he assumed an officious air. "Will
you please have your maid direct us to the Countess Gronska's room
without further delay?"

Anna was glad for the formality. "Of course, Officer." You would
use *me,* she thought, but I have turned the tables.

Lutisha was not long in returning. When Anna's eyes questioned
the servant, she gave a slight smile and patted her skirt.

"Good," Anna whispered to Lutisha. "Now, stay right here. You
may sit down."

"Oh, Lady Stella would never allow—"

"Lutisha, I am giving you permission. Now, sit."

Anna ventured out into the hallway and moved toward her cousin's room. She put her ear to the closed door. The frustrated murmurs of the men and the sounds they made in opening drawers and cabinets, and even in shifting about furniture, confirmed Anna's suspicion that they were searching the room.

She wondered if some enemy of Zofia had warned the king of her writings, sighing in relief that the memoirs were hidden. Still, she would not breathe easily until the guards were gone from the house.

Anna listened for a few more minutes, and when she sensed that their mission was nearly complete, she scurried back to the reception room where Lutisha sat.

The servant pulled her large form out of the chair and stood in attendance.

Anna was seated and composed when the officer came into the room. The other two waited for him in the hall, ready to depart. It is almost over, she thought. Soon they would be gone, leaving the household safe from their prying eyes.

"We have installed the favors from the king for the Countess Gronska," the officer announced.

"How very nice!"

His eyes narrowed at Anna's false enthusiasm. "Tell me, does your cousin have another room where she writes letters or verse?"

Anna could scarcely believe it. They *were* looking for her writings. "No, I don't believe Zofia uses plume at all. She is much too busy for such things."

"I'm certain that she is." His smile was wicked.

Anna held her anger in check. "Is there anything else, Officer?"

"No, we will be taking our leave."

Anna was relieved that they wouldn't be searching the entire house. But when she turned in her chair to tell Lutisha to see the guards to the door, she spied the red diary protruding from the woman's full skirts. *God help us!* The book must have been pushed from the recess of her pocket while she was sitting. Now it was poised ready to fall to the floor with the slightest move of the corpulent servant.

Anna prayed that her face did not register her sense of horror. The officer was bowing before her.

Anna smiled, but where there had been confidence, there was only foreboding that they were doomed. She could imagine the officer's face breaking into a grin at the discovery of the diary.

And yet, he was turning to leave. She held her breath. There was still hope.

Lutisha gathered her skirts and made ready to escort him to the door.

Anna's heart quickened as she watched the diary come to protrude even farther. "Lutisha!" Anna was on her feet.

Startled by the sharpness of Anna's tone, Lutisha halted and turned to her—as did the officer, who watched curiously.

Anna attempted spontaneity. "I will see the good officer to the door, Lutisha." Her eyes burned into the confused servant. "You will please wait for me here."

"That will not be necessary, my lady." The officer's voice was cold. "You needn't exert yourself."

"Oh, it is no exertion," Anna persisted. "Not when it comes to the royal guards!"

The officer stared at Anna in a strange, appraising manner.

Either he suspected something, or he thought her thoroughly crazy. She took his arm and led him from the room. "I do hope I shall see you again one day, Aleksy."

If he didn't think her crazy, Anna realized, Lutisha, who stared open-mouthed, did.

When Anna bade the guards a final good-bye at the door, there was still a glint of suspicion on the officer's face. She closed the door and leaned against it in a posture of relief, hoping never to see him again.

She walked back into the reception room to see Lutisha's broad frame stooping to pick up the red diary from the floor.

22

The Queen's Head was busier than usual for a late Tuesday afternoon. Jan sat alone at his usual table near the window. He was not looking outside. Neither were his eyes focused on the activity in the bar. It had taken two drinks for his nerves to settle.

He was to meet with King Stanisław.

For weeks he had been working closely with his father's friend, Hugo Kołłątaj, who had embraced him like his own son. By now Jan was fully initiated into the Patriot movement. The Constitution of the previous year had laid the groundwork for the real reforms that were only now being proposed and put into effect. Much remained to be done.

Kołłątaj had taken upon himself the task of convincing King Stanisław that labor rents be converted to money rents for the peasants. Jan was to go with him and meet the king for the first time. Convincing the monarch of the need for such a basic and far-reaching change was a formidable task, but Jan had total confidence in his new friend. Jan had watched him turn stones—the unconcerned and frivolous—sympathetic to the cause. Kołłątaj knew how to present, question, contest, rebut, and convince anyone, even the king himself.

This morning Jan had been summoned to Kołłątaj's apartment. Jan arrived to find him in bed. He was weak and deadly pale.

It was influenza, he told Jan. He would survive it. "As you know," Kołłątaj said, "we are set to meet Stanisław tomorrow."

"Shall I get it delayed, sir? Another week?"

"No." Kołłątaj was firm. "Reform has been delayed long enough."

"What are we to do, sir?"

"You, Jan, are to see the king."

"I?" Jan's heart dropped like a weight. He was incredulous. "Alone?"

The man nodded.

"Sir, is he likely to listen to me?"

"Why not? You're wise past your twenty-five years. You're a quick study. You're a man of conviction. I trust you'll make a good case."

"But . . . to the king himself?"

"Yes, to the king himself. He's just a man and not a particularly strong one at that. You've worked more closely with me than anyone else has. You know the proposal, you know the projected numbers, you know the advantages. Just talk straight, Jan."

"Such a search is a standard procedure of the King's Guard," Zofia assured Anna. "The king is a man uncertain of the loyalty of his subjects. I suppose it is the way of most monarchs. If the guards had any real reason for the search, believe me, they would not have confined it to my bedchamber."

The two cousins stood in Zofia's room. Zofia had arrived a scant half hour after the guards had left. Anna had had Lutisha hand Zofia the diary so that her cousin would not think that Anna had even opened the red cloisonné cover.

After Lutisha left, Anna explained that she had the maid search the room on the chance that there might be some writings that Zofia would not want the guards to come upon.

"How very clever of you, cousin!" She waved the diary. "This is nothing more than a journal of silly writing and doodling. I got the idea when I saw you keeping a diary, darling. But, just the same, I would die to have it read at court!"

Zofia dropped the diary onto her vanity and clasped Anna's hands into her own, her black eyes for once serious. "I am very grateful to you, Anna. You are a lifesaver. I shall not forget it."

Anna attempted a smile. While she was at once proud of her little charade, at the same time she felt a stabbing guilt for having made a habit of violating her cousin's privacy.

"Look here!" Zofia said, drawing Anna toward the wardrobe. "I have a little compartment in this." When she touched a hidden spring behind the front leg, a drawer slid open. In it she placed the diary. "I'll keep it in here from now on."

Anna's sense of guilt was sharpened even more by the faith that Zofia was placing in her. She wished that her cousin had not shown her the hiding place. She was not to be delivered from future temptation.

"Why so grim, Anna? The danger is past, thanks to you." Zofia hugged her cousin. "Come, let's see what little gifts the guards have left."

Anna smiled, trying to dispel her mood and silently vowing never again to read from the diary.

Together the cousins explored the room and found the hidden favors. In every drawer, jar, and vase in the room, they found rings, earrings, and brooches. There were even pearl pins placed in one of Zofia's pompadour wigs.

And on the vanity table, under her jewelry case, they found an envelope with the king's insignia. "Why, I do believe," Zofia announced, "it's an invitation to the Royal Castle."

Jan Stelnicki nervously studied the face of King Stanisław II Augustus. He had made his presentation and waited now on tenterhooks for a reaction.

Under the powdered wig was a simple face. Small, colorless eyes peered out under hooded lids. The nose was narrow, the chin nearly pointed. The handsomeness that must have been there when Catherine had taken him as lover was gone. Jan figured that he must have been twenty-five at the time, his own current age. He must be nearly sixty now.

What had Catherine seen in Stanisław, Jan wondered, that made her send an army to the Polish magnates demanding that they elect him king? He seemed so utterly unprepossessing.

Jan had taken more than an hour of the king's time. With as much skill and savoir faire as he could muster, he presented his case for replacing labor rents with money rents for the peasants. He had been trembling with apprehension beforehand, but once he met the king and launched into his argument, some unforeseen power flowed into his veins and pulsed with energy, fueling him with words and confidence.

When the king began to question, the discussion led in a logical digression to the need for a national bank and a paper currency. On these issues Jan felt less secure, but—blessedly—the king did not probe too deeply. King Stanisław retreated then into a quiet meditation and the minutes slowed.

Simple man or not, the king took good time in coming to decisions, Jan thought. The silence was daunting.

Jan could endure the quiet no longer, surprising himself by speaking first. "What it comes down to, Sire," he said, "is the rights of all of our citizens to be paid with a national currency and to trade on a much wider scale in the manner that they please."

"My dear young Stelnicki," the king said, "what it comes down to is this: We have passed a constitution as good as that of the United States and better than any in Europe."

Jan nodded.

The king wagged his forefinger. "But since the Bastille fell, the kind of reform we have undertaken has frightened the jewels out of the crowns of monarchs in Prussia and Austria and Russia. To have Poland in their midst speaking out for the people makes them fear for their autocracies. These countries are not likely to stand idly by."

Jan wondered where this was leading. Was he going to refuse?

"However," the king said with a sigh, "reform is the path we chose last year and there is no retreat. This issue of money rents is just one little bridge in the path. Time brings man ever forward, Jan. Remember that. There may be a step backward after two forward, but the pace of progress is inexorably forward."

Jan's excitement was building. "Then I may tell Kołłątaj–?"

"You may tell him to get well. It is a royal order. Oh, and tell him to move ahead on this thing."

Jan wanted to shout with joy. The pace of his heart quickened, but he fought to hold his enthusiasm in check, struggling against even a hint of a smile. He did not want the king to think him such a novice. "I will, Sire." Within, however, Jan swelled with a sense of accomplishment. How proud his father would have been!

"You hail from Halicz, do you not, Jan?"

"Yes."

"Ah, only yesterday I met another young man from Halicz, a Russian mercenary, damn him. He accompanied the Russian Fyodor Kuprin, who brought some bold threats from Catherine. Although my Russian is merely adequate, Kuprin's Polish is pitiful, so this young man served as interpreter."

"What was his name?"

"His name? Of course, his name . . . Gronski, I believe."

"Walter Gronski?"

"Yes, that's it."

23

Anna could not help but be excited. She was going to the Royal Castle for the first time.

Clarice and Babette spent the entire morning preparing her and Zofia for the royal supper and concert. Zofia had wanted to buy Anna a gown for the occasion, but Anna refused, wishing only to borrow one. She had no desire to be indebted in such a way to her cousin. She would also need a wig, Zofia insisted, arguing that she would appear absolutely naked without an impossibly high mound of powdered white hair. Anna relented.

Louis and little Babette caught the excitement in the air. They were underfoot the entire day, bubbling with enthusiasm. "May we go see the king, too?" Babette asked. The French maids and Zofia found the request quite hilarious and laughed at the children. Louis looked especially hurt. Although he had not given voice to the request, Anna could tell that he dearly wanted to go, but a grown-up pride already taking root in him kept him from begging. Later, while the maids busied themselves in Zofia's room, Anna took the two aside and tried to explain that the event was not for children. Let them learn later about the realities of class distinction, she thought, telling them, instead, of the momentous day she and her father had come into the city and driven past the majestic castle. And she found herself promising that one day she would take them in the carriage to get a closer view of the king's residence just across the River Vistula.

Zofia entered Anna's room fully dressed. She wore a high-waisted gown of pekin, trimmed with gauze flounces, ribbons, and silk flowers. Her dazzling array of jewelry included a sapphire pendant and matching eardrops.

Zofia gaped at Anna's choice of dress. "You can't wear that one, cousin!"

"Really? You don't wish to lend it out?"

"No, it's not that at all. Darling, we're going to the Royal Castle, not to the fish market. It's utterly too simple, too plain, too colorless!"

"The beauty of the dress is in its simplicity, Zofia. Oh, I do wish to wear it!" There *was* some color in the cream-colored gown, Anna insisted, pointing out the faintest pastel flowers that had been brushed into the gauzy material.

This time Zofia relented.

The gown had required only a few alterations—an adjustment to the puffed sleeves and the release of three tucks at the waist to allow for Anna's expanding waistline. Her own white kid leather slippers set it off. She tied her mother's white and blue cameo about her neck, wondering what her mother would have thought of her going to the Royal Castle.

After she was fully dressed, the French powdered wig was fastened to her head. When she looked into the mirror, she was startled by her appearance.

"Anna," Zofia cried, "you look divinely gorgeous! Why, you don't even look as if you're expecting."

Anna did feel a measure of confidence and pride stirring within when she saw her reflection. And she was thankful that her condition was not apparent. Of course, she knew most people would think it quite improper for her even to be out of the house.

"Give me your right hand, Anna. I've brought you a ring. It's only right that you should share in the spoils the King's Guard left."

Zofia slipped onto the third finger a silver ring. The silver had been worked into the shape of a lion's paw which clasped the large stone.

Anna gasped. "What kind of stone is this, Zofia? I can't quite determine its color."

"That is the secret charm of the stone, Anna. It's iridescent. Its color changes with its surroundings. It has something to do with the light. It may appear blue or green or violet or even blood red—any number of colors. It's an opal."

"How wonderful."

"Those *people* who have that same charm of changing are the successful ones. One must adapt to one's own immediate company and situation. Consider it a little lesson from your worldly cousin. Now, I will look in on Mother to say good night."

Zofia had not invited her mother. Anna wondered at the reason. Was it Aunt Stella's recent depression?

Antoni was invited but had some previous appointment. He planned to join them there. Their relationship had not improved. Antoni had made no further advances; this was a blessing that she knew would dissipate after the birth of her child. Oh, he seemed to be trying. He spent much more time at home these days, behaving solicitously toward her. But Anna knew he was up to something, something to do with her estate. She feared how it all might end. If only she could obtain an annulment. She felt like a trapped animal. And she could not, as Zofia seemed to suggest, change her colors.

The maids took Zofia's absence from the room as an occasion to compliment Anna. "*Ah, vous êtes très belle!*" cried Clarice. "You will be the crème de la crème of those women at the palace."

"*Vous êtes magnifique!*" chimed Babette. She then lowered her voice to a confidential whisper: "Madame must be careful or the sudden bloom of her petals will make those of the mademoiselle appear very pale by comparison. You cannot do this, Madame, or your cousin will send us packing."

The maids giggled naughtily.

Anna played down the impertinent joke, but in truth her confidence was bolstered.

A light snow was falling on the gloomy winter afternoon when the carriage stopped for Anna and Zofia. A dwarf attended them as they stepped up on a stool and entered the carriage of Princess Charlotte Sic. Anna met her now for the first time.

The princess had fled France for the safety of Warsaw. She was middle-aged, still rather attractive if a bit overweight. Her high white wig, rolled from the face and curled at the sides and back, presented a cherubic visage, but for a huge beauty mark that hung on one fleshy cheek. She was draped in a wrap of black silk trimmed with white fur. Anna was impressed most by her jewelry. Above the plunging neckline of her gold brocade gown was a three-tiered diamond necklace, fastened tightly at the neck and cascading in shimmering rivulets to cover the exposed area of her generous bosom.

"Your necklace is very beautiful."

"Merci, Anna Maria. It has been in my family for generations. It once belonged to Eleanor of Aquitaine. Ah!—diamonds, they are ageless, my dear."

"Unlike you," Zofia said.

Charlotte became flustered, her cheeks puffing with air. "Why, Zofia, I am but thirty-two."

Zofia nearly screamed with laughter.

The princess eyed her meanly for a moment, then turned to Anna. "Zofia can be most unkind sometimes," she puffed. "I don't know why I have befriended her."

Zofia giggled. "You know very well."

Charlotte ignored the comment. "Your cousin didn't tell me that you were so lovely. With such competition in her own home, it is no wonder she has kept you under wraps."

Zofia's giggles stopped.

"Do you speak French, my dear?" Charlotte asked.

"Just a bit," Anna said. "Usually the conversation is much too swift for me."

"You should work at it, my sweet. It is a necessity throughout Europe."

After some talk of trifles, Zofia and Charlotte lapsed into French, talking and laughing girlishly, confident that Anna could not keep up with the conversation.

Anna sat mesmerized by the lustrous sparkle and glow of the awesome diamonds. While her parents had instilled in her an appreciation of their privileged standing, she was coming to realize there were other nobles who were much wealthier. "There is rich and there is rich," Zofia had once told her. She could not take her eyes away from the diamonds that coruscated to the vibration of the carriage. It must be a wonderful thing, she thought, to be *so* rich.

In time Anna tried to follow the tête-à-tête, pretending to be lost in her own thoughts. They were gossiping about an infamous Italian who had created a scandal at the Polish court a few decades previous. They spoke of how this Giacomo Casanova had beauty and charms that were irresistible to women of all ages; how he tried to start a lottery and failed; how he challenged a member of the prestigious Branicki family to a duel and won; how he was routed from Poland, but not without the compensation of thousands of gold coins from the men's gaming tables and countless gems from the women's jewel boxes.

"Charlotte," Zofia intoned, "is it true he left behind so many red-faced men and sulking women? Surely you're old enough to remember him yourself?"

Charlotte pursed her lips in mock-anger. "You little bitch!"

"They say," Zofia continued, "that he was wonderfully well-endowed where it counts most."

"You are incorrigible," Charlotte said and laughed.

"I know. I know."

Although the distance to the Royal Castle was short, the line of vehicles proceeding across the outer courtyard and into the Great Courtyard was long, and nearly an hour passed before the carriage door was finally opened for the ladies to alight at the Senators' Gate.

Clad in knee breeches and a gold brocade coat, the princess' dwarf helped them down, then led them past the soldiers who stood at attention in their red and yellow uniforms. Their wraps were taken by servants on the ground floor before they followed the little man up the circular marble steps, where they found themselves in the Antechamber to the Great Assembly Hall.

The ornate room was alive with animated talk and laughter. Zofia and Charlotte paused occasionally to nod and speak to nobles they knew. Anna was dazzled by the buzzing chamber; windowless, it was lighted by hammered gold sconces and magnificent glass-and-gem chandeliers, each bearing dozens of gleaming candles.

Anna was glad she'd come, glad that her condition didn't show, and glad, too, that Antoni had not accompanied them. She would enjoy herself tonight, as much as any single and independent woman in the hall. If for only one evening, she wanted to live as if nothing had happened to her the previous September.

Anna regretted for the moment not wearing a more elaborate dress. The women here wore gowns of exotic materials and richly flamboyant colors. Some of the French-influenced dresses covered scaffoldings of metal. Most women wore wigs, and many of them wore their faces heavily powdered and their lips and cheeks rouged; the older the woman, it seemed, the heavier the makeup. Perfume wafted about them and the exposed area of their bosoms were like jewelers' display windows.

The men in the room were no less colorful, Anna noted. Many of them still clung to the traditional Polish garb the men of Sochaczew wore: long coats over tight trousers, colorful sashes—often of Turkish design—at the waist, and ruffs at the neck. The older nobles wore chains and medals in memory of past deeds. Other men wore the Oriental gowns that became fashionable at court about the time King Jan Sobieski defeated the Turks. But Anna could see that the French costume of buckled shoes, stockings and breeches, ruffs, and laces was making inroads, despite stalwart Polish nobles who thought the style effeminate.

Supper commenced at three in the afternoon. Zofia had advised her that the early hour was to allow for the activities of the evening. Tonight it was to be a concert. The dwarf led the women into the adjoining Marble Room where they were seated at one of a score of round tables draped with white silk.

"We have struck it lucky today," the princess whispered. "This is the room in which the king holds his intimate Thursday dinners with artists, literati, and others of the intelligentsia. He uses the round tables to show that all guests are of equal rank."

"Like King Arthur," Anna said.

"Equal rank or not, Charlotte," Zofia corrected, "we aren't so very lucky. Someone just told me the king is dining in the Great Assembly Hall tonight."

"Ah!" The princess was mildly deflated. "Oh well, Anna, you will have to wait to catch a glimpse of the king."

Anna took little notice of the news. She was still taking in the room and its profusion of marble, from the black-and-white diagonally set squares of the flooring to the grays, browns, and greens of the walls, door frames, and entablature that reached to the ceiling. Ensconced in the entablature on all sides were the portraits of some twenty Polish monarchs of the past.

The empty place on Anna's right was reserved for Antoni. She found herself wishing he would miss the occasion altogether. She was thoroughly enjoying herself.

The food was fragrant and delicious. As in even the most modest Polish homes, the preoccupation with good food was wedded to the notion of true hospitality, and the king now called out his best from his kitchens. The Royal Cook, Paweł Tremo, was reputed to be the finest culinary chef in Europe. He combined the exotic French cooking with the traditional Polish fare the king so loved. Zofia warned Anna to eat lightly, and Anna soon learned the reason for the advice. For nearly three hours, a parade of magnificently attired servants carted in course after course of borsch, cold meat appetizers, spicy marinades, fish, vegetables, and an array of roasts, including the king's favorite, roast mutton. Anna, however, was most delighted by the chef's aromatic specialty, grouse in hazel sauce.

The cellar gave up its finest: wines from France and Spain that were suited to the particular courses. Spring water, preferred to wine by the king, was poured into crystal goblets.

"It is all so extravagant," Anna whispered to Charlotte Sic.

The French princess shrugged, as if to say it was nothing.

If a Pole was said to be stingy, it was because he stinted himself only to be generous to his guests. Anna was witnessing firsthand the king's generosity—but she doubted he was ever stingy, to himself or anyone.

Anna was relieved to find that King Stanisław's rule at table went against that of most monarchs of the day: the trend toward conversations in French. Here, only Polish was spoken. For that she was grateful. And proud.

Supper topics centered on mad country days, hunting trips, cruises on flower-covered boats, expensive miniature portraits, and porcelain fixtures from Saxony. There were stories and jokes sweetened and spiced with puns and *des mots à double entendre*. Anna was coming to realize that conversation here was an art. These people were saying nothing of importance, but they were saying it with wit, grace, and expertise.

Fine fruits from the royal orangery were served for dessert. When Anna commented on the delicious apricots, oranges, and peaches, Zofia assured her that there were magnates who surpassed the king with their hothouse figs and pineapples.

To Anna's left sat an elderly baron who had been quiet through dinner. He spoke up now, addressing those at table. "Has everyone heard the story of the Countess Kossakowska?" he asked.

Those who paid attention to him laughed and said they had. He seemed to be deflated for the moment, until his gaze came around to Anna. "You have not heard it, Lady Grawlinska?"

"I have not," Anna said politely.

"Then you must! It is most amusing."

Anna noticed Zofia rolling her eyes but nodded anyway to the man, as if to give him permission.

"Well, the Countess Kossakowska is very wealthy, you know. Wife of a magnate. Oh, this is a very good story."

Anna nodded solicitously.

"Well, it seems that the eccentric countess was traveling in her carriage one day when the cries of an orange peddler caught her ear and appetite. But she soon realized she had not a single coin with her. Can you imagine?"

"What did she do?" Anna asked, only because the old man had paused, just as one actor pauses for another's bit of dialogue.

"I'll tell you exactly what the woman did, my dear. It is extraordinary! She gave that astounded man her pearl necklace, paying him at the rate of one pearl to one orange!"

"Oh, my!" Anna cried.

The baron was laughing at his own story, so he did not take notice that Anna found little humor in it.

She remembered her father telling her that some nobles believed that "to live a noble life was to live an idle life." As she watched the flash and color of wealth this night, she thought that such excess made her more clearly understand the peasants' bloody revolt in France.

After supper, they were escorted by the dwarf to the ladies' lounge, then to the Great Assembly Room, the largest and most magnificent room in the Royal Castle. The dining tables had already been removed, and a performing dais was set up in the middle of the huge room with at least two hundred chairs fanning out in all directions. Windows fronting the River Vistula ran the entire length of the room, and it was near them that Zofia secured the last few vacant seats. "Look!" Anna cried, peering through the darkening sky. "There's your town house, Zofia, just across the river!"

Neither Zofia nor Charlotte was impressed. Anna settled into her thickly cushioned chair, which was positioned behind and a little to the right of Zofia and Charlotte. While most of the tapers were being extinguished, Anna took in the room, from the wood inlaid floor to white and gold walls and some two dozen marble columns.

The statues on either side of the main entrance drew Anna's attention. She tapped her cousin on the shoulder, whispering, "Are those not the likenesses of Apollo and Minerva, Zofia?"

Zofia made no attempt to lower her volume. "It's Apollo, Anna," she said cavalierly, "but if you get up close, you can see the face has King Stanisław's features."

Charlotte turned around, giggling. "And while you're up close, you'll see that Minerva bears a suspicious resemblance to Catherine."

Anna sat back not knowing quite what to think. It was certainly no compliment to Apollo's visage and seemed rather vainglorious of the king. Catherine's features, imposed on Minerva, were fair enough, but the inherent link to Russia was an unwelcome one.

The theme of the room was the divine preservation of order, but Anna had no time to study the mythological ceiling painting *Ordering Chaos* because of the dimming light and entrance of King Stanisław.

The hundreds of nobles stood at once, then knelt in what space they could.

He acknowledged the crowd with the hint of a smile, simple and un-affected, gave the sign to rise with his right hand, then went to his throne, which had been placed at the far corner of the room. He nodded to the French violinist who had taken his place on the dais. The foot-lights around the dais were the primary source of light now. It was not long into the first selection that Anna sensed someone watching her. Was it the dwarf? Where had he gone? A heat came into her face and goose flesh rose on her arms. More than once that afternoon his attention had unnerved her. She drew in a breath and immediately turned around, but behind her there was nothing, nothing but the windows and the river.

Anna thought the musician excellent, and so was surprised that many people continued conversing in scarcely disguised tones. Some even walked around the darkened room, visiting with acquaintances. Even Zofia and Charlotte spoke in gay whispers as they gawked about.

Presently Zofia turned her head to the extreme right and stared shamelessly past Charlotte toward the far side, where a striking, black-haired officer could not help but notice her interest. The man's companion was a large and powerfully built Nordic man, who wore not a uniform but a formal green coat with silver buttons. Anna thought the ruffles at the wrists and neck humorously incongruous to such a mam-moth figure of a man.

"Oh, Charlotte, look at that divine Russian in his red uniform." In low tones Zofia carried on a perverse conversation with her friend without taking her eyes from the officer.

"Why, I suspect he is rather short," Charlotte said.

"He has everything that attracts me," Zofia countered, her head now nodding in his direction.

When Zofia turned to see if her cousin were watching her, Anna immediately fastened her eyes on the violinist, pretending to be lost in the music.

"I tell you," Charlotte said, "that when he stands you will see that he is a short man."

"Why should that bother you, Charlotte?" Zofia asked. "After all, you do keep your dwarf at your beck and call."

The two laughed wickedly.

What was Zofia implying? Anna did not wish to think about it.

Zofia's eyes narrowed at the man in red. Anna could see that he was hopelessly enchanted. "Besides," Zofia said through clenched teeth, "many big men are little men, and many little men are big men."

The two friends rapidly waved their fans to their faces while they tried to control their laughter.

Anna feigned ignorance, but she felt her face flushing hot. She came to accept afresh that what Zofia wrote in her diary was true. The episode with the Baron Driedruski was no fiction. Zofia had romanced him into her web, used him to her pleasure, then after setting in motion a scheme that would secure a monthly income for an imaginary child, discarded the deluded man. How many others had there been?

The handsome Russian looked then at Zofia as though he thought he were the only man ever to win her smile. Enamored men are blind, Anna realized. He was hastily writing a note and soon, of his own free will, would enter Zofia's netting.

The feeling that she was being watched came over her again. Her eyes surreptitiously scanned one row, then another, to no avail. Then she saw a man standing in the door that led onto the balcony. He was scarcely more than a shadow, but she sensed him watching her. And she thought she recognized him.

She reached forward and nudged her cousin, "Zofia, I think that Walter is here."

But when Anna turned to point toward the doorway, the figure was gone.

Zofia seemed irritated. "That's silly, Anna. What would he be doing here? Or in Warsaw, for that matter?"

"Really, there was a man over there looking this way whom I . . . I thought was Walter."

"Well, if it were Walter, he would certainly come up to say hello." Zofia turned back to carry on her flirtation.

In a few moments a courier delivered the Russian's note to Zofia. Quickly inspecting the contents, Zofia promptly stood, whispered something to Charlotte, then turned to Anna. "Darling, I'll be back shortly. I must go say hello to an old friend on the other side."

Were Anna not learning more each day about her cousin, she would have been astounded at the audacity of the lie.

In Zofia's absence, Charlotte patted Zofia's chair, miming for Anna to sit by her. Anna took her cousin's chair even though she feared the countess wished to chat through the poor musician's concert.

Presently, the princess took a silver flask from her purse. "Time for a little drop," she said, handing Anna a small silver cup. "You must join me."

"What is it?" Anna whispered.

"Just take a nice swallow, child."

Anna took the handleless cup. She was distracted then by the sight of Zofia taking a seat next to the Russian officer. The man was fully entranced.

"Well, drink it!" the princess insisted.

Without a thought Anna swallowed it down. The liquor stung like poison as it scorched a path to her stomach. No medicine had ever tasted so strong. She began choking and coughing.

Charlotte laughed. "I'm sorry, dear. Perhaps a sip would've been better."

The fire began to subside. "Is my face terribly red?"

"No more so," Charlotte giggled, "than those of most of the women here. And it's too dim in here to tell."

"What *is* this?"

"It's whiskey, *ma chère*."

"It's like liquid fire."

"I would have thought you'd be accustomed to such a drink, Anna Maria."

"What do you mean?"

Charlotte finished off her cup and dabbed at her red lips. "Zofia tells me that your husband owns a distillery in his hometown. Opole, is it?"

"Yes, Opole." Anna could scarcely believe it. No one had ever mentioned a distillery to her.

"And," Charlotte continued, "he plans to open another one, a huge operation, I hear, very near Warsaw. In Sochaczew, I believe."

Anna's heart stopped. Had she heard correctly?

She watched Charlotte pour another drink.

Was it possible? Was this what Antoni had in mind for her parents' estate? Oh, there were many of the *szlachta* who had small, private distilleries. But to have one as a business enterprise? On the land of her ancestors? The land that her father so loved? He had given his sweat and blood for that property! Her face burned now with a heat that was more intense than her reaction to the whiskey. What was to become of her own garden? And the flowers that were, in a way, her mother's legacy?

She sat in shock for long minutes. The music of the violinist continued as if at a distance, as if from another dimension. Of course, it was true. Anna recalled Jacob Szraber's words to her at his daughter's wedding. He told her how Antoni and his advisors were so concerned with the grain crops. It made sense.

How little I know about my husband, she brooded. Whiskey was no business for the nobility. She was certain that when it was sold to the peasants, who could least afford it, it would become another way of shackling them to a wretched existence.

Anna was relieved when Zofia appeared to reclaim her place next to the princess. She quickly went back to her own seat.

"You will have to be content with August, Charlotte," Zofia was saying.

"August?" Charlotte trilled. "Who is August?"

"He is that big fellow over there with my Russian interest."

Charlotte fidgeted in her seat for a better view. "He is too immense. Why, he looks like someone dressed a huge bear in finery and topped it with a shock of blond hair. He is grotesque!"

"I disagree, Charlotte. He is the tallest and best built man here to-night."

"Then why have you set your sight on the other?"

"A whim—or perhaps the unmistakable scent of real wealth."

The princess grunted. "This August fellow is probably nothing more than the attendant of the one who holds your interest." She took on a pouting tone. "And he looks to be a Swede, too."

"He *is* a Swede! So what? What difference can it make to you? What difference has it *ever* made to you?" Zofia smirked. "Swede or not, Charlotte, he is a bedful."

The princess pretended annoyance but soon fell to giggling with Zofia.

Before Anna could question her cousin about the distillery matter, the violinist paused between compositions, and Zofia and Charlotte used the opportunity to excuse themselves. They were going to visit with the Russian and Swede.

Anna sat numb for some minutes. The violinist resumed his program.

Again, she felt someone's eyes on her. The doorway where she thought she had seen Walter was still empty, however. Her eyes again ran from face to face along the many rows on either side. Her line of vision settled then on a man seated behind and to the left of the king's throne. *He* was watching her, she was certain. Yet, somehow, instinctively, she knew it was not the man in the doorway who had looked like Walter.

Before Anna could study the man in shadow, her attention was drawn to a commotion in the row in front of her. A man was taking Zofia's seat.

Anna was just about to tell him that the chair was reserved when he turned around to face her. Her heart caught. The man was Antoni, her husband.

24

Jan Stelnicki had come to the castle on a whim.

The king had suggested at the end of their interview that Jan attend the supper and sit near him in the place of Hugo Kołłątaj. Jan had no wish to attend the supper. He had no wish to pretend to follow the insipid conversations incumbent on such occasions. Yet, politics demanded that he put in an appearance. He could not turn down the king.

The supper had been tedious, but Jan enjoyed music, for the violinist was hailed as the best on the continent. Jan had attended a concert of his in Paris and thought the man pure genius. He listened avidly, allowing the strains of music to surround him, enter him.

But the lift and swell of the music, however marvelous, could not carry him, for he soon became annoyed by the quiet noise that continued after the musician had begun his program. People wandered in to their seats late, caring little about the commotion they caused. Others talked outright. He began to wish he had not come. Even the patrons of the Queen's Head would have behaved with more decorum.

His eyes absently scanned the long rows of seats parallel to the Vistula windows, whereupon his attention was suddenly caught by two women on the end of an aisle. Their hands, heads, and mouths were in continuous motion. Occasionally, he could hear their voices, too.

The one was Zofia, he realized.

Ah, she is in her element here, he thought. Too bad the concert has no meaning for her and her overly dressed and made-up friend. His eyes came back to them occasionally when some movement or sound of theirs distracted him from the violinist.

Jan was thinking about leaving at the first intermission when he chanced to gaze again in the direction of the windows. Zofia and her friend had vacated their seats. It was then that he noticed a woman who had been sitting in the shadows behind Zofia.

He leaned forward and stared down into the dimness beyond the dais. *Is it possible?*

Unlike the other two, the woman sat still and silent.

He continued to study her.

Suddenly, she leaned forward and looked over in his direction, as if she had felt his eyes on her.

Jan quickly drew his head back into the shadows behind the king's throne. The wig she wore was deceiving, but the flickering light had caught her face in that moment, and her identity was confirmed.

Jan had sat for days, hours at a time, at the Queen's Head watching and hoping, hoping and watching, to catch sight of her. He was amazed now to find her by sheer chance at the Royal Castle, and dressed like a courtesan.

He leaned forward again. Where was her husband? he wondered.

25

Who told you?" Antoni demanded.

"What difference does it make? I know."

Anna had waited for the entr'acte to confront her husband, who had turned Zofia's chair to face her. She knew that she should have waited until they arrived home and probably until the next day or longer, when her mind would have processed the wildly chaotic emotions she felt.

But the shock was too recent and her hurt and anger too great. As it was, she could scarcely wait for the intermission.

"So you know, what of it?"

"It will not happen."

"You think not?"

"Yes. I will not allow it."

"Wait until I give you the details. Hold your outrage in check until then. Please. Anna Maria, we will be rich beyond your wildest dreams. With your estate so near the capital, it is perfect! The demand for good whiskey is growing. Transportation from a distillery on the Vistula at Sochaczew is an entrepreneur's dream."

"There will be no distillery on my father's land. I will die first."

"Listen to me, Anna Maria. Please. We have joined our two estates. We now have greater stature and resources than we would singly. With the income from this venture, we shall become a magnate family. I swear!"

"I have no such interest."

"You will change your mind when you see the respect and power being a magnate's wife carries."

"I tell you, Antoni, I don't care."

"And I don't need your permission, Anna Maria."

"You need my signature to lay your hands on the principal that the Lubicki family holds in trust for me."

"True. You are shrewd. You may delay my plans, but when my father does die, my own inheritance will fund the business. Then I will need only the land. And there was nothing in your father's will to prevent me from using it to my own design."

"Nonetheless, you will not have it!" Anna rose now, though she didn't know where her escape would take her. She was shaking.

Antoni stood and caught her by the wrist, turning her to him.

When she glared at his hand on her, he released it.

"I will concede on the issue of the child," Antoni whispered. "I will . . . I will acknowledge even a boy as my own."

This caught Anna by surprise. She looked up at her husband, whose moustache masked his expression. She wondered whether this were the truth or a concession of the moment. She found herself not even caring. If only she could divest herself of Antoni and live her own life. "You don't understand what the land meant to my father, what it means to me. There will be no distillery on my family estate. I will fight you tooth and nail, Antoni Grawlinski. I will not allow it!"

Antoni raised his hand in anger.

Something in Anna's eyes held it suspended. "Go ahead, Antoni. Strike me. I'll scream down every stone in the castle and deafen the king himself for good measure! Go ahead, let all of Warsaw know that your way of making a point with a woman is to bully her."

The moustache wilted. His arm dropped.

"You struck me once. You will not do it again, Antoni."

"And what power do you think you have?"

Before Anna could reply, Zofia and Charlotte appeared. They gave greeting to Antoni, but their expressions disclosed they had heard something.

"We were just discussing the distillery," Anna said, her pulse pumping with a new daring.

Antoni turned on Zofia. "Who told her?" he demanded.

Zofia's eyes widened. "Not I, I swear."

"Well, someone has. The damage is done!" Antoni pushed between Charlotte and Zofia and exited the Great Assembly Room.

Zofia was just about to question Anna when the obvious came to her. She wheeled about to face Charlotte.

The princess cowered at the sight of Zofia's pinched expression.

"I told you not to breathe a word!"

"I only thought—"

"You fat fool! Your problem is that you *try* to think!"

Zofia reached over, snatched Charlotte's wig from her head, and hurled it through a window that had been opened to let in fresh air.

Charlotte's hands went to her thinning gray hair and she screamed now until Zofia struck her across the face, hard enough only to cause the woman to collect her wits.

Zofia turned and left, paying no heed to those gathered about, their mouths slackened.

"Well, what are you looking at?" Charlotte demanded of the dwarf, who appeared out of nowhere and stood gawking up at her. "Go get my hair!" She looked hatefully at Anna, then scurried off to hide behind a nearby curtain while she waited for her attendant.

Anna was struck silent, as though mesmerized by the horrifying turn of events. She would do nothing to further humiliate the princess, but later, at home, she would find some dark comedy in the episode of the princess' wig, and laugh.

Anna sat alone for some time lost in her thoughts, certain that Antoni would return. If he did, she vowed to leave immediately even if it meant walking home.

She was unaware of someone standing before her, until he spoke.

"Anna?"

At the sound of the musical voice, the hairs at the nape of her neck stood up. She knew immediately who it was.

Her breath was taken from her as she looked up now, into the cobalt blue eyes of Jan Stelnicki.

She had imagined this moment before, numberless times, imagined how she would act, what she would say. Now she could scarcely think. As her condition of impending motherhood progressed, she found that her heart quickened at the slightest provocation. It was now beating so fast she thought she would faint. If King Stanisław himself stood before her, she would not have trembled so. She had once read in a French novel that the heart is the source of romance and love. Today she believed it.

Jan smiled as he bowed before her.

It was not the confident, laughing smile of the previous summer; rather, it was a tentative, uncertain smile, a smile steeped in sadness.

Jan took hold of her hand and kissed it, murmuring, "Anna."

Anna could not speak. She could only think: This is all that I can ever hope for, all that can ever happen between us. But she could ask for no more, her heart was so full.

"It is so good to see you, Anna. May I sit?"

"Of course."

He sat in Zofia's chair, just as Antoni had done not long before. For some minutes, they exchanged awkward pleasantries. Later she would remember nothing of them.

At last, Anna braved the issue they were so circuitously avoiding. "Do you know why I married, Jan?"

"I think so. I questioned the Gronski estate manager—"

"Walek?"

"Yes, that's how I found out about . . . what happened at the pond. It was his opinion that you were pressured into the marriage."

"It's true."

Jan's eyes swelled with tears. "Oh, Anna, if only I had not left you there. I can blame only myself for all you've been through, all of it."

"I behaved stupidly."

"I meant to come back, truly I did."

"Did Zofia catch up to you that day?"

"Yes."

"And she told you that I hurt my foot and could not mount my horse?"

"No, Anna, she said nothing of that."

"Oh."

"By the time I reached home, Anna, I meant to come back, but . . . did you not get my letter the next day?"

"I received no letter, Jan."

He turned pale. "I'm not surprised. Zofia has much to answer for." Jan told Anna now of the events surrounding his father's death, how he had come home that day to find a messenger recalling him to Kraków. "I did try to explain in that letter, Anna," he concluded. "I knew that had you received it, you would have understood."

Anna struggled to hold back her own tears as she realized how the love between her and Jan had been sabotaged. Yet somehow the magic of this moment held anger and bitterness at bay. "I understand now, Jan." She took a deep breath. "You can't know . . . that I am expecting."

"I do know."

"How?"

"Zofia told me one day at the square," he said. "She took great delight in doing so."

"Oh." She took another breath, preparing to tell him the rest of it. "Jan, the child is a result of what happened at the pond."

His mouth dropped a little. "My God!"

"Zofia tried to name you as my assailant."

"Walek told me that, too." His eyes narrowed. "Then *you* never thought . . . ?"

"No."

Jan sighed. "Anna, do you know who it was?"

"No."

"You're certain?"

She nodded.

Jan took her hand in his.

Her faith that neither the attack nor the child would affect Jan's love for her was suddenly validated. Anna wanted to tell him of her loveless marriage and her husband's plans. She wanted to tell him what she had been afraid to say at the pond: that she loved him.

But, before she could speak, before she could unburden her heart, she sensed someone standing behind Jan's chair. She looked up to see that Antoni had returned.

A step behind Antoni stood Zofia. She was whispering something in his ear.

"Oh?" Antoni bellowed. "This is Stelnicki? A bold character it is that will romance a man's wife under his nose and in a place as prominent as the Royal Castle."

"It is no such thing!" Anna said. Both she and Jan were standing now.

"A cozy picture," Antoni continued, "don't you think, Zofia?"

Zofia looked stunned and for once was wordless.

"I merely happened to see Anna from across the way, Lord Grawlinski," Jan said, "and so came over to say hello."

"How many times has this little *coincidence* happened, Anna Maria?" Antoni demanded. "How many times have you met with this man?"

"Antoni, you know that I don't leave the house."

"I don't know that, but I shall be more cognizant in the future." Antoni's gray eyes narrowed as he appraised Jan. "I know by rights I should call out this man." His eyes shifted to Anna. "What is he to you, Anna Maria? Zofia tells me he was at the pond last September. Is he responsible for your belly?"

Anna's mouth fell open in a silent gasp; she was unable to mask her humiliation.

"No, I am not, sir." Jan's face was reddening. "I *was* at the pond that day. And I do blame myself for leaving Anna in the care of her careless cousin. I shall blame myself for that until the day I die. But if you wish to pursue this other line of questioning, it is I, sir, who shall call you out . . . now."

Antoni stood rigidly silent, and for the first time Anna saw fear in those colorless eyes.

No one spoke for what seemed a full minute.

"I will take my leave, Anna," Jan said at last, "before I cause you further trouble." He bowed before her, shifting so that his back was to Antoni. He whispered: "Any message sent to the Queen's Head will find me."

She nodded, as if she understood. There was no time to try to understand the riddle: a few seconds were all she had to imprint his image upon her brain and heart. She might never see him again.

He turned and left the Great Assembly Hall, causing Antoni and Zofia to step aside. He took no notice of Zofia.

"Anna, how could you—" Zofia started to say.

"Never mind!" Antoni shouted. "Leave us, Zofia!"

Anna knew that Antoni meant to vent his anger and shame at having backed down.

Zofia started to say something, thought better of it, and retreated.

Antoni turned on Anna. "Your cousin coaxed me into coming back to talk sense to you, and this is what I find!"

"Do not waste your words on me, Antoni."

"Perhaps there was no rape at the pond. Perhaps there was only mutual consent."

"You're despicable. You have only to ask Lutisha, who cared for me in the days after."

"What is this man to you, Anna Maria?"

Anna tried to catch her breath. Her throat was dry and tight. "He is a man for whom I once cared. It seems a lifetime ago."

"And now?"

Anna thought. Of course, she loved him, ached for him. The strength of her love was so strong that she thought perhaps she and Jan had loved in some previous existence, or that they would love again in a future life. She dared not hope for that in this life. Anna wet her lips and looked into her husband's eyes. "Now, Antoni, I am married to you. I will honor that commitment. But do not think that you can establish a distillery on my estate, the estate my father lived and died for. And do not think you can strike me. I see the temptation in your eyes. If you dare, you will regret it."

"What would you do, Anna Maria? Send Stelnicki after me?"

"No! I will fight my own battles."

"You can fight alone then! I'm leaving for Saint Petersburg tonight."

"Leaving?"

"Oh, don't raise your hopes, Anna Maria. I see that in *your* eyes. No, you won't be rid of me as easily as that." He smiled. "Fate has brought our paths together, yes?"

Anna stared wordlessly as Antoni left the hall. She slowly sank into her chair.

The audience had returned to their seats, she suddenly realized. How long had the occupants of the rows all about her been staring?

Numb, she sat, her face burning, the strains of the violin filling the chamber.

Well, I have found my voice, Anna thought. *But at what cost?*

26

As the carriage rumbled across the wooden bridge from Warsaw to Praga, Zofia stared at the sullen Anna. She surprised herself with the level of animosity toward her cousin she felt surging within her. She had brought her to the Royal Castle as a reward for having saved the diary from the king's eyes. What a wretched mistake it had been! But who could have anticipated that doing so would facilitate a reunion with Stelnicki?

It had been no easy task, either, to keep Antoni from leaving the palace and convince him to return to his wife. Zofia wanted Anna's marriage to be successful, even if Antoni's ambition did propel them into a magnate status above her own. She didn't wish Anna any harm, not really; in fact, she held affection for her cousin.

Let Antoni and Anna be successful! Zofia had her own lofty ambitions. And she had confidence enough to attain them. But her spine tautened as she thought of the moment at the castle when she came upon Anna and Jan together. That sickening feeling came again in dizzying waves. It was like seeing them together in the forest so many months before. The image filled her with dark, nameless emotions that seemed to make her capable of anything.

Zofia was heedless of time and the motion of the carriage. She tried to make order out of the myriad feelings that eddied and boiled up within her, tried to measure the strength of one in relation to the next. Though she would not fully acknowledge the hurt to her heart and the affront to her pride, she felt deep anger all over again that her plans the previous September had been foiled by her country cousin. She had assumed that with Anna married to Grawlinski she had permanently severed her cousin's attachment to Stelnicki. But now, to see them together, her hand in his, revived and inflamed powerful emotions. Was it jealousy? she wondered. Did she love Jan?

She wanted him, she knew that. Somehow, too, when she saw at the castle the interest that Anna inspired in Jan, she wanted him all the more. And watching him stand up to the pitiful Grawlinski, she realized now, brought her desire to a white-hot heat.

If only I could have him once, she thought, just once—make him yield—it would be enough to satisfy me. And it would ruin him for Anna—in his own eyes and in hers. Jan and Anna were cut from the same dull cloth of honor.

With her cousin still on the scene there was no chance of seduction, however. Worse, there was now the very real danger Jan and Anna would reignite their little affair despite Anna's marriage. Zofia realized she had discounted Anna's boldness, underestimated their passion. There must be a way to be rid of her.

Zofia thought herself clever enough. She had been so with Walter that very night. She smiled with self-satisfaction. She was surprised to find her brother at the Royal Castle, but she had expected that he would appear one day, indignant that she had done him out of land and fortune. She also suspected he would resurrect the doings at the quagmire where her father died, attempting blackmail. It was all so predictable. But wasn't he just as guilty as she? He could not accuse her without implicating himself. She made certain to counter him at every move, for though they were not brother and sister by blood, *they* were cut from the same cloth, one not nearly so dull.

Zofia's smile widened. She was the smarter, however. When the threat of blackmail ricocheted, poor Walter had to settle for the promise of a tiny fraction of the cash trust, money that she would give only to salve his pride and keep him quiet. She was doing him a favor, she reasoned. Despite her parents' objections, he had had the ambition to get out and make his own way years before. She was allowing him the opportunity to continue to do so.

At last, the carriage arrived at the Gronski town house.

Zofia watched wordlessly as Anna, who had been seated next to the large Swede named August, stepped down from the carriage, assisted by the dwarf who would see her to the door. Anna made no reply to the good-byes given her by Charlotte and the two men. Wouldn't she be surprised, Zofia mused, to know she had been right about Walter's presence at the castle? But Zofia knew it was best not to bring them together.

Zofia and Charlotte were sitting on the opposite side with the Russian officer between them. Zofia motioned to Charlotte, who took Anna's place next to the Swede.

The carriage retraced its way back to the city proper.

"Oh, do let's stop at the fountain in the Market Square," Zofia said as the carriage rolled off the bridge and started up the incline toward the city walls.

"But it is so late already," Charlotte protested. She was tired, inebriated, and eager to get to the inn where the officer and his companion had rooms.

"It won't take long, Charlotte darling," Zofia said. "Why, if it were summer, we could dunk our toes." Why had she trusted Charlotte with the secret about the distillery? Zofia might not be able to vent her anger at Anna right now, but there was nothing to keep her from avenging herself on Charlotte.

Momentarily, Zofia called to the driver: "Do as I told you at the fountain!"

"Oh, you planned this?" Charlotte asked.

"Hush, Charlotte, it'll be fun."

When the carriage wheeled into the square and stopped, they prepared to alight.

The dwarf helped Charlotte onto the footstool and then to the ground.

Instead of alighting, Zofia reached over and pulled shut the door. "Go!" she screamed at the driver.

The driver cracked the whip at the team of horses. The wheels turned and the carriage lurched forward, clacking along the cobblestone square, quickly picking up speed.

"Stop!" Charlotte shrieked. "Stop! Zofia this is not amusing!"

Zofia put her head out the open window. "Wait there, darling, and we'll send your carriage back for you."

Charlotte's cries were amplified by the emptiness of the dark plaza. The little man next to her was calling out something, too, in his strangely deep voice. Zofia's bribe to the driver, however, had been sufficient to deafen him to their plight.

Zofia laughed, calling out, "Hush, or you'll wake all of Warsaw!"

Now she turned in her seat to look at her two quizzical companions. They had been too drunk to offer resistance to her scheme. She giggled at their stupid looks. "Charlotte's voice certainly does carry, doesn't it?"

Zofia settled back into her seat. Her fingers drummed the windowsill. "Don't look so sad, August. I will be able to please you both."

The man brightened as he and the officer exchanged glances.

The officer turned then to Zofia. "What about your cousin?" Perhaps it would pick up her mood to make it an even foursome? She's very beautiful."

Zofia turned to him now, not with desire any longer, but with loathing.

Anna slept little that night and moved through the next day as through a fog-laden fen. The memory of the meeting with Jan was the only thing that carried her along. She still loved him—there was no denying that reality. In fact, separation had deepened her feelings. And he loved her—she knew it, *had* known it. Thoughts of him lifted her and helped her through the day, if only for minutes at a time.

Then came the thoughts that numbed the happiness of her heart, as if with ice.

The thought of Zofia for one. Though Anna and Jan had no time to speak of it, Anna was convinced that Zofia had lied at the pond when she accused Jan of attacking her. Had she also intercepted Jan's letter? One thing was certain, however: Zofia had engineered Anna's marriage to Antoni.

Anna thought how in a strange way the Fates had been kind twice to Zofia while cutting down the lives of others: were it not for Uncle Leo's death and for the rape at the pond, Zofia would be leading a very different life. She would be married to Antoni and deprived of the independence and power she now enjoyed.

While it was true that at times Zofia projected what seemed a sisterly bond and looked out for Anna's interest, something mysterious and dark clouded her behavior, too. Anna vividly recalled how at the Royal Castle Zofia had stared silently at her and Jan. For once the mask that her cousin presented to the world—one of wit, humor, confidence—fell away, revealing what appeared to be jealousy and hatred.

Anna wondered if Zofia secretly loved Jan. If that were the case, why had she encouraged Anna in her attraction to him? Was her cousin even capable of loving any one man? Zofia herself had told Anna how she longed to pick all the flowers in the garden. Anna's head spun. She could make no sense of it.

What did make sense was to get away from Warsaw, away from Zofia.

Anna was plagued by thoughts of Antoni, too. His leaving for Saint Petersburg had brought an inward sigh of relief, but she knew that the conflict with her husband was very much in the beginning stages. She was all but certain he would not agree to an annulment. Unless, of course, she gave up everything.

Anna was not about to do that. Her standing among the Polish nobility was modest. Although her father had parlayed the farm into a profitable operation and had invested wisely with the Lubicki family, he had had only the one estate, with no city mansion. He had placed that home and land at Sochaczew above everything. For Anna, no sacrifice was too great to protect it.

Anna's stomach tightened now to think that her wretched marriage had put both finances and land in jeopardy. She could not care less that Antoni's scheme might provide magnate status for them and their heirs. She *would* die before seeing her family home turned into the site of a distillery.

Sochaczew! She seized upon the thought. *That is where I should go. Home!*

Antoni must be made to relent on this whiskey business. She would write to Lord Józef Lubicki: perhaps she had some legal recourse. If not, she would be there at the estate to fight him to the end.

But to what end? she wondered. What chance did she truly have to beat Antoni at his own game, a game that men played?

Women had roles to play, had to wear masks and heavy dresses emblematic of their station in life, like actors in the Greek dramas. Men, with their trousers and age-old license for power, had all the advantages. For once Anna could not blame Russia's Catherine for seizing opportunities usually forbidden to her sex.

She chuckled to herself then, suddenly realizing the bitter paradox: in the Greek dramas, even the roles of women were awarded to *men*.

27

A distillery?" Countess Gronska looked up, dumbfounded, her knitting dropping to her lap.

Anna stood before her. "Yes, Aunt Stella, a distillery. It's true. And were it not for the Princess Charlotte, I might not have found out until after the fact."

The countess struggled to compose herself. "And you knew this, Zofia?" Her tone was accusatory even though she knew in recent days her own opinion carried little weight with her daughter.

Zofia shrugged. "I did." She stood staring out the French windows.

"And you said nothing?"

"I didn't think it my place."

The countess sensed an unpleasant electricity pass between her daughter and niece. "But it does concern Anna Maria's welfare."

"If the venture makes Antoni and Anna rich beyond measure, what can come from it other than good?"

"I did not raise you to think that money is what constitutes nobility."

"It is a sad noble who has none," Zofia said, turning to face the countess. "Money is the way of the new order, Mother. With the kind of wealth Antoni hopes to acquire, Anna will not have a care in the world. I should be so lucky as Anna."

"I don't want that kind of money," Anna said, displaying an uncharacteristic abruptness.

Zofia's gaze shifted to her cousin. "What you want, Anna," she said, "is impossible."

The countess saw some masked tension pass between the cousins. "What is there to do?" she asked, to no one in particular.

"I plan to go to Sochaczew," Anna said.

Zofia's reaction was quick: "You can't do that."

"I can. I will quite literally stand my ground. It is right, too, that I have my baby at home."

"Anna Maria, I, too, must oppose that plan," the countess heard herself say. "Your husband will no doubt return here and he should find you here." She paused a moment. "And there is the baby, dearest. Here in Warsaw you have midwives and doctors. Why, even *I* could provide more expertise with your confinement and delivery than you would find on your estate."

As it did in moments of distress, the countess' heart beat irregularly, surging in rapid little fits, then slowing to skip a beat. Countess Gronska was truly torn. This man that she had encouraged Anna to wed had plans to destroy the Berezowski estate and tarnish the dignity of Anna's family name and parents' memory. What's more, he had left her, running off to his mother in Saint Petersburg. And now the countess found herself telling Anna to await her husband's return. It was the conventional advice, the advice that a noblewoman had been bred to give. But she could not help but wonder: is it the best advice?

"And there is that Paduch culprit, too, Anna," Zofia was saying. "I won't have you alone on that estate while that man runs free. It's too dangerous."

"Danger," Anna said, "is not always outside the home."

Again, the countess detected a taut current flowing between Anna and Zofia. Again, she didn't understand.

Zofia's solicitude suddenly took on a hardened edge. "Well, it would be a futile trip for you. You would only have to turn around and come back."

"Why?" Anna asked.

"Because, Anna, your home at Sochaczew has already been razed."

Neither the countess nor Anna could respond before Zofia opened the French windows and bolted from the room.

Although Zofia had been thinking of ways to rid herself of Anna, her cousin's scheme to go to Sochaczew alone was unacceptable. The little chill of fear that ran through her at the thought was not fear of Feliks Paduch.

No, it was fear of Jan Stelnicki. At such a short distance, a morning's ride from Warsaw, Sochaczew was entirely too close for a husbandless Anna to be to a stupidly determined Stelnicki. There must be no recurrence of the catastrophe at the Royal Castle.

If Antoni were at Sochaczew, it would be a different matter. Or if Anna were to join Antoni in Saint Petersburg, that would be better yet!

Telling Anna of the demolition of her home was perhaps impulsive, Zofia thought, but it had given her time. How much time? She was certain that at that moment Anna was scribbling out a letter to Jacob Szraber, asking for verification.

Zofia sat down to pen her own letter. It should not be hard, she hoped, to find someone in the capital who, for the right price, would go to Saint Petersburg on the spot. Anna might get her reply from Sochaczew within the week. Zofia knew she had to do better despite the great distance her correspondence would have to travel.

28

T he morning was rainy; heavy, gray clouds pressed down upon the River Vistula. The only customer at the Queen's Head was Jan Stelnicki.

Jan sipped at his coffee. The sight of Anna at the Royal Castle played in his head for the hundredth time. The visualization of her sweetly surprised face when she turned to see him had sustained him for days.

She still loved him, her expression told him. He would never again attempt to lock outside his mind those wide and deep-set green eyes. They were filled with a love that spanned place and time.

Jan stared at the house across the river through a dirty glass window that threw back at him his own reflection. His hair was mussed. The dark pouches under his eyes betrayed the lack of sleep. He was tired. And he was tired to death of thinking *if only*: if only Anna had not married; if only she had not been attacked; if only there were not to be a child. Most of all, he thought, if only he had gone back that day to the pond. He had had to assume the responsibility for that, and live with the guilt that came with it. Still, he knew that most of the suffering was Anna's.

It was so unfair that one rash decision, one moment of pride and anger, could alter lives forever. But it was so.

On days when his guilt was too much for him, he wondered about Feliks Paduch. Was he the one who attacked Anna? Was it his child she bore? How was one to find such a man, a man running from the law? Jan fantasized how he might one day confront Paduch and avenge Anna.

For the present, he admitted to his love for her, to their mutual love. But he would not have the audacity to hope for a future. He would have to live without her.

And he would marry no one else. He would pursue his politics. He forced his mind onto that path now.

The Commonwealth's general election was coming up in a matter of days. It was imperative that the Third of May Constitution be affirmed by the people as a whole. But he knew that Catherine was busy sowing bribes and threats in order to gather the votes that would overthrow it, or at least enough to sow doubt in the minds of the Polish people. He knew, too, that the most important mind, that of King Stanisław, sometimes was easily swayed. Would he stand by the cause?

In recent weeks Jan had quickly learned the art of public speaking. He spoke daily, often several times a day. He spoke to every manner of group willing to listen. No potential political pressure group was too small, no single citizen too insignificant.

Often his speeches evolved into debates with hard-edged characters. Jan enjoyed these best. Responding at the moment to an accusation or philosophy at odds with his own sharpened his mind and enabled him to elucidate his views on democracy in a way more emotional and emphatic than with mere oratory. At these times he held his own and relished the pace at which his heart pumped and thoughts ran.

In such moments, thoughts of Anna, the pains of heartbreak, and the image of the thin-moustached Grawlinski were dispelled. A pervasive sadness clung to him, however, in moments removed from discussion and debate. It was a sadness that some observers in his political circle might have misconstrued as a quiet pessimism for the cause.

Jan wondered: Had Anna understood his entreaty to her concerning the Queen's Head? He doubted that she even knew the Queen's Head was an inn. Would she ask someone? Would she write?

In a quick movement, Jan stood, pushing back his chair and reaching into his pocket for a coin to leave Hortenspa, the old proprietress. He was shaking his head. He had caught himself at it, he realized: thinking of a future where there was none.

Anna paced her room, wondering when the letter from Jacob would arrive. She suspected that Zofia had been lying about the destruction of her home. She *had* to be lying! Little building or demolition took place in winter. Yet, why would she say such a thing?

Anna would never forgive Antoni if he had razed her family manor house. She grew dizzy thinking that her childhood home might be gone. What was she to do if it were true?

And as for Zofia, Anna would never forgive her, whether she told the truth and had kept the secret from her, or whether she had lied for some selfish reason of her own.

If the letter from Jacob affirmed the well-being of her home, she would go there and not look back. She would have her child there. She would deal with Antoni somehow, give up whatever it took—other than home and land—to divest herself of a foolish marriage. As for Jan . . .

A horse that had been clip-clopping along the cobblestones seemed to slow at the Gronski town house. Anna rushed to the window. A man carrying a leather letter pouch was dismounting.

Moving as fast as she dared for her condition, Anna moved out into the hall and to the staircase.

Halfway down the stairs, she realized that Zofia had been quicker. Her cousin was just closing the door, letter in hand.

Anna arrived at the bottom of the stairs. She wondered if Zofia planned to hide it, as she must have done to Jan's letter so many months before.

"I believe that's for me," Anna said.

Zofia turned it over in her hands. "So it is," she said, her almond eyes assessing her cousin. "You were expecting one?"

"Yes, from Jacob Szraber."

"Oh?" Zofia smiled. "This one seems to be from Saint Petersburg, Anna. Your husband, perhaps?"

* * *

At supper, the Countess Gronska came right to the point. "What does Antoni say in the letter, Anna Maria?"

Anna glanced at Zofia, who feigned disinterest, yet she must have spoken to her mother about the letter. "He apologized for his behavior."

"Did he make mention of your home?"

"No."

"Is he to return soon?"

"No, Aunt Stella. He says his father is ill again and that they wish me to join them in Saint Petersburg."

"Saint Petersburg?" The countess was surprised.

"I'm sure he means to patch things up," Zofia said. "Perhaps you should go."

"I don't want to go," Anna said. "And there is the baby to consider."

"There is that, Anna Maria," the countess said. "You're nearly five months along now. Traveling is no easy thing. Still, it may save your marriage, dear. Why don't you wish to go?"

"Physically, I think I can weather it fine. But I have a bad feeling—"

"You know," her aunt interrupted, "how I am suspicious of everything Russian. I cannot help it. We have always been dealt a crooked hand by Catherine and the ones that came before her. I don't like that Walter became her mercenary or that your husband has his city residence at Saint Petersburg rather than here or Kraków. To send my niece there at this politically explosive time is not an easy thing for me to do, Anna Maria. But I think that you and your husband come first. Before there are countries, there are families."

Anna flinched. "You think it's my duty?"

"I do."

"Mother is right," Zofia said, after the countess had left the table. "Antoni is not inflexible. You will come to terms over your differences, I'm sure. *You* should not be too inflexible, either. You are a woman, Anna. And a woman with charms. Do not be afraid to use what charms God has given you."

"I would rather use my head."

"Ah! rightly so. It is the woman who uses both head and charms who achieves. Antoni is, after all, only a man."

"Were it in my power, I would wish never to see him again."

"Nonsense! Is he expecting a response?"

"No. He has had the presumption to hire a coach." Anna fumed at the thought. "It is to arrive in three days."

"Well, it's settled then. If you need any help packing, you can borrow Clarice or Babette."

"Am I to take it, then, that I would be unwelcome if I stay here?"

Zofia smiled and leveled her dancing, dark eyes at her cousin. "Oh, Ania darling, I don't see that as even an option."

On her own, Anna had already decided to go to Saint Petersburg. Her decision to do so was not out of any sense of duty to a loveless marriage; rather, it was in the hope that she might bring her marriage to some conclusion. She planned a final confrontation with Antoni. She wanted her baby, her home and land, and—after the baby was born and given a name—an annulment, if the Church would allow it. Otherwise, a separation would have to do. She could not imagine herself living with Antoni, having to submit to him . . . in every way. She was repulsed at the thought of sharing a bed with him and everything that entailed. She would not do it!

Anna recalled one of her least favorite tales. A wife was beaten regularly by her husband for such things as not having meals prepared on time. One day, for help and guidance, the woman called on the guardian angel Betojinka, named for the herb commonly known as wood betony. The angel's advice was simple:

> Don't cry, don't holler
> Because it's your fault.
> When others prepare breakfast,
> prepare breakfast
> When others prepare dinner, prepare dinner
> Supper must be prepared at suppertime, then
> Your man will not beat you.

What moral was to be found here? For Anna, Betojinka's advice for women was no advice. In her own retelling of the tale, the shouting and vodka-infused husband chased his wife from her kitchen, brandishing a heavy spoon. Crying, the woman ran across the dark yard and took refuge behind the well. The drunken man went to leap upon his terri-fied wife but fell screaming into the deep shaft. His echoing shouts did not last long, however, and it was this story—Anna's story—that she claimed gave birth to the phrase "silent as a well."

Anna laughed to herself. No, she would not throw Antoni down a well, much as she would like to. She *would* sacrifice some of her assets, however, to have finished with him. She would give up any holdings—other than the Sochaczew estate—that Lubicki held in trust for her. It was a considerable fortune and Antoni was a greedy man. Perhaps he would take it.

But Anna worried that the stakes involved in his distillery business were higher. He had hopes of becoming a magnate, and she knew what she could offer him, outside of the estate, would not accomplish that.

She sat down at her desk to pen two letters.

The first was to Baron Michał Kolbi, informing him that she could not attend an election day party and that she would be in Saint Peters-burg for a short while. She confided in him some of her vague fears re-garding the trip.

Her aunt's words about Russia came back to her and she felt trai-torous. Her father had had no kind words for Catherine, either. A chill came over her when she thought that her baby might not be born on Polish soil. She vowed to herself that her stay there would be brief.

The second letter she addressed to Count Jan Stelnicki. Her hand trembled as she wrote. Would she even have the nerve to send it?

She had learned from Michał that the Queen's Head was an inn al-most directly across the river from the Gronski town house. It was fre-quented by commoners and some political partisans. Her heart quickened at she thought of Jan so close to her at times, with only the current of the Vistula between them.

Anna sighed. Even if she had known, however—given their circum-stances—the river might as well have been an ocean.

Only the day before she had hired a carriage, asking the driver to take the capital's riverfront streets. Peering out of the coach window, she saw it for herself, then. It was a dingy first-floor tavern in a three-story, red-brick building. No doubt in the summer the business spilled out noisily onto the narrow street. A faded green sign bore the name in red letters. Under the arched lettering was a sketch in black of a queen's head, amateurish and silly.

But Anna thrilled to think of Jan sitting behind one of those dirty windows. Out of the opposite coach window she could see across to the Gronski town house, rising on its little bluff across the river. Had he chosen the place because of its close proximity to her? She dared to think so.

She now wished that she had had the driver stop the carriage at the inn and inquire whether Jan were there. But her caution had cost her a lost moment.

Anna finished the letter and read it over. She frowned. Of course, she could not write of her feelings for him. She wrote of her health and asked of his. She mentioned the next day's election and its importance. Finally, she told him of the trip to Saint Petersburg that she would take in three days' time, providing a little schedule of mundane events leading up to departure. Jan would glean the letter's purpose: a hint that he could visit the morning after the election, between ten and twelve. Her frown did not abate. Overall, it was an insipid note, but she doubted she could do better and had no time to try.

What would her aunt think if he visited? she wondered. Or Zofia?

She was leaving the Gronski home now, so she threw caution to the four winds. Without allowing for second thoughts, she had Babette see that the letters were delivered within the hour.

I cannot, she thought, as she watched Babette hurry down the walk, spend my life always taking the cautious way. Her father had told her: *"Sometimes you must put yourself in the way of destiny."*

Part Three

The roots of learning are bitter,
but the fruit is sweet.

–POLISH PROVERB

29

The carriage for Anna arrived on the morning of Election Day, February 14th. It was two days early.

Anna spoke a little Russian, but she could understand little of the low dialect of the two men who came to collect her. Yes, she was packed, she told them, insisting also that she didn't wish to leave for two days, as had been planned.

It must be after Jan's visit.

Impossible, they said, with a minimum of respect. They were paid to pick her up and return immediately, allowing no time for a stopover in Warsaw or on the way back. These were gruff, lowborn men, she realized, little acquainted with the ways of gentility.

Zofia and the countess were of little support. She would have to go. She retreated to her room.

Holding back her tears now at the dissolution of her plan, Anna stared at the crystal dove, still debating whether to take it on the long and rough journey. Intuition told her to leave it. She packed it away in its box of wood inlay and gave it to the countess for safekeeping. It seemed that, like her dreams, she was always tucking it away.

Her meeting with Jan had been scuttled. She was certain that he would come, only to find her gone. Twenty-four hours were all she would have needed.

But it was not to be. She sat down to pen a second letter to him.

Anna went to the side entrance where the ramshackle carriage stood ready. She had said her good-bye to her aunt when she gave her the box with the crystal dove. She had no desire to say good-bye to Zofia. The letter from Jacob Szraber had arrived only that morning, contradicting her cousin's contention that Anna's manor home had been razed. Zofia *had* lied. Relief and disdain coursed through Anna. She wanted nothing more to do with her. After dealing with Antoni, she would return to Sochaczew as soon as possible.

She was seated within the coach and the two Russians were lashing her trunk to the roof when Babette came running. "Wait, Madame!" she cried. "Oh, please wait!"

Anna looked out to see the maid hurrying down the driveway, her two children in tow.

"Oh, Madame, please—" she said, struggling for breath. "If you would be so kind, I wish you to take Louis and little Babette with you as your little servants. You may have them as long as you wish or until they come of age."

"What?" Anna's mouth fell open.

"I know they like you, Lady Anna. You are such a good influence on them! And they so love your stories. Here they merely get underfoot and Mademoiselle Zofia has so little patience with them. She tells me I must send them away or that I must go myself."

Anna stared in disbelief at the young mother. Were her own flesh and blood of such little value to her? How like Zofia she was, so fully self-absorbed.

Anna trembled to think of the awesome responsibility, but she took the children without a second thought. They were spoiled and unmannered and unloved; Anna hoped to undo some of the damage. *Poor little souls.* She realized now that Babette had taken her answer for granted because the children's little satchels were already packed.

The children climbed into the coach and settled into the seat across from her. Anna stared at their little round faces. Until they come of age? What had she gotten herself into now?

As the carriage began to descend the driveway to the street, Anna looked to Zofia's first-floor window. She was certain that she saw the slightly parted curtains stirring. Was she secretly standing there, watching the departure? Were Zofia's feelings for her as mixed as her own toward Zofia?

Babette stood in the drive waving and calling adieu to her children. Anna turned back to see Louis and little Babette motionless and dry-eyed.

It began to snow. The carriage moved down to and across the bridge to the city proper, turning left onto the riverfront street.

Well, Anna thought, at least the two Russian bears possess the intelligence to understand a bribe when they hear one.

The wheels ground to a halt on the stony earth in front of the Queen's Head. Momentarily, one of the Russians clumsily helped Anna to alight.

Election Day was a hectic one for Jan Stelnicki.

He was one of a party who were traveling from town to town, *sejmik* to *sejmik*, to check on voting irregularities and to bring out any men sympathetic to the cause who had not yet voted. It would be very late before he got back to Warsaw.

The spirit of the patriots was up. They were confident that the Constitution passed the previous year at the Great *Sejm* would be ratified this day at *sejmik*s all over Poland, guaranteeing a democracy within Stanisław's monarchy. With the exception of some greedy, power-hungry, and shortsighted nobles, it would be a grand moment for Poles of all classes when the results were announced, presumably some time in the next two or three days.

What made the hard day an effortless and memorable one for Jan, however, was the letter he carried in his breast pocket. On the morrow he would see Anna. Never mind that it might be the last time for a long while. He would see her. Alone, he hoped.

He could imagine no future after that. Tomorrow *was* his future.

30

Not long after the carriage was out of the city and upon the icy country roads, Anna began to feel ill. She had had a sense of foreboding ever since Antoni's letter, but this illness she put down to her delicate state and the rough travel conditions.

Antoni *would* attain magnate status, she thought, if his parsimony regarding the hiring of the carriage and men were indicative of how far he could stretch a ducat. He must have found the best bargain in Saint Petersburg. The carriage was worn and evidently older than the invention of springs. Anna felt every bump and pebble in the road. There was no glass in the windows, merely shades. These were fastened as tight as possible but still let in an unhealthy draft. And the two characters above who took turns at driving were as buffoons from some comic play.

Anna tried to make the best of it. The snow was continuing. A wintertime journey did have its advantages in that the carriage wheels did not spew up the dry dust of summer, nor were they hampered by the mud of spring. The countess had provided goose-down comforters that shielded them from the icy air, head to toe. At their feet were two covered pans of hot coals.

Lutisha had tied a tanned goatskin around Anna's belly as extra warmth for the baby. At the time, Anna could not have guessed how valuable such a measure would prove.

They were not long on the road when Anna began to doubt the wisdom of taking on the two children. They were impolite and chattered incessantly in their low French. Though their clothing was fine, they were dirty, as they were unaccustomed to frequent washing. Louis was eight and Babette six, and Anna worried that training the two, who had been without discipline for so very long, would be a thorny and thankless task.

Late in the day they stopped at a hovel of an inn to rest and feed the horses. The men ate inside, but Anna preferred the foods from the basket Lutisha had prepared to the stench and rat-infested inns, the bad food, and the prying eyes. She did use the privies, filthy as they were. Had she been alone, she would rather have relieved herself in the snow.

It was getting colder as night drew on, and before Anna reentered the coach, she asked Louis to go into the inn with the foot-warmers to see that the coals be replenished. The mindless Russians hadn't thought to ask.

The boy shook his head. "No, I want to get in the carriage where it is warm."

"It will not be warm long if you do not get us coals."

"No!" The boy was obstinate.

Babette was just behind him. "No!" she mimicked in her tiny voice. She sidled up to her brother now.

"Louis!" Anna spoke sharply.

The boy stopped on the command. He looked up at Anna from beneath a mop of brown, curly hair, his eyes enlarging. This was the first time Anna had ever raised her voice to the children.

"Come here!"

He hesitated.

"This minute, Louis!"

The boy moved slowly toward her, his eyes defiant, yet fearful. Babette, her cherubic face pinched in fear, huddled close to his side.

Anna tried to collect her thoughts as the boy approached. Her silence was making him uneasy.

"I am your guardian," Anna said in French. "Do you understand?"

He nodded uncertainly.

"If we are to get along, we must come to an understanding. While you are with me, I am to take your mother's place. If I make demands of you your mother did not, or do things in ways different from hers, then that is my business. Yours is to obey. I won't ask so very much of you, but when I do request something, I will expect you to respond. Without a word or a comment. Is that quite clear?"

"Oui." There was still a trace of defiance about the mouth and in his voice.

"Oui?"

"Oui, Madame."

"Good. In return, I will take care of you. We will be fast friends, will we not, Louis?" Anna's smile coaxed him to abandon his insurgency.

"Oui, Madame," he said, smiling sheepishly.

"Now, see to it that the warmers are replenished with coals. I'm quite certain you will not freeze to death in the time it takes to do your task."

The boy went to get the pans from the coach.

Anna turned to the girl. "Babette, you must never answer me in such a manner again. Do you understand?"

The blond girl looked up at Anna, her wide, blue eyes brimming. Her tiny mouth, little more than a slash between her chubby cheeks, trembled and turned down. "Oui, Madame," she said.

Anna longed to take them both into her arms. Instead, she said, "Now run along to the inn with your brother."

Anna knew that they were testing her. She knew also that she had met their challenge and had risen in their eyes. She felt that children often possess an uncanny awareness and that just then the foundation of their relationship was established. Anna was certain that Louis and Babette would respond to the love she would give them. First, though, she would have their respect.

Soon they were back on the road. Anna's uneasy stomach found no comfort. Her misgivings about the trip multiplied, even as the snow fell and the sky darkened. Her mind kept coming back to one question: How was it that the two Russians had arrived two entire days earlier than Antoni predicted? Did he mean to take her by surprise? Was he afraid she would leave the Gronski home before the carriage arrived?

It is a queer thing, she thought.

Jan and his party of patriots, noble and common, arrived at the Queen's Head after midnight, the long day behind them. Jan had secured the use of the inn for their celebration although the election results would not be known for two days. Because this was a private party, the inn could stay in operation well past its usual midnight curfew.

At least a hundred men crammed the little tavern. Jan felt great satisfaction at having brought together the mighty within the cause—his mentor Hugo Kołłątaj, as well as Ignacy Potocki, Stanisław Malachowski, and Tadeusz Kościuszko—with citizens of all types. Franciszek Karpiński, the renowned Polish poet and friend of the king, regaled everyone with a poem written for the occasion.

Jan was ebullient about the expected confirmation of the Third of May Constitution, but his mind could not be drawn from the happy prospect of meeting with Anna the following morning. He would drink no alcohol tonight, he vowed. His mind must remain clear. He was counting the hours.

Hortenspa, the stout-bodied and stouthearted proprietress, bustled over to Jan. "Milord Stelnicki," she cried breathlessly, "I almost forgot what with all the excitement."

"What is it?"

"A lady came in this morning to see you."

"A lady?" Jan asked. Though some women frequented the place, ladies did not. Jan's heart quickened.

"Yes," Hortenspa said, "a stunning woman, she was, brown hair and deep eyes, very serious."

Jan's heart thumped now with foreboding. He watched as the woman reached into the front of her apron. "Green eyes?"

"Oh, yes! Very beautiful, sir, but a sadness about the mouth that would break your heart. She left this letter for you, milord."

Jan took the envelope, turning it over in his hands. "Thank you, Hortenspa."

"I do hope it's not bad news." The woman turned, vanishing into the crush of people and noise.

Jan sat down, his pulse racing. It was from Anna! The envelope matched the one held in his breast pocket. What is it, he wondered, a change of plans? He tried to avert a nameless panic swelling at his core.

He opened it quickly. It was nothing more than a note and he read its few sentences with one scan of his eyes.

Anna had already left Warsaw! She was to meet her husband in Saint Petersburg. Russia! His stomach tightened. She was gone. There was to be no meeting the next day. He felt as if his heart had been ripped from his chest.

He read the note again as if doing so would change the words. Her sadness was there in between the lines. An economical three sentences to tell him. She had left in a hurry, it seemed.

When am I to see her again? he brooded.

He ordered a drink. He tried to disguise his sadness, so as not to call attention to himself or throw a pall on the party.

After several drinks and the time for the news to sink in, he came to marvel at Anna's pluck to come into such a place by herself. He could easily imagine Zofia doing it, but Anna? He smiled to himself. Anna

Maria was becoming a woman, full of poise and confidence. He was terribly proud of her and touched that she had gone to such lengths to let him know about her departure.

Godspeed Ania, he prayed, and keep her safe from harm.

Jan had never used Anna's diminutive before, to her directly or even in his thoughts. It came freely now, for he had never felt so close to her—despite the great distance that would keep her from him for a space of time only God could foretell.

31

An unrelenting winter storm pummeled the carriage with snow and icy wind for days. On the fourth day, with the shrill gale at fever pitch, Anna and the children sat silently in the rocking coach.

Their progress had been reduced to a mere plodding. Anna hoped they would come upon an inn soon. If the Russians had half a brain between them—which she doubted—they would seek refuge as soon as possible.

Louis was strangely subdued, but Anna put this down to his awe of the storm or mere boredom. He began to mumble in low tones as he perused a little French book; his voice lacked its usual ardency. Anna doubted he could make out the words in the dimness of the single lantern. Little Babette lay next to him, scarcely visible as she was curled snugly into the cocoon of her comforter. She had not stirred for several hours, not since their morning inn stop.

Anna thought how the traveling must be exhausting for such young ones. She was thankful they were not as concerned as she about the storm that raged about them. In this, she envied them.

At dusk the carriage came to an abrupt halt.

What did it mean? Anna wondered. Her heart leaped at the thought of a warm inn. She would not complain even if it were dirty, odorous, and rodent-infested—as it was certain to be.

No one came to open the carriage door.

Anna tried the window flap; it was frozen fast. She tried the door next, but it would not budge, either. They were locked in, it seemed, by a thick caking of ice and snow.

A feeling of claustrophobia enveloped Anna. She tried to decipher voices in the howling wind. What was happening?

"What is it that you want?" The muffled voice from above belonged to one of the Russians.

Of course, Anna thought they were addressing her. She started to call out, but the sound of other voices, Polish voices, took the sounds from her throat.

Who was this band of Poles hailing them?

Anna strained to hear what was being said. With the winds and the noise of the horses' hooves, she could understand little. Using a spoon that Lutisha had packed in the basket, she chipped away at the ice under the window flap. In a few minutes she was able to lift the flap slightly and thereby see a fraction of the scene unfolding outside.

It was evident that the Poles and Russians were having great difficulty understanding one another. Anna saw three mounted Poles. Behind moustaches that drooped with icicles, they wore angry, demanding faces.

She became frightened now. She remembered what her aunt had instructed her to do in case of robbery, something not uncommon these days on the road. Aunt Stella cautioned her not to resist, to hold out her valuables in one hand, the little crucifix she had given Anna in the other. She warned her niece to hide only her food, which might be her salvation should she become stranded.

Anna did not look for the crucifix. Instead she looked to the children. Babette remained motionless despite the loud commotion. Louis sat with his open book, but he had stopped reading. His eyes were dark and vacant, more an old man's than a child's.

"Are you afraid, Louis?"

Slowly he shook his head.

Something was wrong with the children, Anna realized. Very wrong.

One vociferous Pole kept demanding of the Russians their destination.

Anna could hear the Russians murmuring above, conferring between themselves. She was just about to call out that they were going to Saint Petersburg when a Russian spoke. "Opole," he said.

Anna thought she had not heard correctly.

The question was repeated.

Again, the reply: "Opole!"

Anna's heart contracted. They were not going east to Saint Peters-burg, but southwest to Opole, where the Grawlinski family had their country estate.

Why? And why the deception?

Anna tried to open the door again. She would have an explanation from the Russians. The driving sleet, however, had sealed the coach tight as a tomb.

"Whom do you carry?" came a Polish voice.

After several misunderstandings among the men, Anna heard her name.

"Get down, then. Open the door. We will talk with her."

Anna stifled a cry in her throat. Louis looked frightened, too. She tried to speak in a light tone. "Louis, won't you come sit by me?"

The boy ignored her.

"Louis, please!"

He stood up and dropped himself on the seat next to Anna.

Her patience was being tested, and she thought for a moment she would slap the silly child.

"I don't feel well," he said.

"There, there, you're merely frightened," Anna said, enfolding the child in her comforter as a bird would shelter its young. "Everything will be fine." Anna was certain of no such thing. She prayed now for the two that had been entrusted to her and for the life of her unborn baby.

Minutes passed. It seemed that the Russians had no intention of opening the carriage.

A crescendo of angry shouts jarred Anna from her thoughts and prayers. Then a pistol shot rang out, splitting Anna's ears. A man in-stantly screamed.

Louis scrambled away from Anna and fell to the floor, crouching near the door.

Anna looked out the narrow opening to see a riderless horse.

She could not fathom what was going on. Why would the Russians kill and risk death themselves rather than show her to the Poles?

Another shot rang out and then came the sound of hand-to-hand combat with swords or cutlasses.

"God help us!" Anna called out.

Still another pistol explosion sent a bullet into the carriage, where it lodged in the wood above the sleeping Babette's head.

Anna suddenly smelled smoke. She looked to the floor. Louis had upset one of the pans of coal and the wooden floor had caught fire. It burned slowly, without flames as yet, so Anna thought she would have time to put it out.

Louis was distracting her, however. He kept nudging his sister, calling, "Babette, Babette." How had she not heard the noise and gunfire?

Outside, chaos had broken loose.

Anna lost control herself, screaming and crying at the same time, at a complete loss as to what she should do.

Suddenly, someone tugged at the door. Anna instantly sobered. The whole carriage shook with the effort, but the door didn't give.

"Push against the door!" The voice was Polish.

Anna sat stunned in fright, staring at the door. She didn't know whether to trust the Poles or the Russians.

The carriage stopped shaking. The Pole's effort ceased.

Anna attempted to pull herself together. In order to protect the children and herself, she would have to act. She reached over to the still form in the comforter. Something within her told her that little Babette was dead even before she touched the doll-like hand and found it cold as ice. In a state of shock, Anna thought that if she were to lift the chilled and lifeless body to her, Babette might regain her warmth.

"Louis, help me lift your sister."

The boy's eyes were transfixed on Anna, but he didn't move. Even in the dimness of the dying taper in the lantern, Anna could see that there were deep blue-black depressions beneath his eyes. The boy was sick.

At the inn that day the Russians had brought to the coach a casserole of eggs and mushrooms. The children had eaten it, but Anna ate only the sausages, yogurt, and hard, leftover bread from Lutisha's basket. She realized now that the children had been poisoned by the Russians, who no doubt assumed she would eat the casserole, too.

It came to her then with the clarity of a sunrise: *Antoni has hired these Russians to kill me!*

On her own power, Anna turned Babette, lifting her torso and head upright. She gasped when she saw the face. Babette's still eyes stared out of their deep, dark sockets. Her gaping mouth, ringed by purple lips, was a tiny black pit. Babette would never regain her warmth.

Anna pulled Louis to her now and held him as if in a vise. It would do no good: he was dying, too. There was no reserve in his manner as he clung to her, his wide, blue eyes staring into hers. The boy knew.

The carriage started to pitch and shake violently. Anna could hear the frightened coach horses rising up in fright.

They had to get out. If the carriage did not tip over, the fire or smoke would kill them. The opportunity to extinguish the fire had come and gone: it was spreading rapidly. Escape was the only way to safety.

Anna left Louis to try the door away from the fighting men—if, indeed, anyone outside was left alive. They were both coughing now. She could feel the heat of the floor against the soles of her boots.

Anna threw her weight against the door. On the third try, it gave way, and as it opened out, she had to catch herself from falling into a roadside ditch. She saw that a rear wheel was already on the incline so that the carriage was perched precariously, ready to tumble from the road.

The carriage lurched suddenly, throwing Anna onto the seat. The incoming air seemed to fuel the fire, and flames began to feed hungrily in the smoke-filled compartment.

Louis had stopped coughing.

"Louis! Louis!"

Anna found the boy's wrist and felt for a pulse.

There was none.

There was no time to cry now for the children or even to think. Anna moved to the door and climbed as far down on the coach as she could manage, then let go, dropping like a wingless bird into the cold and wet—but snow-cushioned—ditch.

32

ountess Stella Gronska felt as if she had been drawn through the eye of a needle into some dark place, but somehow had come to escape. She was feeling much more like the woman she had been in the days before her husband's death.

Oh, she was aware that Zofia and Anna thought her eccentric and peculiar. It was strange, but some part of her, too, was cognizant of the cloud that had attached itself to her. Sometimes she felt as if she were a prisoner in her own body watching herself do and say the most outlandish things. She talked to herself, knitted shapeless garments, tore them apart and started again. She snapped at the servants with little provocation.

Still, her ordeal had led to a kind of self-discovery. She had been born and raised to be a noblewoman. This, in effect, meant being a nobleman's wife. Her relationship to her husband was the same as her mother's to her husband: both listened to and obeyed their mates without question, often with little or no investigation into the reasoning of a decision or opinion. She had not learned to truly think.

Stella had been taught always to rely on a man. The transition from relying on her father to relying on her new husband in an arranged marriage had been carefully prepared for and seamlessly executed. It was not, she had been instructed, for her to question her place in the family, or for that matter, in the world.

She had been lucky. Leo had been a good mate. He had never mistreated her, and they had come to love one another. There were sometimes heavy drinking incidents and occasional violence against their adopted son, Walter, but she had learned how to exert a quiet influence on her husband that helped to neutralize such behavior.

Stella had not been prepared for life without a man. She had not been prepared for the sudden violence of his death, the decisions regarding Anna, or the behavior of her two children. The sum of these things accounted for her downward spiral—but what precipitated her return? She thought it was, in part, her concern for Anna. She regretted now letting her go to Russia, to Antoni Grawlinski, who, she had come to realize, was a poor specimen of a husband. The Minka episode was proof enough of that. What danger had she sent her niece into this time? The recurring thought that Anna Maria was indeed in danger raised goose flesh on her arms.

Stella also gave credit for her recovery to prayer. Through these past months she had not abandoned her faith. Prayer had allowed her to endure and survive. It was a Pole's best friend.

She sat now in her sewing room, absorbed in a special issue of the *Monitor*. It was good news. In only two days the word had come back from *sejmiks* across the Commonwealth of Poland and Lithuania: The Third of May Constitution was to stand! The vote, though still not officially tallied, was overwhelmingly in favor of democratic reform.

As she read now, the countess hummed to the music and joyful noise she heard coming from the streets of Praga and Warsaw. It was a happy day. Poland was the first country in Europe to adopt such a progressive document. Despite the ruffled feathers of some of the magnates, the Constitution was vindicated. She felt very proud.

Her pride had to do with herself, too. Before Leo's death, she had accepted his political views without question. In these past weeks, however, she had become politically inquisitive and aware. Hours once devoted to knitting useless garments were now spent reading about Kościuszko and his cause. She came to see how wrong it was to keep whole classes of people from attaining a decent quality of life. All men should be able to live to their full potential, as Thomas Paine suggested in *The Rights of Man*. This simple philosophy she discovered and embraced. She was thinking for herself, and a new, quiet dignity settled over her.

In celebration, some men were setting off pistols across the Vistula, jarring the countess into a more fearful train of thought. She remembered the Partition of 1772. She had been thirty-nine. Even then Poland's long push toward democracy had begun. King Stanisław, a young man, supported it then, as now. Unfortunately, this current quest was coming at the very time Poland's three neighbors were putting together the most powerful autocracies Europe had witnessed in a millennium. The Hapsburgs in Austria, the Hohenzollerns in Prussia, and the Romanovs in Russia were creating their empires at the expense of common citizens and the peasants. Ninety-five percent of Russians, it was said, lived as serfs in abject misery. In the city there was a saying that defined the contrast between Poland and Russia: "In Russia as one must; in Poland as one will."

The countess remembered how, with that partition, Austria, Prussia, and Russia—afraid that Poland's more humane and democratic nature would encourage the hunger for reform in their own peoples—conspired to divide up portions of Poland among themselves. Polish lands and people were traded off like livestock and were not returned.

By God, she thought, the Constitution is to stand! Only now, after the countess' personal rediscovery, could she fully understand this vote, its importance, its history, its potential.

But the countess could see its danger, too. If anything, those three empires were stronger than ever these twenty years later. Were they going to stand by and allow the rose of democracy to flower in their midst? They would see only thorns.

She shivered, as if overcome by a chill. She knew they would not stand idly by. They would act.

How might Poland respond to their aggression?

True to its peaceful nature, the Commonwealth had no standing army. The treasury paid for some eighteen thousand troops, a small enough force. But rumor had it that a corrupt military and political system inflated that number for personal profit and that the true number probably did not exceed eleven thousand.

The countess worried as the happy explosions continued. What could eleven thousand troops do to allay the advance of three powerful autocracies?

She prayed that she would never bear witness to the sounds of enemy gunfire in Warsaw.

33

Anna lay stunned for what must have been several minutes.

The snow stung her hands and face, slowly awakening her to her surroundings. She had fallen into a deep, natural ditch at the side of the road. She looked up. Above her, against the darkening sky, the carriage was dangerously perched at the road's edge. Its underside was ablaze, and the frenzied horses stamped and whinnied in their panic. The immediate danger of the teetering vehicle brought Anna to her senses.

She crawled along the ditch, burrowing into the high drift of snow. She moved slowly, fighting for every bit of ground.

The blizzard was increasing in strength. Sleet, driven by a fierce wind, lashed at her face and gloveless hands.

She was not twenty paces away from the carriage when she heard the crash. She looked back to see that the horses had been cut loose: at least one of the men must still be alive!

The carriage lay in the ditch upside down, flames leaping up now, like the scarlet petals of a poppy around its pistil. Anna stared blindly at the sight. Her first thought was to return to the children. But Louis and Babette were dead. There was nothing she could do for them. *May God take their innocent souls!*

Her hands moved instinctively to her belly. She had to protect her own child at all costs. Anna looked about. Here, she might be easily sighted. She needed a safer shelter.

Over the sounds of the wailing wind, she could hear nothing. Of the two Russians and three Poles, who had survived? Praying she would not be seen, she crawled up the slope opposite the road, where spruce trees would provide a shield.

Once hidden, Anna knelt and hunched over, burying her head and hands in her cloak, as a turtle might retract into its shell. She lost track of the minutes.

She dared then to peek out between branches. It was fully dark except for the area lighted by the fire, which had already weakened. She watched for a very long time. She saw no human movement, no horses. Through the white blur of snow, she could make out the dark forms of the bodies on the ground. Anyone who survived, it seemed, had fled.

Slowly Anna eased herself down into the ditch again and pulled herself up onto the other side. Cautiously she stood and went to check the bodies. There were four, as well as that of a horse.

Anna's mind took her to that day her murdered father had been brought home. Why must things such as this happen? she wondered, shivering in the cold. She pulled the wool cloak around her, one hand holding the collar to her mouth as protection against the cold, the other grasping her belly.

The carriage was still throwing off enough light to identify the men. Anna went from one to the next. They were all bloodied, all wearing grim expressions, as if the world into which they just ventured was an unwelcoming one. The first was a Pole, then a Russian, then another Pole. The last one lay facedown near the dead horse.

Anna thought. Although there might have been more, she had seen three Poles through the narrow opening in the carriage window. Was this the third Pole? Or was it the other Russian? Anna drew in a deep breath. She bent now and pulled at the bloodied overcoat. With a great effort, she was able to turn over the body.

Anna screamed. The man's face had been shot away by a pistol at close range. His lower jaw was missing.

Still, she knew from his clothing that this was not the other Russian. The other Russian had escaped. Her heart stopped. *Where is he now?*

She looked about the ever-darkening scene. Might he come back? Was he out there even now, watching her? He had been paid to kill her. Would he come back to complete his mission?

No, she decided. He undoubtedly thought she had died in the carriage, if not by poison, then by fire. Perhaps, too, he had taken all of the surviving horses: that would be a pretty bonus for him.

Thinking was about to drive her mad. The cold night wind tore into her as if her cloak were a gown of gossamer. She was exhausted. Pulling at the dead horse's wool blanket, Anna opened it and draped it off the animal's back so that it formed a crude shelter. After pulling the gloves from one of the dead Poles, she bent down and crawled into the little tunnel the horse and blanket formed. Shivering with an intense inner chill, she sidled up to the still-warm carcass. She lay there shaking, thinking only of her child and praising Lutisha for having had the foresight to gird her stomach with the warm goatskin. If only it would prove sufficient to save her baby.

In time, she felt herself being drawn toward a cold, blue blankness—as if she were a tiny skiff caught up in the powerful current of the River Lethe.

When Anna awoke, the horse had stiffened into an ice sculpture, its warmth gone. She pulled herself from her shelter. To lie there was to yield to death.

The night was fully dark. She cursed herself for her stupidity. Hadn't she realized that the horse would not warm her for long? Instead of sleeping, she should have kept alive the fire that had burned the carriage. She looked to the ditch. The fire seemed to have gone out long ago.

She was hungry, too. She had not remembered the crucifix, nor had she thought to save the basket of food from the coach. Aunt Stella's advice had gone unheeded.

She guessed that an hour or two had passed. The blizzard had moved on, leaving the white landscape eerily serene. Nothing stirred. Anna began to pace back and forth to keep her circulation going. How was she to survive this? Where was she? How far from any human settlement? Would daylight give her some direction? Would she live to see the dawn? Tiring quickly, she paused and listened to the frigid stillness.

She was about to start moving again when she heard something. It was indiscernible, but she had heard *something*. Her numbed feet carried her back to the ditch. Her eyes moved over the charred carriage.

She heard the noise again. It was the crackle of a tiny fire, she realized, for a small flame exploded now, as if feasting on some part of the carriage that had not yet been burned.

Hope dared to tempt an almost hopeless Anna. She hurried down into the ditch. Before she could build on that tiny flame, she knew what she had to do. The body was host to the immortal soul, and even in its lifeless state, deserved a respectful burial. Of course, she could not bury the children herself, but—God willing—someone would see that they be laid to their final rest in Christian fashion.

Anna reached into the overturned carriage, and—with great difficulty—pulled from it the remains of little Babette, dragging her some distance farther down the length of the ditch.

She returned for Louis. The boy's body was hideously burned; eyeless sockets stared out of a featureless face. Anna pulled his body some thirty paces, to where his sister lay.

She turned now and fell to her knees. A spasm of retching overcame her. What little she had eaten earlier spilled out into the snow.

Why did two innocents have to die? Life had scarcely begun for them. She could not help but think that they were dead because *she* had been targeted by her husband.

Knowing that the cold could kill with no further help from Antoni, Anna focused her mind on one thing: survival. She rushed back to the carriage, praying that the flame had not gone out. She found it quickly and nursed it with bits of wood and other flammables that had escaped the fire. It responded with a modest vigor, sending up a little stream of smoke. She scrambled about in the deep snow, searching for branches and twigs. It was not long before the fire was radiating real heat.

Doffing what stays remained in her hair, she let her long brown tresses swing before the warmth of the fire. It mattered little if it were singed, as long as it became dry again. She was cold and wet through and through, but those modest flames kept her alive that February morning.

Hours passed. The black night turned to blue. Daylight would not be long in coming.

Anna kept moving to keep warm and to keep the fire from going out. Each search for firewood took her farther along the ditch or deeper into the spruce forest. Each step tired her more than the last. Like the fire, she was weakening. Through it all, congestion began to develop in her lungs and head.

As day dawned in the east—a *cold* red, it seemed—Anna could see that this road indeed had been taking them in a southwesterly direction. The rising sun seemed to intensify the whiteness that lay all about her. The spruces were at her back and before her was nothing but a wide expanse of flat, wild fields laden with white. Farther south, a great distance away, stood a forest of strong birches, like tall, thin, snow-spattered soldiers.

Anna began to tremble with a chill that came from within. How far am I from a settlement? she asked herself, trying to hold down a new panic. How far from another living soul?

Was it best to stay and hope someone happened upon her, or should she follow the road? There was nothing the way they had come, she thought; they had covered too much distance since the last inn. Or had it only seemed so? Should she move ahead? That thought gave her pause because she knew she did not wish to find herself in Opole and at the mercy of Antoni.

As Anna prayed to make the right decision, she experienced the same sensation she had had at the pond: her spirit seemed to disengage itself from her body. She floated upward, upward until she felt as though she were high above, looking down at the trees, the snow—and herself. She was but one of a few dark specks in an enormous bowl of the whitest yogurt.

With this experience came feelings of insignificance and helplessness. A sense of profound despair enveloped her. Whole minutes seemed to lapse while she watched herself moving about aimlessly on the blanched landscape below.

Suddenly, spirit and body became one again when she heard a noise! She listened to the deathly calm. It had sounded like a dog's bark.

There! It came again, and yet again. The distant sounds of dogs barking came from the birch forest, so far to the south. It was the sound of hunting dogs, tamed hunting dogs. Men must be near!

As if to assure her, a hunting cry sounded on the light morning wind. They would be peasants, she thought, praying that they were God-fearing.

She waited. No one came into sight. Though she sorely wanted to call out or scream, her upbringing as a noblewoman precluded such behavior.

Minutes melted away. She knelt because she could stand no longer. A half hour passed; the morning remained silent as a tomb.

The cold was so fully in her head and nose that she had to breathe the icy air through her mouth. Her throat was raw and sore, her lungs tight.

No sign of life in or near the birch forest. Help had been near, but had passed her by. Anna was too cold to cry. *How could I remain so stupidly silent?* It would be the last time she would place the fine delineations of her class above her very life. But was it too late?

Countess Anna Maria Grawlinska stood. She screamed without

thinking: "Jesus Christ, help me!" Her hoarse voice seemed so very small on the wind. It would not carry far. Panic, held at bay for so long, surged within her. She and her child were as good as dead. She repeated her urgent call. And then again.

Anna was so chilled that she thought of jumping upon the fire, but she looked down to see that it had died. There was not a single ember to warm her.

"Help me!" she cried. "Help! Let someone hear!"

She kept moving about in circles. Every part of her was becoming numb. She clapped the huge gloves together to revive her hands.

"In the name of a merciful God, help me!"

Anna stumbled now and fell to her knees. If there were no one to help her, she prayed that death would be quick in coming.

The dogs barked again.

Anna raised her head to the far-off birches, pulling her hair back from her face. The sounds seemed louder than before.

There, just emerging from the trees, were a half-dozen dogs, bounding now toward her. Behind them came the figures of perhaps ten men, three on horseback. They, too, began to move in her direction.

Anna had no time to rejoice, so fearful was she that the men would not respect her because she had screamed out like some madwoman.

She stood and collected herself in the long minutes it took for them to reach her.

"I am a noblewoman," she told them when they finally stood before her, their faces stricken by her appearance and the sight of the bodies. She stood rigid and spoke with an authority she didn't feel. "I am in need of your aid."

She nervously surveyed the group of crudely clad men who gaped at her. Their silence unnerved her.

"My carriage was set upon and two children were killed." As she spoke, she became filled with humiliation to hear her own teeth clicking and chattering from the cold. "I . . . need dry clothes and food. Then I wish to . . . return to Warsaw."

One of the mounted men was clearly the leader. With surprising agility for so large a man, he jumped from his horse and approached Anna. The small blue eyes above a black beard seemed opaque. "Who are you?" he asked.

"I am Anna Maria Berezowska, Countess of Sochaczew." Anna dared not use the name of Grawlinska. If she were close to Opole, he would know the name.

"And your destination, milady?"

"That does not matter now." The question had caught her off guard. "I only wish to return to Warsaw."

He studied her for a minute, then turned away.

She stood tall and erect, secretly quaking, while she watched them move about, looking at the bodies.

The leader barked out orders to his men in a swift and low dialect Anna could not follow. When he returned to her, he held in his hand an unsheathed hunting knife. With their backs to the leader and Anna, several of the men formed a circle around the two. Anna shook, as much from fear as from cold. She said nothing, praying that they would not dare touch a noblewoman, but knowing that times were changing. Peasants were bolder now. She had only to think of her own father's death.

Anna's heart moved to her throat as she saw him reach for her. He forced her to remove her sodden cloak. The dress underneath was just as wet. His large hands gripped her shoulders and turned her so that her back was to him.

Anna started to protest, but he ordered her silence. He went on speaking to her, but her mind raced so fast she couldn't comprehend.

What was he doing?

Anna felt his hands take hold of the folds of her dress at her waist. His knife now ripped through the bodice of the dress in one long, up-ward stroke.

She screamed and wheeled about. "Stop! What are you doing? I am a noblewoman, do you hear? You are not to touch me with your filthy hands!"

The man gripped Anna's arms and held her until her hysteria waned.

"Lady Berezowska, we will do you no harm." He spoke slowly and deliberately and with peasant common sense. "We heard your plea on the wind and we will not refuse help. You are ill with the cold. You may die if you do not obey. We will help, milady."

Anna was powerless to resist. He was right: she was very ill.

The man removed all of her clothing, even the wet goatskin that had protected her belly. Anna stood with her head on her chest, her wet, tangled hair blessedly hiding the degradation that made the cold of secondary importance.

The men worked together, silently wrapping Anna in warm bearskins.

"We will take you to our home," the leader said.

"I cannot ride."

"You are with child, I know. Two of my men have prepared a litter for you."

In a short while, they were ready to leave the site where so many had died.

Anna lay on the litter constructed of two spruce spines and leather wrappings. A flap of bearskin came down over her head to shelter her face.

Two men were designated to be the first to carry Anna, and the slow trek began. She wondered how far they had to go.

As time went on, she fell asleep and dreamt.

Anna stood in Warsaw's Market Square. It was filled with shouting, laughing people. As she was pushed and shouldered by the crowd, she nearly slipped on the wet stones. She looked down to see that the wetness was blood.

The people were clamoring about a huge platform upon which had been erected the facsimile of a French *guillotine*.

All of the Polish nobles of the kingdom were being put to death. One by one, they stepped up to the slicing machine, and—one by one—their heads fell to the ground.

There was no basket to catch the bloodied heads. Instead, they rolled across the square, prodded by the feet of the jeering peasants, who had cleared a pathway for them.

As the heads rolled past where Anna stood, it seemed as though the eyes and mouths were still moving in lively fashion. The heads passed into a winding hillside street above the River Vistula. Down they rolled, spinning in the spiral street like a released cache of marbles, until, one after another, they splashed into the river waters.

On the stairs leading to the *guillotine,* Anna saw acquaintances of her parents and her few childhood friends. She saw Baron Michał Kolbi. Next in line was her aunt. "Aunt Stella!" she called. But her aunt didn't hear.

Behind her was Zofia. "Zofia!" Anna screamed. "Zofia!"

Her cousin turned her imperious head at the cry, the dark eyes dilating. She smiled in recognition. Raising her arm now, Zofia did not wave but pointed in Anna's direction.

The executions were immediately halted. A hush fell over the crowd as the last head wheeled past Anna. Every eye in the square turned upon her. Men in strange, disheveled uniforms were moving toward her.

They roughly picked her up, and while the mob cheered wildly, they began carrying her—held high in a horizontal position—toward the scaffolding.

Her throat was tight and raw and sore. *No!* she wanted to call out, but the voice would not come.

34

Anna was jostled into consciousness when the peasants carrying the litter placed her near a hearth in a large stone and timbered room. With his blue eyes, somehow less opaque now, the leader of the men stared down at her. "You will be safe now, milady. I leave you to our women."

Anna made an effort to speak, but her throat had closed.

He put his finger to his lips. "There, no talk. Only rest."

Anna closed her eyes. She was aware that many had come to see her. She sensed them hovering over her, speaking in low tones. She did not try to understand what they said.

She slept deeply, feeling herself being moved about at some point, but she did not allow herself to come fully awake.

When Anna did awaken, only one other person remained in the huge room. A woman stood a few feet away busily preparing something at the hearth. No sooner had Anna opened her eyes than the woman hurried over to her. She was blond, not yet forty; Anna thought her attractive. She spoke in the same strange dialect as the men. "I am Lucyna . . . Does the Countess wish to use the chamber pot?"

Had Anna the strength, she would have laughed at the greeting. As it was, she could only shake her head: her throat, like her forehead, felt as if it were on fire. When Anna raised her hand in a gesture of refusal, she saw that she had been dressed in a peasant nightdress.

Lucyna seemed to read her thoughts. "We women dressed you, milady."

Soon other women in colorless, sacklike dresses came into the high-ceilinged room, setting to work around the huge hearth. Their ages varied. They seldom spoke to one another, and when they did it was in a quiet, respectful tone. Anna sensed they occasionally chanced to steal furtive looks at her.

When the meal was prepared, everyone gathered in this room that served both as kitchen and dining hall. Clearly, several families lived and worked together in what seemed to be a very large dwelling. It was a clan, Anna realized, and for all appearances, a rather harmonious one. She had thought clans such as this belonged to some bygone era, but here was proof to the contrary.

"Does the Countess wish some soup?"

"Will the Countess eat?"

"Some milk, milady?"

Anna was too ill to answer. She put her head to her pillow and fell back into a feverish sleep.

The next thing Anna knew someone was gently shaking her. The clan's meal had ended. "Open your mouth, child. Open your mouth."

Anna looked up to see a thin old man whom the others called Owl Eyes. He pinched her cheeks, inducing her to obey. He peered into her mouth. He squeezed her cheeks again. "Open wider, child."

Anna silently cursed him, wishing he would go away.

He placed a vile smelling herb against her nose, and she immediately sneezed. The paroxysm racked her body. A woman held a cloth over Anna's mouth and nose, wiping away the matter that escaped. Anna sneezed again and could taste blood in her throat.

The old man made soft-sounding comments as though pleased. "Now, child," he said, "baby tears will better your wind-sore and bleeding throat."

Anna could not imagine what he meant. She wished only to be left in peace.

His thin but authoritative voice called out to one of the women: "Sylwia, bring your child here."

When Anna opened her eyes, she was startled to see Owl Eyes holding a naked baby above her. He slapped its rump now and the straining and reddened face was held over Anna. One of the women held Anna's mouth open.

Anna could taste the warm, brackish tears falling onto her tongue and trickling to the back of her throat. She tried to resist this old folk practice, but the hands holding her head and mouth were strong.

Owl Eyes struck the child until Anna thought the shrill and pitiful cries would drive her mad. Soon, a second child was employed in this same manner.

Afterward, Anna lay physically and emotionally exhausted, the cries still ringing in her ears. She recognized, though, that the sprinkling of salty tears had given blessed relief to her mouth and throat. She slept again.

A heavy knocking, a persistent metal-against-wood thudding, resounded through the cavernous dwelling.

Anna huddled at her place by the hearth, fearing at once that the safety the clan afforded was to be taken from her.

A huge stone-faced man stood before her now while the roused peasants clustered behind him in the chilled room. He was Russian.

"I've come for you, Lady Grawlinska," he said in poor Polish.

"Who are you?"

"I've been sent by your husband to take you on to Opole."

"Like the others?"

"Unfortunately, they met up with highwaymen."

"It was not the highwaymen who poisoned Louis and Babette!"

"You must come, my lady. The Grawlinski family awaits you."

"No, you mean to kill me."

"Come along quietly, won't you?"

"I will *not* go quietly!" Anna pulled herself to her feet and ran to the clan leader. "You mustn't give me over to this man. He has been hired by my husband to kill me."

The leader did not appear to understand.

Anna's desperate eyes scanned the room for the others' faces. The peasants' expressions were inscrutable. She ran from one to the next, begging their help.

They stood unmoved and unmoving. They did not understand. Suddenly, Anna thought that perhaps they *did* understand: perhaps they were merely relishing the sight of a countess, a member of the often-hated nobility, receive her comeuppance. Her heart dropped in despair.

The ugly Russian moved toward her. His massive arms, like a vulture's wings, swooped down and upon her.

Anna awoke in a sweat. The women were starting to filter in quietly to make breakfast.

Physically, however, Anna felt a little better. She could swallow. And for the first time in a long while, she felt as though she could think.

The despair of the dream did not abate, however. She could not forget that her husband had arranged for her death and was responsible for the deaths of two innocents. Anna recalled his warning: he had said that if she dared stand in his way he would kill her. Or had *she* put those words in his mouth? Whichever the case, she believed it now.

Antoni was serious enough to do it. He wanted only her property and wealth. He did not want her, and he certainly did not want a child not his own. Her death would be a windfall for him. He could do what he wanted with her inheritance, perhaps even realize his dream of catapulting himself to magnate status.

Who were the dead Poles? she asked herself. She knew that they were not highwaymen. They had asked for her. Someone had sent them to rescue her, but who?

How close was she to Opole and the Grawlinski estate? The thought that one of the Russians had survived sent a chill along her spine. That Antoni would soon find out she had escaped the carriage seemed likely. He would then search for her.

As long as she remained here, her identity must be kept secret. She now wished she had not used even her maiden name.

Her return to Warsaw must be arranged as quickly as possible. Out of fear that Antoni would find out, she dared not write for Zofia or Aunt Stella to send a carriage. She knew, too, that she could make no effective accusation in a letter. Her aunt and cousin would be skeptical.

She would get to Warsaw on her own. But what then? Would she be able to convince her aunt and cousin? The authorities? What real proof would she have if she accused Antoni? Who would believe her? Her heart caught at the thought that she might even arrive to find Antoni there waiting for her.

Perhaps she should go to the Lubicki home. The banking family had always been close to her parents. But would they believe her? Might Antoni have thought of that? He would have prepared a story already.

Neither would going to Sochaczew be wise. At her family home she would be isolated and an easy target.

What about Jan Stelnicki? A message might be sent to the Queen's Head. But what assurance did she have that he would be in the capital? She could not just wait about on the chance that the letter got to him.

Anna's head spun. The possibilities had come full circle with each cancellation. No, she would find her own way to Warsaw. But she knew that once she got there, Jan was the only one she could safely seek out. He would know what to do. Her heart warmed at the thought of him.

Anna suddenly felt the baby kick. It was the first time she actually felt the life within. It seemed the best of omens. Her whole body seemed to pulse with warm life. She smiled to herself. *I must get well.* After eating a breakfast of milk and buttered bread, she slept.

When Anna awoke at midmorning, she was startled to find that there was only one other person in the hall, a young man of eighteen or nineteen. He sat with a steaming mug, staring at her.

She sat up slowly, warily, the aroma of his chicory reviving her.

He put down his mug, stood, and approached Anna.

"Who are you?" she asked. He was shaven and well dressed. He was no peasant.

Anna's stomach tightened. She feared that he would start speaking Russian, that he had been sent by Antoni, that her dream was becoming reality.

He smiled, still moving closer.

Finally, he stood before her. "I am sorry if I alarmed you, my lady," he said.

His speech was Polish—high Polish.

Anna sighed. "Just for a moment."

"I'm sorry. My name is Antek."

Anna nodded. "I am Lady Anna Maria Berezowska."

"Hello, my lady." He bowed. "May I sit down?"

"Of course." Anna watched as he fetched a stool. He was a handsome young man: muscular body, brown hair, good features.

"You've come from Warsaw?"

"Yes."

"Where are you going?"

"I only wish to go back to Warsaw now."

"I see," Antek said. "I've not been to the capital. I imagine life there is very different. I should very much like to see it."

"I'm sure you will one day. Just how far am I from Warsaw, Antek?"

"Five or six days in this weather."

Anna let out a little gasp. They had come farther than she had imagined. Had they been traveling east as she supposed, they would have been into Russia by now. *How am I to get back?*

"You look stunned, Lady Berezowska."

"What? Oh, I'm sorry. Just distracted for the moment. Tell me, Antek, where are you from?"

"Why, this is my home."

"What?"

"You've met the patriarch here, Witek?"

"Yes, though I didn't know his name."

"He is my father."

"Your father?—But surely you are not—" Anna could not find the words.

"Like the others? A peasant, you mean? Ah, but I am." He smiled boyishly. "You are mystified by my clothes and speech?"

Anna nodded.

"I must explain. My mother died giving birth to me and my brother. Oh, I have a twin: Stefan. Witek was devastated by my mother's death, and, I think, intimidated by the prospect of raising two infants. As it happened, Baron Galki, the landlord of this old ruined castle and all the land you can see from its tower, struck up an agreement with Witek. He and the baroness were childless. Stefan and I were given over to them and, in return, the clan is allowed to make their home here and live in freedom."

Anna had never heard anything quite like it. But the young man seemed beyond deception. "So you don't live here, then?"

"No, I live at the Galki family manor, a distance south."

"You came to visit Witek?"

"He sent for us, so that we might discuss what to do with you once you are on your feet."

"I see. Stefan is here, too?"

"He'll arrive tonight."

Anna let out a nearly silent sigh. Here was hope on the horizon. "How far are we from Opole?" she asked, attempting a casualness she didn't feel.

"Opole is the nearest city. It's under a day's journey west."

Anna was relieved. She wished it a hundred days' away, but one was enough distance between her and Antoni—for now, she hoped.

"Is there another city or town nearby?" she asked.

"Just south of here is Częstochowa."

Anna felt her jaw go slack. "Oh, Antek, have you seen it? The Black Madonna?"

"Of course. Many times."

"They say the painting has miraculous powers."

"So they say . . . Tell me, Lady Berezowska, are you in need of a miracle?"

"What?" Anna smiled. "Perhaps, I am."

"Don't worry. Stefan and I will devise a way for you to return to Warsaw. Is that the miracle you need?"

If only that would be miracle enough, Anna thought. "Perhaps," she said. "It is funny, Antek. You've seen the Black Madonna and wish to go to Warsaw. I've seen Warsaw and would like to see the Black Madonna."

They laughed together like old friends. The name *Antek*, Anna suddenly realized, was the diminutive for *Antoni*. How strange that it only just now came to her. She had never called her own husband *Antek*. She doubted that she ever would.

After Antek left, Anna thought about the Black Madonna. More than any fairy tale, more than any of her favorite myths, it had always fascinated her. Originally a Byzantine icon, it found its way to the cloister of the Pauline Fathers in the fourteenth century. During the next century, it was painted over after it was damaged by the Hussites, thus accounting for the darkness of the picture and the two sword cuts on the Lady's right cheek. In 1655 the site of the cloister provided the turning point in the war against Sweden. Since then Poles looked to the Black Madonna as Queen of the Polish Crown and patron saint of Poland. For the moment Anna forgot about her many difficulties and longed only to see the Dark Lady.

Later, the hall became a hive of activity. Some women prepared sausages. Others cleaned fowl that had been newly caught. Three or four older women sat sewing and talking in the warmth of the hearth. While Lucyna and another woman prepared the noon meal, Owl Eyes stood, at some distance, hunched over a table, cutting leather.

Only one person was watching Anna: an old woman sitting alone working on a piece of leathercraft. Anna had noticed her before. Unlike these other women, she hadn't shown Anna the slightest deference or courtesy. The many lines of her weathered face seemed to meet in a scowl at her thin lips. Whenever she chose to speak to the others, it was with a quick and slicing tongue.

Anna returned her gaze. Even a smile did not break the ice. In time, the woman looked away. But every so often, Anna could sense the saucer eyes beneath sparse and wiry hair spying in her direction. She was like an old cat, Anna thought, half-frightened and half ready to pounce.

Lunch and supper were substantial meals, and Anna ate what she could. Her health was slowly mending.

In the evening, Stefan arrived.

Anna sat at her place by the hearth. She stared in amazement as Antek introduced him. He was the mirrored reflection of his brother: the same brown, wavy hair, sculpted features, muscular physique.

"One of you must grow a beard immediately," Anna said. "Otherwise, I shall not be able to tell you apart."

The twins laughed.

Stefan kissed Anna's hand. "You don't see any difference between us?" he asked.

"Let me see," Anna said, her eyes moving from one to the other. "Of course! Antek, you have a little mole on your cheek. Stefan, where is yours?"

"I was cheated, if you must know," Stefan said. He draped his arm around Antek. "You see, the girls adore that little mole, don't they, brother?"

Antek colored in embarrassment.

Anna silently concurred that the mole did give Antek the advantage, but she sensed immediately that Stefan possessed a gregariousness and forward sensuality that probably more than evened the score. Both brothers were striking. They had gotten their height, strength, and masculinity from Witek, she supposed, but it must have been their deceased mother who had willed them her good looks.

"I was sorry to hear of your accident," Stefan said.

Antek shot a sidelong glance at his brother, a reproach that only Anna noticed.

"A tragic thing," he continued. "I understand two children died at the site. They were not yours, were they?"

"No, but they were in my care. They were innocent victims."

"It is all very sad, but it is in the past now," Antek said, attempting to sideline his brother's conversation. "The countess is expecting her first child and must look only forward."

"Of course," Stefan said. "Forgive me. I trust you are feeling better."

"I improve a little each day," Anna said, "though you wouldn't know it to look at me."

"Nonsense," Stefan said. "You are very beautiful. Wouldn't you say, Antek?"

"Indeed."

"Thank you." It was an awkward moment. Anna had not meant to fish for compliments. "Now if you both don't sit down, I shall get a stiff neck looking up at you."

The brothers drew up stools. While they did so, Anna noticed for the first time that they were not alone in the hall. A movement in the shadows near the far door drew her eyes to a shrouded figure there. An inner sense told Anna it was the old woman who had seemed to take an instant dislike to her.

Anna ignored the chill her presence inspired and addressed the twins in a serious tone. "What is to be done about the bodies at the carriage site?"

"That has already been seen to," Antek said. "They have been given burial. You are not to worry."

"It is at least one worry I can put aside," Anna said. "Please thank those men responsible."

"I understand you want to return to Warsaw," Stefan said.

"Yes, as soon as possible."

"Is that where your husband is?" Stefan asked.

Husband. Anna felt her face flush hot. "No, he will not be found in the city."

"Is there someone there who would send a carriage?" Antek asked.

"No."

"We would take you ourselves, my lady," Antek said, "but our father will not allow it. He's afraid the city life would be too appealing to two country boys."

"Men!" Stefan countered. "We are eighteen."

"I would gladly pay for the carriage and driver's service, of course." Anna was trying to hold back despair. The longer she stayed here, the greater the chance of Antoni's finding her.

Antek could see her concern. "There is the monastery at Częstochowa, my lady. They have carriages and the abbot does go to Warsaw on occasion."

Anna's heart lifted.

"Father Florian, a priest from the monastery, will be here on Sunday next," Stefan said. "He comes every other Sunday to attend to the clan. He holds Mass in the old chapel."

"We'll approach Father Florian with your situation," Antek explained. "I'm certain he'll help you get back to Warsaw."

Thank God, Anna thought.

The old woman came out of the shadows now. Shouting what seemed gibberish to Anna, she seemed to be upbraiding Antek and Stefan. She fired off a question, spit out a retort to their answers, then demanded something else.

The twins answered her respectfully in the low dialect, nervously casting glances at Anna. They were embarrassed.

At last the old woman's babbling exploded into a barrage of curses leveled at the brothers.

Antek grew angry now. He spoke sharply to the old woman.

She shrank back slightly at his words, the cat's eyes assessing the situation.

She turned on Anna, pointing an accusing finger and letting fly another spate of unintelligible syllables. Then she wheeled about and fled the room.

Anna stared after her.

"I apologize for Nelka, my lady," Antek said, turning to Anna. He seemed upset and humiliated.

"Who is she?" Anna asked.

"She is Witek's mother," he said, his eyes lowered, "our grandmother."

"It would seem she doesn't like me," Anna said.

"Don't worry about her, my lady," Stefan said. "She doesn't like anyone not of the clan."

"My brother understates the case," Antek said. "The fact is, Nelka has difficulty getting along with a good many people *in* the clan."

"But what is it that she harbors against me?"

"It is only that you are an outsider," Stefan said.

Anna was doubtful. "Isn't it that I am a noblewoman?"

The twins looked shamefaced.

"Yes," Antek said. "Her one experience at the hands of a noblewoman . . . well, it's useless to go into. It led to tragic consequences."

"And," Stefan added, "she has never gotten over Witek's giving us over to Baron Galki."

"I see. But I am sure I detected some specific animosity toward me."

The brothers hesitated to speak.

Anna's questioning eyes persisted.

Antek finally spoke up. "She was listening to our conversation. When Nelka learned that your husband would not be coming to take you home, and that he was not to be found in Warsaw . . . well, she has quite an imagination."

"And what does she imagine?" Anna asked.

"She suspects," Stefan said awkwardly, "that you are not wed at all and that you are running away because of your fatherless baby."

"Oh." Anna was stunned. "You can be certain that my husband does exist." It was strange, she thought, to attest to a marriage she wished did *not* exist.

Still, Anna could not help but think there was more. "When your grandmother pointed at me, what was she saying then?"

The twins were silent. Stefan's face was a mask, but Antek wore his heart in his hazel eyes.

"Lady Berezowska," Antek said, "I beg you to overlook Nelka's eccentricities. The clan still holds to many old and groundless superstitions. What she said can only hurt you. It is better to–"

"I want to know," Anna insisted.

Antek grimaced in defeat. He sighed. "She said that your child was sired by the devil and . . ."

"Go on."

". . . that such a one as you should be treated as witches once were by the ancients–driven out with lighted candles and a hearth poker."

35

Zofia was bored to distraction. She paced from room to room, waiting for Count Henryk Literski. What was keeping him?'

She walked to the window of the reception room and pulled back the lace curtains. Dusk was settling its violet shadows on the Vistula. Still no sign of Henryk. She swung around in irritation. The house was so quiet, so damnably quiet.

She missed Anna. The realization surprised her. Without Anna and the French children, the house was a crypt. There had been no word from her, either. Zofia smiled, thinking of her poor cousin saddled with those foreign brats. One of my more clever maneuvers, she thought.

Anna's going to Saint Petersburg was for the best. She would be reconciled to her husband in the end, of course. She had no choice. That was the way of it, Zofia decided, women who were too slow to choose for themselves would always have their choices made by others.

Zofia heard a door close nearby. She was certain it was her mother, floating about the house like a quiet specter. Oh, she had seemed to return to normal, to her daughter's surprise, but she spoke only to the servants. She could not resign herself to the life Zofia had forged. Now, the dowager countess was no doubt secluding herself in her sewing room as she characteristically did these days after supper. She seldom sewed, however. Her current interests were exclusively political. Zofia would hear her musing to herself or anyone who would listen. What might Catherine do? What would Austria and Prussia try next? How was Poland to protect herself? Would Stanisław stand firm with the Constitution? Zofia wanted to scream when she found her mother knee deep in *Monitor*s and preoccupied with one political move or another. And it was not only her mother: Warsaw was awash in nothing but political talk and rumors. She hated it.

Baron Michał Kolbi had spoken politics, too, one day when he came calling, asking for Anna. He asked question after question about her welfare and seemed quite concerned that they had had no word. But why should *he* be so concerned? Zofia could make nothing of it. Did Anna have a power over men? Zofia had not forgiven Kolbi for failing to respond to her flirtation at Anna's little party, and so she answered his questions in the most perfunctory manner, wishing to herself that she actually had some information about Anna to suppress from the pompous ass.

For every little failure like Kolbi, however, Zofia could produce a ledger of successes. She could juggle flirtations with three men in one night, intimating to each that she was ripe for the picking. Sometimes she was. Inevitably, she chose to pursue the most challenging of the lot. If he were married, fine. If he were married and had a mistress, even better. There was even one who had a wife, a mistress, and a male lover. Oh, the delight in upsetting that little menagerie! She had learned that with the right precautions against conception she did not have to deny herself to anyone she found attractive. But she was finding fewer and fewer attractive in recent weeks. The sexual aspect of the liaisons seemed to actually bore her now; no one man held her interest for long.

There was but one chase, one challenge, that had not abated: Jan Stelnicki. Why couldn't she get him out of her mind? No other man had ever so dominated her thoughts. She smiled to herself. Perhaps it was merely that he had been denied to her.

Jan lived in the city now. And with Anna gone, she thought, there must be a way to entice him. Jan became for her the Golden Fleece.

Her answer to this self-imposed quest had come in the form of

Count Henryk Literski. Zofia found the young man repulsive: ugly, classless, hopelessly simple. But he was smitten with her, worshipped her. What could she do but take advantage of him?

Henryk, a landless noble with neither occupation nor interest, lived on the profits of a modest trust. He became a willing spy for Zofia, daily observing the comings and goings of Count Jan Stelnicki. He recorded everything in a little yellow journal and reported regularly to her. If he had an inkling that it was some inner passion for Jan that drove Zofia to such measures, he didn't show it. Zofia occasionally hinted at some vague political motive. He asked few questions. When she appeared satisfied with some bit of information, his thin, pockmarked face beamed. This was enough for him, this and the vague, unspoken promise that one day he might expect more than a light brushing of her lips against his pitted cheek.

From Henryk, Zofia learned that Jan's world was relatively small. Any excitement in it was political excitement, an oxymoron in her view. All of his friends were connected to the government and king in some way. Many of them seemed old enough to be contemporaries of his father. They were all male; he did not seek out the companionship of women. When not giving speeches at political functions, he was writing them at the small town house he had rented. There, he was served by a middle-aged woman named Wanda.

Often, he went down to the riverfront and sat brooding in a tavern called Queen's Head, one Henryk called a hellhole. From there, Zofia surmised, he could see the white Gronski town house across the river.

She turned back to the window now, again drawing back the curtains. Her gaze searched the modest shop fronts across the Vistula. She could imagine him there in the weeks before her cousin's departure staring across the river, hoping for a glimpse of Anna.

Zofia felt her face flushing hot with jealousy. How had Anna won that kind of allegiance from a man such as Jan? How had *she* lost it? Where had she gone wrong?

How was she to read his current Spartan behavior? Was he adjusting to life without Anna? To life without hope of Anna? Was he facing up to reality?

Here at least was a chance, she thought. Her heart quickened at the challenge. She fantasized herself seducing him, even marrying him.

Thoughts of missing Anna were suddenly dispelled by the old anger at her for foiling the plans for Jan. She thought of a dozen ways to tell Anna that Jan was now her conquest. She *would* triumph in the end.

Zofia had written to him, a letter that skirted an apology and hinted at her interest. He failed to rise to the bait, however. Henryk found its burned remains in an ashtray at the tavern.

Zofia was not surprised. She assumed it was his pride that kept him from responding. She was not to be discouraged. His reticence merely piqued what was becoming for her an obsession.

She would resort to more pointed measures. The opportunity would come, and if she could not win him, she would at least avenge herself in full measure against him and against Anna, whose appearance in her life would have ruined everything, were it not for her own ingenuity. They would both pay.

Henryk arrived at last. Had he known, Zofia would later muse, that the news he brought her this day could have bought for him an afternoon of delights in Zofia's bedchamber, he would have played it to his advantage. But his simple mind was too thickened by her beauty.

The information came after Henryk produced the most recent litany of Count Stelnicki's activities. Henryk spilled it out without an inflection or blink of the eyes: "Oh, and in a fortnight Lord Stelnicki is to attend the ball of the Countess Lubomirska."

"What?" Zofia gasped. It was so unlike Jan, who didn't go to purely social events. "How do you know?"

"I was at the next table. I heard everything. He doesn't want to go, but his friends convinced him. They seemed to imply that this would be the last of the great parties for some time." Henryk looked puzzled. "Do you know why that is, Zofia?"

"No, I don't. And I don't care. Tell me about this ball, Henryk, before I turn you upside down and shake the words out of you. You took your sweet time to get to this news."

Henryk appeared startled and confused by Zofia's sudden zeal. "It's to be held in a fortnight."

"Yes, yes, you said that."

"It's to be a masquerade."

"What?"

"A masquerade," he repeated, "You know, Zofia, when the guests all come in—"

"Idiot! I know what a masquerade is. Did you learn anything else?"

Henryk looked hurt. "Only that the count is to go as Emperor Justinian."

This is too good to be true, Zofia thought. Her chance had come. If she couldn't fish an invitation, she would go anyway. Masquerades were incredibly easy to infiltrate. She had done just that a half dozen times. It was always the most marvelous fun.

While Henryk droned on about some insipid costume ball he had attended once, Zofia began to plot: the invitation, the costume, the pleasurable snare that would at once bring down Jan and Anna.

"Zofia," Henryk said, "just who is this Justinian? Is he emperor of some tiny continental nation?"

"Why, Henryk, you *are* a fool." Zofia laughed. "Justinian ruled the Byzantine Empire in the sixth century!"

"Oh."

Poor oaf, Zofia thought. Henryk was incapable of discerning the meanness in her laugh.

36

Anna slept fitfully, awakening to find herself alone in the hall. The hearth's fire flickered weakly. It must be very late, she thought. For a moment she was certain she heard something stir in the darkness. Her first thought was of the old woman, and her heart tightened. Long, long minutes ticked by, with the only sound a faint sputtering from the hearth. She found herself staring up at the blurred and swaying shadows on the timbered ceiling, slowly losing thought.

It was then that she felt a strange heat at the base of her spine. Some minutes passed and the warmth grew feverish, radiating down through her thighs to her legs to the very bones of her feet and toes and simultaneously up through her upper body, streaming along her spine and into her head. The heat carried with it an intense energy that rendered her captive. She lay there, helpless, unable to move or speak.

The force that ran through her body suddenly caused her to shake uncontrollably, as if with palsy. White light exploded in her head like so many capsizing stars. Her heartbeat accelerated and a strange, erratic breathing pattern took over. She experienced then what seemed like a hundred emotions at once, some delightful, some terrifying. She plunged into a swirling labyrinth of love and hate, fear and desire, strength and weakness.

Visions flew at her. Multitudes of people. Loving faces, angry faces, blank faces. Strange as well as familiar visages loomed in front of her, moved down toward her, dissipating, one making way for the next. Anna stared at them as if in search of a particular one. Or perhaps in search of all of them and a life gone by. She saw her beloved grandmother. Childhood friends. Peasants from the Sochaczew estate. And then her parents—her father's face radiant like a god's, her mother's with the smile that was not a smile. Had they come for her? Were they to be reunited? Was she to have a family once again?

Her parents' faces seemed then to fuse, their features blending into one image, unrecognizable, dark and threatening. The eyes were neither that of her father's blue nor her mother's violet-gray. Now, the hooded brow sheltered eyes of fire. Still, these were the eyes of *someone* she knew. Someone she hated and feared. Her heart convulsed. Who was it? The red eyes glowed and though Anna realized eyes could not laugh, she knew that these orbs of evil were laughing at her.

The eyes moved down upon her as if to possess her. "No," Anna wanted to scream, then did scream. Or did she?

Somehow, she slowly gathered within herself a strength that grew and grew, until she forced out of her body the foreign energy that had fired the hideous vision. Her body stopped shaking. Her breathing fell into a normal rhythm. That she was able, of her own power, to dispel the sensation amazed her.

Anna lay for a long time inert and spent. This had not been a dream, of that she was certain. She had been awake, yet in an ethereal state of complete helplessness and subject to forces beyond her imagination. It was only when she recalled the eyes of fire that her memory colored them with another hue. Yes, they glowed with a kind of red heat, but they were brown. And Anna suddenly knew to whom they belonged. Where minutes before a heat had run along her spine, a chill now encased her. She could hear her teeth chattering.

The eyes seemed diabolical, indeed. She could not help but wonder whether Nelka hadn't put the notion into her head with her talk of the devil. Anna knew of forbidden books that narrated lurid accounts of the devil violating bodies of virgins and inseminating in them seeds of corruption. And weren't the eyes of the devil reputed to be red? A shudder ran through her.

Were such things truly possible? Had the woman somehow sensed the conditions of her impending motherhood?

Anna tried to put Nelka out of her mind. No, the eyes were not the devil's. They were the eyes of one born of flesh and blood, eyes more brown than red. They were the eyes of her attacker at the pond.

Anna's hand moved up involuntarily to her parched lips. The eyes in this dream that wasn't a dream might be the key to the identity of her assailant—and of her child's father.

Whose eyes were they?

She had never met Feliks Paduch, the peasant who had sworn retribution on her father's house and family. What color were his eyes? Were they his? Was he the one?

The chill permeated her body. She pulled the heavy fur up around her neck. In truth, she knew she had no fervent desire to see those eyes again. Even if it meant not ever knowing to whom they belonged.

Beneath the fur, her hands moved down to caress her stirring womb. Of one thing she was certain: this was not the devil's child.

Anna's strength grew as she waited out the days until the arrival of Father Florian and her return to Warsaw. She lived to see Jan again. The longing for him was there, always there, even if it were attached to a guilt that would not let her relish the thought of him for any length of time.

The nourishing foods, herbs, and potions with which Owl Eyes plied her coaxed the return of her health. The soreness in the throat, the heaviness in the chest, the coughing and sniffling were all on the wane.

Anna observed the daily rituals of the clan. While old Owl Eyes, the women, and the young ones tended their tasks, the men hunted. Supper was the social event of the day, a time of good spirits. The clan kept a stable of horses, numberless hunting dogs, and several falcons. Preserved fruits and vegetables attested to large summer gardens. The families supplied Baron Galki with a portion of their yield in game and harvest.

Anna was surprised that such a feudal clan existed in modern times. But, for all their backwardness and simplicity, these people seemed more secure and happier than any she had known, peasant or noble.

Nelka was noticeably absent though Anna still sensed her presence somewhere about. Antek and Stefan stayed with the clan in the days before Father Florian's arrival. They were glad to do it, they assured her, as it gave them time with their father and the opportunity to hunt with the men. Day by day, they kept her company, each taking a shift, and in this way Anna got to know each one.

While they were twins, so alike in appearance, Anna was to find how unalike they were beneath the skin.

Antek was a talker. He and Anna conversed incessantly. Fascinated by her tales of Warsaw and the nobility there, he never exhausted his store of questions for her. He even seemed interested in Anna's life with her parents on the estate at Sochaczew. She found him remarkably well versed in politics, too; and that he shared Anna's support of the Constitution. In a brief span of time, she grew close to him and found herself confiding much of what had happened following her parents' deaths.

Anna spoke of her unhappy marriage, her love for another, her concern for her child. But she couldn't bring herself to relate the attack at the pond or the knowledge that her husband had arranged her murder. She felt relieved in what she did tell him, however. Antek was warm and understanding. He was, she felt, the brother she had never had.

Stefan was a stroke of a different brush. And it was not long before Anna felt uncomfortable in his presence. He was charming and attentive, but he and Anna had to struggle to find common ground. And there was more to it than that, she came to realize. Each time she allowed herself to look into his serious eyes, she could see his attraction.

This unnerved her.

Oddly, Stefan seemed to regard her as if she were not married and five months with child. Sometimes he made some awkward or ill-timed comment, too, that was nothing less than flirtation. Anna put this down to the lusty nature she had spied in him from the first. He was a man much concerned with women.

His behavior was out of place, she told herself, but certainly harmless.

*   *   *

Preparations for Father Florian's coming began long before the Sunday dawn.

While the women of the clan plucked wild fowl and carefully seasoned their soups and the stew that would simmer for hours, the men, who didn't hunt on this day, occupied themselves with minor household tasks. There was a quiet excitement about them that was not lost on the children, who were quick to express their glee. This was an occasion eagerly awaited by the peasants, a break from the sameness of their days.

Magda, an older daughter of Lucyna, braided Anna's hair. Then she and Lucyna led Anna to a wooden tub. The men had prepared the heated water and Anna was the first to use it. She luxuriated in the pristine warmth, assured that her return to Warsaw was imminent.

When the clan members assembled in the unheated chapel at midmorning, they were all well-groomed and dressed in their simple but immaculate Sunday Mass clothes. The twins' garments were considerably more sophisticated. The sashes at their waists, emblematic of the proud Polish male, were particularly striking.

Anna detested her own appearance. The women had attempted to sew and clean her dress, but it remained a sad sight. Over it Anna wore a homespun shawl and on her head a lace covering.

A fine impression I will make upon Father Florian, she thought. Most likely I'll be mistaken for a charwoman.

The twins were on either side of Anna as they knelt on the chipped stone floor awaiting the priest.

The customary arrival time came . . . and went.

"How are you feeling?" Antek asked.

"Fine," Anna said. Actually, she was famished. Everyone had been fasting since the previous night, so as to receive Communion.

After kneeling for some time, the worshippers sat on the hard, backless benches.

Antek excused himself, saying he was going to keep a lookout for the priest.

Anna worried that Father Florian would not come. If that were the case, how long would it be until some other travel plan were worked out for her?

To occupy her mind, she surveyed the ruined chamber. Parts of the high-beamed ceiling had rotted away and had not been replaced so that she could see—and feel on her hands and upturned face—faint flurries of snow. In gilded niches along the side walls were life-size statues of saints and apostles, the heads of which were nearly faceless from age. The marble altar was in deplorable condition, but the golden tabernacle gleamed.

In the wall behind and above the altar was a gaping circular hole where a stained glass window once had been. Anna could see out to where the bleak, white hills fused into a hazy meeting with the endless, gray winter sky.

Shivering, Anna pulled her cloak about her.

Suddenly, a faint, steady, rustling sound drew her attention again to the rafters. There, a bird—a ring-dove—was winging its way about in confusion. Stray birds must have been a common thing, Anna thought, because it seemed that only she took notice of this one. Trapped, the beautiful bird was becoming increasingly frightened. Anna watched as it flew from beam to beam, then in swift circles, in its random search for a way out. When a few feathers fell noiselessly to the ground, some of the clan members looked up.

Anna's heart tore. She feared the dove would kill herself in its panic.

Just then the dove descended into a whooshing decline and glided the length of the chapel, disappearing through the glassless aperture behind the altar.

For the moment, Anna's heart soared, too.

"Stefan, is it often that the priest . . ." Anna stopped before she could complete her question about the priest's tardiness. Nelka had turned about in her place and shot her a dart of hatred that halted her in midsentence.

Anna stared back.

The sound of the heavy chapel doors swinging open broke the silence. Anna and the others turned to see Antek with the priest.

Silently, neither looking left nor right, the tall man took long strides up the aisle, moving directly to the sanctuary.

Antek came to his place at Anna's side.

Everyone stood. With his back to the little congregation, the priest immediately concerned himself with the business of setting the altar for Mass. His tonsured hair was graying, and the crown of his head shone like a looking glass. His large frame was draped in a dark brown robe that fell to his sodden boots.

Anna assumed that Antek had already told him of her predicament.

She had thought he would seek an introduction before starting the service. He did not. Neither did he acknowledge the faithful clan he had kept waiting so long.

Anna's heart seemed to pause for the moment. Was this the man who would help her return home?

The priest turned around then to face the congregation. The Mass was about to begin. He was probably fifty, she guessed. His face was florid and plain. He had small eyes, so deeply set as to hide their color and intent. Anna judged him to be in an ill humor. His actions had seemed perfunctory; his face fell into stern folds.

Anna's attention was brought up short when she realized his eyes had stopped on her. Her first impulse was to look away. Then she steeled her nerves and returned his gaze.

The red of the priest's face deepened. He turned around immediately to finish his preparations.

He thinks me audacious, Anna thought. In his demeanor she detected conflict. What if this were but a blind wall in the labyrinth into which she had somehow stumbled? She worried that each day might be bringing Antoni closer.

Anna prayed.

The priest now descended the three short steps and strode to where Anna stood.

Antek drew Anna out into the aisle and introduced her to the priest.

"May Jesus be merciful to you," he said "and to the souls of your traveling companions." He held his hand out for Anna to kiss his ring. "Of course, I will do whatever may be in my power to see you restored to Warsaw."

Anna was weak from fasting and waiting in the cold chapel, so she remained standing. This must be shocking to the peasants, she thought, but she could not help it.

"Would my lady wish to make her confession before Mass?"

"Yes, Father."

Perhaps her first impression of the priest had been too harsh. After all, this man had come to her from the chapel of the Black Madonna. Might he be her miracle?

The confessional, situated at the front of the chapel, consisted of nothing more than a chair for the priest and a wooden kneeler for the penitent. Anna whispered to him of the carriage ordeal, describing it in

detail only at his request. She tried to be brief, knowing that the peasants were as tired and hungry as she.

Anna told the priest of Louis and Babette and her own guilt at her
impatience with them. Father Florian assured her she was guiltless. "Often, when one survives and others do not," he said, "there is this sense
of guilt. Put it aside, my child."

Anna could not bring herself to tell of her terrible suspicions about
Antoni. They seemed too unreal to put into words. And she sensed that
the priest would not believe her.

"Is yours a marriage of love?" the priest asked.

The question came unannounced and Anna could only stare
blankly. What strange power had possessed him to ask her such a
thing? "No," she said at last, "my marriage to Antoni was a . . . a kind of
arranged marriage."

"Has he beat you?"

"He struck me . . . once."

"I see." His eyes assessed her. "My dear," he sighed, "you are
young. Marriages are not like those of a young girl's dreams or those
depicted in romantic books. A marriage is a marriage when both partners bring to that relationship their fullest cooperation. It is a communion of spirits. The wife should be more concerned for her husband's
happiness than for her own, and in this way happiness will find her."

"Should the husband not be concerned with his wife's happiness?"

"Yes, of course." The priest's eyes held Anna's "But sometimes the
woman makes the bigger sacrifice."

Anna wanted to ask why it should be so, but didn't dare. Neither
did she dare to speak of how hopeless her marriage was . . . or that she
loved another.

"I am certain you have no real cause for complaint, Lady Berezowska. You should be loyal to your husband in both mind and body."

Anna cringed at the sound of her maiden name, but before she
could tell him her married name, he was absolving her. Lying about her
name would be one sin that would remain on her soul.

"I will say Mass now, then I will go with the men to the place where
your companions and the others were killed. Their burials must be
made Christian." The priest immediately announced that he was unable
to hear any other confessions that day.

As Father Florian proceeded to say Mass in what Anna thought a cursory manner, she wondered whether the peasants would resent her because the priest had no time to offer *them* Penance. The only person of nobility present had been the only one to receive the sacrament.

When the ceremony came to an end, the enigmatic Father Florian and the men of the clan took their leave.

"The Countess is not feeling well?" The words penetrated Anna's consciousness as though drawn through a tunnel. The palm of a hand was touching her forehead. "Milady?"

"What? Yes?" She lay not far from the hearth.

"You are ill?"

She opened her eyes to see Owl Eyes withdrawing his bony hand. "No . . . just a bit dizzy, I think."

"You are hungry?"

Anna could not deny it. She was famished.

The old man turned, calling to Lucyna, "Bring here a plate of your deer stew."

The woman turned from her task at the hearth and mumbled something Anna could not make out, but her tone and narrowed eyes indicated her dissent.

Owl Eyes lost patience. "It is for the countess, woman. Hurry on with it."

When Lucyna looked to Anna, her defiant manner melted away. She immediately ladled steaming stew into a wooden bowl and brought it over to where Anna lay.

But before Owl Eyes could guide the first spoonful to Anna's lips, Nelka appeared. "She will wait!" she screeched. "She must wait!"

Anna immediately understood Lucyna's initial reserve: no one was to break the fast before the priest and the other men returned from blessing the burial site.

"She is to wait!" the woman hissed. "No special privileges here!"

"The countess must eat!" Owl Eyes said. Anna was becoming more familiar with the low dialect and understood his speech now. "The Countess Berezowska is with child. Like me, you are old, Nelka. But you are a woman and cannot have forgotten what it is to bear a child. She will eat—not because she is of the nobility—but because she nourishes the helpless one within her. Am I understood?"

The old prune's face puckered hatefully. "It is the devil's child she carries!" And in an instant the woman was gone from the great hall.

"Eat now, child," Owl Eyes said softly.

Anna lay on her side, looking down at the bowl brimming with good broth, vegetables, and deer meat. Its aroma filled her nostrils. Her mouth watered. But then she looked to the several faces watching her and the several more feigning indifference. Lucyna's little daughter, Wera, stared hungrily.

"No," Anna said, pushing the bowl away. "I will wait for the men to return."

Owl Eyes protested, but she remained adamant.

A short while later, he lifted her head and pressured her to drink a strange, dark-hued brew of some kind. She found a peculiar tang to the taste, but the potion wasn't wholly disagreeable. Within moments, it seemed, she felt her eyelids become weighted.

Anna's imagination burst colorfully alive. In her mind's eye she viewed a beautiful snowy landscape, one more real than any art created by man. She could feel the cold, cold sting of the air and smell the brisk freshness of the snow.

Then came movement on this canvas. Figures of men moved about, working at some task, and as they did so, their forms and faces came into focus. She realized who they were and what they were about.

There in the icy-hard earth were the graves dug just weeks before by the peasants. This surrealistic vision emitted no sounds, but she could see one man's mouth moving in prayer, while his right hand made the sign of the cross over one grave, then the next, and the next. It was Father Florian, Anna realized. Then she spied two smaller mounds: Louis's and Babette's resting places for all eternity. Tiny, frigid graves without markers.

Anna struggled now to stay awake. The priest—her link to the outside world, her link to home—would be returning. *I must keep my wits about me,* she thought, even while descending into a drugged sleep. *I must keep my wits. . . .*

It was Stefan who, hours later, informed Anna that the priest had returned to Częstochowa without her.

Anna sat up and stared in disbelief. "But . . . why?"

"It was decided that you were in no condition to go. You didn't have the strength for the journey."

"I was merely hungry . . . and then I was given that potion. . . . Oh, Stefan, how long before he comes again?"

"He comes every other Sunday."

"Two weeks." Anna felt overcome with despair. She could not allow two weeks to go by and do nothing. Even now, Antoni might be looking for her. *What am I to do?*

"You needn't think of going, Lady Berezowska," Stefan was saying. "You needn't think of going at all."

"But I must—and soon." Suddenly Anna realized that Stefan's face was subtly contorted and tense, as if he were screwing up his courage.

"I . . . my lady, it wouldn't matter a damn to me whether you have no husband or whether your marriage is not a good one."

"What do you mean?"

"Well, you haven't once spoken of love for a husband or of returning home to him—to Warsaw, yes, but not to a husband."

Anna bristled, not yet seeing where the turn in the conversation was taking them. "This is not your concern, Stefan."

"I wish to make it my concern."

Anna's eyes spoke her question.

"I want you to stay, Lady Berezowska. Not in these ruins of course, but in a home. Let me be the father to your child . . . and husband to you."

"You're not serious!"

"I am."

And he was, Anna could see. "It's impossible, Stefan." She could not suppress a smile.

"Because I am not of the aristocracy?"

"No, it's not that—"

"It is! I may not have been born noble, but I have been raised in the same fashion by Baron Galki and have had as much education as many nobles—"

"These are not issues. I cannot consider such a thing."

"Lady Berezowska, I have fallen in love with you."

"But I cannot return your love. You must believe that I do have a husband."

"Can you tell me that yours is a happy marriage? Can you?"

It took some moments for Anna to answer. She thought of the incongruities between her hopes for her life just a few months before and her life as it was now. The convoluted series of events that was her existence for the past months played before her like some perverse Greek play. She could interpret it either as comedy or tragedy, and so wishing to avoid tears, she chose to laugh. "Oh, Stefan, I cannot begin to consider—"

"What is so humorous?"

"Nothing . . . it is impossible to explain." She was laughing openly.

Stefan's face was reddening by the moment. "I suppose it is very comical to have some bumpkin like me make a fool of himself?"

"Oh, no, Stefan. That's not it at all." Anna suddenly realized that this was not Antek, who could read into the subtle textures of one's face and words. Antek would have sensed the irony of her words, seen through the laughter, felt the pain. But Stefan, whose emotions fed him and spilled out like blood at a moment's notice, had not. Anna's dark mirth immediately died away as she prepared to assuage his hurt.

But Stefan was gone.

37

Two weeks later Anna sat again in the chapel awaiting the priest's arrival. They had been painfully slow weeks. Stefan stayed away from the clan. After Anna confided in Antek the nature of that last unfortunate meeting, he tried to speak to his brother, tried to bring peace, but to no avail. Whereas Antek could and did speak of feelings, his twin—whose feelings, Anna was certain, ran as deep—was unable to do so. How was the damage to Stefan's pride to be undone?

Now, sitting with the clan in the cold chapel from midmorning until early afternoon, Anna's worst fear was realized: the priest did not come.

"We will wait no longer," Witek finally announced. "Something has kept our priest from coming today."

"It's that one," Nelka hissed, loud enough for most to hear.

Anna didn't turn around to look at the old woman. She sat stiffly, feeling her face flood with heat. She knew that others, though, had given the woman their attention.

"It is the evil one," the hiss continued. "*She* is who keeps the priest away! He will not return until she is gone. Let us send her from us!"

"Enough, Nelka!" Witek's command was more intense than loud.

"Witek, you must see. She is the instrument of the devil."

"Go with the other women now, Nelka, and help with the meal. And cease your grumblings."

The woman bristled sourly at her son's command but obeyed.

Anna lay sleepless at her place near the hearth long after midnight. She was alone. It was true, she brooded: the priest had not returned because of her. She could not say why it was so. It was a mystery. How was she now to find her way to Warsaw? She thought of Jan Stelnicki and her heart quickened. If only he knew of her circumstances. But such thoughts were useless.

Antek had assured her only that evening that he would construct a plan. While she prayed that he would be able to help her, another question loomed, one that was never far from her conscious mind: Would Antoni find her?

Suddenly a noise jarred her from her thoughts.

She sat up immediately, every nerve on edge. She strained to peer into the shadowy chamber, her heart thumping irregularly. It's nothing, she thought, perhaps just Lucyna, come to check on me, as is her custom. Or it might be nothing more than a mouse scurrying beneath the table in search of crumbs.

Then, Anna saw a candle that seemed to fairly float through the far door. Then another, and another. And still another. She stared dumbly at the tapers.

Hooded figures were holding the candles. Slowly, abreast of one another, they advanced, like Druid priests.

Stricken with fear, Anna could not speak until they stood before her. "Who are you?" she asked at last. "What have you come for?"

"We have come for you, *Countess.*"

Anna recognized the voice at once. "What do you mean?"

"The time has come for you to leave us." Nelka pulled back her hood now, freeing her puff of wiry hair. Her eyes, catching the light of the fire, were menacing discs.

Anna watched numbly as the old woman went to the hearth and lodged the poker between two red-glowing logs. Anna looked to the other figures. These were Nelka's cronies. Their faces were like grim masks.

She tried to disguise the panic rising within her. "Why do you hate me?"

"You are evil!" Nelka spat.

Nelka stopped only a foot away and Anna could feel the spray of the woman's saliva on her face. "It's because I am of the aristocracy, isn't it?"

The woman laughed. "Your veins will bleed as easily and as red as anyone's."

"Why, Nelka? Why do you hate me so?"

"Your kind has trampled on the poor for as long as I can remember." Her eyes grew distant for a moment. Her voice dropped to a monotone. "We would do well to rise up like those in France and slay you all."

"Have you been so ill-treated by Baron Galki?"

The woman caught herself, as if shaken from a trance. "Stand up and put your shawl around you. It is cold outside."

"They will not permit this, Nelka. Neither Witek nor your grandsons."

"They are blind. Enough talk! Get up!"

Nelka nodded to the others and two women pulled Anna to her feet. Anna started to cry out, but a hand came quickly from behind, silencing the alarm.

It was while she was struggling in this manner that she realized a fifth figure had entered the chamber, moving now out of the shadows and toward the hearthlight.

It was Stefan.

Thank God for Stefan, Anna thought. He would be able to control his deranged grandmother. Unable to speak with the hand over her mouth, her eyes pleaded with the youth.

His face inscrutable, he slowly approached the women. Why is he hesitating? Anna wondered. Why doesn't he say something?

Nelka turned around now and noticed him. But she registered no surprise. "Is the horse ready?" she asked.

Stefan nodded.

And Anna understood. Her hope had been the briefest of comets. Stefan would be of no help to her. He was there to aid his grandmother in banishing her.

While Nelka moved closer to the hearth, Anna snatched the opportunity to again silently implore Stefan's help. His stonelike stare seemed to weaken for a moment at her expression, but by the time his grandmother returned with the poker to the semicircle of figures in front of Anna, his expression had again hardened.

The poker's end was glowing red. Nelka held it a half finger's length from Anna's forehead. Anna could feel its heat singeing her eyebrow. "If you struggle or call out," Nelka warned, "no one will ever look with pleasure upon you. Silence her, Stefan."

The woman who was keeping Anna silent withdrew her hand, and Stefan forced a rag into her mouth. Anna could only wonder at the depth of Stefan's hurt.

Prodded by Nelka's bony fingers, Anna was directed out of the chamber and along the deadened rooms and down the stone steps into the stable area. Then Stefan bound her hands.

"Put her on the horse," Nelka ordered. "Take her deep into the forest and leave her."

"And the horse?" Stefan asked.

"Bring it back. She has the devices of the devil at her command and the forest is the devil's home, everyone knows that. She can call on *him* for help."

Anna wanted to cry out. She could not ride a horse in her condition. It would kill the baby, she was certain. And left to her own defenses in the middle of the forest during winter, she knew she had no chance of survival.

Anna could not believe this was happening. Her eyes passed over the faces of the other women. They knew that the crazed Nelka was sending her to her death, yet they stood as statues. She thought she detected sympathy or regret on one of the faces, though, that of Janka, one of the women who had been kind to her in the first days of her stay. Still, Anna knew that any hesitation on Janka's part would not stand up against the crusty Nelka. She had bewitched and bullied all of them.

And Anna knew that she could expect no help from Stefan, no last-minute contrition. Her unconscious cruelty and thoughtless laughter had sealed her fate. Nonetheless, as he lifted her onto the horse, her eyes searched his for some sign of empathy.

His eyes were colorless and cold. She hated him now and knew—God forgive her—that she would go to her death hating him.

When Stefan mounted his own horse, the women circled around Anna's, their candles held high. Nelka held the poker ready as if to strike the horse.

What kind of ancient superstitious practice was this?

"Throw open the door, Janka," Nelka ordered.

The woman obeyed and a gust of cold air rushed in. As Janka started back toward the waiting group, something caught her eye and she immediately halted, hesitating long seconds. All eyes followed hers to where someone stood in the timbered doorway. One of the women let out a quiet gasp.

Antek.

38

As Zofia's hired carriage pulled into the drive of the Wilanów Palace, King Jan Sobieski's one-time summer residence, she drew back the shade. For a moment her self-confidence began to wane. Here was a sprawling residence magnificent enough to rival the Royal Castle itself. Set against Italian gardens and camouflaged by intricacies of design that could only be French, the yellow building some-how—paradoxically—maintained the simplicity of a Polish manor home. Her driver drew the carriage into a long line of carriages that slowly moved toward the main entrance, where the masqueraders were alighting. Would she be admitted? For the first time, a doubt took root.

She had spent two weeks researching and seeing to the making of a red dress and elaborate bejeweled tunic. For the hooded robe she knew to wear purple. Theodora had risen from the street—she had been an ac-tress, equivalent even then to being a prostitute—to the wearing of the royal color, and Zofia thoroughly relished playing the role. The robe, of the plushest velvet, draped majestically.

She knew that some masqueraders wore full masks, some half masks, and some no masks at all. She thought on this for a long time before making a decision. She did not want Jan to recognize her until the moment she chose. In the end she decided upon having a mask made that covered her entire face except for her mouth and chin. She knew that her mouth was most expressive; she would have that at least to work her charms. The mask was made of purple felt and the upper border, ear to ear, was fitted with semiprecious gems and white feathers.

Only the day before she had taken the dress and gone to Princess Charlotte Sic's to borrow appropriate jewelry for the occasion, and her friend had been willing to loan her the three-tiered diamond necklace. Zofia was tempted but felt a twenty-six-stone ruby necklace and matching clip earrings were somehow more Byzantine.

"You don't seem to worry," Charlotte had chided, "that your plunging neckline is so . . . so *un*-Byzantine."

Zofia laughed. "You're right. Perhaps I'm afraid that the waterfall of diamonds would distract from . . . *other* assets."

At last Zofia stepped down from the carriage and fell in with the arriving throngs of partygoers. In no time she stood in a reception line at the entrance to the ballroom, wondering how she might avoid greeting the Countess Lubomirska. The line moved surprisingly quickly, however, and before she knew it she stood in front of the countess herself.

The countess was draped in an elaborate robe of white that made her appear as wide as she was tall. A wreathing of myrtle leaves circled the high mound of powdered hair that sat upon a round, puffy face. Zofia thought her perfectly ridiculous.

"You are, no doubt," Zofia exclaimed, "the great goddess Hera."

The woman's round, red mouth flattened into a smile. "How did you guess?"

"I'm an avid student of mythology," Zofia said, failing to mention she had overheard the countess announcing her identity to the party ahead of her.

"And just who are you? My, you're a lovely creature."

"Empress Theodora."

"I see. How delightful!" The woman's small eyes narrowed. "Now, who are you truly? I swear I do not recognize you." Her chubby hand reached out toward Zofia's mask.

Zofia drew back, smiled. "Ah, but Lady Lubomirska, isn't that the point?"

The woman was taken aback for a moment, her mouth forming a round circle before emitting a little laugh. "Oh, I suppose you're right. But I must know before the night is over, do you hear?"

Zofia was then announced as Theodora, Empress of the Byzantine Empire, and a thousand pairs of eyes turned to see her make her entrance.

Even with her face hidden, Zofia was the talk of the ball, and she knew the stir she created. It was easy then to play up to an old baron at Jan Stelnicki's table. She affected a French accent, charming him and insinuating herself into his group. A chair was acquired where there had been none. The group found it astonishing and amusing that Emperor Justinian's wife should so miraculously appear and so she was made to sit next to a maskless Jan. Sitting stiffly in his purple Byzantine robe, he was merely polite at first, but as the evening wore on and the French wines flowed, he began to warm.

Several of the men at the table and even a few women seemed political by nature, and conversation often came back to the subject of the Constitution. Zofia hated such talk and did her best to speak of more pleasant and pleasurable things. Her pretense at a poor Polish was fun for her.

Zofia and Jan danced several times. Jan was as handsome as ever, and Zofia was certain they were the subject of much talk. She spoke in an exaggerated whisper, one that she hoped disguised her identity yet held an allure.

"Are you certain we haven't met?" he asked once as they were returning to their seats, nearly breathless from the triple-time steps of a polonaise.

"I am your wife."

"No, really. Have we?"

"You must marry one day."

"How do you know I'm not already married?"

For a moment Zofia found herself entangled in a web of her own making, yet instead of fear at being found out too soon, she felt only the excitement of the chase. "Someone told me." She smiled confidently.

"Who are you?"

They reached their table now and Zofia was spared further questioning. Did he have a suspicion?

Jan's behavior toward her, while polite and warm, was a disappointment. When the evening grew late and it became clear that Zofia could have any man in the room except for Jan Stelnicki, she resorted to the final stage of her game plan. She had hoped it wouldn't be necessary.

While duty called Jan to dance with the old pockmarked baroness on his other side, Zofia took the opportunity to remove from her tunic a small cobalt-blue vial. She took his half-filled wineglass now, nonchalantly, as if it were hers, held it in her lap as she surveyed the room for anyone watching, and when she was certain no eyes were upon her, she removed the tiny cork and poured the contents of the vial into his glass.

The nighttime streets of Warsaw were silent except for the sounds of an occasional carriage carrying its tired merrymakers home from the magnificent Wilanów Palace on the outskirts of Warsaw. Out of fear of being recognized, Zofia had chosen not to use the Gronski carriage—with its emblazoned coat of arms—and, sparing no expense, hired one many times more magnificent.

Jan sat slumped in his place next to her. It had been so easy, she thought, so very easy. Well, why not? Theodora had been an actress, hadn't she?

When he seemed unwell at the table, she had offered her carriage. She herself was leaving just then, perchance—no, it was no inconvenience at all, she told his friends—and two of the men even helped Jan to the carriage.

She had asked Jan for his address, though she had known it—Henryk was very thorough in his reports. She knew, too, that one old servant woman lived in the back of the premises of the town house and that she was hard of hearing.

Jan was still in a stupor when the carriage arrived at his home. The driver, clearly thinking Jan drunk but knowing his own place and saying nothing, helped Zofia get him to the door. Jan fumbled with his keys, and finally the door opened. Zofia and the driver struggled to get him up the stairs to his bedchamber.

Zofia dismissed the driver, rewarding him well. She returned to the bedchamber. Jan lay on his bed now, seeming to sleep. The bed is so narrow, she thought, coming to stand at its foot. The bed of a single man. Unconscious, Jan was more handsome than ever. Like a sleeping blond angel.

Zofia removed her purple robe. Of course, he would be useless tonight. But in the morning, when he awoke to find her naked in his narrow bed . . . well, he was a man, wasn't he? She would show him pleasure he hadn't imagined. She would have him. *I do have him.* And even if he might somehow overcome temptation, the damage would be done. They will have had a night together. He will know it and at the right time Anna will know it and she will at last give up her obsession with him. And perhaps Zofia, too, would be able to relinquish her own obsession.

Zofia pulled the mask off now and threw it to the floor. She looked up and was surprised to find his eyes open. He seemed to be watching her through drug-dilated eyes.

"Zofia?" he whispered.

She smiled. She waited for him to say more; desire stirred, eddied, and coursed through her. She would enjoy undressing before him. But he disappointed her, slipping again into sleep.

Zofia walked to his dresser, glancing at her reflection in the mirror that hung over it. She was still smiling. It had been so easy. Too easy, she thought for a moment, allowing a fleeting sense of foreboding to alight. She dispelled it at once.

She reached behind her head to remove the ruby necklace. Unclasping it, she placed it on the dresser. She reached now for the ruby earrings—only to find them gone!

Her heart dropped. She grew dizzy, holding on to the dresser for support. Dear God, she thought, where are the earrings? The room seemed to spin about her.

And then she remembered.

She had gone to the lounge just before departing from the ball. She had taken off the mask and the earrings while she freshened her face. It certainly wasn't her custom to remove her earrings, but the clips had been pinching her all evening and the chance to take a respite from them had been too tempting. *Sweet Jesus!* She had left the priceless rubies in the lounge just before her departure. Her preoccupation with getting Stelnicki out of the Lubomirski palace had superseded everything.

She breathed deeply now. What was she to do? Had some other guest taken them? She prayed not. There was hope: there had been an attendant and the Lubomirski servants were known for their honesty—the count would not tolerate anything less. With luck, the lost rubies needed only be claimed.

She looked at Jan, felt the desire moving in her veins. Would the rubies be there in the morning? And if she waited would she be able to sleep—or make love with any abandon—while worrying about them?

Zofia put the necklace back on. Wearing it would prove that it was she who had lost the earrings. She would race to the Lubomirski mansion and return as if on wings. Picking up the mask from the floor, she looked to Jan before leaving. Yes, he sleeps like an angel.

Downstairs she folded her mask in half for thickness and wedged it between the door and its jamb so that she could admit herself when she returned.

39

Antek's face was hard and questioning, yet Anna found his gaze somehow opaque as he surveyed the little group, fastening on her for a split second, then looking to his grandmother.

Nelka glared back at him for long seconds. Then her voice broke the brittle quiet. "The time has come for the evil one to be sent from our midst." The pursed mouth twitched slightly. She saw at once that her careful plans might be impeded.

Anna looked to Antek, wondering if he had the courage to go against family members. While she sensed that he was not in any way physically attracted to her, she worried whether the bond she thought they had formed was strong enough for him to come to her aid.

Antek was speaking to his brother now: "You are prepared to do this thing?"

"I am." Stefan sat on his stallion.

"Why?"

"She is evil. Nelka says—"

"Since when do you believe in the old ways?"

"There may be truth in the old ways. I have not been so brainwashed as you."

"You know that Nelka's hatred of the aristocracy is a blind one."

"And you should not forget your—our—birth, Antek. We will never be accepted as aristocracy, brother. The baron may provide for us, but he is forbidden to pass on his title. His ancestral line dies with him."

"We don't need titles, Stefan. The Commonwealth is a republic! These are not the real issues here and you know it."

Stefan sat rigid and silent in his saddle.

"Isn't it true," Antek continued, "that your reason is a more personal one?"

Anna could sense Stefan tensing at her side.

Antek was unrelenting. "For God's sake, Stefan, the countess is married and with child. What could your expectations have been? You would forfeit her life now to salve your pride? Answer me!"

Suddenly, Nelka screeched, "To the devil with her!"

Anna turned to see the woman raising the poker into the air above her horse's flank.

"Stop!" Antek shouted.

Nelka raised it still higher and started to bring it down. For Anna these things seemed to slow in time . . . and she braced herself for the sudden reaction of the horse.

In a flash, however, Antek fell upon Nelka and wrested the instrument from her clawlike grasp, flinging it across the room.

At that moment Stefan leapt from his horse onto his brother and they crashed to the floor.

For a few moments Antek lay stunned, sprawled facedown on the straw-strewn floor. Stefan was atop him, forcing his brother's hands together at the small of his back. "Nelka," he called, "fetch some rope!"

But before she could even process the command, Antek pulled his arms free. He drew in his knees and bolted upward, disengaging Stefan's hold.

Stefan was on his feet now, too, and the twins squared off, moving in a slow, winding circle, each doggedly eyeing the other. They moved cautiously close to one another, their arms shooting out then withdrawing, while each searched for the advantage of first contact. Anna suspected that this had been for them a ritual game while growing up. The ferocity in their expressions now, however, indicated that this time it was more than a rite of passage.

As if by design, each gripped the other by the wrists now, their bodies arching backward and starting to revolve, faster and faster. It was like some bizarre Russian dance, Anna thought, a dance of competition.

Nelka and her cronies moved back to give room. Janka closed the large door and then—unobserved by everyone except Anna—she fell back into the shadows and slipped away.

Round and round, the twins continued in a blinding swirl, until the legs of one began to falter slightly. Amazingly, the other—who was it?—was able to increase his speed and take the advantage now. He was soon dragging his brother for several revolutions until, with one final and deliberate stratagem, he released him and sent him crashing into one of the stall's wooden supports.

Upon impact, there was a bone-crushing sound and the beaten brother slid to the floor. The head lay in defeat on his chest, but Anna could distinguish the mole on his cheek.

"Get up!" Stefan commanded. "I'm not finished with you yet."

Stefan walked over to where Antek lay, dazed but conscious, and kicked him in the ribs. "I said to get up!" He lifted his leg to kick again, but as he swung it forward Antek grasped it, and holding to it, started to rise from the floor.

Stefan's arms flailed about as he tried both to strike Antek and to keep his balance. Antek was standing now, and with one strong pull on the captive leg, he brought his brother to the floor with a heavy thud. He instantly fell upon him, and they rolled and thrashed in the straw.

Stefan came up perched on Antek's stomach, his knees pinning down his twin's arms to the floor. His fists, one then the other, slammed into Antek's face. Blood began to flow.

Anna was struggling to free her hands. The rope loosened slightly, but she could only watch the scene unfold, unable to do anything, unable to look away.

The battering continued. Finally, Antek was able to topple his twin off to the side. In seconds they were on their feet and face-to-face, not touching, moving in a slow, calculating circle. The room was silent as a catacomb. Antek was bleeding heavily.

Anna's bonds were loosening. She suspected that Antek had been reticent to come to hard, fistic blows with his twin and would have preferred wrestling as a means to a settlement. Now, though, his body straightened, signaling a new determination. It was as though he knew that if he didn't fight on Stefan's terms he would be beaten.

Stefan thrust his fist toward Antek's face again. His hand sailed through empty air, though, as Antek shifted swiftly to the side. This afforded Antek the opportunity to seize the offensive, and he propelled his fist into his brother's middle. Stefan immediately doubled over. At once Antek's fist crashed into Stefan's already contorted face, springing his brother once again into an upright position—and still another blow pitched him backward seven or eight paces. He fell to the floor.

When Stefan pulled himself to his feet, he held the poker in his hand! And he had murder in his eyes.

Anna's hands were almost free now and she worked feverishly. She would not be the cause of one brother killing the other.

Nelka and the others didn't stir—they stared as if hypnotized by the violence. They didn't notice that Anna's hands had come free.

Stefan staggered like a drunk toward the alerted Antek, who stood to face him. As Stefan rushed the last few steps, his powerful arm and the poker cut through the air in a wide whirring arc.

Anna pulled the rag from her mouth and screamed.

No one paid any attention to her.

Antek proved just agile enough to jump aside, and the poker slammed down on the rim of a water trough, splintering the wood. Anna's voice fell silent at the sound.

Before Stefan could lift it again, Antek's foot came down and wrenched it from his brother's grasp. Antek caught hold of Stefan by the scruff of the neck now and thrust his head forward and downward into the full water trough.

After some seconds, Stefan's face bobbed to the surface and he gasped for air. Antek forced him under again. The drowning Stefan struggled awkwardly to lash out behind him, but Antek stood clear of his reach and leaned more heavily upon his brother's neck and shoulders.

Stefan could not bring his head up again.

Anna suddenly became aware of her own silence. "Stop, Antek!" she called out. "Stop it at once! You're killing him!" She continued to scream, scarcely aware of what words she used. She had no way to alight from the horse or she would have run over to stop him.

At last, Antek looked back at Anna. "Please Antek," she said in a calmer but intense voice, "please!"

His eyes widened as rationality seemed to flow once more through his veins. He pulled his twin from the trough and laid him facedown on the floor. Stefan had stopped struggling. Anna was certain he was dead.

A little gurgle, however, then a faint gasp told her otherwise, and she thanked God.

Stefan's breathing was nearly regular when Witek entered.

"What is happening here?" he boomed. Janka hovered nervously in the shadows behind him. Anna silently blessed the woman for going against Nelka and bringing the clan leader.

Silence.

"Will not one of my sons speak?"

Stefan was picking himself up from the floor, his eyes averting his father's.

"They meant to banish the Countess Berezowska," Antek said.

Except for Nelka, the women shrank back.

As Witek came farther into the stable, Nelka moved forward to meet him. "She has brought bad luck with her. She must be driven out. See how she pits brother against brother? She has used the devil's charms to beguile Antek—"

Witek lifted his hand to silence his mother. "Can't you see, woman? *You* have set brother against brother. Not the countess. Would it have pleased you if one had killed the other? Get you from me before I forget you have a place in this family—before you shame me further!"

Nelka opened her prunelike mouth to speak, but she thought better of it, shot a last look of hatred at Anna, and whisked from the stable, the other women—except for Janka—following sheepishly.

Antek helped Anna from the horse.

"You were aiding your grandmother in this?" Witek asked Stefan.

Stefan voiced no answer.

"Make ready to return to Lord Galki's at once, Stefan. You are more his son than mine, it seems. But we will talk before you leave."

Head bowed, Stefan limped from the stable.

"I'm ashamed and very sorry, milady," Witek said. "I did not retrieve you from the winter wilderness to submit you to this. Forgive me."

"You are certainly not to blame, Witek. I will be fine. I'm only grateful for your intervention . . . and for Antek's."

Witek turned to his son. "Are you all right?"

"Yes."

"You've become a man." The simplicity and straightforwardness of the statement made it all the more poignant. "And you've already proven your worth," he said now to Anna, "as a countess and as a woman. Tomorrow, I think, my son Antek will escort you to Często-chowa, where you should be able to find a way back to Warsaw."

Anna's heart raced at the thought. "Oh, thank you," she said. Later she would wish that she had said so much more to show her apprecia-tion. Witek and his clan had plucked her from certain death in the snow.

"Were you not mending, I should have done so at the first. It seems I placed too much faith in the priest, too. I'll see you in the morning, then."

"Witek," Anna piped, putting her hand on his sleeve.

"Yes, Lady Berezowska?"

"Don't be too hard on Stefan."

He studied her for a moment, then smiled. "When you leave us, milady, it will be our loss." He turned to leave, and Janka timidly fol-lowed suit.

"Janka," Anna called softly.

The old woman turned, her face a composite of curiosity and fear.

"Thank you," Anna whispered. She knew that Nelka would not be quick to forget her friend's betrayal.

The woman's oval mouth spread into a thin, toothless smile. She curtsied clumsily and retreated, close upon Witek's heels.

40

Zofia sat complacently in the carriage she had been lucky to hail for her return trip to Wilanów. She looked down and smiled. There in the cup of her hand were the two earrings. The atten-dant had gone to look for her, or so she said, as soon as she found them. And it may be true, Zofia thought, for she had left the ball almost im-mediately after stopping in the lounge.

Just a minor setback, she thought. Now her thoughts returned to

Jan. Wouldn't it be ironic if this little interim allowed him to become more responsive? What kind of lover would he be? The cold air and the exhilaration at losing and finding the rubies had breathed new life into her own desires.

For the second time that night Zofia dismissed a driver at Jan Stelnicki's door.

She was already reaching for the door handle when she realized there was no trace of the mask she had used to keep the door from closing. Heart racing, she pulled at the heavy door.

Locked!

Zofia stepped back to look at the windows. They were dark on all three levels. Returning to the door in disbelief, she tried it again, to no avail. She felt her temper rising. What had happened? Had the old woman risen in the middle of the night and found the door wedged open? Or had Jan recovered enough to find his way downstairs?

She sounded the knocker several times and waited. Nothing. She sounded it again. The old woman had probably locked her out, Zofia decided. Jan couldn't have done it; he was too drugged. And now she had gone back to her room in the back of the house and gone to sleep. Even if she were awake, Henryk had told Zofia that she was hard of hearing. Damn her!

Something on the ground flashed in the moonlight. Zofia bent over and picked up the crumpled mask.

She turned back to the door and knocked again, knowing even as she did so that this little venture had come to an unforeseen end. Angrily Zofia picked up her skirts and started down the long cobblestone incline winding to the bridge that would take her across the river to Praga. Her temples pulsed in pain at the thought that the propitious evening had come to such ignominy. She could only hope no one she knew would see her walking home. It would be the final humiliation.

Two days later, when Zofia returned the necklace and earrings, Princess Charlotte Sic told her, between fits of laughter, that the jewels were glass, beautifully colored and faceted, but glass nonetheless.

41

Anna and Antek made steady progress toward the city of Często-chowa, where it rests on and among the limehills that extend from Kraków to Wielun on the River Warta. Antek told her a great many details about the monastery Jasna Gora, or Bright Mountain, situated on land given to the Pauline Fathers in 1382. The Black Madonna, the icon of the Virgin that Anna so longed to see, found its home there years later, and the site became the place of pilgrimage for generations of Poles.

"There's the bell tower!" Antek announced as the sleigh came to an arc in the road.

Anna stared in amazement. They were still some distance away, and yet the chapel's majestic steeple rose out of the white wilderness like a statue sculpted from a mountain.

"It has over five hundred steps should you like to see the bell, my lady."

"We haven't the time. And it is the Black Madonna I want to see."

"They say that the icon is a guide for those who have lost their way."

"Then I shall be glad to see her."

Anna thought back to her parting from the clan that morning. It had been bittersweet and tearful.

Around her middle, Anna had strapped the goatskin that Lutisha had given her—a lifetime ago, it seemed. The old woman was as shrewd as Owl Eyes, she realized, for the skin had proven a lifesaving device when she stood alone against winter's harshest elements. Anna dressed then in her brown traveling dress that the women had repaired and restored. Still, she vowed to destroy it upon arriving home because she wanted no such memento of the trip or what happened at the carriage site. Magda and Wera braided Anna's hair as directed by their mother, encircling the braids around her ears as protection from the cold.

Lucyna approached Anna during the braiding process, her face a vision of doom.

"What is it?" Anna pressed. "Tell me!"

"Oh, milady," she moaned, "look what's become of your lovely boots." The woman clutched them to her ample bosom. The boots were discolored, misshapen, and shrunken; utterly useless. "Oh, I am so sorry," she wailed as if she were to blame, "we've tried to clean them and oil the leather, but . . . well, you see how they are." She started to cry now.

"Ha!" Anna laughed. "Aren't they a sight? Don't worry, Lucyna. I didn't plan to wear them. I've always hated those boots." She laughed now in a conspiratorial tone. "They pinched my toes! If it's all right, I'll wear these marvelous fur slippers you've fashioned for me."

Lucyna blinked back a tear, nodded, and gave a faint smile.

Anna took one of the boots and held it up to Lucyna's daughters. "Look, Wera and Magda, it would take a strange foot to fit this now, don't you think?" Anna and the girls laughed together, and soon Lucyna relaxed and joined in the mirth.

Anna wished that Nelka's defenses could be melted as easily, but she was nowhere to be found that morning. Neither was Stefan. Of course, a part of her hated Nelka for the happenings of the previous night, but she would not leave the clan, who had restored her to life, with ill feelings. Nelka had acted out of ignorance, Stefan out of emotion. Anna would not sit in judgment of either.

After a hearty breakfast, the rest of the clan assembled in the stable area to see Anna on her way. Antek was seeing to the horses and sleigh.

Anna had broken in pieces the fine gold chain that had held her mother's cameo; there were six gifts to be given and Anna dared not give up the coins that still might be needed for the trip back to Warsaw. She had decided to present the gifts to the oldest woman of each family.

The women were astonished at the gesture, refusing at first to accept the little lengths of gold, and Anna had to catch their hidden hands and slap the tokens into their palms. Janka, too, balked at the gift, but Anna succeeded at last in prying open her fingers. When the woman looked down, she stared dumbly at two lengths of chain, then looked to Anna, who shushed her with only her eyes. "Take the second length," Anna whispered, "and after I am gone, give it to Nelka."

Janka nodded, her eyes as large as moons.

Old minds and hearts are difficult to change, Anna reasoned, but that should not preclude the attempt.

When the gifts were given, she approached Owl Eyes. "No amount of gold would be enough to repay you, my friend. I owe you my life."

The bushy eyebrows lifted. "Godspeed, milady. May yours be a happy and healthy life. Above all, above everyone, trust your heart, milady."

Anna hugged him.

"I owe you no less," she said to Witek as she embraced him in front of his clan.

His face turned bright red. He shifted from one foot to another, like an anxious horse.

"Fair is fair," she said. "If you remember, it was I who nearly died of embarrassment at our first meeting."

"Good-bye, Lady Berezowska." It was all he could bring himself to say.

Then it was Anna's turn to be surprised. When she climbed into the sleigh, Lucyna, Janka, Magda, little Wera, and two other women crowded into the cushioned seats with her. Not understanding their intentions, she could only stare dumbfounded.

The women giggled at her puzzlement. It was Lucyna who explained: "It is good luck, milady, for people to crowd themselves into a sleigh or carriage with the traveler. Good sense, too, because on such a cold journey the warmth of the persons will linger."

Anna laughed appreciatively while the chattering women enfolded blankets and furs around her. For a moment, it seemed to her that the clanswomen and she were as one, unaware of classes designated by society.

"It is time," Antek said, his preparations made.

Anna disregarded social boundaries now and insisted on kissing the women on both cheeks. Tears were flowing freely down the clanswomen's faces by the time Antek helped them to alight the sleigh.

When only Anna was left, Antek climbed in.

Little Wera looked up at Anna with great sorrowful eyes. "Are you coming back, milady?" Her tiny voice broke with emotion.

"I don't know, little one," Anna said.

Suddenly, the great doors were open and the men were pushing the sleigh out to where the snow made the effort unnecessary and the horses started at a lively gait. Anna turned around to wave.

Years later she would remember the clan huddling there against the cold: men waving, women holding rags to their eyes. "Godspeed!" they cried. "Godspeed the countess!"

"I'll not forget you!" Anna called. "If you ever come to Warsaw, come see me!"

Anna turned around in her seat. Antek was absorbed for the moment in the horses and pathways. Anna silently called herself a fool to have said such a thing. She knew that it was doubtful that anyone of the clan had ever been to Warsaw or would have reason or inclination to travel to that faraway city in the future. The women, especially, had probably rarely ventured farther than the huge gardens surrounding the castle. Such limited confines are theirs, she thought, until the earth, which they have tilled, becomes for them the most limited of confines, their graves. She envied them, but at the same time she knew that she wanted more out of life—for herself and for her child.

Now, as they neared Częstochowa, Anna asked a question that had been haunting her. "Antek, how is it that Nelka hates me so?"

Antek sighed. "It isn't you, Lady Berezowska. Really, it isn't."

"Oh, you think not?"

"It's the whole fabric of the aristocracy she hates. She can't be rational about it. You see, years ago when she was a young and vital woman there lived a magnate's widow in the next parish who took a fancy to Nelka's husband—my grandfather. The noblewoman connived with the nobles upon whose estate my grandparents depended and he was made her footman." Antek shot Anna a meaningful glance. "Of course, her real motive was very different."

"What happened?"

"While he was away, my grandmother gave birth to Witek. My grandfather wanted only to return to his little family, but the noblewoman wouldn't hear of it. When he attempted to leave, he met with a riding accident. He died. Nelka never believed it an accident, of course."

Anna thought it a wretched story, a throwback to the Dark Ages. "And Nelka's life was ruined," she said. "So there lies the explanation."

"It was a terrible thing my lady. But she was a young woman and it needn't have ruined her life. She might have put her energies into creating a new life. Instead, she allowed the tragedy to harden her, to embitter her. The story may explain her behavior, but it doesn't excuse it."

"One's first love can be the strongest, Antek. Never to be forgotten, never to be replaced."

Antek's silence seemed to attest to his surprise at Anna's role of apologist for his grandmother.

They traveled in silence for a short while. Anna thought that the story of Nelka and the noblewoman might be transformed into a wonderful myth. But what happy ending might she be able to supply?

Antek broke the silence. "While my grandmother might never forgive, I must tell you that Stefan is sorry he ever listened to her."

"Is he?"

"Most ashamed, my lady. He was too humiliated to come this morning to see us off. He was certain you would not forgive him. He thinks himself unworthy of forgiveness."

"I see."

"It seems a cowardly thing, I know. But Stefan is not really a coward. We are both joining the Patriots' Army."

Anna's mouth fell open. "Oh, God be with you, Antek. God be with you both! And you are to tell your brother that I harbor no ill feelings, do you hear?"

Antek's appreciative smile told Anna just how much he loved his twin.

Further talk of the patriots' cause inevitably led Anna to think of Jan Stelnicki. She wondered if she would become another Nelka, an old woman bitterly unhappy because her love had been scuttled.

The sleigh now passed through the gates that led to the chapel. The trip had taken less than a day.

On the very day after the masquerade, Count Jan Stelnicki became a commissioned officer—a lieutenant in the light cavalry—by the sword of Tadeusz Kościuszko himself. He felt proud and richly honored, but he celebrated little because the effects of the drug, nausea and headache, had stayed with him all day.

What had been placed in his drink at the masquerade? It certainly wasn't mere alcohol that had such effects. He remembered nothing of the trip home.

Of course, he remembered Theodora, the mysterious French guest seated next to him. And his friends told him later of how she had taken control when he appeared ill at the table. She assured everyone she would see that he got safely home. No one knew who she was.

So, Jan thought now, she took me home, somehow got me to the second floor and into bed. And then disappeared. It was the strangest thing.

To make it even stranger, all day—even during the ceremony—he kept having a hazy and half-remembered vision of the woman portraying Theodora standing at the end of his bed. The disturbing thing was that the unmasked woman's visage was Zofia's. The laughing dark eyes would be hard to duplicate. How was it possible? No, of course it wasn't she, he decided. It could only have been some drug-induced delusion that caused him to transpose Zofia's features to the mystery woman's mask.

That he should have such a delusion about Zofia, however, disturbed him in no little way.

"Welcome, pilgrims!" It was a very tall and lean priest who met Anna and Antek at the entrance to the chapel. "I'm sorry, but you've missed the services."

"That's all right, Father," Antek said. "The countess would still wish to see the icon of the Black Madonna."

The priest seemed surprised at the mention of Anna's title. He appraised her with skepticism, then glanced at the unpretentious horse and sleigh. "I've only just locked up. The next service will be at six."

"Oh, but I've so longed to see her," Anna said. "Father, might you give me but a few minutes?"

"You see," Antek said, "the countess is . . . in frail health. She is to have a child."

"I see," the priest said, glancing at Anna. "And what is the countess' name?"

"Anna Maria Berezowska, Countess of Sochaczew." Anna answered formally because she suspected he was looking for some proof of her nobility in her speech or manner. She tried to appear assertive. And yet she hoped he didn't misinterpret for insincerity her nervousness at not using her married name.

"Sochaczew is not far from Warsaw, is it, Lady Berezowska?"

Anna smiled. He *was* testing her. "A morning's ride in good weather. I am spending the winter in Warsaw."

The priest's suspicion seemed to abate, and Antek pushed the issue before he could devise another question. "Might the countess have just a few minutes for a prayer and the lighting of a candle?"

He studied Anna another moment, then nodded. "Yes, of course, she may." He turned and unlocked the door. "Go in, Lady Berezowska, and do not feel rushed. I am in no hurry. There are five altars. Follow the main aisle all the way down and you will find her."

Anna thanked him and entered the dark and cold chapel, her fur-wrapped feet making her steps eerily silent. She passed through the vestibule and paused at the entrance to the chapel proper, allowing her eyes to adjust to the dimness. An iridescent glow from the stained glass windows and the flickering of many votive candles supplied a magical kind of light.

Anna could hear Antek conversing with the priest. She heard the mention of Father Florian's name. She knew Antek was asking about Father Florian and possible plans to restore her to Warsaw. Despite the importance of those things to her, she didn't attempt to listen further or process the information. The chapel already had a mysterious hold on her and some force drew her forward.

Anna walked slowly up the aisle. The chapel was quite elaborate. She had never seen anything like it. There was the cathedral in Warsaw, of course, but it was so huge and grand that within it one felt merely lost or insignificant. It did not have the sense of warmth and immediacy that she felt here. The walls of the chapel were filled with votives—chasubles, tapestries, fabrics, embroideries, weapons, crowns, and precious stones—all given in thanks for the grace and miracles received. And there was some indefinable and mystical presence to the place.

Anna came to a great war sword in a special niche. She moved closer and saw that it was the sword King Jan Sobieski had used to relieve Vienna from the Turkish onslaught. Her heart quickened. Her own ancestor—her father's great-great-grandfather—had been there at Vienna, Anna remembered. He was there fighting side by side with Sobieski, and for his reward Count Waldstein, the Viennese Imperial Ambassador to the Polish Court, recommended to the Austrian king that he be ennobled. Anna felt faint at the thought. She was who she was because of men and events from a century ago. And despite the years and distance in generations, she felt connected to her courageous forefather. Pride surged within her. What had he been like? Perhaps he was a hero of mythic proportions. Or perhaps he was one of millions of Poles who through the centuries had risked everything and often paid with their lives for their homeland. They were heroes, too. In any case, she prayed to her ancestor, imploring him to watch out for her well-being.

Anna continued her slow walk to the icon. She came to the very high presbytery grill that kept her from proceeding into the sanctuary. Stepping up to the grill, she saw the icon—a simple painting on wood— there on an altar of ebony and silver. Anna's gaze was drawn immediately to Mary's eyes. They seemed so real, as though they were watching Anna, reading her. There was something so strange and ethereal about the painting that Anna's breath was taken from her.

In time, she was able to make note of other details. The painting depicted only the upper portion of Mary, dressed in a dark robe and mantle, the fabric woven with the images of many lilies. A single six-pointed star decorated her head covering, just above the middle of the forehead. She was holding the infant Jesus; both figures had gold auras that contrasted with the dark facial coloring. What had the painting looked like before the damage done to it by the Hussites and the subsequent repainting that had no doubt caused the dark tones? Yet what did it matter, she thought, when it was such a beautiful thing today? And one was always drawn back to the powerful gaze of the Virgin's eyes. They seemed to know and tell the story of the world, not in confinement of words or ideas, but in the largeness of emotion.

Anna remembered that the Black Madonna was known to be a "guide along the road." She knelt now, praying for her guidance. Minutes passed. She became aware of a hush behind her. The priest and Antek were waiting for her. She had been neglectful of the time. She took a flame from a small votive candle and lighted her own. Then she took one last long look at the Madonna's eyes, daring to think her prayer had been heard, rose, and retraced her steps to the vestibule.

Anna was shocked to find, in place of the thin priest, the imposing figure of Father Florian. She had distrusted the man from the first, and then after his failure to show for Mass, she had become doubly critical. Somehow, she immediately sensed this meeting boded no good.

"It is so good to see you again, my lady!" he exclaimed. "Let me first tell you that I regret my having missed Sunday Mass. I do beg your pardon!"

Anna smiled. "There is no need to—"

"You see, I was quite ill. Taken to bed in fact, I was. I wasn't able to make it."

"You're better now, I hope," Antek said.

"Oh my, yes."

"Good. Father, circumstances became such that we thought we should come here to see about getting the countess transportation to Warsaw. Will you help us?"

"I can do better than that!"

"What do you mean, Father?" Antek asked.

Father Florian turned his gaze on Anna. "I mean that my missing Mass has actually facilitated the Countess Grawlinska's return. Some heathens would call it Fate. I, however, believe that such random happenings are God's happenings."

Anna's heart tightened in fright. Father Florian had used her married name! She knew immediately that the priest had had some contact with Antoni. When? How? Her eyes began to dart about the shadows of the chapel. Was Antoni here now?

"That is not the countess' name, Father," Antek said.

"It most certainly is, isn't it, Lady Grawlinska?"

Anna nodded. She felt nausea rise up within her. "It is my married name."

"Why the charade, Lady Grawlinska?" Father Florian asked.

Anna's lips tightened. It was as if the priest had dropped one mask for another, like some shapeshifter, transforming from one who spoke of her well-being to one who acted as an antagonist. "I wish nothing to do with my husband."

"But you are married, my dear," the priest said. "And with child. Your husband is most concerned."

"I'm certain that he is." Anna tried not to let her bitterness show. "Where . . . where is Antoni?"

"Ah, that is where the random happening comes in. Had I not been sick, I would not have been here when he came through looking for his wife. The confusion of names forestalled our understanding, but at last the little mystery was solved. The runaway wife was using her maiden name."

"Runaway wife?" A puzzled Antek turned to Anna.

Anna smiled weakly. How was she to explain in a few words—and in front of the priest?

When she paused, Father Florian launched into a litany of wifely responsibilities and ended by expounding on the duty Anna owed her unborn child.

Antek at last asked the priest the question uppermost on Anna's mind. "And where is the Lord Grawlinski, Father?"

The priest's face dulled. "Unfortunately, I sent him off early this morning for the Galki estate. They, of course, will tell him you've come here. He will then either turn about immediately or stay the night and come back in the morning. I suspect that he will stay and the happy re-union will occur tomorrow."

Anna's head reeled. She was safe for the moment, but no more.

"Now, Antek," the priest said, "you take your horses to that shed beyond and turn them over to the ostler. Then come join us in the monastery for a hot meal. Come along, Lady Grawlinska."

Anna exchanged glances with Antek. He could not know the level of her distress, but her lack of enthusiasm for the impending reunion had not been lost on him. He looked at her with puzzlement. He seemed to be waiting for some direction from her.

Anna nodded, releasing him to do as bidden by the priest.

By the time Anna and Father Florian arrived at the outer door of the monastery her plan was formulated. She knew Antoni would not stay the night, that he would immediately turn about for Częstochowa. She sensed a clock inside her, ticking, warning, urging. "I'm sorry, Father," she blurted, attempting spontaneity, "but I've left my mother's cameo in the sleigh and I'm never without it. It will only take me a moment."

"Nonsense! As soon as Antek comes in, we'll send him for it."

"Oh, he hasn't a clue as to where I've hidden it! I'll only be a moment!" Anna was running down the incline before the priest could protest further.

Antek was just leaving the stable when she came upon him.

"What is it?" he asked. "You shouldn't be running."

"But I must!"

He took her meaning. "You *have* run away, then."

"Not until now. Antek, will you trust me to tell you everything once we're well removed from this place? We must leave now!"

"But the horses need rest and we both could use a meal, my lady."

"To take the time to do that now will cost me my life. I know that sounds absurd. I know that I'm asking much of you, that you will be expected back home . . . but will you help me get to Warsaw?"

Antek didn't hesitate. "Of course, my lady."

"We'll have to take all the farm roads, no highways."

He nodded.

"Bless you, Antek. And please . . . call me Anna."

Much later, along the desolate and treacherous and bumpy by-roads, her escape a fait accompli, Anna wondered whether the Black Madonna had not, after all, worked for her a secret miracle.

Part Four

Push not the river;
it will flow
on its own accord.

–POLISH PROVERB

42

I t was on a cold day in mid-March that Anna once again set eyes on the streets of Praga. She and Antek arrived in a horse-driven carriage they had rented the day before when the melting snows began to make the sleigh's going impossible.

Their journey of several days had been long and tedious, the roads scarcely good enough to warrant the name. They had stayed the nights mainly at private homes out of fear that Antoni would be searching them out at the more usual inns. Both plain peasant cottages and the more lavish manor homes extended the customary Polish hospitality.

Lutisha opened the door. At the sight of Anna, her face lit up like the sun. "Oh, Lady Anna!" she croaked, her large hands flying to her face. Then, forgetting her French schooling in the art of running a home, she called into the house: "The Countess is home! Praise God, the Countess is home!"

The corpulent servant impulsively hugged Anna to her, then withdrew in embarrassment at the show of familiarity. "Excuse me, Madame—it was the excitement."

"No one could be happier than I," Anna said, returning the hug as proof, then introducing Antek.

"Come in, come in, it's cold out here. The storks made their return to the roof only today. Marta said it was a lucky omen—and so it is! Oh, I'm sorry to babble . . . Are you well? And the child?"

"I am, Lutisha. And the child is also. The travel has made him very active, you can be sure." Anna was delighted to once again see the servant's toothless smile.

"We heard . . . that is, Lord Grawlinski said that you were dead, that the carriage had been set upon by highwaymen."

"I escaped, Lutisha." Anna then whispered: "Where is my husband?" Her heart beat erratically.

"I don't know, Madame. He left some weeks ago."

"I see." They stood in the entry hall. Anna calmed herself. "How is Aunt Stella?"

"Fine."

"And Zofia? Is she at home?"

"She is not!" The answer came from Countess Stella, who was descending the stairs with the dexterity of a young woman. "She's off on some damn river cruise! Sweet Jesus, Ania, you are a sight for these old eyes!"

Anna lay awake, life and energy slowly reentering her cold and travel-wearied bones. Her room was dark, the time of night indecipherable. She knew she must have slept for many hours, waking occasionally when Lutisha prodded her to take nourishment.

She tried not to think of Antoni or how long it might be before he would show, as he must.

Anna prayed that Antek was safely making his way back to his family. Parting from him had been difficult, for they had grown so close at the clan's home and especially on the journey to Warsaw. They had come to speak with such ease with one another. She had told him about everything: the attack at the pond, the expected child, her husband's attempt on her life, her love for another, her suspicions regarding Zofia. He listened and believed what she said. He had wanted to stay and help her deal with Antoni, but Anna would not allow it. His family was awaiting him, as was the patriots' cause. She insisted she would have enough help, showing a confidence she knew to be hollow.

It was an attraction of the spirit that Anna held for Antek: he was the brother she might have had. If she were physically attractive to him, he had never given any indication. He was very proper in that way. She had stood in the doorway as he walked to the carriage, watching him turn back only once to smile sadly and wave. She waved, too, wondering if she would see him again.

Anna reached for the glass of water Lutisha had left on the bedside table. How strange, she thought. Antek had been so important to her life. Though lowborn he had shown such nobility, doing no less than a knight would have done. Twice. It was a lesson she had been learning all along: one's strength of character was instilled by learning and by life's tests, not by birth.

And yet he left her life like an actor exits the stage at the end of his part in a play. Here was another lesson. This is life, she mused, people pass through your life—and you through theirs—and then it is finished, the scene written and played. There was something immeasurably sad about that.

Would it be so with Jan? Was he to pass out of her life, too?

Anna wondered if Jan had received by now the note Antek had promised to deliver to the Queen's Head before leaving Warsaw. She tried to estimate the number of hours that had passed, but her brain was cloudy. What did it matter? She was certain he would come.

Anna finished the water and fell back against the pillows. She was not yet done with sleep, it seemed. Her aunt had been the one to put her to bed so many hours before.

"What cruise has Zofia gone on?" Anna had asked.

"On the Vistula," the countess replied. "On some huge and elaborate ship. Can you imagine? Why, the ice isn't even completely gone. Some magnate or other with too much gold in his purse, I suppose. Think what good such money would do Kościuszko! It makes my blood boil!"

"Aunt Stella, where is Babette?"

"She's there, too, God help her, on that ship of sinners. Attending your cousin and witnessing who knows what kind of merriment!"

"Oh."

The lines in the countess' face were at once transformed from bitterness to sympathy. "Oh, my dear . . . the children. Are they truly . . . ?"

Anna nodded. "They did not survive."

"How terribly sad. It is as we feared. We heard there were two small graves among the others. What a world it is. Well, you must sleep now. You can tell us about it another time." The countess stood to leave. "It means little now, I suppose, but Babette was not a good mother."

"Nor I a good guardian."

"You did everything in your power, I'm certain. Children are difficult. Look at mine, Anna Maria. Perhaps it was our fault, mine and Leo's. Perhaps parents are the least qualified to raise children."

The countess left the room.

Anna's hand moved down to cradle her belly. What a strange thing for her aunt to say about parents. It took a very long time for sleep to claim her.

Anna heard a voice calling her. A man's voice. It seemed as though she had only just fallen asleep.

It was an angry voice, familiar in its impatience. "Anna Maria! Anna Maria!"

She sat up in bed, her back straight as a rod, perspiration beading on her forehead, heart thumping against her chest. The day was only just dawning and the room was a canvas for the interplay of nighttime shadows and tenuous light. She sensed the ethereal silence of breaking day. She felt, too, the palpable presence of danger.

Then she heard a faint sound, metallic in nature. She turned to stare in astonishment at the door. The door handle was slowly, almost imperceptibly, being depressed! Her heart seemed to stop. A click set the door free, and it started to move inward.

Suddenly, a tall figure was standing in the shadows a few feet into the room. She had not seen the steps that propelled him there.

"Who . . . who is it?" Anna could scarcely recognize the reedy voice as her own.

He moved silently and deliberately toward the bed.

In the blink of an eye, the man was standing over her, smiling insidiously. Anna looked up into Antoni's face. She drew in a long breath.

Her eyes fell now on the corded rope he was holding in his hand. She knew its purpose.

Anna tried to rise from the bed. "No, Antoni!" she called out.

In an instant, he was upon her, pressing the cord hard against her throat.

She struggled to call out again, but her breath was already stifled by his hand. Her arms flailed about helplessly.

She felt the cord tightening by degrees. Long seconds passed. Her world went black. She felt herself falling, falling, as though into some abyss. His hand was suddenly gone and the great fear within her was expelled in screams like those of a lost soul.

Slowly she became aware that someone was slapping her lightly upon the cheeks. "Wake up," a voice was saying. "Wake up, my child."

Anna's eyelids opened. Lutisha was staring down at her, her gray eyes full of concern.

"You were having a nightmare," Lutisha said. "I've never heard anyone scream so. Don't you know you're home safe with us now?"

Anna tried to smile. Home. Yes, she thought. But safe?

"It's already midmorning, Lady Anna," Lutisha was saying, "let's get you up and moving. You've got company!"

The news jolted her awake. Her ghostly dream dissipated at once. "Who?"

43

Anna walked into the reception room to find Aunt Stella conversing in low tones with Jan Stelnicki.

They both stood. "Jan tells me," the countess said, "that you have written him."

Anna's heart raced with excitement at seeing Jan even as she steeled herself for her aunt's reaction. "I did." Here at last was the confrontation with her aunt regarding Jan. Was there to be a terrible scene?

"I see." The countess appraised Anna. "Oh, don't worry, child, I'm not going to scold you. After all, this is a man who has taken up Kościuszko's banner."

Anna had no time to react to her aunt's seeming change of heart. Jan was crossing the room to her. His uniform consisted of black boots, white trousers, and a dark blue coat that intensified the blue of his eyes. He kissed her hand, his expression darkly serious. "You've been through so much."

Anna smiled into those eyes. She had doubted she would ever see him again, ever look into those eyes again. And yet, here he was. "There is more to the story than what Aunt Stella has told you."

"Anna Maria," her aunt asked, "shall I leave you alone for a bit?"

Anna turned to detain her. "No, Aunt Stella. What I have to say, you must hear, too. It's about Antoni."

Anna seated herself opposite her aunt and Jan. She wondered whether they would believe her. She wondered if she herself believed that her husband had tried to kill her, and had in fact killed two innocent children. Perhaps there was an explanation; perhaps circumstantial evidence had made her draw conclusions that were untrue.

The story took no more than half an hour's time. Anna watched the stricken faces of her aunt and Jan. As she spoke and recreated the experience for them, she relived the harrowing nightmare herself.

A little silence fell over the three when her story was told. The remembering and telling had confirmed her own suspicions anew. But what about Jan and Aunt Stella? Anna studied the faces across from her. Did they believe her?

"So," Jan sighed, "the Russian who escaped no doubt reported to Antoni. He must have hoped you were dead, but when he went back to the site he could come to no conclusion. He investigated and stumbled upon the priest."

"Dear God in Heaven," the countess gasped. "Is it possible, Anna Maria? Your *husband*?"

"What other explanation might there be, Aunt?"

The countess could only shake her head.

"Who could have sent the Poles?" Jan asked.

"Yes, there is that," the countess rejoined.

Anna shook her head slowly. "I don't know. They were on a mission to rescue me, I'm certain. I thought perhaps one of you might have sent them . . . or was it Zofia?"

"Had I known you were in trouble," Jan said, "I wouldn't have sent anyone, Anna. I would have gone myself. One day I hope to shake the hand of this Antek."

"And I had no clue, dearest. I think I may say the same for Zofia."

"Then it is a mystery," Anna said.

"Well, what are we to do?" the countess cried. "What if Antoni is to come here?"

"Oh, he will come here, Aunt," Anna said. "And I don't think our wait will be long."

"If this is true," the countess said, "we must bring charges. He must be kept from you, Anna, and he must pay for the lives of those two children. Isn't that so, Jan?"

"In a perfect world, yes."

"What do you mean?" the countess asked.

"I mean that all we have here are circumstances, conjectures, nothing else. Anna is the only living witness. And she has been eyewitness to nothing that involves Antoni directly."

Anna's blood chilled. It was as she had feared. Jan was right. There was no real evidence against her husband. Nothing tangible. And now he moved about at will, able to strike when he chose.

The countess became flushed and agitated at this news, and Anna found herself soothing her. "It's nothing," the countess insisted, "just my palpitations. They'll pass soon enough."

Nonetheless, Lutisha was summoned, and the three assisted the countess to her bedchamber.

"I'd better go now," Jan said as he and Anna came out from the Countess Gronska's room.

Anna felt a familiar emptiness as she walked him toward the door. How she longed for him to turn to her, to hold her. How had it all come to this? Perhaps it would be better never to see him, rather than having to seize the briefest of moments and then part. Always parting.

He turned then and took her hand. "You know that I would have come, had I known?"

She nodded. "Of course."

"You must do as I ask now, Anna. No matter what, I will stay in the city until Antoni does make his appearance, as he must. You are to have a letter already written—and at first sight of him you are to dispatch it immediately to the Queen's Head, do you hear?"

"Yes."

"I am not always there, of course, but I will leave word always as to my whereabouts. If the tavern is closed, have your messenger wake the proprietress who lives above stairs. She has a young son who will get it to me in quick order."

Anna nodded.

"You will ask Zofia about the Poles who came to your aid?"

"I will."

"Be brave." Jan kissed Anna's hand. "I should go."

"But . . ."

With the door open, he turned back to her. "What is it, Anna?"

"But what can you *do* . . . when Antoni arrives, I mean?"

Jan's smile was enigmatic. "I shall confront him." He turned then and began moving down the stairs to the street.

"But what does that mean?" Anna called.

He pretended not to hear.

Zofia arrived that afternoon, bursting into Anna's room in an effusive display of surprise and delight. "Why, dear Anna, we thought you dead!" she cried, at last releasing her cousin from a long embrace. "Is it truly you?"

Anna smiled. "It is."

"And the baby?"

"Fine."

"What wonderful news! I've just come from the most delightful cruise, though the ship never left its docking. Too much ice still in the river. But it was delicious. Oh, Anna, I'm overwhelmed to find you home and safe. Antoni did not hold out much hope for you. But he found you! How wonderful! Is he here?"

"Come let's sit down. I must tell you . . . about Antoni."

"What is it?" Zofia asked, seating herself across from her cousin.

For the second time that day, Anna lived through the story. What the enigmatic Zofia felt as she listened to the details of Anna's close call and the deaths of the children was impossible for Anna to decipher. However, she was openly skeptical about Anna's conclusions regarding Antoni's role in all of it.

"I find the whole thing improbable, Anna, highly improbable," she announced at the story's conclusion.

"Then you did not send the party of Poles to take me back from the Russians?"

"I? No, of course not. They may have been highwaymen. Perhaps you misunderstood. Surely Antoni will explain himself when he gets here."

"Zofia, should he be allowed into this house, my life is forfeit. Perhaps not immediately, but in time he will find a new way to rid himself of me."

"Don't you think that if you just give yourself over to the marriage and—"

"No! Even if I gave him my estate at Sochaczew to do with as he wishes, all the cards are on the table now. He has made up his mind that I am a hindrance. You must understand, Zofia. I must convince you. Your mother understands the danger, as does Jan."

"Jan?" Zofia's face bled to white.

"Yes."

"He's been here?"

Anna nodded.

"On whose invitation?"

"Mine."

Zofia gasped. "Why, you little minx! No wonder you want to divest yourself of your husband! Perhaps it is you who wishes to dispose of a spouse. Not even home a day and you have him sniffing around. When will you give up your pipe dream of possessing Jan Stelnicki?"

"I have no hopes of—"

"Don't even try to deny it." Zofia's face was reddening now in anger. "And just what does Count Stelnicki think he can do to remedy the situation?"

"I don't know what he plans to do."

"I suppose you would like it if they dueled and Antoni was killed. Would that solve all your problems, cousin?"

"I do not wish for—"

"You do not have permission to invite Jan Stelnicki into my home. Please remember that." She started for the door. "Oh, and I'm having company tomorrow night. If it becomes too raucous downstairs, just send me word." At the door, she turned back and appeared to warm slightly. "Oh, as for Antoni, I will set about my own investigation. Leave it to me should he be guilty."

"Zofia?" Anna called.

"Yes?"

"Will you send Babette upstairs?"

"I will." And she was gone.

Anna had the unhappy task of telling Babette the details of her children's deaths. How is it, she wondered, that Zofia had shown so little emotion at the tragic story of the French children? Where is her heart? If Babette had been telling the truth when she entrusted her children to Anna—that Zofia insisted she give up the children or her position as maid—how could she not realize that the advice she had given Babette led to their deaths?

Anna thought back to Zofia's reaction to the mention of Jan. There was emotion enough then! What motivated her to such disdain of Jan? Anna had to admit to herself now that she had deliberately baited Zofia, waiting and watching for her cousin's reaction to Jan's name. Did Zofia really think him the one at the pond? Or might it be that she herself loved Jan and wished to scuttle his love for Anna? Yet, how could that be? She had denied any attraction to him and actively *encouraged* Anna to pursue him.

Anna recognized an irony in that the countess was no longer an obstacle to Anna's relations to Jan, or so it seemed. It was Zofia now who forbade Jan to come to the house. Anna knew that whatever Zofia's real motives were, one day she and Zofia would have a terrible confrontation. It was a day to which she did not look forward.

Babette was a long time in coming. At last, she opened the door with a tentative air and slowly entered. "It is so very good to see you, Madame."

"Oh, Babette, it is good to see you." Anna approached her, kissing her lightly on the cheeks. She cared little about breaking with custom. She had learned that Marzanna knows no classes. "It is good to be home."

The pretty French maid stood before her, her lustrous dark hair cascading about her heart-shaped, small-featured face. Anna found it difficult to read her mood.

"Oh, Babette, I only wish that Louis and little Babette were with me. I'm so sorry for that."

Babette smiled slightly. "I am resigned. We heard some weeks ago about the tiny graves that Lord Grawlinski found. Madame must not blame herself. It was I who conscripted them into your service. Whatever happened was God's will."

"Perhaps. Do you wish to know the circumstances?"

"Of what use could it be, Madame? I think not."

"I think you should know," Anna insisted, motioning for the woman to sit down.

Babette hesitated but obeyed.

Anna calmly told her of the truce she had formed with the children and the hopes she had had for them. These were good children in need of firm direction and love. Families would reach their full potential if only a parent's eyes sparkled each time they beheld a child.

Anna wanted Babette to know the full extent of her loss. And she realized, too, on some deeper level, that she wanted to share her own pain and guilt.

Anna told Babette about the plot on their lives, the poison, the fighting, the burning carriage. By the time she was finished, Babette sat quietly stunned.

Anna immediately regretted having told the woman everything. What possible good could it do to so break the woman's heart anew? To go into such detail had been mean-spirited and selfish of her. After all, she and her own child had survived.

Anna rose now and walked to the alcove that housed her desk. From a drawer, she withdrew some bank notes placed for this occasion, a goodly sum, and brought them to Babette's accepting hands. "I want you to have this, Babette."

The woman nodded soberly and rose to withdraw. "It is exceedingly generous of you, Lady Grawlinska."

Anna smiled, thinking that her speech had touched her.

"Madame should not be so distressed," Babette said, moving to the door, then turning around. "They were not good children. They had no father. And I think I was not a good mother. Neither were they happy children. I suspect that they sensed they were not . . . planned. Maybe, Madame, it is all for the best."

Anna could only stare in disbelief at the door as it closed behind the maid. Aunt Stella's words came back to chill her: *"Perhaps parents are the least qualified to raise children."*

44

The message came at dusk.

Jan's hands worked feverishly at saddling his horse, his mind a web of thought and emotion. That the note had come from Countess Stella and not Anna was unsettling. *Antoni is home,* it read, *come at once*. Why hadn't Anna herself written? Had something already happened?

He mounted now, adjusting the pistol hidden by his waistcoat, and directed the horse out of the carriage house and into the night.

Anna had said it would not be long before Antoni turned up, and she had been right. Had she been right about everything else? He had believed Anna's earnest suppositions about her husband, yet in retrospect they seemed like something out of fiction. What kind of man plots to kill his own wife, risking the lives of children in the bargain? Of course, there were such men, men who valued themselves above everything.

He spurred the horse through muddied streets.

He was incensed to think anyone would attempt to harm Anna. Since he had met her, she was all he could think of. If it were true, he felt capable of dispatching Grawlinski on the spot. What need was there for a formal duel? What need was there for the slow and haphazard workings of the law? If he could only be *certain* of Antoni's malevolent intent for Anna, yes, he would do it. Gladly. But what if Anna had let her judgment become colored by her dislike of the man, her resentment of the arranged marriage, or her love for another?

A perfect world, he had told the Countess Gronska. In a perfect world, Antoni's guilt would be proved. But this is not a perfect world, he knew. "To meet an angel, one had to go to heaven," his own mother had often said. Earthly reality was different. How many guilty go unpunished daily? Would it be so with Antoni?

Jan pulled on the reins, slowing his horse as he moved into a heavier flow of traffic near the bridge to Praga. His hands were perspiring, he realized. He was nervous.

His options were twofold and simple on the exterior. He could kill Antoni. Or he could allow Antoni to live. What was it to be? To kill him would make it all so neat. The husband of the woman he loved would be dead and out of the way. In time, she would be free to marry another, himself. But how would the law see it? What if Antoni were *not* guilty? Or what if his guilt were never proved? Could he live with himself, having taken the man's life—and his wife? No, not with any integrity.

And if Antoni were to live, was there some way he could be prevailed upon to give up his sham of a marriage? Could he be intimidated into releasing Anna? Might he be bought off? Anna's religious ties, too, were to be considered. As long as Grawlinski lived, she and her church would deem it a marriage. Jan knew divorce was forbidden in the Catholic Church, but in cases where a marriage wasn't a marriage, might annulment be a possibility? The ways of churches were often inscrutable to him.

The thundering echo of the horse's hooves on the wooden bridge seemed to further jumble Jan's thoughts. He had only minutes now to rethink his options.

Presently he arrived at the Gronski town house. Countess Stella Gronska met Jan at the door, a lamp in her hand. Evidently, she had anticipated his arrival, for he had been about to lift the knocker when she opened the door and motioned him in.

They moved noiselessly to the open doors of the reception room. Jan could hear a man's low tones.

Stepping in, he saw Anna's face first. She was seated. She looked neither frightened nor angry. Just passive in some vague sort of way. The amber-flecked green eyes were lifeless pools. Antoni was pacing in short steps, never moving far from his wife. He seemed agitated, his voice quietly impassioned.

It was Anna's expression—Jan thought it more alarm than relief—that gave away Jan's presence to Antoni. He turned about, startled at first to see someone not of the household, startled again as he took in just who it was. But by the third beat he had masked his displeasure. "Stelnicki, is it not?" He forced a smile.

"Sir!" Jan responded, bringing together the heels of his boots and bowing slightly.

"Why, Anna Maria," Antoni cried, "we have a guest!"

Anna nodded silently.

The countess remained in the doorway as Jan moved into the room. He had expected Anna to be in tears or raging in accusation. What did this passiveness portend? Were things as she had made them out to be? Or had her mind been changed somehow?

Anna looked at Jan, nodded expressionlessly.

Antoni's gaze went from one to the other. "Ah, you two scarcely act as though you have not seen each other since the Royal Castle. If I'm any judge, I would say you two have met recently, in fact." Antoni behaved as though Jan and Anna were two children found at some forbidden mischief. "Am I right? It's true?"

Jan attempted a polite smile. The man was astute, he thought. "I made an initial visit yesterday to welcome Anna back. I only learned then what she has been through."

"Purely a social call?" Antoni asked, the corners of his dark moustache rising. "And only just hours after her arrival in Warsaw? What coincidence!"

Jan braved it out. "Yes, indeed!"

"You've become a soldier in the interim."

"Yes."

"Infantry?"

Jan was well aware Antoni knew better, but he was not going to be baited. He smiled. "Light Cavalry."

"You know, my dear Stelnicki, I really should be angry with you. The last time I saw you was the last time I saw my wife. We had—you and I—our words then. Now she and I are happily reunited after so much . . . distress . . . and here you are again. Strange, isn't it? If I were not in such a relieved and ecstatic frame of mind to find Anna Maria after I had every reason to give her up, I might not find room in my heart to be polite to a rascal like you. But then, she is an easy woman to like, is she not?"

Anna stared at Antoni as if he had just quoted the Bible, but she did not dispute her husband. She looked back to Jan and said nothing.

"Yes," Jan answered. "She is an easy woman to like."

"And to love?"

Jan grew angry. Later he would realize that the truth had angered him so. Of course, he had long ago opened himself to the intensity of his love for her, but to hear Grawlinski speak of it coarsened it. He tried to keep up a cool front. "You could have no better wife, Grawlinski."

"Yes, I agree. Anna Maria has, however, a predilection for fantasy. It is her chief failing. She read too much as a child, I think."

Neither Jan nor Anna spoke.

"It's the most amazing thing, Stelnicki. My wife has imagined that *I* have been behind the terrible things that have befallen her. Can you imagine? Why, now I can only guess that it was her lack of faith in me that must have taken you away from whatever heroic deeds you are about these days."

Anna squirmed in her chair. Jan could only wonder at her protracted silence.

"And you have assured her—"

"That I am innocent? On my father's grave, I have! It pains me to the quick to have her think and give voice to such things. But, alas, she has listened to reason. We are a family once again."

"I see."

"I will not let Anna Maria wander off into danger again. She shall stay under my wing. You see, Stelnicki, we will be happy."

Anna stood now, and both Jan and Antoni turned to her. "That is not possible, Antoni." Her voice was soft but even.

"Anna, dearest, to find your tongue only to say such things! This is talk of the moment and talk not meant for others' ears."

"I won't have you stay in this house."

"I am your husband, and do remember that the house is Zofia's."

"Then it is *I* who will not stay!"

"To do what?" Antoni was losing his patience. "To run off with him? A soldier? To disgrace your aunt's name? Your father's memory?"

The mention of her father seemed to startle Anna. Her head tilted in her husband's direction, green fire in her eyes. She could not bring herself to words.

"I've told you!" Antoni continued. "I've explained."

"What?" Jan pressed. "What has he explained, Anna?"

Antoni turned on Jan. "You've worn out your welcome, Stelnicki. But go ahead, Anna Maria, tell him. And when you've been told, Stelnicki, you are to disappear from our lives. Go back to playing soldier."

Anna stared at Antoni. Jan couldn't read the emotion playing out on her face. What was this that she kept so subdued? Anger? Then she turned her back to both of them.

"Anna Maria?" Her husband was affecting a loving tone. "Tell Stelnicki."

With her back to them and her words bereft of emotion, she said, "He says that he was the one who sent the Poles."

Jan took a moment for it to sink in. If it were true, it meant that Antoni had *saved* Anna's life. It was a dizzying thought. No wonder Anna seemed so torn. She, like him, wanted nothing more than to have done with Antoni Grawlinski.

"I most certainly did send the Poles," Antoni said. "The Russians were kidnappers who meant to ransom my wife."

"Kidnappers? Why?" Jan asked. "What proof is there of that?"

"Proof? Who needs proof, Stelnicki? Evidently *I* was tried and found guilty without any proof."

"Anna," Jan asked, "do you believe it?"

Anna did not turn around. A long moment passed. Anna's answer came as a mere whisper: "Perhaps . . . I don't know. . . ."

"Listen to me, Anna Maria," Antoni said as he moved toward her, reaching for her arm.

Later, Jan's memory would replay that move as one that hinted violence, but for now there was no time to interpret, only time to act.

Jan took three quick, precise steps and struck his fist flush into Antoni Grawlinski's face.

45

Anna lay sleepless. She could hear what seemed a hundred servants milling about in the street beneath her windows. Inside, Zofia's guests danced and made merry. The orchestra had abandoned the processional-like polonaises and stately minuets of the early evening for rousing mazurkas and polkas. The effervescent laughter had swollen, too, to a near riotous din punctuated by high shrieks and an occasional tinkling crash of what Anna supposed must be her aunt's crystal glassware.

The disturbance downstairs was not the only reason sleep would not come. The duel was a mere thirty-six hours away. Someone would die, and there was no calling it off. When men set such things, Anna knew, neither God nor nature can dissuade them. Antoni had been shamed into making the challenge. He had had no recourse. He had gained consciousness only to look up from the floor to Anna to Jan to Countess Gronska to the several servants in the room. He took it all in, his gaze going back inexorably to Jan, his voice croaking out, "When?"

And so it had been set. Midmorning Thursday in a patch of forest outside Praga. Pistols. Jan and Antoni were each to have two men attending. No one else was to be present, as these things were not sanctioned, and hadn't been for decades. Jan or Antoni would likely be killed. Perhaps both.

What had made Jan strike Antoni? She remembered that he could be rash. At the pond he had let anger get the best of him when he thought she had believed Zofia's account that he had made advances to her, tearing her blouse. Oh, yes, he had been angry enough to leave Anna there.

Where was her husband now? He had not insisted on staying at the Gronskis', not after such a scene. Anna wondered at first if he might run away, but she suspected that his desire to be a magnate kept him in Warsaw even if his bond of honor did not.

At midnight Anna pulled herself out of bed, drawing on a blue wrap. Lutisha had cautioned her to stay in bed, but her dark thoughts and the sounds of merriment made her restless. The whole house seemed to vibrate with music and voices. She wanted to take just a quick look from the balcony.

She had seen Zofia only briefly after the duel had been set. Her cousin's reaction had been impossible to read. Anna had been certain that she would cancel her party, that it was quite inappropriate under the circumstances. Evidently, however, such a notion had not occurred to Zofia.

Neither had it occurred to Zofia to invite Anna to her party. Anna put it down to the fact that she was now a full six months along. Expecting women were not to be seen socially, of course. Still, Zofia was not one to obey custom.

It took little more than opening her door for Anna to realize why she had not been included among the guests. As she took a half-step into the hallway, a young woman raced by, followed by an old man with great bushy whiskers of white, yet hair as black as ebony. The woman stopped at the balcony, allowing the man to catch up to her. When he did, she danced a delicate sidestep and dipped her body to escape his grasp. The woman then turned and started to race back toward the stairhead, but stopped in her tracks at the sight of Anna.

"Oops!" she blurted. "Excuse me, I hope we didn't disturb you." Her highly powdered wig was tilting to the side and the curls were coming undone. Her orange ball gown with its many flounces of pale green was so disheveled that one of her breasts was exposed.

"Caught you, you twit!" The old man's arms encircled the woman's thin waist from behind.

"Stop it, fool!" she said. "Are you as blind as you are old?"

He noticed Anna now and smiled stupidly.

"You are Zofia's cousin, are you not?" the woman asked, nonchalantly adjusting her bodice.

Anna could only stare as the woman pattered on with one silly comment after another. A beauty patch, too large to be attractive, hung precariously on her white cheek, like a wart. Her lip paint had been so smeared that her moving mouth looked aslant, as if it would slide off her face at any moment.

The old man had come to attention with all the aplomb and charm he could muster. "Good evening, my lady," he said, to comic effect. "It is a lovely party. Will you not join it?"

Before Anna could think of some excuse, the woman drove both of her elbows backward, into the man's appreciable paunch. Caught off guard as he was, he released her and fell into a coughing spasm.

The woman took the opportunity to escape and disappeared down the stairway, singing some inane French parlor song as she went.

The old man straightened, collecting himself. He eyed Anna uncertainly, his black toupee askew on his head, like a dead raven. He smiled oddly and Anna sensed, horrified, that he was about to transfer his affection to her.

She immediately tucked in the folds of her wrap above her protruding stomach so that he could see her condition. The effect was not lost on the man despite his drunkenness.

His eyes enlarged slightly and he suddenly stiffened. "Madame," he said in a slur that he no doubt thought dignified, "will you be so good as to excuse me now? I go to rejoin the divertissement."

Seconds later Anna watched the black hairpiece descending the stairs in quick little jolts.

Anna was not ready to retreat. She walked out onto the balcony, at first keeping her distance from the rail so as to reduce the likelihood of being seen. Only half of the candles on the huge chandelier had been lighted so that the main hall of the Gronski home was bathed in semidarkness. Emboldened by the dimness, Anna moved to the railing. Below was a tapestry of Satan sprung to life. All the condemned of Warsaw were here this night, it seemed, lounging and cavorting on the steps, on the carpet, on the bare marble. Those still dancing would trip and tumble over those reclining. Anna recognized a number of these people, some half dressed, as undoubtedly noble. It seemed a paradox.

Anna wondered where Aunt Stella might be found. How could she allow this?

She caught sight then of the plump Charlotte Sic. As on the occasion when she had met her—on the way to the Royal Castle—the French princess was bedecked in a glittering array of diamonds: a tiara set into her high golden wig, long pendant earrings, and her fabulous three-tier necklace. This time she wore nothing else above the waist.

Anna blinked in disbelief. And either she let out a little cry, or the princess merely sensed someone's eyes on her from above because she looked up suddenly, her eyes narrowing in appraisal of Anna.

As fate would have it, a mazurka came to an end at that moment so that when Charlotte called out for everyone to look above, she was heard quite distinctly. "Zofia!" she exclaimed, with the seasoned air of an actress. "You didn't tell me you had invested in statuary!"

The woman was pointing at her now. Anna's instinct was to run, but her feet would not move.

"Why, that's no statue," sang some woman who had taken Charlotte literally.

"Why, then," said the princess, "if it is no statue, it must be a vision, and all in blue. Zofia, come quickly! Damn, where is she? We are being visited by the Virgin herself and in the months before she gave birth!"

Anna would not wait to see if Zofia were one of those souls below pushing their way from other rooms to see what the commotion was about. Her heart pumped a terrible heat into her face. Then the hellish laughter at last loosened her from her spot at the railing and she raced back to her room.

What had possessed Princess Sic to speak to her like that? She had been nice to Anna previously. Perhaps Zofia had found some way to make Charlotte regret having told Anna about the liquor business Antoni wanted to set up at Sochaczew.

The party continued until dawn.

At midmorning the next day, a count Anna had never met was shown into the upstairs sitting room.

"Lady Grawlinska, I am Paweł Potecki."

Anna nodded, wondering what business he had with her. He possessed a sturdy frame, good features, black curly hair.

"Zofia has spoken so often of you," he said. "I am so glad to finally meet you."

"Thank you." Anna could think of little to say. She had never heard Zofia speak of *him*. What was this man about?

The man glanced at Lutisha, who had stayed after ushering him in and played now at dusting the furniture. Anna immediately realized that he was hesitant to speak in front of a servant.

"Would you leave us now, Lutisha?" Anna asked. "I will ring should I need you."

The large woman bristled at the request, her eyes momentarily daring to question. Anna's cool stare, however, was unwavering and the servant left the room, but not without leaving the door open wide. No doubt the servant had heard much in recent weeks. Anna suspected that she hovered nearby, ready to play protectress.

Anna and the count looked at each other and laughed.

"She is a treasure," he said.

"No doubt she thinks I should be closeted as my term goes on. But I don't know what the household would do without her."

The count grew serious. "Lady Grawlinska, I—"

"Lady Berezowska," Anna corrected, "please call me by my family name, not my married one. I no longer consider myself married."

His eyes opened a bit at the distinction, but he acceded with a nod. "As you wish. Lady Berezowska, Zofia has asked me to speak with you about last night."

"Oh?"

"She is heartbroken about how everything seemed to get out of hand."

"I see. Tell me, Lord Potecki, were you present?"

"No, I just now rode into the city."

"Oh." Somehow Anna could not imagine him present. She sensed him to be a man of some character.

"But I understand it got a little lively."

"Is that how my cousin put it? She hardly does it justice."

"Oh, she's quite ashamed. I am to intercede on her behalf. Some comments were made about you, I take it."

"Oh, they were silly, drunken things said by a silly, drunken woman."

"You will forgive your cousin, then?"

Anna thought a few moments while the count patiently waited. "Lord Potecki," she said at last, with an air of resignation, "I am not in a position to excuse my cousin. Zofia is not accountable to me. I am for the time being but a guest in the Gronski home."

"Then you bear her no ill feelings?"

"How could I? Zofia and her parents have done so much for me. And perhaps her father would be here today to discipline her if it hadn't been for me and a day long ago when I chose not to obey my aunt and uncle. No, I can't judge. I only wish . . ."

"I know," the count said. "Zofia is at once a weak and wild creature. She's like an untamable bird from the tropics. All the primary colors, you know? But her intentions are good, Lady Anna, and her love for you runs deep. She would do anything for you. Sometimes we must accept those we love as they are, rather than attempt to make them over."

"You mean rather than tame them?"

"Yes."

"Perhaps you are right." Anna instinctively knew then the Count Paweł Potecki was in love with Zofia, and that he must often have occasion to excuse her for much. Love, Anna thought, now there is a *power*.

The count stood to leave. "Then I may tell Zofia that nothing has changed between the two of you?"

Anna smiled. "Yes." She could not say why she was so trusting of one of Zofia's associates, but it was so.

The count kissed her hand. "I wish you a strong child, Lady Anna, strong and healthy."

"And if it is a girl?"

He laughed. "Girls, I sometimes think, need more strength than boys."

After he left, Anna sat in thought. He was to tell Zofia that nothing had changed between Anna and her cousin. She wanted to laugh. Why, even if they were to live, God willing, into their old age, they were worlds apart. Things most certainly had changed.

46

Jan was up long before dawn. His body felt heavy, his mind cloudy. He had slept little that night. He had needed all his rest in order to be quick in every way this morning. Now, despite his avoidance of liquor the night before, he still felt compromised by the lack of sleep and lingering fatigue. Had Grawlinski gotten a good night's rest?

As he shaved, Jan watched himself closely in the mirror. The thought occurred to him that this might be the last time he shaved. He tried to put it out of his mind.

He was confident in his skills as a marksman. He had practiced regularly at the farm and kept up with pistol practice and fencing at the university. One never knew when one of his class might be called on to lead in war. What about Antoni? Could he shoot worth a damn?

Jan had never dueled before. Did Antoni have any experience? What was it like to kill someone? Would he be able to do it? More and more, it looked as though Poland would have to fight to keep her independence. Her continuing steps toward a democracy were not taken lightly by Prussia or Austria or Russia, neighbors that had already raised arms against her in the recent past. The next time he would be in the thick of it, he knew, and killing would—for a time—be a way of life. How he knew this, he wasn't sure, but he already saw himself in battles, fighting for his country, his heritage.

But to kill someone in a duel? To kill Grawlinski? That was different. And yet, could he allow Antoni to live? Was he the threat to Anna that she thought? He remembered the very moment he had struck Antoni. And he had to be truthful with himself. What had driven him was not fear that Anna was at that moment in any real danger from Antoni. He could admit to himself now that it was the crushing disappointment that Antoni might be *innocent*.

From that, it had come to this, he thought. And what if Antoni were the better shot?

His housekeeper knocked at the door with the news that his friends Józef and Artur had arrived. They were to be his seconds.

"Bread and coffee for three?" she asked.

"No, Wanda, something more substantial. An omelette, perhaps, a huge omelette with sausage or ham—no, both!"

The woman turned to hurry down to the kitchen, smiling at the break in the routine. She knew nothing about the duel.

Countess Stella Gronska seated herself in the downstairs reception room with her niece and daughter. There they would await the outcome of the duel between Antoni Grawlinski and Jan Stelnicki. Both Anna and Zofia averted their eyes each time she looked at them. The tension in the air was palpable. What had transpired between them? There was the party, of course. The countess fumed at the thought of it. The house was still not back in order. And so many broken crystal wineglasses!

She had not felt well that evening and had retired early. In the morning she had been told that she slept through it. But to look at the shambles in which the house had been left, she could not believe it. No, she had not merely slept through it. She suspected she had been drugged. It was no use bringing it up to Zofia, not with what was going on in the forest right now, but she would be on her guard in the future. Imagine that, she thought, having to watch one's back against a daughter. There was, however, one fuzzy memory of that night that came back to her now. She dreamt she had awakened from a deep sleep to find a man's face peering into her doorway. The man could have been Walter's double. *Had* it been a dream?

"Zofia," the countess asked, "was Walter at your party the other night?"

"Walter?" Zofia's expression was at first inscrutable. Then, as she looked from her mother to Anna and back to her mother again, she arranged her face into a mask of light mockery. "Why, Mother, it was a *party,* for pity's sake. One does not invite a brother like Walter to a party."

Morning had broken by the time Jan and his companions entered the forest. It was cool and crisp. Thick morning vapors rose languidly from the forest floor. Jan watched his own frosty breath as he exhaled, glad for the cold that shook him awake. He spoke little.

Józef was the guide. He had been here once before on a similar mission. Jan did not ask how that one turned out.

Soon they came to an area where the undergrowth and overhanging branches were too thick to pass on horseback. "This is where we leave the horses," Józef announced. "The clearing is maybe three hundred paces or more. It looks as though we're the first to arrive."

The three dismounted and secured the horses. They moved off then through the dense foliage, Józef first, then Jan, then Artur, who carried the case with the pair of pistols.

The forest was quiet and the thick mist rendered it eerie as a painting. The three friends fell silent again. Jan thought about the lengths to which Grawlinski had gone to kill Anna and take her land. If it were true, of what else was he capable? Would he even show himself today? If he did, was he prepared to fight honorably? And did fighting honorably mean shooting to kill?

Somewhere in the interior of the forest a cuckoo bird sang its strange lament. Jan thought then of the day in the forest that he and Anna had heard it. He had asked her if she had any coins to jingle so that—as the superstition went—all would be well. Neither of them had any coins. Jan was not superstitious, but their lives changed so that day. Now he found his hand had moved, involuntarily, toward his pocket. He had brought no coins this day, either. And he did not succumb to the temptation to ask his friends if they carried any.

Antoni and his party should have arrived by now. Where were they?

He thought he heard some noise then, like a horse's hoof crushing a twig. The others heard it, too. They stopped and listened.

All was quiet.

Józef assured him he knew of no good path that would accommodate a rider to the clearing. Artur suggested it was some small forest animal foraging its morning meal.

They began to move on. But Jan's nerves, already on edge, were sharpened. What if Antoni were taking no chances? What if he had planned an ambush? What if he had hired men to kill him, as he may have done with Anna? His heart caught at the idea. He knew that if such were the case, he had brought two good friends to their deaths. No one would be allowed to live to tell the tale.

The cuckoo moaned again. The bird seemed closer.

Jan knew that his two friends had been put on guard, too. The three fell silent.

As they pushed on, he heard Artur behind him, gently, almost surreptitiously, rattling change in his pocket.

Her polished nails drumming the wooden arms of her chair, Zofia sat watching her mother knit and Anna pretend to read. They were attempting to mask their nervousness. What was there for *her* to be nervous about? And yet she was uneasy. She stood and began to pace.

She knew her mother glanced over at her from time to time in disapproval. The countess still seethed over the party and the condition of the house afterward. Oh well, Zofia thought, she will have to get used to the changes around here. She is merely a dowager now. The house is not to be eternally hung in crepe. And if it is all too much for her, she can go back to Halicz. Zofia smiled to herself then, thinking how well the laudanum trick had worked. Charlotte had been right: a little sprinkling of it into her mother's evening glass of sherry and she was off to her own private party!

Anna had not said a word about that night. Zofia had given Charlotte a verbal drubbing afterward, but the damage had been done. Zofia did not want to see Anna needlessly hurt. Indeed, she would see her cousin get anything she wished, barring one thing. Commissioning Paweł to soften her had paid off. There was always someone to take care of untidy things. Today, for instance, provided the supreme proof.

Lutisha bustled in with a coffee tray.

"Coffee?" Zofia sang. "I think we all need a drink!"

"Zofia!" the countess cried. "How can you be ready to drink and be light-headed about things when others may be dying at this moment?"

Zofia looked to Anna, whose mouth appeared as though it might smile at any moment, but whose eyes seemed set on tears. "I'm sorry," Zofia said, "I only meant that coffee puts one on edge and you are both already on edge."

"And I suppose you are not?" her mother retorted.

"No," Zofia lied.

Anna looked up. "Do you think the duel a foregone conclusion?"

Zofia sat down again. It seemed an objective and sincere question. As if Zofia had the answer to the future. "No, Anna, I suppose not."

"It is in God's hands," the countess said.

"Whatever the outcome," Anna sighed, "no good can come of it."

"You're right, I'm sure, Anna." Zofia looked at Anna's distant green eyes and thought something very different. *Ah, cousin, your husband or your love, is that it? And I know whom you would choose!*

Jan's uncertainties regarding Antoni Grawlinski were unfounded. He and his attendants arrived only a few minutes after Jan and his men found the clearing. The usual civilities took place: introductions, handshakes, clipped and polite conversation.

Jan found Antoni difficult to read. The gray eyes seemed placid, but something else lurked there, too, a kind of suppressed fire. Was it determination, or fear?

Józef went over the protocol: the signal to begin, the fifteen paces, the turn to fire.

The second of each duelist examined the guns of the other. There was talk of reducing the distance to ten paces because of the thick mist. No agreement was struck, so it remained at fifteen.

Jan wanted to tell Antoni he would shoot only to wound. He had come to that conclusion only half an hour before. He needed more proof that the man had tried to kill Anna. It wasn't that he didn't believe Anna. It was just that he needed proof before taking a life. He could not help but be struck by the painful irony that one might, in certain circumstances, doubt one's beloved—just as Anna had doubted for a moment at the pond. And he had not understood.

He could not bring himself to say anything. To do so would break with tradition. Today only the seconds and guns were to speak, and he suspected Antoni meant to shoot to kill. But he knew that his own pride, too, kept him from speaking. He wouldn't have Antoni thinking that he was trying to obtain quarter by giving it.

The two men were asked to take their places. They did so, each man selecting his gun. Neither looked the other in the eye now.

They came to stand back to back, ready to walk in opposite directions.

They would be a total of thirty paces apart, Jan thought. Would they even be able to make out each other's outline in the morning vapor? What good would marksmanship matter then?

If one shot from each did not resolve the duel, protocol called for the second pistols to be used at ten paces closer, twenty in all. It would take some doing to miss at twenty.

The tiniest noise—the rustle of a mouse in the leaves or the flailing of a bat—echoed strangely in the cathedral of the forest. Jan heard a faint drumming that seemed to come from miles away, vibrating along the forest floor and up into his being. Before the signal was given, he realized that it was the beating of his own heart.

"No man knows courage," his father had told him, "who has not known fear."

The signal, merely nods from a Stelnicki and a Grawlinski attendant, came and the men parted, moving off as the paces were counted by one of Antoni's attendants.

One . . . two . . .

Jan tried hard to concentrate. Not to do so meant his death. There would be no working for the democracy.

Five . . . six . . .

There would be no life within Anna's sphere, in whatever form it might manifest itself.

Eight . . . nine . . .

He tried to call upon all his powers now. He would wound Antoni, wound him and somehow make him give up his claim on Anna. But how?

Twelve . . . thirteen . . .

Something caught his ear now. What was it? The snap of a branch? Where? Nearby? What *was* it?

Fourteen . . .

What it was suddenly didn't matter to him. It had been enough to destroy what concentration he had.

Fifteen. Turn and fire!

Jan turned, his mind working just the fraction of a second behind. But it was enough of a deficit: Grawlinski got off his shot first.

47

The three women waited. No one had spoken for what seemed an hour. Anna thought she would scream out of frustration. Why hadn't she defied custom and gone herself? Why was it women were relegated to sitting in reception rooms waiting while men went about such lethal business?

The painted porcelain clock on the mantle held her captive. Half of an hour remained before the assigned time of ten o'clock. The timepiece ticked away slowly, so slowly Anna thought it was surely running down. She came to realize that she was not the only one to note every tick of the minute hand; her aunt's and cousin's eyes swept to and from the mantle at regular intervals, like search lanterns.

What if Jan kills Antoni? she thought. What then? Would her husband not come between her and Jan in death? And if he lives? What will have been solved by this primitive rite of honor?

And what if Jan is killed? Her mind went blank. Life without him was unthinkable. Even if they were never to marry, life without Jan seemed no life at all. She found herself catching her breath at the possibility. She should have gone, she thought, she should have gone.

At ten minutes before ten, the front door knocker sounded. The three women looked up in wonder, each moving her gaze from one to the other. What news could this be? The duel was only now about to take place, and then it might be two hours before they heard the outcome.

In a few minutes Lutisha ushered a man into the room.

Anna looked up to find Baron Michał Kolbi striding toward her. She tried to disguise her astonishment with a smile. She had hardly given him or his patriot friends a thought since arriving back in Warsaw. There had been no time.

She stood to greet him and introduced him to her aunt. Zofia, of course, needed no introduction, and her silent nod to him now indicated that his chilly attitude toward her overtures at the patriot celebration still rankled her.

Beaming, he turned to Anna. "I thought you dead, Anna, despite my measures. Praise God! I am so happy to see you."

Anna smiled. "It seems I have more lives than a cat, Michał. Will you be seated?" The baron brought up a chair to the women's circle and they all sat, Anna stealing a look at the clock as she did so. This was a happy distraction, but merely a distraction nonetheless. There were only minutes now.

"What measures?" Zofia asked.

Only now did Anna process what he had said. "*Despite my measures . . .*"

"Anna was right in her presentiments about Antoni," Michał said. "After she left for Saint Petersburg, I set to work and it did not take long to unravel the man's plot."

"Plot?" the countess asked.

The baron's gaze shifted to Countess Gronska. "I questioned after those men who had been conscripted to take your niece to Saint Petersburg. Her letter to me raised my suspicions. I found a man, a Russian, who had turned down the job because . . ."

Anna suspected that he had shocking news to relate and that he paused now out of deference to the Countess Gronska.

"Yes," the countess said, "do go on."

He nodded and drew a breath. "Because Grawlinski had no intention that Anna get to Saint Petersburg at all. The carriage was to be taken to Opole, to his family farm, but Anna was not to arrive . . . alive."

Countess Gronska gasped. "It's true, then. My God, it's true!"

"So, Antoni," Zofia said in a strangely flat manner, "did, indeed, mean to kill Anna."

Both the countess and Zofia turned to Anna, who seemed to be taking the news with silent equanimity. "And it was," Anna said, "*your* men who attempted to take me from the Russians?"

The baron nodded.

"God take their good and brave souls," Anna said.

"I've been scouting out Antoni for weeks, but he's an elusive devil. I've been as far as Opole and Częstochowa and have always come up just a step behind him. I do know he's now here in Warsaw. I intend to call him out and take a just revenge. I take it he hasn't shown here as yet?"

The women exchanged glances, suddenly remembering where Antoni and Jan were at that moment and what they were about. Before Anna could even shift her eyes to glance at the clock, it struck ten.

Antoni Grawlinski's shot whipped past Jan's left ear. He *had* meant to kill, Jan realized. He had aimed for the head. But he had missed.

Jan took in a mouthful of air now and aimed his own pistol. He felt confident that he could kill him—the heart was a more sensible target than the head—and yet, without solid evidence that damned him as Anna's would-be murderer . . .

He took his aim now, moving away from the heart, and fired.

Antoni was struck in the upper right shoulder. He remained standing. His left hand went protectively to the wound. There was blood on his hand when he withdrew it, a small amount. He looked up at Jan and smiled, as if to say, *You may have come off the better today, but not by much.*

I've had my chance, Jan thought, and I may regret not having taken it. He may yet be a threat to Anna.

At that moment an explosion rang out. Another pistol shot! In the blur of a few seconds Jan saw Antoni's chest open up and spill out a geyser of blood. His eyes enlarged in surprise and pain, and he crumpled to the ground.

"There! There!" Józef screamed, pointing to where a cloud of smoke hovered near a large oak. "It came from there!"

One of Antoni's friends ran to his aid. Jan and the others rushed to the spot where the foliage had concealed the sniper. Jan remembered hearing a noise from that direction, the noise that had put off his concentration. He took his extra pistol from Artur as they ran. But they heard the horse's hooves before they could get a clear line of vision. There *had* been a path of sorts, after all, and with all their horses many yards behind them, the man's getaway was a near certainty.

Still, Jan quickly aimed his loaded pistol and took his shot, its sound reverberating loudly through the forest. Its mark, however, already well out of range, cleanly escaped.

They returned to Antoni Grawlinski's lifeless form.

48

He is dead and that's that!" Zofia said. "Who *cares* who did it, Anna?

"A man like that," Michał offered, "does have his share of enemies." The baron had stayed to wait for news of the duel, news that reached Praga with the arrival of Jan just short of two hours after the event.

Anna had looked up to see Jan in the doorway, and her soul opened at the vision, filling with warmth and light. She had prepared herself for the worst. After all, if her father could desert her through death . . .

Jan was solemnly subdued. This was no surprise to Anna. He had seen death that day and in the most disturbing circumstances. Meeting the baron now for the first time, he listened to the case against Antoni with no little interest. Anna sensed that he shared Zofia's opinion: that what mattered now was that Anna could live her life without fear of her husband. The opportunity for them to speak privately did not arise before he took his leave.

In the days that followed, Anna wondered about Jan's reaction to Antoni's death. And with as much honesty as she could muster, she plumbed her own reaction. She wished no one dead, but she knew that she and her child would live now, thanks to some nameless assassin. Who was it? Feliks Paduch? Michał had solved one riddle, but now there was another, perhaps equally as worrisome.

She initiated no service for her husband, though she felt compelled to dress in mourning. She sent his body back to his mother in Saint Petersburg with a formal letter giving up any claim to the Grawlinski title and fortune. Let his parents keep everything, she thought. She wanted nothing to do with them. While the baron was old and probably harmless, Michał had seemed quite convinced that the Baroness Grawlinska knew very well what her son had been up to. Who knew what the mother of a man like that might be capable of herself? Anna wanted all ties to that family severed.

The third week of April found winter but a memory. The virgin rains and vapors of the new spring swept through the grateful kingdom, carrying off the sediments of the harsh months.

Anna heard nothing from Jan for some days, and she wondered if Zofia's interdict against him were the reason. Some of Anna's patriot friends visited her, lifting the impatient discomfort of the final months of her term. Because many of them were commoners, she was careful to keep such meetings from her cousin and aunt.

Halicz, under the jurisdiction of Austria since the Partition of 1772, and all of Poland mourned the death of Leopold II, Emperor of Austria and brother to Marie Antoinette. He had remained favorable to Poland's Constitution, maintaining that it might prevent revolution in Central Europe. Anna's compatriots clung to the hope—some judged it a thin one—that his successor, Francis II, would honor his father's alliance with Poland.

Aunt Stella's mind seemed steady during this time, and like Zofia, she was kind to Anna in the weeks following Antoni's death. Zofia, however, continued her entertainments at the town house, and Anna became determined to leave the city soon after her child's birth.

Anna was napping one afternoon when Lutisha came up to her bedchamber to say that Count Stelnicki was below in the reception room. "Shall I tell him you are indisposed, Madame?"

"Indisposed? You may not! Bring me my mirror."

"But Lady Anna Maria—"

"But what?"

"You are only six or seven weeks from coming to term," she said, handing Anna the mirror. "And your husband has died so recently. It is not appropriate for you to see Lord Stelnicki." The servant stopped, blushing at her own forwardness.

"Lutisha, I catch your meaning. I know what is said below stairs about Lord Stelnicki. Listen to me: it's not true. Uncle Leo was mistaken; Jan was not at fault for what happened at the pond last September. Do you understand?"

"Yes, Madame."

Jan stood and complimented Anna on her appearance as she approached him.

"What a cool liar you are, Lord Stelnicki."

"Lord Stelnicki? Is this what we've come to? Back to such formality?"

Anna dropped her happy retort when she saw that Zofia sat in the countess' chair near the fireplace. She was knitting. Knitting! Anna could not help but emit a little gasp. She had never seen her knit. She knew immediately that this was merely a bit of stage business and that her cousin planned to remain for the entirety of Jan's visit. Anna felt the seeds of fury take root within her at the thought of her cousin's intrusion.

Jan was questioning Anna now on her health, showing sincere concern as her time came due.

"What? Yes, I'm fine." Anna spoke absently, drawing her eyes away from her cousin, who sat feigning disinterest.

"You won't be for long, Anna, darling," Zofia said, without a glance up from her work, "if you don't take care of yourself. You should be in bed."

"I am fine, Zofia," Anna said. "Shouldn't you be in preparation for tonight's festivities?" Anna attempted a light tone but knew her meaning was clear and caustic. What had the two been talking about before she came into the room?

"Oh, there is a wealth of time," Zofia rejoined in the same false lightness. "I have all afternoon."

Jan and Anna seated themselves on the sofa. Jan told her that he had been in Kraków on political business and that he would have to go back within a day or two. Anna knew that it was Zofia's presence that inhibited him from kissing her hand, or even taking it into his. They were meeting for the first time since Antoni's death had freed Anna, yet she knew that neither of them would be able to say the things that only their eyes dared to communicate in the most surreptitious manner.

For half of an hour they attempted conversation that was polite and stilted. Anna's angry distraction with her cousin grew in proportion to the time lost.

At last, she had had enough of Zofia's meddling. She spoke directly to Jan, disregarding Zofia. "Jan, childbirth always involves a risk. Should something happen to me—"

"Why, Anna, you look splendid! Nothing will happen to you."

"Nevertheless, I want you to take this." Anna withdrew a sealed document from her skirts. "It is my will and statement of intent, should my child survive me."

Jan's face darkened. He reached for the document.

Anna sensed Zofia's steady gaze upon her. She ignored it. "Before you take it, Jan, I must ask you to become my child's guardian, should I die."

Zofia took in an audible breath and pitched in her chair, but Anna gave her no notice.

"Of course, Ania," Jan whispered.

She gave him the document. "My child's wealth will be left in your hands. I ask that you see to his education. I should like him to learn four or five languages. Knowing languages will be key to his future. Will you see to these things? It is much to ask, I know."

"It is not, but we needn't worry about such things. Why, you will teach him Polish, Russian, and French yourself!"

"I'm not worried for myself, Jan. I want my son to be a man of character."

"How can you know it's a boy?"

Anna shrugged. "A presentiment, I suppose. I shall be surprised if it is not." She felt a faintness overcome her then.

"Anna . . . are you all right?" Jan asked. "You're turning quite pale."

"It's nothing. A dizzy spell. It'll pass in a moment."

"She's too weak to be out of bed," Zofia said. "I knew this little interview would be too much for you, Anna Maria. My God, you're as pale as Marzanna!"

Like Anna, Jan ignored Zofia. "I'll stay here in Warsaw, Anna, until your child is born."

"No, that's not at all necessary. The birth is weeks away and you have important business to be about."

He nodded reluctantly. "I would be useless anyway, I imagine. But

I shall keep you informed of my whereabouts so you may send word of the birth . . . or if, in some way, I might be of help."

"Thank you, Jan."

Jan smiled and for a moment Anna was completely happy in the warmth of those lips above his dimpled chin.

"Anna, dearest," Zofia pressed, "I think it is time you return to your room."

"Zofia is right," Jan said, before Anna could protest. "I should be taking my leave." He rose and bowed to Anna, then to Zofia, saying his good-byes.

Zofia rang for Lutisha.

Just as the servant lumbered in, Zofia stood. "I'll see Lord Stelnicki to the door, Lutisha," she said. "You are to help Anna back to her room."

Anna seethed at Zofia's interference. She was left to wonder what Jan might have said, were it not for her cousin's presence.

Her mind's eye would cling to the look Jan's cobalt eyes cast in her direction as Zofia led him from the room, a reassuring glance from which she would draw strength during the ordeal of giving birth.

49

Although the Third of May Constitution had divided the ranks of the nobility, its first anniversary was greeted with unreserved, joyous celebration throughout the capital.

On that day Anna received several selling women and seamstresses in the downstairs reception room. Despite her continuing estrangement from her mother, Zofia attended and surprised Anna by seeming to enjoy helping Anna and Countess Gronska select from an assortment of babywear.

Countess Gronska had knitted a few things for the baby, but there were many more to be purchased. Anna preferred reading to sewing and so appreciated the painstaking craftsmanship that attended the making of the silken caps, the lace and cotton gowns, the tiny knitted booties, and, of course, the diapers. Each piece had some little flourish in design or coloring that was its maker's signature, so Anna purchased at least a few items from each seller.

"Oh, Anna," Zofia gushed, "you must let me buy this silken white robe for your child. Why, it's fit for a crown prince!"

Anna could not answer, for she was holding her belly and gasping in pain. The searing sensation had come on unannounced. She became uncomfortably warm as a cycle of hot blood warmed her face, then drained away.

The paroxysm seemed to pass, only to flare up again. Anna cried out in pain. The women around her buzzed like worker bees around their queen.

Anna was coaxed to lean back in her chair. Her breath came and went fitfully. Her aunt and cousin were on either side of her, plying her with questions and reassurances. Lutisha and Marta bustled about her with grim faces. Anna was gripped with a sense of suffocation that threatened to overwhelm her. She became very faint.

The pain struck a third time and Anna panicked. Was this usual? Had she come so far only to miscarry now, as her mother had done several times? Fear enveloped her.

She pointed to those clothes she had chosen and they were placed in her lap. She clasped them to her, closing her eyes, feeling warm and alien movements within herself.

"Lean forward to breathe, Madame," Lutisha ordered, her hand pressing down on her head. Then the servant's other hand—so large, Anna thought—was held to her belly. During the next several minutes, the pain came and went, came and went.

"The Countess Anna," Lutisha announced at last, "is about to give birth."

"It's impossible!" Countess Gronska said. "She isn't due until next month."

"You must be mistaken, Lutisha," Zofia said.

"In no time, Lady Zofia, you can tell that to the child itself," Lutisha dared to say. "It is ready to enter the world."

Anna listened absently to the buzz of conversation and whirr of activity. Suddenly, she became aware of a warmth spreading over her legs. She opened her eyes to find her lower body awash with water. Lutisha was right: she was about to give birth!

While she marveled that a child could come into the world so quickly, she was filled with fear, not so much fear for the pain she knew would come, but fear for the child. She knew early babies did not often survive.

The selling women were being dismissed, and each time the door to the street was opened, Anna could hear the festive music playing throughout the capital. That her child was being born on the third of May gave her confidence. Her father had once told her to look for signs in small things.

"The countess must go to her bed," Lutisha said.

"We'll not attempt the stairs," Aunt Stella replied, her mind never clearer than in this crisis. "Take her to my room."

While the Countess Gronska and Marta rushed away to prepare the bed, Zofia and Lutisha supported Anna in her walk to her aunt's room.

Hours passed. Anna was nearly unconscious when a priest appeared at the bedside. He told her what prayers to say, but the searing pain left her unable to speak. Before departing, he placed a rosary in her hand; however, she soon lost hold of it.

"Can you hear me, Anna Maria?" It was her aunt's voice.

"Yes."

"We've sent for the physician, but he may not arrive in time. Lutisha will deliver, if need be. She has experience. Do you understand?"

Anna nodded.

The room seemed unbearably hot. Perspiration ran from every pore of her face. The combs had been taken from her hair, freeing it to fall about her shoulders in wet strands. She did all that was requested of her.

Lutisha prepared to serve as midwife. The countess and Marta would assist. Zofia excused herself, whispering words of encouragement to her cousin, then removing herself from the room.

The pain heightened.

Outside, the Third of May celebration escalated, the lively polkas and mazurkas providing a surreal background to Anna's ordeal. Anna began to move to the music in the bed, not caring what those attending her would think. Later, she thought she only dreamt she was able to move to the music.

That she called out in pain no one could contest. Anna had never known such pain. For a time she felt certain her own death was near. She knew that many women did not survive childbirth. Her first prayer, however, was for her child. Through the fiercest paroxysm, she heard her aunt at her ear: "God gives nothing freely," the countess whispered, "but opens everything, and everyone takes from God as much as she wants."

She felt the women touching her, directing her, urging her. She placed her faith in God and in Lutisha. Neither had disappointed her before.

Push, Anna, push! Again. Harder, Anna! It's coming, Anna. Push! The baby is coming!

The greatest effort, the greatest strain she could ever imagine came, endured, and finally passed. This time was short, she was told later, yet it seemed an eternity.

Anna's eyelids flew back at the sound of a high-pitched screaming. An infant's sound! Lutisha was holding the child high in the air. The cord had been cut.

The screaming child was drenched in blood and other matter, and at first sight Anna thought it was dying. Lifting her head, she tried to call out in alarm.

"It's the most beautiful baby boy," her aunt announced.

"He's bleeding—"

"We need only to wash him off," Lutisha said. "He is a wondrous babe!"

Anna tried to smile as she lay back upon the pillows. *I have a son!*

The women seemed to take forever in their separate attention to Anna and the child. She longed to call out, to demand she be given her baby, but she couldn't speak because she was so weak and light-headed.

At long last, the child was placed in her arms. For a moment, she thought the women were mistaken. The infant seemed so small and fragile she thought it a girl. Though she would have welcomed a daughter, she saw for herself now that it was indeed a son.

"Do you have a name in mind, dearest?" her aunt asked.

"Yes. This is Lord Jan Michał." She hugged the squirming pink body to her naked breasts, lightly fingering the fine wet wisps of blond hair. After a time the child slept. Anna, too, was exhausted by the ordeal of birth and soon fell into a peaceful sleep, her child in the crook of her arm.

Later, she would notice that Lutisha had tied a red ribbon around the baby's wrist, a protection against the evil eye.

50

It was a source of immeasurable happiness to Anna that she was able to nurse her child. As each week passed, Jan Michał seemed to grow more beautiful, more precious. Or so it must appear to every mother, she thought. "Let me see your little blue eyes," she would coo, pulling a face. His eyes were wide, inquisitive and quick as a falcon's, Anna thought. He would stare up at her as if he were trying to fathom what she was saying. He was several weeks old when he suddenly smiled toothlessly at her antics, then broke into a fit of giggles at the faces she made over him.

Anna felt somehow transformed by motherhood. Certain vague and unfounded fears—which used to wash over her like dry desert breaths—ceased. Oh, there had been some very real anxieties rooted in the dark turn of events that had started with the deaths of her family and shadowed her through to the end of her unhappy marriage, but now she dared to think that her luck had changed.

Motherhood seemed to make her heart always content, always glad. A sublime sense of peace descended on her, a peace, she was certain, that men with their warring ways could not know. Homer had gotten it all wrong. Yes, Odysseus had stood in the stern of a majestic ship and cut through the shimmering waves, propelled from one adventure to the next, along the way falling into the pleasurable snares of Circe and Calypso. It was he whom history called brave. But Anna knew that it was Penelope who endured a woman's pain to give birth to their son. And it was Penelope who summoned from within herself a reservoir of courage and cleverness in order to fend off suitors while raising him for the twenty years Odysseus was gone. And it was Penelope who had to wait. Homer doesn't speak nearly so highly of her for her quiet domestic deeds and faithfulness. How heroic she was, though, and how heroic is every woman who has ever risked life to give birth.

Often, Anna would take her son down to the kitchen—womb of the house, she called it—and there spend a part of her day with Lutisha, Marta, and Marta's daughters, Katarzyna and Marcelina. The huge room had wide windows that were a source of light and life to a variety of potted herbs lined up on the sills. She loved the tantalizing aromas of baking bread and puddings, simmering soups, and skewered meat in the fireplace, the fat of which made the fire sputter; it was always a lively place, a warm and healthy environment that renewed her enthusiasm for life.

Sometimes, while the women played with Jan Michał, Anna assisted with simple kitchen tasks and meal preparations. At home she had helped Luisa with a few dishes, but her culinary skills were enhanced sevenfold under the tutelage of Lutisha and Marta. While she relished the diversion, she took care to keep from her aunt and cousin the extent of her association with the servants.

One day Anna was kneading the dough for dark bread while Katarzyna held Jan Michał, singing lightly to him. Her young brother Tomasz came in and began to make a fuss over the child. Anna could not help but smile at the scene they made. It was like children playing out the manger scene. Jan Michał made a perfect Christ child.

"May I hold him, too, Lady Grawlinska?" Tomasz asked. He was not shy.

"I'm holding him now," Katarzyna said.

"Well, you won't have him all day, will you? Let me see him . . . What color are his eyes, Lady Grawlinska?"

"Blue," Anna said. She saw no reason to deny the boy his request. "You may, in a few minutes . . . Tomasz, you are to address me as Lady *Berezowska*."

"Yes, Lady . . . Berezowska."

"Now go away, Tomasz," Katarzyna was pleading. "Look, he's making a face at you."

"Is not! I think his eyes are brown."

"They're blue. Didn't you hear the countess?"

Anna looked at the boy. He seemed uncertain whether he should say anything more, and when he caught sight of Anna his lips tightened.

He knew not to contradict. Anna thought it most appropriate that he was named for the apostle who doubted.

Marta came up to her son as if to shoo him from the kitchen when she stopped for a moment and stared at the baby in rapt attention. "Why, Madame, Tomasz may be right. The eyes do seem to be taking a turn for brown . . . they do! It happens that way sometimes, blue when a baby's born, only weeks later they change color."

Brown—Anna felt a sharp sensation at her heart. The word was a knife and it had done its damage before she could take the five or six steps to her child. Brown eyes. She became dizzy. *The child had his father's eyes!* She had known it. She had seen the change begin. And yet she had denied it, praying it was not true. But for someone else to confirm it now, denial was impossible.

In her panic to get to her child, Anna stepped away from the table so quickly that the large bowl that held the dough crashed to the floor with a great clatter.

Anna watched Babette as she entered her room on some errand. It seemed that each day the maid wore some new article of clothing or jewelry, so Anna came to suspect that she was quickly spending the money she had given her. If she felt any grief for her children, her deportment gave no evidence of it. Anna had planned to give her another sum, one large enough to make her old age comfortable, but she thought better of it now. She was a free woman, Anna reasoned, and servant on occasion to other noblewomen besides Zofia, so that with her makeup and hairdressing talents, she could accumulate her own reserves for her later years. Perhaps she was doing so, but such did not appear to be the case.

Anna noticed that Babette held a package neatly wrapped in white paper and held with red ribbon.

"It is a gift," Babette was saying, "from Lord Stelnicki."

Anna's heart raced. "Jan?" She had thoughtlessly blurted out his first name. "Is Lord Stelnicki here? Downstairs?"

"No, Madame. It came by messenger."

"Oh." Anna smiled, hoping to mask her disappointment.

She waited until Babette was gone before she opened the package. In it she found the most beautiful silk baptismal gown and cap for Jan Michał. Anna had been putting off Aunt Stella, declining to set the date of the baptism until Jan answered her letter asking him to attend and act as godfather to her son.

Anna found her answer in the form of a written note. She opened it, taking in Jan's neat and broad strokes. For just a moment she thought about the letter that Zofia must have intercepted so long before, the letter that would have made her wait for Jan, the letter that would have kept her from marrying Antoni. She continued to be haunted by it.

The message was short. It was the Stelnicki family christening gown, and he hoped she would use it for Jan Michał. Anna was touched. She held it up and admired the skill it had taken—how many years ago?—to make something so beautiful. There was a yellowness to the white silk, of course, but that only enhanced its worth. She held it to her cheek for a moment.

When she glanced back down at the note, her heart dropped. Jan was needed in Kraków. Something to do with the cause. He would be honored to act as godfather, he wrote, but he was not a Catholic. She must have forgotten.

Anna sat quietly for some minutes. No, she hadn't forgotten. She just hadn't made the connection. The only thing that mattered, then and now, was that should something happen to her, her son would be in Jan's hands. She sighed. Of course, he was right: the Church would not allow him to stand for Jan Michał. The baptism would go forward and Jan was not even able to attend! Disappointment coursed through her. She could hear the sounds of a carriage in the street, her son in the next room giggling at something, the cheerful maids in the kitchen preparing supper. The moment held significance only for her. Everywhere else about her, life went on.

She pressed the soft silk cloth to her lips.

Anna had chosen the baby's second name in honor of Baron Michał Kolbi, and it was he who stood as godfather for Jan Michał. A friend of Anna's, Helena Lubicka, stood as godmother. She was daughter to Lord Józef, who managed Anna's family assets.

Before the group had left for the cathedral, Zofia begged off. "I just know," she laughed, "the place would fall in on us should I attend. And who would pay for the breakage of all that splendid stained glass?"

But Anna suspected that she was miffed at not being asked to stand as godmother. Even though Zofia had come to show a genuine attachment to the child, Anna had not considered her. Neither did she regret her decision.

Jan Michał Grawlinski was baptized and proclaimed free of the devil. He did not even whimper as the water ran over his head and face.

The cathedral was chilly though it was late May, but there was some unnamable warmth there in the iridescent light that shone in through the windows, falling on statues of saints and the great gold cross above the altar. It was a warmth that made Anna mindless of any cold. It was, she thought then, the presence of God.

During her son's christening, she herself felt something like an awakening stirring within. She remembered how her father had taken her aside one day to tell her that the founder of their house—the man ennobled at the recommendation of King Jan Sobieski—had come from a Jewish background. It was something of which her mother, a living act of devotion to Catholicism, never spoke. And it was something that had unsettled and confused Anna, carving into her heart doubts about faith. How could she carry within herself the history and tenets of two religions? She sometimes cursed the day her father had told her.

But the sublime peace that had descended on Anna with motherhood seemed also to aid her in her thoughts about religion. Her belief that there is a God flowed from that same Elysian center within her with such a surety that she thought she could face Satan's army alone and without fear. Jan was right. She had felt it at the Szraber wedding and she felt it now. God *is* in all the churches, she thought. The members of other faiths believe, as do Catholics and Jews. And, Whoever God is, He is there because we believe Him to be there.

Anna thought back to that gloriously alive field in Halicz where Jan had told her that his God was there, in the meadow, in the fields, in the sky. Now she understood.

51

Anna had to consider her future. Zofia's behavior had not changed. She often stayed out the whole evening and occasionally held wild entertainments at the town house. Aunt Stella, reduced to a dowager countess, was powerless over her daughter, her objections giving way to a brooding silence. The countess moved upstairs, into Antoni's old room, in order to keep distance from her daughter and her goings-on.

While Anna tried not to be judgmental about Zofia, she knew she must leave soon. Her father had once told her that if an animal is born in the forest, and not tamed, it may kill a man. Who, then, could hold this animal fully responsible?

So it was with Zofia. If she were somehow tamed, she wouldn't be as she is, nor would her friends. Neither would the robber steal, nor the killer kill. But for some inexplicable reason, her parents had been unable to tame her.

Once the spring rains and flooding, which had come late this year, subsided and the roads were dried by the summer sunshine, Anna would take Jan Michał to her home at Sochaczew, where he would grow up unaffected by the kind of life found in the city.

Anna wondered if perhaps Aunt Stella would accompany her.

In the interim an invitation arrived from Lord Józef Lubicki, the family friend who managed the Berezowski finances. A Mass and reception was being held to celebrate his mother's eightieth name's day.

On the day of the celebration, Anna squeezed herself into an ill-fitting mourning gown of black taffeta and lace, thinking it was itself a coffin for anyone living. Clarice had arranged her hair in a pleasing upswept style, held by amber barrettes, but once the black veil was in place the maid's handiwork was hidden.

Lutisha knocked and entered. "Madame, Lady Helena Lubicka has arrived."

"Show her up, Lutisha. Does Marta have Jan Michał ready?"

"She does."

Helena had been only too willing to pick up her childhood friend. Anna had not wanted to ask Zofia for the use of her carriage; doing so would have meant having to extend the invitation to her, something she wanted to avoid at all costs. It was a safe wager that her cousin would refuse going to Mass, but she was unpredictable.

Helena swept into the room.

At Jan Michał's christening, Anna had been taken by surprise with the appearance of the old friend. It had been two Christmases since she had seen her, and the transformation was profound. Even if Helena were a bit too large of bone to be considered classically beautiful, Anna thought her stunning, with her shimmering black curls that framed a face with sculpted features. Her complexion was as white as porcelain, her cheeks pink roses. A tiny maid dogged her footsteps, tending the train of a gown of ivory lace.

"You look lovely, Anna, even in black."

Anna stiffened slightly. "Thank you, but look at *you*, Helena, you're so beautiful!"

Downstairs, another maid of the Lubicki family already held Jan Michał, who was dressed in blue. The stout maid waddled off to a carriage that would take her and Jan Michał directly to the Lubicki mansion, rather than to the cathedral.

Anna and Helena sat alone in the two-seat carriage headed to the cathedral.

"Your child is beautiful, Anna," Helena said. "Such an alert baby."

"Thank you."

"These days must be hard for you. For so much to happen in such a short time." Helena pursued the subject of Anna's unexpected marriage and the untimely death of her husband.

Anna's responses were evasively minimal, and she steered the subject toward Helena and the two suitors she was keeping at bay.

Presently the carriage came to an abrupt halt amid the din of a crowd.

"Help!" a muffled voice called out. "Help me!"

Helena lifted her window shade and the two friends peered out at the street scene. A little bridge just ahead was crowded with animated people.

"What is it?" Helena called to her driver.

"Someone has fallen into the gutter, milady, and they're trying to fish him out."

The refuse-strewn trench was filled to overflowing because of the spring flooding, and the luckless man had fallen in at a deep point. His blackened face was scarcely visible above the fast-moving mucky stream, but his terrified voice made his presence known.

The victim was holding onto a rope held by several men on the bridge. Slowly they pulled the man up the several feet to the bridge, laying hold of him then, and lifting him to safety.

When he stood shakily on the little bridge, his head a sheep's wool muff of black ringlets, he tried to free the grime from his eyes with his fists.

The tension of the crowd lifted. One woman called out in a shrill voice: "The fool was dancing across the bridge," she screamed, punctuating her words with robust howls, "and danced himself—right into the gutter!"

The crowd roared with laughter.

"To cleanse himself," someone shouted, "maybe he should dance himself into the Vistula!"

In contrast to his blackened face, his white teeth were revealed now in a silly smile bearing witness to his own comedy.

The happy throng slowly started to disperse, as if hesitant to go about the drudgery of their daily lives. While the bridge was being cleared, Anna thought how splendid it was to witness the good nature of the Polish people. Could these same simple souls take part in anything as bloody as what was occurring in France? No. This little episode made her realize that people in Warsaw were like those in Sochaczew, or Halicz. The disposition of the peasants, even in hard times, was uniquely peaceful.

Helena was just about to draw the shade when an open carriage pulled next to theirs in a rude attempt to get to the bridge first. Seated amid a variety of gaily wrapped packages and in an orange dress that mushroomed up around her was Zofia. Next to the hatless countess sat a handsome young gentleman who must have been her current companion and gift-giver. Zofia held her head high and her gaze forward, her apple red mouth moving in lively conversation.

A number of the peasants paused to gawk at the sight.

"I wonder who that vulgar woman can be," Helena whispered.

Anna drew back from the window. "What does it matter?" she asked. "I do hope this delay hasn't made us late for the service." She sat very straight, her shoulder blades touching the cushioned support, which started to vibrate now with the first forward motion.

Anna and Helena were the last to arrive for the noon Mass. The Angelus bells were already tolling their final notes as the two friends hurried up the stairs of Saint Jan's Cathedral. Helena ushered Anna up to the front where the family sat.

The cathedral was warm and stuffy, the service interminable. That Anna had to leave Warsaw was clearer than ever. She had been ashamed to witness her cousin Zofia's boldness in dress and manner. And now she was ashamed that she had not acknowledged Zofia's identity to Helena. What should she have said? *Yes, Helena, that vulgar woman is my cousin.*

She would leave Zofia to her own devices. One day, Anna was certain, Zofia's beauty would fade, and her men and fortunes would fall away from her like leaves from a tree in winter. She would need Anna's help then. Would Anna be so selfless as to give it? She hoped so.

The priest's monotone was passing over Anna like steady waves on a distant seashore, until she heard mention of both her maiden and married names come from the altar. The Lubickis, it seemed, had instructed him to say prayers for the soul of her husband.

She knelt straight as a rail, sensing many eyes upon her, and wishing she were anyplace but there.

Outside, Anna drew in the cooler air. It was sunny and the brisk winds of late spring swirled around them as Helena guided Anna to her parents on the cathedral steps. The elderly dowager countess wasn't present, as she rarely left the family home.

Helena's mother, Lady Ada Lubicka, was still beautiful at fifty, and a high brown wig added to a youthful effect. When she smiled, the years fell away. Always very emotional, she was now on the verge of tears. "Oh, Anna Maria," she whispered, clasping her, "my dear, dear child."

Lord Lubicki seemed much older, with his milk white hair and deeply lined face. Anna's father had always chided him for worrying too much about business matters. Anna thought it was just such concerns that had aged him. He offered Anna his condolences on the loss of her husband.

Anna thanked him, attempting to smile. She hated the charade of mourning Antoni. It was, like the ignorance she had to assume earlier when she did not acknowledge Zofia to Helena, another mask she had to wear, more uncomfortable than the constraints of the tight black dress.

"Who could have predicted," Lady Lubicka was saying, "on that last Christmas together, your family and ours, that it would come to this?"

Such sympathy chafed. While Anna dearly loved the Lubickis, her mourning made her feel so duplicitous that she asked to be excused from the reception, saying she would collect Jan Michał and go directly home. The Lubickis, however, would not hear of it.

And so began the descent down the cathedral steps with the Lubickis, Anna watching the cascades of men and women moving down and away in waves of reds, yellows, blues, and greens flowing down toward their carriages, their coachmen at attention. She had not seen such a group since the king's supper.

Anna thought the newly built Lubicki city mansion more a palace. At the entrance her eyes were fastened to the geometric designs in the neat brick walk. Several of Warsaw's red squirrels caught her eye as they romped on the thick grass, chasing one another from tree to tree. On every side of the house were shaded gardens—crazy quilts of lush, spring flowers—alive with chattering guests.

Helena hurried Anna upstairs, where the hostess pulled from her wardrobe a lovely dress, a gauzy creation in royal blue.

"It's beautiful!" Anna said.

"I'm glad you like it. Put it on."

"What?"

"Put it on. I'm uncomfortable just *looking* at you in that black crepe."

Anna smiled. How had she known? Discarding the black might

mean answering fewer questions about her *loss*. And the blue gown was so beautiful. She acquiesced.

When Anna stood facing the full-length mirror, Helena stood behind her, beaming. "You look wonderful, Anna!"

"*Merci*," Anna said, turning and dropping in a mock curtsey.

Helena laughed but quickly sobered. "Anna your parents have been gone for some time now. Over a year, yes? And you may contradict me or even hate me for saying this, but I have the feeling that the loss of your husband is not so terrible. I'm speaking out of turn, I think—"

"You are, Helena," Anna said, "but you've made your point and I promise you I shall enjoy myself today!"

The friends descended the curved staircase, their gowns sweeping across the ebony floor of the massive reception room, as silk over glass, Anna's eyes lifted in distraction by the relief of painted cherubs flying against the azure of the ceiling.

Anna visited her son in the servants' quarters and nursed him before the meal was announced.

The luncheon might have rivaled any at the Royal Palace. Anna had a place of honor at the Lubicki table, which fronted many long rows of elegantly set tables accommodating at least two hundred guests. The tall, elegant French windows ushered in glorious light and spring scents from the garden.

The venerable Lady Lubicka, with her toothlessly winning grin, seemed a delighted child as the endless parade of platters and trays began.

Later, the dowager motioned Anna toward her, as if in confidence. "They think my eightieth may be my last," she clucked, "but I shall fool the lot of them. I'll see eighty-five yet!"

Anna laughed. "I have no doubt you'll see ninety. Tell me, Lady Lubicka, what is the secret to your long life?"

The woman grinned. "Whimsy!"

"Whimsy?"

"Yes, Anna. Follow your heart. Indulge your whims. They are usually correct. And when they are not, do not allow the world to judge you overly much."

"It is a good philosophy," Anna said, watching the woman swallow a small glassful of Polish vodka. But it was one that Zofia had already carried to the extreme.

After the meal, when most of the guests had retired to other rooms or the gardens, Lord Lubicki presented Anna with a wooden box, its top carved with the Berezowski coat of arms, a half-moon rising above a swan. Anna blinked back her surprise; she had never seen the box before.

"It was your father's, Anna," Lord Lubicki explained. "Now it belongs to you."

Anna opened it to find documents with her father's signature.

"These are the complete records of your father's investments with us."

"There seem to be so many—"

"It amounts to a great deal of money. . . . You are a wealthy young woman, Anna Maria."

"I'm delighted. But why are you giving these to me now?"

"For your signature. I knew that you and your late husband had plans for the money these investments will bring. I assume that you still wish to divest yourself of—"

"No," Anna said, "there are no plans. Not any longer. I would like you to continue to see to my financial affairs. You are to take, of course, whatever fees—"

"There are no fees. Your father repaid me with his friendship." Lord Lubicki smiled. "I'll continue, if that is your wish."

"It is."

"You and your son should be able to live handsomely on the interest generated by your inheritance."

Helena came then to collect Anna and take her to the gardens.

Outside, groups of lively, loquacious guests stood on and near the huge dance floor, a temporary device of stone squares enameled in red. Birch trees graced two of its sides, forming a living, vaulted roof above the dancers, who were squaring off in the formation of a German cotillion. A cooling breeze lifted the leaves now and then, allowing the jewelry and rich finery of the dancers to sparkle in the mottled sunlight.

If only Zofia's parties were like this celebration.

Leading the cotillion were a striking woman in white silk and lace and a foreign-looking gentleman whose movements were elegant, if somewhat strutting. The woman was the height of style, from her petite, bejeweled slippers to the crown of her great white pompadour. Anna thought her well into her thirties, but she certainly commanded the eyes of the men. Her smile, while serene as the Madonna's, indicated she was aware of the stir she was creating.

When the dance ended, the woman hurried over to Helena and Anna, her partner in tow. Helena introduced her as Lady Wielopolska. Her dance partner was Guy Mornay, a French count.

"I'm delighted to meet you," Anna said to Lady Wielopolska. "You're well known in Warsaw circles."

The Madonna smile widened slightly. "And I have heard of you, Lady Grawlinska."

The woman's delicate, feline features were hard to read. Anna was certain, however, that there was an undercurrent in the woman's tone.

Helena had introduced Anna using her married name. Anna chose not to correct her. It was still her legal name, after all, and that of her son.

The count stepped up to Anna. "Will the Lady Grawlinska consent to dance?"

Anna looked into the slightly pinched face. She would not use the bereavement excuse. "I . . . I don't know how to move to these Germanic dances."

The count turned back to Lady Wielopolska. "The good countess says that she cannot dance to these 'Germanic dances'!" His voice was nasal. Anna thought it an affectation.

Someone nearby snickered. Anna flushed in embarrassment.

"Nonsense, my dear," said Lady Wielopolska, her tone condescending. "It is one of the easiest. The only way to learn is to do." The woman took Anna's hand and gave it over to the Frenchman, who guided Anna out onto the floor before she could protest.

Anna's first steps were uncertain and awkward. She felt as if all eyes around her were watching every faltering move.

She regretted now having put off the black mourning dress, regretted having come to the reception.

Soon, though, she fell into step and found herself dancing with the count as though they had done so a hundred times, the couple gliding gracefully among the quadrilles of dancers.

"You're doing wonderfully," the count said. "It's almost time to change partners."

"What?" But before fear overtook her, she found herself partnered with another. And then another. Surprisingly, she lost not a step and continued to enjoy herself.

Anna passed near to where Helena and Lady Wielopolska stood watching. Helena waved. Lady Wielopolska's smile seemed unchanged, but her eyes betrayed her surprise.

Anna was reunited with Count Mornay before the dance ended. His arm went around her waist as they moved off the dance floor. "You are very beautiful, my lady. May I call you Anna?"

"Let me go," Anna whispered.

He did not remove his arm. "Zofia is not as lovely as you. Why have you kept yourself out of society for so long?"

"You know my cousin?" Anna asked, turning to him.

He smiled wickedly. "Of course."

Anna pushed him away and hurried over to Helena.

"I must leave at once," Anna announced. "Thank you for your kindnesses. Give my best to your parents and grandmother."

"What is it, Anna? What happened?"

"Nothing. I'm sorry. I'm not well."

"That's too bad," Helena said. "Don't you wish to say good-bye to my father yourself? He may have some last caution—"

"Yes, I should. I must thank him. Where is he?"

"Lord Lubicki," Lady Wielopolska said, "retired to the library not long ago with my husband and some other men."

Anna hated the woman's arrogance. The count was rejoining them now, two glasses of wine in hand. She ignored him, quickly making her move toward the house.

Inside, Anna heard hastening steps behind her.

"Anna," Helena said, "ill or not, that was rude of you to so abruptly leave Lady Wielopolska and the count."

"I'm sorry," Anna replied without missing a step, "but I don't care much for Lady Wielopolska, nor the French count without manners."

"What happened? Did he say something, do something?"

They entered the house.

"It's nothing," Anna said and sighed, stopping before great double doors. "Forgive me, Helena. Perhaps I'm oversensitive today, but I must go home. Is this the library?"

"Yes."

Absently she knocked and the two hurried in.

The ten or twelve men in the room were caught in the midst of a heated discussion. The names of several men were being roundly scorned. Anna's interest was immediately piqued, her irritation with the count and Lady Wielopolska forgotten.

As the two young women advanced, slowly, uncertainly, the men's voices died in their throats. The impatient looks in their eyes made Anna feel an intruder.

Lord Lubicki, seated at a large desk, noticed them now. "What is it, Helena?" He, too, had little patience.

"I'm sorry, Father," she said. "We didn't know—"

"It's my fault, your grace," Anna said. "I merely wanted to say good-bye."

Lord Lubicki smiled. "Then it is no interruption."

Anna just wanted out of the room, but Lord Lubicki insisted on protocol and introduced her and his daughter to everyone present.

The last man to be named was a frail, elderly gentleman sitting near the desk. Anna had to disguise her reaction when she found out that this was Lord Wielopolski, husband to the woman with the Madonna smile—and decades older. If Anna showed her surprise, he seemed not to notice. His manner was serious, his mind clearly on other things.

Anna addressed herself to Lord Lubicki. "*Adieu, adieu,*" she said, turning to leave. On impulse, she turned back. "Forgive me, Lord Lubicki, but when we entered, I thought I heard the names of several magnates. Has something happened?"

Lord Wielopolski came suddenly to life now. "The names you heard, Lady Grawlinska, were Feliks Potocki, Seweryn Rzewuski, and Ksawery Branicki. You will hear of them again."

"I see." Anna nodded, thinking that he spoke with the weight of the mythical Greek seer Tiresias. A chill came over her.

"They are nobles," the elder continued, "that lack even the crudest peasant sense."

Anna committed the names to memory as she and Helena made their retreat. Something of the greatest importance was occurring in the Commonwealth, and it had to do with these men. No doubt her patriot friends would know something.

"What has happened, do you suppose?" Anna asked, once the library doors closed behind them.

"I haven't a clue," Helena said, "but it isn't good. I'm going to make short work of finding out. Won't you stay now, until this meeting is over?"

Anna declined.

"Friendship is like wine," Helena called out to Anna as the carriage began to roll down the driveway, "the older it is, the better it is!"

Anna waved. Helena's words were ironic. She looked at little Jan Michał, already asleep in her arms. His origin was a secret she had not confided to Helena. Zofia's behavior was another. No longer did she feel close enough to her friend to unlock her secrets at a moment's notice. Time and circumstance had come between them.

Anna realized now that the music had ceased and that the voices from the gardens nearby were charged with excited talk and a sense of alarm. Guests were already streaming out into the driveway toward their carriages. She recognized a few of the men that had been present at the meeting.

What kind of disclosures had gone on in the Lubicki library?

52

Anna was told she'd find Zofia in the reception room.

Her cousin lay face-up on a fainting couch that had been covered in a fur and placed next to the open French windows so that the sun might warm and lend a pinkness to her skin. She was naked.

"Come in, Anna! Come in, it's not for you to be shy, if I'm not."

Anna adjusted her line of vision away from Zofia and toward a table with a plate of roast beef and a hand mirror. Eventually, it was drawn back to her cousin.

"Ohhhh," Zofia crooned, "isn't it wonderful to have at last a warm afternoon?"

Anna moved slowly to the sofa opposite Zofia. She sank back into the cushions, still at a loss for words.

"Tell me about the feast day party, dearest. Who was there? Was it terribly boring?"

"No, it was quite nice." Zofia's body was perfection itself. What a woman is this, Anna thought, one who lounges unattired and unashamed in the sun, while eating meat from the noon meal or gazing at her reflection in the mirror.

"Imagine, a name's day celebration for a woman eighty years old. A farewell party, more likely!"

"Zofia!"

"You know what they say: 'The young may die, the old will.'"

At Zofia's insistence, Anna described the Mass and reception, as well as the Lubicki home and guests. She watched for a flicker of recognition when she made mention of the French count's name, but it went unrewarded.

"It sounds tedious to me, Anna. Many of the guests you named are dull and stiff-necked nobles who cling wistfully to a bygone era. But I'm glad if you were entertained by it."

"It was lovely, Zofia. But it came to a strange end."

"What do you mean?"

Anna related then in detail what had gone on in the Lubicki library, what had been said.

Zofia's interest was fully aroused by the time Anna finished. "The names, Anna, what were the three names? Do you remember? You must!"

"Yes."

"Because I hate politics you and mother think I am a dunce. I know what I must know . . . Now tell me their names."

"Potocki and Branicki and Rzewuski."

"Ah, then the time has come," Zofia muttered.

"Time? What is it? What's happened?"

"Oh, Anna," Zofia said with a sigh, "you act as if you haven't a clue as to what you've just told me." She was on her feet now, taking short steps about the room.

Anna was uncertain whether her cousin was pleased or agitated. "I *don't* understand."

"Ha!" Zofia laughed, the black eyes appraising Anna. "It is so like you, cousin, to give a flawless account of something you have witnessed firsthand, yet be unable to interpret it. Why, you would be a priceless associate to the king!"

Anna shrugged. "From those little bits of facts, I could hardly—"

But Zofia wasn't listening. "Lutisha!" she screamed. "Lutisha!"

The servant appeared promptly, opening the double doors. Her eyes bulged at Zofia's nakedness.

"That letter, Lutisha, the one that came for me this morning! Where is it?"

"I left it in your room, Mademoiselle."

"Fetch it immediately!"

The servant made for the rear stairwell.

Anna thought she detected a buoyancy in Zofia's attitude.

But it soured quickly. Through doors that opened into the main hall, Anna could see Marcelina opening the front door to six or seven women who evidently had been sent to help prepare for a midnight supper Zofia was to host that night.

"Good God!" Zofia shrieked as she ran toward the hall. "Doesn't one of you have a particle of a brain in those piss-pots on your shoulders?"

Already in the vestibule, the maids huddled together like does, their eyes dilated at the sight and sound of Zofia.

"Don't stand there wiggling like a swarm of maggots! If you can't enter this house through the servants' entrance, you can go back to your mistresses."

The women scurried out the door.

"You should know better," Zofia chastised Marcelina. "Don't ever let a servant in through the front again!"

The horrified girl nodded and retreated to the kitchen, her red apron held to her face.

When Zofia returned to the reception room, she glanced at Anna, down at herself, then at Anna again. A smile played on her lips. She seemed to recognize the farcical quality of her little scene: naked and ranting, she had demanded strict decorum from the servant class. Suddenly, she started laughing aloud.

Anna could not help but join in.

Zofia bent to pick up the fur, and she had only just draped it about herself when Countess Gronska came down from her room.

"What is all this shouting?" the countess asked, her gaze catching on Zofia.

"It's nothing, Mother. Merely stupid servants."

"Is this some new style of attire?" The countess took her usual chair.

Zofia left the question unanswered. Anna saw that she was surreptitiously picking up some item from a table. Anna hadn't noticed it before; it was a piece of blue velvet that encased some small article. With her back to her mother, Zofia sidled near to her cousin, placing it in her hands and whispering something about *safekeeping*.

Lutisha appeared with the letter, flushed in embarrassment about her granddaughter's gaffe. She was about to make an apology, but Zofia was already hungrily tearing open the letter. Anna winked and waved the servant away. Zofia might flare and fume at such an infraction, but it was usually quickly forgotten.

Zofia devoured the contents of the letter, the impatience giving way to smug satisfaction. "Well! It is done."

"What is?" Anna asked.

"Potocki and those other nobles you mentioned, Anna, have formed a confederacy at Targowica—with Empress Catherine!"

"No!" the countess cried. "It can't be true!"

"But it is, Mother."

"What is the aim of this confederacy?" Anna asked.

Zofia tilted her head arrogantly. "To subjugate the bourgeoisie, destroy the Constitution, and restore the kingdom to what it once was! That is what you failed to grasp, cousin. That is what set those weak-kneed nobles at Lubicki's to grumbling."

"But we stand for the Constitution," Countess Gronska said, "just as your father did."

"Father was wrong, Mother. It was one thing Walter was right about. The Constitution is no friend to the nobility. It allows commoners to own land!"

"Is that so bad?"

"Yes, Mother. Through their accumulating wealth, they would finally destroy us. Now, the possessions of the kingdom will remain in rightful hands, in our hands."

"And all done with *her* help, I suppose?"

"Catherine's? Indeed. Hail the Empress of Russia!"

"The Empress-Whore!" the countess spat. "Was it so much to give commoners land, something to sustain them, something in which they could take pride?"

"Yes, Mother, yes. Tell me, what part of our holdings would you wish to part with?"

"If needs be, we could do with less. The constitutional reform will ease the kind of tensions that account for travesties like those occurring in France."

"Then I am only too glad that I am in charge of the Gronski purse strings. The Constitution *created* unrest, Mother; it didn't reduce it."

The countess had winced at the reference to the disposition of the estate. Nevertheless, she drew in a long breath to sustain her reply: "The unrest has come from nobles who are disgruntled at giving up *anything* to the lower classes. Zofia, even if the reform would prove to be the means of our demise, as you seem to think, that does not warrant our asking Catherine for assistance. It is like a trapped mouse asking a hulk of a hungry she-cat for help. She may give it . . . but then what?"

"Then," Zofia sang, "there will be no Constitution and no Third of May celebration for the rising of the scum. Only feasts and festivities for the true sons and daughters of kings!"

"We will be the cat's supper," the countess said, "and she will lap us up like rich cream!"

"Let's ask Anna her opinion." Zofia turned to her cousin. "What do you think, Ania?"

"I agree with your mother, Zofia. It's wrong to rescind the Constitution by force and doubly wrong to employ Catherine in its undoing."

"You're a bit of a cretin on the quiet, aren't you? Well, I can see I'm outnumbered in my own house."

"And were your father here," the countess said, "we would lend our support to the Constitution duly enacted by the Polish *Sejm* and signed by King Stanisław."

"Ah, but he's *not* here, Mother. And I shall lend our support where I see fit."

Countess Gronska looked as though she had been struck.

Zofia's face folded into a mask of contriteness. "Forgive me, Mother, but I'm not a political animal like you with your pamphlets, and you, Anna, with your little group of patriots. I am a realist, and a realist casts her fate to the strongest wind . . . Now, I should rest before I

begin my *toilette*. Thank you, cousin, for your information, however in-
complete. I never would have opened Pawel's letter detailing the confederacy, and at my supper I would have been the last to know of it.
What a pretty pudding on my face!"

Zofia kissed her mother, then Anna, and started for the door, adding
flippantly, "I thought Pawel's note merely another one of his proposals."

Anna and the countess sat for a while in silence.

Anna excused herself then, kissing her aunt on both cheeks. Upstairs, in her room, she unfolded the blue velvet and stared in wonder at
a gold-mounted emerald stickpin.

Jan Michał giggled as Anna twirled his golden hair into curls. She had
only just dressed him in his knitted leggings and shirt, each trimmed
with blue ribbons.

A knock came at the door. Zofia peeked in. "Anna, may I come in?"

"Yes, of course."

"Oh, let me see the little man!" Zofia walked over to where Anna
lay with him on her bed. "Oh, isn't he darling in his little clothes? Like
a little prince. And the curls are delightful!"

Anna sat up at the side of the bed. "Zofia, why have you given me
such a stickpin?"

"Oh, it's a trifle."

"Then it's not genuine?"

"Oh, it's genuine. It's just that I would like you to keep it for me . . .
I'm afraid that I would lose it."

"Lose it?"

"Or gamble it away, who knows? Must you ask so many questions?
Is it too much to ask, that you take care of it?"

"No, I guess not."

Zofia tempted Jan Michał with her forefinger. When he would
reach for the polished nail, she withdrew it and laughed. Her infectious
laughter brought him out in giggles.

"Anna, why don't you hire a wet nurse for your baby and send
them off to the country? Your life as an unattached woman here in the
city would be so much freer. I have plans for you."

The suggestion that she send her baby away carried with it the
force of a slap. "Zofia, my baby does not clutter my life."

"I didn't mean to offend you. It's just that, well, sooner or later, you will have to think about another match."

"The tradition of my parish is that I must wait a full year."

"Tradition! What is tradition but some old people telling you what to do. Tradition is meant to be broken."

"I have no intention of going husband-hunting."

"Anna?"

"Yes?"

Zofia looked her in the eye now. "Why did you name him *Jan?*"

It was all Anna could do to return her gaze. "I believe it is an old family name."

"That won't wash. There is no one, on your mother's or father's side, by that name."

"Oh, but there is. Your mother says that King Jan Sobieski is an ancestor of the Gronski clan."

"Ah, yes, Jan Sobieski. A great patriot."

Anna looked away. Zofia went back to teasing Jan Michał.

Anna felt her temples pulsing. She knew her cousin wasn't about to drop the subject.

"Anna, when will you give up your infatuation with Jan Stelnicki?"

"I am not infatuated."

"Oh, very well. You think you are in love with him, don't you?" Zofia kept her eyes on the child. "And do you think he is in love with you? A man like that? Do you really think he'll wait even a year?"

Anna said nothing.

"It puzzles me, cousin, why you have named this child so. I think about it sometimes. Why, you don't think Stelnicki *is* the father, do you? You claimed another attacked you at the pond."

"*Claimed?*"

"Yes, and we accepted that story."

"It was not a story, Zofia."

"Well, why would you name him thus, unless . . ."

"Unless what?"

Zofia's gaze turned now to hold Anna's. "Unless you conceived his child *before* that night at the pond! What with all those meetings in the meadow, there was ample opportunity. And little Jan here *was* born prematurely. Or so we supposed."

Anna could not believe what she was hearing.

"And," Zofia continued, "why would you use the Stelnicki christening gown?"

Anna felt her teeth clench in anger. "Jan is not the father."

"Ah, no, I suppose not. It was silly of me, I admit. You were too innocent then, weren't you? Listen to me, Anna. You were hurt, too. I know that. But every young girl has at least one ill-fated romance. Jan was yours . . . You must forget him. I shall see that your next is a great success."

"Like my marriage to Antoni?"

"Touché! No, we'll do better this time."

"Zofia, I intend to go to Sochaczew."

"Oh? When?"

"At the end of the week."

"I see." She stood. "Well, that's that, then, isn't it?" She moved to the door and paused. "You'll come winter with us again this year, won't you?"

"I don't know."

"You must." Zofia turned to face her cousin. "You know I do love you, Ania?"

Anna attempted a smile.

"Perhaps Sochaczew would be a nice respite for my mother, too. What do you think?"

When Anna did not respond, Zofia went back to her room to prepare for the midnight supper.

The Countess Gronska and Anna sat together for breakfast.

"Anna Maria, Zofia tells me you are off to Sochaczew."

"I had planned to go, and I was going to invite you, but . . ."

"Yes?"

"Well, I thought if you were going to Halicz for the summer, I might join *you*."

"You certainly may. I shall be glad to have you." The countess smiled. "Tell me, dearest, did the letter you received so early this morning have anything to do with your decision?"

Anna felt chilled. "How did you know?"

"Intuition. It was from him, yes? Jan?"

Anna nodded.

"He's going to summer in Halicz at his family estate?"

"No, aunt. Politics are moving much too swiftly. He's tied to the cause now. He'll be there only for a short time before he rejoins Kościuszko. If we leave at the end of the week, our time at Halicz and his will overlap by just a day or two. . . ."

"Such a long distance to travel for a day or two. . . . I once gave you some very bad advice, my dear. I should never have imposed marriage to Grawlinski on you." The countess was near tears. "Anna Maria, can you ever forgive me?"

"The decision to marry Antoni was my own."

"Zofia and I led you into it."

"No one is to blame. Antoni was not the man he pretended to be."

"I should have known. I should have seen! The clues were there. But you saw them, didn't you?"

Anna stretched out her hand across the table. "We all hoped for the best."

"I only pray that I live long enough to see you happy, Anna." The countess clasped her niece's hand, and she blinked back her tears.

"I have Jan Michał. I'll not be too quick to ask for more."

"Together we'll go to Hawthorn House," the countess said, brightening, "and we'll forget what goes on here in Praga and have a wonderful summer." The countess paused, standing abruptly. "Oh, Anna, why wait until the end of the week? We can prepare today and leave in the morning!"

In the afternoon, Anna slipped into Zofia's room after her cousin had gone out. The diary was still in the hidden compartment of the wardrobe. She could not help but wonder what plans Zofia had for her.

While she found no new mention of her own name, she did discover how Zofia had come across the emerald stickpin and why she thought it safer with Anna.

My experience with the rich beast from The Hague happened thusly: Baron Vahnik was brought to my party by the thin Garbozki, and when he was introduced to me his tiny dark eyes stared boldly. His nose and lips are overly large, but somehow voluptuous just the same. I invited his hungry glare, not because he is so respected for his musical genius as a violinist, but out of admiration for his great wealth and his pinchable round buttocks at the base of a rather hunched back.

His eyes would follow me as I moved among my guests. When I would glance at him, he would be staring at me like a hungry calf eyes its mother. When I went into the dimly lighted music room to get a particular red wine, he followed me. Like a fat moth to a dancing flame. He overtook me from behind, embracing me roughly.

From where we stood, we were in danger of being seen by the other guests in the adjoining reception room, so I pushed the stout man away and walked toward the double doors, saying in a loud voice, "Tell me, Lord Vahnik, what is it that makes The Hague such an important city?"

Click! The doors were closed and he was upon me. Grasping the wine decanter, I pulled away playfully, moving around the piano, past the bookshelves. He caught up to me, of course, and held me tightly. It was only with the greatest effort that I didn't cry out in pain. Although I was delighted by the whole affair.

"I must bring this wine to my guests," I said.

"*I* am a guest," he replied, pressing me against a cove in the bookshelves.

"Then take a taste," I said.

"I'll have a taste of your lips instead."

"It'll cost you."

"You like to play too much!" He clutched me then, so tightly that I lost hold of the decanter and it went crashing to the floor.

"Look what you've done!" I cried. "That decanter was crystal and over a hundred years old, and the wine was the last of my father's favorite."

"You must meet me later," he said.

"Perhaps . . . if you bring something to make up for my losses."

"I will."

"I believe you will, but to be certain, I'll hold on to this." It was then that I withdrew the emerald stickpin from the ruff at his neck.

"But . . . it was my father's."

I slipped it carefully into my bodice. "And a fair bargain for my father's antique decanter of priceless wine, not to mention the pleasures I have in store for you."

And so I received a glorious emerald in return for a vintage wine that was mediocre at best and a decanter of mere cut glass. At the conclusion of our rendezvous the next day, he asked about the pin, but I claimed to have lost it. I must make certain that it stays well out of sight.

The Praga town house came alive with preparations for the trip to Halicz.

In the afternoon, Anna could not find the countess, so she went down to the kitchen. Despite the frantic buzzing that went on there, Jan Michał, exhausted by the ordeal of his bath ritual, slept soundly in a crib hanging from a rafter near the open door.

"Where is Lady Stella, Lutisha?"

Lutisha was just removing two large loaves of spicy sweet rye. "She's gone off to the apothecary, Madame."

"Oh." Anna could see that Lutisha had been crying. Her heart went out to the servant, who was to remain in Praga to train another support staff for Zofia. Her daughter Marta and grandchildren Marcelina, Katarzyna, and Tomasz were to go to Halicz. Marta's husband, Walek, had gone months before to see to the planting.

"Would Madame wish the heel?"

"You know I won't refuse *your* bread . . . We'll miss you, Lutisha."

"The seasons are a circle," the servant said, smiling bravely. "The fall will come soon enough."

"So it will." Anna chewed at the bread. She would not tell her she had no intention of ever returning to Zofia's town house. "What business did the countess have at the apothecary?"

"She needed a supply of her medicine to last the summer."

"What medicine is that?"

"I don't know, Madame."

"How long has she been taking it?"

"Only recently. Here, take another heel. My granddaughters always ask for the soft middle slices. They don't know what's best."

As Anna took the bread, she saw the heavy tears in Lutisha's gray eyes. Before leaving the kitchen, she surprised Lutisha by kissing her on one cheek, then the other.

53

In her room, Anna was just packing her treasures. Into the inlaid box that contained the crystal dove, she placed both the opalescent ring—it seemed ruby red today—and the emerald stickpin, carefully cushioning each item in soft cloth.

Marcelina appeared in the open doorway. "Mademoiselle Zofia asks that you come down to the dining room."

"Zofia? You mean she's up so early?"

"*Oui*, Madame. Do you wish me to bring that box down to your carriage?" The girl was excited about the trip.

"No, Marcelina. I'll carry this myself. Tell my cousin I'll be down momentarily."

Anna went downstairs and out to the driveway to secure the box in the coach. Dawn was only just now breaking. Katarzyna waved from the carriage that had been hired for the servants. All seemed in readiness.

Anna went back into the house. In the dining room, she found her aunt, attired in a dark traveling dress and sitting stiffly at the huge table that had been cleared of the early morning breakfast items. Anna seated herself to her left.

Across the width of the table, Zofia stood behind her chair. She wore a morning wrap. Her hair was untidy and dark half-moons were evident under her eyes. Anna wondered if she had been to bed. "I'm sorry I took so long," Anna said.

"What is this all about, Zofia?" the countess asked. "We did want to get on the road before the heat of the day."

"And so you will, Mother." Zofia's smile, set against her dark beauty, was a mirrored image of Anna's mother's nonsmile. "I pray that you both, as well as the baby, have a God-safe journey and a wonderful summer. I'll take care of any needs you might have, should you send me word. I intend to take care of all of your needs until such a time when we have a good man to care for us."

Anna watched her cousin with interest. Zofia's hands played nervously on the posts of her chair, the knuckles whitening against the dark wood. She was nervous. Her little speech was leading to something, but what? Anna had never seen her behave so formally.

"I believe," Zofia continued in measured tones, "that I will do my best for the interests of both of you, whom I love so dearly."

She paused now. Anna and the countess waited.

"It is because I love you that I have taken care to sign our names with those of the other nobles who stand in support of the Confederacy of Targowica."

The countess gasped. "You have done *what*? How do you dare to presume—"

"I pray," Zofia pressed, "that you let me continue with what I have to say, Mother. If we do not sign, as all the wisest nobles of Warsaw and Poland are doing, the empress will not guarantee our welfare."

"In the name of Sweet Jesus, I will not have it!" The countess sat forward, her face defiant and flushing, her body rigid.

"For your life, and for the lives of your family and the continuation of its name and title, you must consent to that which I've already seen to. If our names are not recorded, the empress will regard us as subversives. We could be exiled or killed. Unless, of course, we choose now to flee to some foreign kingdom. That certainly is not your wish, is it, Mother?"

"I will not bow to the whims of a Russian empress. I am a God-fearing subject of the King of Poland!"

"And Stanisław is, in turn, a Catherine-fearing subject of Russia!" Zofia exploded with angry disdain. "He is but a ripe berry beneath the jeweled slipper of the empress."

The countess flew into a rage now, ranting both at Zofia and Anna. "The Russians are half-wolf animals!" she screamed. "Even the Lithuanians held up trees and snakes as gods until we showed them the ways of God and civilization. The Russians may no longer live in holes or caves like wolves—Oh, they may live in fine palaces and dress in silks, but their disposition is unchanged. Now they war, Zofia. They have learned that cutlasses and pistols are superior to spears. And they have learned how to march men, so now they war."

"Yes," Zofia quickly answered, "now they war. And most likely they will have the armies of the royal houses of Prussia and Austria marching with them! If they war, and we do not, then we must consent to being protected by them. When the Constitution is repudiated and the peasants and others are put in their place, the war will be over. We are the nobility and we will survive. It is only the rebellious cattle who will die, Mother. Only those who resist will be punished. The nobility must suppress the peasants and those who would usurp our lands and wealth. When the Constitution is destroyed, we will be left to our true heritage."

"Such a wish is not my wish," the countess hissed. "I will not stand against the Constitution. Leo would not have done so, either. I will not let those who stood bravely for it now die in my name!" The countess stood. "I'll wait for you in the carriage, Anna Maria," she said, hurrying from the room.

"Then you will die!" Zofia called after her. In a softer tone unheard by her mother, she added, "Had I not the wisdom to see that you do not die."

"I have been silent, Zofia," Anna said, "but I speak to you now as your mother spoke to you. We are all God's children, noble or not. Our citizens should not die for the rights established by the Third of May Constitution. No one should die in our name."

"Anna, our names have already been listed with those of the Confederacy."

"You were wrong to do that, Zofia. I know there are many who do not agree with the Confederacy, many who will not sign. I have many such friends myself, the Lubickis among them."

"And Stelnicki, too, I suppose, with his fine uniform! They are all fools inviting their own doom." Zofia moved around the table to Anna, speaking in a tone at once pleading and superior. "If you don't think that I am right, tell me, Anna Maria Berezowska-Grawlinska, what should be done!"

"All that I can answer is that we should have no part in this. I ask that you see that your mother's name, my name, and that of Jan Michał are removed from any document supporting the Confederacy of Targowica."

"Must you see things so simply, Anna? Must you be a fool, too?"

"Your mother and I must follow our consciences. We do not seek the protection of Catherine."

"But the Poles will not be able to stand up to her!" Zofia stooped near to Anna and took her hand. "Perhaps you and Mother are right. Perhaps the Poles are too much closer to God than other men to fight and make war. Or, perhaps the Polish nobles have been sitting on silks for so long that they no longer know how to make war."

"Does not being able to fight mean decadence?"

Zofia shrugged. "What all this is, I cannot say. I told you and Lord Michał Kolbi once that I didn't believe women to be political animals. I still hold to that. What men do in matters such as these, you and I cannot control or influence. . . . But much of Poland will fall, Anna, how much I cannot guess, but it will fall and I will not let us fall with it." She knelt in front of her cousin's chair, her black eyes imploring. "You and Mother must comply with me, should you be confronted by the forces of the Confederacy. If you do not, you may die, and my mother may die, and because of your ignorance or stubbornness, we all may die. You have Jan Michał to consider, too, darling."

Zofia quickly squeezed Anna's hand and stood. "It's good that you're going to the country for the summer. I only hope that you will be secure there once this matter becomes unsafe, as it surely must."

"I shouldn't keep the others waiting," Anna said. She felt torn. There was no use to argue further. They would come to no compromise. While she didn't agree with Zofia, she felt the genuine concern Zofia had for her mother, her cousin, and little Jan Michał.

"Ah, well, be off and away then!" Zofia gave Anna a quick hug.

"But if I should come scurrying to Halicz with angry Russians, Poles, or *both* biting at my buttocks, please don't lock your cousin Zofia out of her own home!"

Anna had to laugh with her at the vision.

"Seriously, Anna, if the Russians confront you, tell them you are under the protection of the Confederacy of Targowica. If it is your own Polish patriots, tell them your first love is Poland. But favor the Russians, darling, because in the end the whore will triumph." Zofia kissed Anna on either cheek. "Godspeed, Ania."

Anna made ready to leave. "Good-bye."

"Just one more thing, cousin."

Anna turned back. "Yes?"

"You *will* forget him, won't you?"

"I have few expectations regarding Jan Stelnicki. But, Zofia, what is your interest?"

"My interest?"

"Why are you so concerned? Tell me, do *you* love him, Zofia?" How long she had waited to ask that question!

Zofia stared at her cousin for several long moments, then shrugged. "Perhaps I do."

It was Anna's worst nightmare suddenly realized. The answer she had just heard was the very reason why she had waited so long to ask the question. She felt dizzy. "And when I came to Halicz . . . ?"

"Why did I encourage you to court him?"

Anna nodded.

"It was stupid of me, I admit. Jan and I had argued and I didn't think your interest in him would harm anyone. It was your first taste of romance and—"

"And you thought your naive little cousin from Sochaczew would pale in comparison to you, is that it?"

"Don't be so unfair to yourself, Anna."

"But you have so many men."

"Jan is uniquely attractive."

"Then . . . you still have thoughts of having him?"

Zofia's lips lengthened into a thoroughly wicked smile. "Don't *you*?"

Anna stared vacantly. The horses could be heard restlessly stamping outside; the carriage that would take her away from Zofia was ready. She was tempted to run outside without another word.

But she took in a deep breath and faced her cousin. "I don't under-estimate you, Zofia, your beauty or your charm. If it is within your power to win him, so be it. But it seems you underestimated me, once. I suggest to you that you do not make that same error again."

Anna turned then and walked out of the room, out of the house, leaving a silenced Zofia.

It was on the first of June that she and her son and the countess set off for the south of Poland, a little retinue of two carriages.

Part Five

If there is no wind,
you must learn to row.

–POLISH PROVERB

54

The sky remained cloudless and the roads blessedly dry so that the two carriages made good time as they trundled to the far south of the Commonwealth.

Anna could only wonder what her stoically silent aunt was thinking. She had to know, as Anna did, that Zofia would never remove their names from the document. Zofia's presumption, after everything else that had transpired, could only widen the chasm between mother and daughter.

Anna's own break with Zofia was now political and personal. What right had she to affix Anna's and Jan Michał's names to the Confederacy? And did she truly have a notion she could still have Jan? Was it a silly fancy or was it based on anything in fact? Jan had never said a word about any past alliance with Zofia. Why not? Had he been a conquest of hers? If he had cared for her once, might he still?

Now Zofia's behavior at the pond made sense. Anna had told her cousin of Jan's proposal, and Zofia reacted by pretending to believe that Anna wished no such serious courting; in fact, she must have been horrified to think he had taken Anna seriously. When the two were left alone picking raspberries, they must have argued—perhaps Zofia had made the advances—and she lashed out at Jan's indifference by tearing her own blouse and claiming he attacked her. And that charade had ini-

tiated a chain of events resulting in the attack on Anna, the child that
she carried, and the doomed marriage to Grawlinski. There was, too,
the missing letter from Jan that must have been intercepted. Zofia must
have taken it without so much as a twinge of conscience! Anna's eyes
were opened now to what lengths Zofia would go in order to have her
own way.

Days later, the sight of the white limestone manor house at Halicz with
its columned portico was a happy one for both Anna and her aunt.

On the first morning after their arrival, Marta came up to say that a
guest awaited her in the reception room. Anna guessed the identity of
the visitor but did not question the servant.

She glanced longingly at one of her favorite summer dresses, blue
with lace at the neckline and sleeves, then donned her black mourning
dress. How glad she would be to be done with mourning.

She collected herself at the top of the staircase, where a large stone
eagle rested on the upper newel post. It was a representation of the white
eagle, symbol of Poland. As many times as she had passed it on her previous summer's stay with her relatives, she had never given it any
thought. Now she paused to think about the safety of her homeland,
touching the rough surface and wordlessly asking the bird to be vigilant.

She imagined now that one of the glass eyes was winking at her, as
if to confirm who the visitor was. She smiled to herself at the capricious
thought, then quickly moved down the stairs.

Anna came to an abrupt halt at the foot of the staircase when she
came face-to-face with Jan Stelnicki. The deep blue of his eyes seemed to
laugh at her.

He bent immediately to kiss her hand. Lifting his blond head, he
said, "You were not moving so fast at our last meeting, Anna."

She laughed. "I was swollen with child then!"

"Swollen, perhaps, but beautiful, nonetheless."

Anna felt herself blushing. She took in a breath, savoring the dulcet
sound of his voice more than the compliment. "Oh, Jan, it's so good to
see you again."

They were wordless for the long moments he held her hand. Then
he led her into the reception room where Countess Gronska was waiting.

Anna could not help but be disappointed. How she longed to talk with him alone! She wanted to absorb his presence. And there was so much to ask him.

"I've come to say good-bye, Anna," Jan said.

Anna had no time to respond to the sting of those words because Marta entered the room, carrying a tray with three glasses of wine.

No one spoke while the servant was present. For Anna, the delay was interminable. Her heart pounded fiercely. What did he mean? Had she waited so long and come such a distance for another good-bye? Was this all life had to offer them? A series of good-byes while the greater parts of their lives were spent apart?

After the three held their glasses and the servant was gone, Anna said, "Wine in the morning—I shall get light-headed!"

The countess' smile lasted only seconds. "Jan is to go against the Russians, Anna."

Jan looked at Anna as if to confirm it. He raised his glass. "To Poland!"

The countess echoed his toast.

Anna scarcely whispered hers. As she raised her glass and sipped, she watched Jan for a long moment. He was going off to fight the Russians. She knew she should be concerned for the country, but all that she could think of was that he might be wounded or killed. Only Jan Michał would ever rival him for an equal portion of her love; however, that was a mother's love and different from her love, her *passion*, for Jan. Knowing that he would be in danger brought the fullness of her feelings into focus. Little else mattered. She knew that she would never have such feelings for any other man. She would gladly die for his safety.

Jan was watching her. "Empress Catherine has dispatched troops to Poland to uphold the Confederacy of Targowica and destroy the Constitution. I am to rejoin Kościuszko's forces sooner than I expected."

"When do you leave?"

"At noon tomorrow."

Noon! So little time.

"A Mass is to be said at ten," he continued, "before we depart."

"A Mass?" the countess asked, unable to hide her surprise.

"No, Lady Gronska," Jan laughed, "I haven't suddenly converted. I may one day, but it hasn't happened yet. Most of the men from my farm are to join up with Kościuszko, so in deference to their leaving, I've asked a priest to come to the estate."

"I see," the countess said.

"But I will attend and I was hoping that both of you would come to the house for it."

Neither Anna nor her aunt had to be persuaded further. The matter was quickly decided.

"I know you two have only just arrived, but I must counsel you to return to Warsaw as soon as possible. Things may become unsafe here in short order."

"Sweet Jesus," the countess said. The fear and disappointment in her face mirrored Anna's.

"How is Jan Michał?" Jan asked, as if to shift to a happier subject.

"Fine," Anna said. "Would you like to see him?"

Jan brightened. "Of course."

"I'll call Marta."

"No, Anna," the countess said. "Let me go fetch the little one."

Anna silently blessed her aunt, suspecting that she was deliberately giving her some time alone with Jan.

The two sat on the sofa. Her heart started pounding again. She suddenly became afraid to trust her own emotions.

Jan, however, took the lead in conversation, speaking mostly of the nature of the Russian invasion.

Their little time together was being spent on very important, but public, matters. How was she to divert the conversation to the private concerns of her heart?

Eventually, he realized she wasn't wholly following him. "What is it, Anna?" he asked, taking her hand in his.

"Do you know of Zofia's intention?" Anna herself was surprised at how quickly the question came, rolling involuntarily off her tongue.

"Zofia?"

Anna nodded.

"What has she told you?"

"That she loves you."

Jan gave out with a strange laugh. "Is that what she said? She doesn't love me. Her great pride's been hurt, that's all."

"Then there *was* a time when—"

Jan put his finger on Anna's lips. "Do *you* love me, Anna?"

"I am only recently a widow. A full year must pass before I can marry again."

"There are some conventions that would do well to be ignored."

Was he of the same mind as Zofia? That Anna could flaunt tradition and marry when she chose? "What do you mean?"

"You could come to Kraków. It is safely in the hands of the patriots."

"Kraków?" Anna's head spun. What *did* he mean? That they marry? Or that she merely live with him?

"I ask you again, Anna: Do you love me?"

At that moment, Countess Gronska came into the room, Jan Michał in her arms. Anna could give Jan no answer.

They stood and Jan fussed over the child, the countess joining in. He took and held the baby, making funny faces at him, much as Anna sometimes did. If only this child *were* his, she thought.

"I must take my leave now," Jan said after a time, giving the baby over to Anna. "You will both come tomorrow, at ten?"

Anna nodded. Her opportunity to tell Jan that she loved him had come and gone. But there was tomorrow.

"Oh my, I've given orders for a good meal," the countess said.

"My apologies, Lady Gronska, but there is so much to do. With my men joining the cause, I'm closing down the estate."

"I see," she said, accepting a kiss on the cheek in reparation. "We'll see you in the morning, Lord Stelnicki."

"Good. And with luck, it will never be *Citizen* Stelnicki." Jan turned to Anna. He kissed the baby first, then Anna on both cheeks. "Till midmorning, then."

"Till midmorning," Anna heard herself say. She would tell him then.

After he was gone, Anna turned to her aunt. "What did Jan mean when he said he wished his name might never be *Citizen* Stelnicki?"

"He didn't sign with the Confederacy, Anna. If the Kościuszko forces should lose, both his estate and his title will be lost. He will merely be *Citizen* Stelnicki."

Anger flared within Anna. "Only God can take his title!"

"Perhaps, dearest. But the long-gathering storm has been unleashed and I fear our way of life will never be the same."

55

Anna slept very little. The meeting with Jan played and replayed in her mind. He had not answered her question about his feelings for Zofia. But then she had not been able to complete it before he put his finger on her lips and asked whether *she* loved him.

And she had not answered him. Of course, she loved him more than life itself. But what if he and Zofia had been in love? What if *she* had broken it up? What good could come of that? Or what if Zofia had never declared her love? Might his knowledge of it now make a difference?

By dawn, she could focus on only one thing: she must tell him of her love. And if Zofia loved him, too, well, then it was his choice to make.

The Countess Gronska and Anna ate an early breakfast. Before clearing the dishes from the table, Marta addressed the countess. She was in an agitated state. "Oh, Madame, Walek is insistent on joining the patriot forces though I need him here, and God knows, you do, too! He is no soldier and he is not young anymore."

"I know, Marta. He and several of the other men spoke to me earlier. I would like to keep them here, but there is too much to lose at the hands of the Russian she-wolf."

"Yes, Madame." Tears began streaming down her full cheeks. "I know."

"Take heart, Marta," the countess said. "They say 'Peace does not last without conflict.' Marta, would you like to accompany us to the Stelnicki home for the Mass?"

"Oh, yes! Thank you, Lady Gronska."

"Very well. See to it that Stanisław makes ready carts to accommodate any of the other women who also wish to go."

Marta nodded, wiping at her tears.

"Be glad, Marta," the countess continued, "that your son Tomasz is too young to go soldiering."

Marta nodded. "Oh, Madame, that hasn't kept him from pleading to join his father."

* * *

Anna stood in the downstairs hallway, anxiously awaiting her aunt, who seemed so slow in her preparations. She resisted the urge to call for her, wondering anew about her health. Walek and the other men had already left for the Stelnicki estate. A cluster of women could be heard gathering at the side of the house.

Finally, the countess emerged from her room in her black gown of shining satin. They left the house, Jan Michał in Anna's arms, a light blanket covering his face against the heat of the morning sunshine. The covered two-horse carriage stood waiting, old Stanisław holding the door. Behind the carriage were two carts, each drawn by a single horse. Seated in them were a number of peasant women, Gronski servants whose serious whisperings died away while they watched the countess, Anna, and Jan Michał enter the lead vehicle. Anna could hear one of the women sobbing for the loss of her man.

The Stelnicki manor home at Uście Zielone was not far, but the single road allowing for the little caravan was not a direct one. Stanisław took the carriage slowly because the women who drove the two carts had little experience with horses. Anna grew impatient, immediately wishing that she had taken her horse directly through the patch of woods separating the two estates. How she longed to feel the freedom of the ride again, the wind running past her face and through her hair, the furrows flying fast beneath! But only that morning she had given Pegasus to Walek so that he might have a good horse to take him to Kościuszko. It occurred to her now that she had not ridden since that day at the pond.

The air inside the coach was thick and stifling. Anna undressed Jan Michał and the countess joined her in fanning the red-faced and restless infant.

After more than half an hour on the circuitous route, the carriage came to a sudden halt.

The window shade had been pulled to keep out the heat and flying dust. When Anna opened it, she was disappointed to see that they were not yet at the Stelnicki estate.

Momentarily Stanisław opened the door. "Father Janewicki will bless us, Lady Gronska."

Anna's heart sank. She knew immediately that something had gone wrong.

Anna alighted from the coach while the countess remained seated, holding Jan Michał. The old and humble priest who had married Anna and Antoni a lifetime ago greeted them warmly despite his serious manner. "I was sent this way to speak to you," he announced. "I'm only sorry that I didn't get to your estate before you left."

"What is it?" Anna pressed.

"Mass has already been said, Lady Grawlinska. You see, the Russians are already on Polish soil."

"And the men? Jan Stelnicki?"

"Gone. All gone. If you will allow me, we will say a prayer for their safety right here at the side of the road."

The priest led them in saying the entire rosary. The countess remained with the baby in the carriage. Kneeling in the dust, Anna, Stanisław, and the stalwart peasant women chanted their replies to the Polish landscape which seemed to promise a summer like any other. But it would not be a summer like any other, Anna thought. Her mouth moved mechanically through the prayers, but she could only think: *I didn't tell him . . . I didn't tell him . . . I didn't tell him . . .*

"Follow the road forward," the priest said when they were finished, "and make a left into the Stelnicki driveway. The maids have a meal waiting. You'll need the rest before you return. Besides, the road is too narrow here to turn these vehicles around. There will be ample daylight to see you back to your home. Peace be with you."

Countess Gronska motioned him over to the carriage. "Peace be to all of us," she said, dropping some coins into his palm.

The vehicles turned into the Stelnicki estate, passing through the gates of a high wooden fence. The inviting two-storied house was wooden, too, unpainted, with a steep evergreen-shingled roof from which jutted hooded eyelike windows.

All of the male Stelnicki servants had joined the cause. The maids who waited upon Anna and the countess were polite, but sourly silent. Anna felt as if an invisible pall had fallen upon the house, upon the country, numbing its inhabitants with sadness and the knowledge that one's nation was at war. How many women of high or low birth, she wondered, through how many centuries, have shared the same destiny of watching their men march off to war, keeping an interminable vigil for their return? And how many men had not come back?

Anna and the countess were shown to an upstairs bedchamber to wash before the meal. The room, like most of the manor, was clean but lacking in subtle, feminine touches. Anna put this down to the fact that Jan's mother had died many years before.

The countess sat on the side of the bed. "Oh my, I'm faint, Anna Maria."

"The heat is oppressive, Aunt Stella. Would you like to lie down for a while?" Anna could not help but notice that her aunt's face was as white as the porcelain pitcher on the washstand.

"No, it will pass. It's a spell I sometimes get. I didn't think to bring my medicine, either." The countess pushed herself up from the bed. "I think it might help if I eat something."

Marta was allowed to sit at the dining table so that she could hold the baby while Anna and the countess ate. The other women who had come ate in the kitchen.

Bowls of a rich and creamy potato soup were placed before them. The meal consisted of thickly sliced dark bread, pierogi stuffed with mushrooms, and braised venison. The mere aroma of the food seemed to revive the countess.

Anna's eyes moved around the large room, taking in the plate rail that extended the length of each wall, at a height above the windows and doors. The shelf held a wide variety of dishes, pans, decorative plates, and platters organized in no particular way, but homey just the same.

One thought cheered her: this was Jan Stelnicki's home. Anna dared to hope that she and her son would eat countless meals in this dining room.

Before the meal was over, the strange weakness overcame the countess again. "You and the others go back, Anna Maria," she urged. "I think I should stay the night. You can send Stanisław for me in the morning."

"I won't hear of it." Anna was not about to allow her aunt out of her sight. "I'm equally exhausted, however short the distance is. We'll all stay the night."

Much later, after a lighter meal, Countess Gronska and Jan Michał were settled into separate bedchambers, and Anna explored the manor. While the Stelnicki home was of good size, it was plain to the eye, and certainly no mansion. The whiteness of the plaster walls had darkened over the years. Tapestries hung in almost every room, but furniture was sparse and mostly functional. It had been a man's home for some time.

After dark, Anna retired to the small room she shared with Jan Michał. One of the maids had earlier provided the crude crib in which he now lay. He slept soundly.

The evening seemed no cooler than the day, unusual weather for June. Anna had no nightclothes and so laid herself, fully clothed, upon the blankets of the narrow, feathered bed. Lutisha would have scolded her, had the servant known that Anna left both windows open to the un-known spirits of the night. But Anna's fears were not fears of spirits.

Eventually she fell into a fitful half-sleep.

By morning, Anna slept more deeply, coming awake only when she heard noises at the side of the house, the sounds of horses and muffled voices.

Jan Michał awoke then and began to cry. Anna took him to her bed and began to nurse him, wondering what the activity below was about. Unlikely as the prospect was, she prayed that for some reason Jan had come back to the house.

She was not to wonder long at the commotion.

Suddenly, the door was flung open, and a soldier in red took some four or five steps into the room. Anna immediately recognized the Russ-ian uniform.

The man didn't blink or turn away when he saw Anna was nursing. Anger overcame her embarrassment. "Who are you to behave like this?"

"By order of the Empress Catherine," he growled in low Polish, "you are to follow me immediately."

"Turn aside!" Anna demanded in Russian.

He stared in surprise. Anna's eyes met his uncompromisingly, and he turned away his gaze.

When her dress was buttoned, she stood, and holding fast to Jan Michał, followed the tall figure in the long coat and high black boots. He carried his pistol in his hand.

The two entered the countess' room. Anna's aunt stood facing them, Bible in hand. Marta and her daughters stood behind her, all clearly terrified.

"Countess Gronska?" the Russian asked. "Which of you is the countess?"

The countess slowly brought her eyes up to meet his. "Whom am I addressing?"

"A captain of the army of the Empress Catherine of Russia." His manner was haughty.

"I am the Countess Stella Gronska," she said with quiet dignity. "Mine is the neighboring estate."

"And you?" He had turned to Anna.

"I am the Countess Anna Maria Berezowska-Grawlinska." She hoped she appeared as unruffled as her aunt.

"Have the names of your husbands appeared in agreement with the Confederacy of Targowica?"

"We are widows," Countess Gronska answered.

Anna knew that answer would not suffice. She knew, too, that to spare her aunt, she must be the one to say what she said next: "Both of our names have been affixed to a document supporting the Confederacy." The treasonous words tore at her heart.

"Ah, then you most gracious ladies are free to leave this house. I must ask you to do so without delay, for this is the home of a traitor. It is to be destroyed."

Anna felt angry blood rush to her face. But this was not the time to defend Jan or his home. There were others in more immediate danger. "These are our servants here. We have others downstairs. They will accompany us back home."

The Russian eyed Marta, Marcelina, and Katarzyna. He shrugged his indifference.

Just then a great disquiet arose in the yard. Soon, a second Russian appeared in the doorway. He told the captain that another detachment had arrived.

"Ah, well, then," the man said, "you ladies will please keep to this room for the time being."

As the captain left, he turned and gave Anna an appraising glance, one that lifted the little hairs at the nape of her neck.

The four women were left to their prayers and dark imagination.

The day's heat rose. The sounds of pistols, drunken shouts, and screams of women put everyone on edge. Jan Michał cried. The others were too frightened to do so.

What was going on downstairs? Outside? Why hadn't they been released? What was this delay? Anna's mind conjured the worst possibilities. "Aunt Stella," she whispered, "should anything happen to me, I know you will see to Jan Michał's safety."

"The baby will come to no harm, I guarantee you, Anna. And neither shall we. These barbarians would not dare injure a titled Pole."

Anna was not nearly so sure. She worried especially for the physical safety of the two young girls. What was happening to the Stelnicki maids below? Men at war were capable of anything. She worried for herself, too. If one of them violated a noblewoman, she suspected he would kill her to suppress the crime. And if he didn't kill her, she would wish he had.

By midafternoon, there was only silence, oppressive as the heat. An exhausted Jan Michał finally slept.

They heard heavy footsteps on the stairway, then along the hallway. One man's. The door was unlocked and thrust open.

"Lady Gronska," the young officer said, seeming to know at once which of them was the countess, "you and your servants are to come with me. You are free to go back to your estate." He spoke perfect Polish.

"And my niece, the Countess Grawlinska?"

"I have no orders for her yet."

"Then I will not go."

"You must, Aunt Stella. Don't worry about me. Hurry now, take Marta and her daughters. This is your chance for safety."

"I will talk to whoever is in charge downstairs. Don't worry, Anna, you will come with us."

Anna was alone then, and minutes ticked by. Perhaps half an hour. She put her ear to the door. She could hear her aunt raging downstairs. "But why are you doing this?" her aunt said. It was strange, but there was something in the countess' tone that hinted at her knowing her enemy. Yet how was that possible?

Things went quiet then for many minutes until a commotion arose in the side yard. Anna went to the window. The Gronski carriage and carts were being readied.

They would come to collect her presently, Anna thought, carefully readying the sleeping baby.

She again heard steps on the stairs, then moving toward her chamber. The lock turned and the door opened.

Katarzyna entered, tearful and shaking. A guard remained outside the door. The girl carried with her the large canvas satchel that held the countess' knitting and needlework. It seemed to be empty.

"What is it, Katarzyna?" Anna whispered. "Tell me!"

"I am to take the baby." The girl spoke as though in a trance. "Lady Gronska said they aren't to know that he was here at all." The trance broke and she started to sob. "I'm so frightened. Oh, I don't think I can do it, Madame, I don't!"

"Why are you to take the baby, Katarzyna? Where? What's to become of me?"

"I'm so afraid, Madame. So afraid."

Anna realized it was useless to try to elicit information from the girl. She knew nothing. Anna went to the window. She could see Marta and Marcelina below. Then the countess came into view. Anna retraced her steps to Katarzyna. "You are to take Jan Michał in the satchel, is that it? Katarzyna!"

The girl nodded.

"My baby's life may depend on you, do you understand?" Anna shook the girl. "*Do* you?"

"Yes, Madame." She seemed to gather her wits, sniffling.

The child was still sleeping when Anna placed him in the satchel, quickly kissing him on the forehead.

"Very well, Katarzyna, take him and go. God will grant you the courage. Be certain not to awaken him."

Katarzyna left.

Anna heard the door's lock click into place. Holding her breath, she listened to the sound of voices at the foot of the stairs. Was the girl being questioned? Would the baby awake and cry out in terror?

Instinctively Anna's hands moved up to pull at her hair in the nervous way she had done as a child. She stopped herself as the voices dropped away.

Anna ran to the window and had to lean out at a dangerous angle to see where the carriage had been moved. The carts were filled with the Gronski servant women. She assumed her aunt was already in the carriage.

Anna stared unblinking as she saw Katarzyna appear now, delicately picking her way, holding tight to her cargo. *Sleep, Jan Michał. Sleep. Just a little longer.* Stanisław took the satchel and handed it up, Marta's strong hands reaching from the coach to take it. The door closed and Katarzyna made her way to her place with Marcelina in the first cart.

The carriage wheels started to turn then in the dusty drive, moving slowly at first. Anna watched until they were gone from sight . . . then from hearing. She slipped to the floor underneath the window, spent.

It was only now, with all the others on the way to safety, that Anna feared for her own self. Why had she been singled out to stay at the Stelnicki estate? The Russian captain had told her that this place was to be destroyed. What was to happen to her?

Hours passed. By nightfall, she was hungry and in need of using the chamber pot. There was none in this room.

Anna knocked at her own door. "I must be attended!" she called.

She could hear the sounds of boot steps thumping to and fro and distant voices.

She called out again.

Finally, the door opened to an unfamiliar guard and a Stelnicki maid who cowered behind him. "After you are attended, you will follow me," he said.

Anna questioned the woman once they were alone in the little room Anna had occupied the night before, but she stood facing the wall, not answering. Anna thought she must be simpleminded, but came to realize the terrified woman was praying her heart out. The maid was dismissed when they left the chamber, and Anna followed the guard down to the reception room. "I am very hungry," Anna said.

The Russian ignored her.

A candelabra with six tapers lit only the far area of the room. A small group of men was gathered about the sofa that supported a man who appeared to be badly injured. An army surgeon worked over him.

Anna's guard stood behind her, prodding her now to move closer to the group. She did so, trying not to focus on any one thing or face.

Several men stepped aside, allowing Anna to catch sight of the bearded man's chest wound. It was a gaping hole, red and hideous.

Anna was pushed to the very edge of the sofa, but she kept her gaze away from the patient.

"She is here," someone said, as if to the prone man.

The man's head rolled on the pillow, and Anna could sense his eyes on her.

She kept her own averted.

"You will hold my hand while the wound is attended to," he said, in a simple but demanding way. His hand reached up quickly, taking Anna's captive, and holding it with a crushing tightness. It was all she could do not to call out. Why was she being subjected to this?

While the physician worked, the pressure on her hand increased unbearably. When a glowing iron was used to cauterize the wound, the patient screamed out in agony and his body heaved upward.

Moved by pity and the kindness she might have for any injured beast, Anna at last looked down at him.

What she saw made her forget his vicelike grip and the fingernail cutting into the cuticle of her thumb. Neither did she smell anymore the stench of burning flesh. The man's eyelids had opened wide in pain and shock—and Anna saw his reddish brown eyes.

The man was no stranger to her. He was the one . . . the one that last September . . . at the pond. She tried to catch her breath. He was grinning through his pain at her recognition.

Anna fainted dead away at the sight of her cousin Walter.

56

Anna's senses were slow in returning. The first sounds she recognized were those of a door creaking open and footsteps approaching, then retreating. After she heard the closing of the door, she dared to open her eyes.

She was in the room where she had been held captive earlier. She had been placed upon the bed with no particular care, so that her head hung over the side. Lifting her head onto the pillow, she noticed that a tray had been left on the bedside table.

She lay there, desperately hungry, yet without appetite and lacking the will to sit up and eat. She could think only of Walter.

Her own cousin had raped her. She had since found out that Walter was not the blood son of the Gronskis, but what did that matter?

And why hadn't she figured out that it had been Walter? Guessed as much? The memory of those penetrating eyes at the pond should have made her realize they were the same brutish eyes that stared at her from across the dinner table. Something, some part of her, had kept her from making the connection.

Well, it was out now. And to compound matters, the father of her child still worked for Catherine, who sought to overrun Poland. Countess Gronska *did* know the man with whom she had been arguing. It was her son! No wonder she flew into a rage. Walter must have told his mother that he was the father of Jan Michał and that he would detain Anna here. When she saw there was no dissuading him, she adroitly saw to it that the baby was secretly removed from his influence. Anna would never be able to repay her for that remarkable bit of cleverness.

With the greatest exertion, Anna sat up at the side of the bed, near the table that held the tray. She thought the meat pie wretched but swallowed it down, lubricated by small swallows of the watery and sour milk. Not long after, she called out to be attended because she was ill.

Anna awoke the next morning to the voice of Lilka, the Stelnicki housekeeper. "I've brought some breakfast, Lady Grawlinska."

"Thank you," Anna managed to whisper before the maid slipped out. The old woman reminded her of a very thin Lutisha.

Anna did feel better.

At midmorning the officer who had come for Countess Gronska reappeared. His Polish was too good for a Russian. Anna suspected he was, like Walter, a Polish mercenary.

"All women are being summoned at once."

Anna followed him out of her room.

Downstairs, she was brought to stand in a line with the servant women, and once assembled, they were marched into the reception room, where Walter lay on his sofa, propped up by several pillows.

Anna was mortified to be standing before him, like a beggar. She wanted to spit upon him but held her anger in check.

Eight or nine women stood stiffly with her in this line, several of them sniffling or crying out of fear of the man lounging on the sofa, his shirt open to reveal the black-haired chest and bloodstained bandage.

He took immediate notice of Anna. "Come here!"

Several of the women showed surprise at his demeanor toward her.

Anna moved to within two paces of him. She fought to stand erect and hold her head high.

"I said, *Come here!*" Walter attempted to reach out and take hold of her, but his wound caused him to recoil in pain.

Anna stood her ground.

He angrily reached out again, laying hold of her wrist and pulling her to him.

Anna struggled to release his grip and pull free. When his strength pulled her forward so that she almost fell atop him, she threw all of her weight backward, falling onto the floor when he released her.

Despite his obvious pain, he laughed and reached for her arm again, swinging around into a seated position on the sofa. He then put his booted foot against her side even while he continued to tug at her arm. "I'll drive my foot through her," he announced, "and through all of you who are stupid enough not to respond to my commands!"

The room became quiet as a cave. The women stood in speechless fear. All but for Lilka, whose disdain lurked in her blue eyes. This woman seemed to have her wits about her. It occurred to Anna that this servant must certainly have known Walter from his days of growing up on the neighboring estate.

Anna fought not to cry out, not to shed a tear.

"I am Captain Gronski," Walter said. "You will all attend to me and do my bidding exactly as I say! This home has been taken over in the name of Catherine, Empress of Russia."

The women stared, their faces like those of a tragic chorus.

"Old one," he barked.

"Lilka," she dared to say, stepping forward.

"Lilka, you will see that food and supplies be provided for my men. There are twenty of us. You are all to work from sunrise to dark, do you hear? At night you are not to waste candle or torch. For every one who runs off, the others will lose one finger. Am I understood? You will take no orders from the countess here; she is to have no freedom in this house. Should she escape, you will *all* die. Now move along. Go!"

As the women scurried into the kitchen, Walter released his hold on his cousin.

Anna crawled a few steps away and got to her feet. "I have been allied with the empress," she cried. "My name is on the document of the Confederacy. You have no right to detain me!"

"You have been allied?" he scoffed. "Zofia's idea, no doubt. And who do you think gave her the idea?"

"You?"

"Yes."

"At the Royal Castle that night. I *did* see you staring!"

Walter laughed. "Have you forgotten an alliance of our own?"

"You were . . ."

"Yes, Ania, I was the one, for God's sake. Now, where is my son? Go upstairs and get him."

"He isn't here."

"What do you mean? You're lying. Bring him to me at once!"

"My son is in Warsaw."

"In Warsaw? You keep him as a *bastard*?"

"Isn't that what he would be, had I not married Antoni? *Your* bastard."

Walter glared at her, then laughed. "You have more spirit than I remember, *cousin*."

"*My* son is not kept as a bastard. He is well cared for by all of us."

His eyes narrowed. "Then why didn't you bring him with you to the country?"

"I wanted to, but the countess and Zofia were adamant that I recoup my strength here. The child is sickly and too young for such a journey. He stayed in the city with a wet-nurse." Would he believe her? What was his temper capable of should he discover that the child left the estate under his nose with the countess, his own mother? Anna prayed that her aunt had taken him back to Warsaw; Halicz was safe now for no one.

After more questioning, Walter grudgingly let the subject of Jan Michał pass.

A chair was brought and Anna was made to sit at his side. He went on at great length bragging about his promotion to captain, his power, and his work for the empress. Anna answered his occasional question in as few words as possible. She no longer felt that he would physically harm her. In fact, it was as if he were striving for an intimacy of some kind. What was his game? Anna was afraid to think about it.

Periodically he gave orders to his men. Anna learned that the first captain she had met had left with the first detachment, leaving behind Walter and his own small force, some of whom also nursed wounds. She breathed a sigh of relief to think that captain gone, not only because of his leering glance at her, but also because he had taken notice of Jan Michał's presence.

At that moment the Polish-speaking Russian officer came in to speak to Walter. Anna's heart caught. Had he noticed the sleeping Jan Michał when he came to collect her aunt and the servants? She prayed not. If he had, what were the odds that he would have some occasion to mention the baby to Walter? And what about the Stelnicki maids? All of them had seen the child, fussed over him . . .

For now, Walter seemed to take notice only of his pain or perhaps he grew tired of his own voice; in any event, Anna was dismissed.

At the first opportunity, Anna spoke to Lilka, imploring her and the other maids not to mention Jan Michał.

The woman nodded knowingly. "Your aunt already instructed us. The other women have sworn their secrecy, too."

"You recognized him?" Anna asked. "Walter?"

"Yes, Lady Grawlinska. From the time he was a boy, I knew he would turn out bad. Forgive me, but he was born with the evil eye upon him."

How true it was, Anna thought, that no one knows more about what goes on in a house than a servant.

As the days passed and the Russian officer said nothing to Walter about the presence of Jan Michał, Anna came to believe the child had escaped his notice.

Anna remained a prisoner in the little upstairs room. Lilka brought word that Countess Gronska and Jan Michał had returned to Warsaw. For that Anna was relieved and grateful.

Summer passed. From her window she watched the landscape revel in its final burst of color before its seasonal death. The weeks, like the leaves, fell away and the wheel that was the seasons turned.

Only the Russian soldiers were allowed to eat meat. Anna suspected this was a kind of mental torture Walter was inflicting on her, but she said nothing, refusing to allow him to think it bothered her. After a while, it became a moot point because what livestock had not been butchered died from neglect.

Lilka did her best to see that Anna had enough to eat, but the Lenten-like menu varied little. Breakfast consisted of *kasza* with thin milk and sometimes a piece of fruit, fresh or dried. There was no lunch. For supper, it was black bread, a vegetable, and *żur*. *Żur* was the main meal throughout Lent, and at Sochaczew Anna had often helped in the preparation of the sour soup made from fermented, raw bread dough and served over boiled potatoes. It was traditional at the end of Lent to happily break the large bowl used for making *żur*, so tired was everyone of the soup. For Anna and the other women on the Stelnicki estate those many months, there was no breaking of the bowl or their routine.

On occasion, Anna was allowed to borrow books from the library downstairs, where her real nourishment took place. She read every title the Stelnickis had by the French author Voltaire. She loved that his stories were cleverly stated parables highlighting the foibles and flaws of man's character. In writing about man's intolerance, Voltaire implied that there was little to be done in ebbing its eternal flow. "Escape if you can," he wrote.

Escape.

Each day, Anna was made to sit at Walter's side while his health improved. The man was full of ambition and pride. He went on at great length about his role as liaison between the empress and King Stanisław. Anna suspected that he was merely an interpreter, but to hear him tell it, he personally had Catherine's ear and one day he would be a force in Russo-Polish politics.

Anna would say little in response to his pontificating. This irked him to no end.

One day, his gloating attitude suggested that he held some secret. Anna refused to give him the benefit of drawing him out on the subject— even if she were curious.

"You might be interested in the latest news, Anna," he said at last. "Kościuszko's forces have been repelled by the army of the empress."

Anna didn't believe him. She didn't want to believe. How could the hearts of patriots be brought low by the likes of Walter? Where was Jan? Was he safe?

"I expect that I will be returning to Russia soon," he added, when she didn't respond.

Anna knew he was baiting her. She tried not to appear hopeful. Would she be allowed to return to Warsaw?

"You are to send for the child," he said.

"What?" The single word was scarcely more than a breath.

"He is to be brought here immediately."

"Walter, he's too young . . . and he's in poor health."

"No child of mine could be sickly. Look at us, Anna. His parents are survivors. He will be, too." His plans came out, then. Anna and Jan Michał were to live in Saint Petersburg. Jan Michał's name would be changed to Walter, but he would remain Walter's bastard. Walter was determined not to marry because marriage might jeopardize his position in the court of Catherine.

Anna's head reeled with what he said, and didn't say. She thanked God he did not have marriage in mind. But what was she to be to him? A mistress? Did he think she would stand for it?

"I prefer to have my son raised as a bastard," he was saying. "History has documented that bastards make the most powerful of men."

"And you expect me to go to Russia and raise him for you?"

"You disappoint me, Anna. Of course, it would be entirely your choice. I thought certain you would not allow anyone else to raise your son. But, seeing how you left him in Warsaw, maybe you aren't the maternal kind?"

It was a game for him, she realized. He had checkmated her long ago and now enjoyed toying with her, forcing her from one blind square to the next.

Her anger brought her to her feet. "I would kill my son and myself before we would go to Saint Petersburg with you!"

"You, Anna?" he laughed. "In the role of Medea? It doesn't suit you."

As Anna raced upstairs to her cell-like chamber, she could only think that her bravado had done nothing, except to amuse him further.

She threw herself onto her bed.

Escape if you can.

In the afternoon, Anna was forcibly brought downstairs when she refused to go on her own. Pen and paper were placed before her. She was to write to Aunt Stella and Zofia, requesting that they send Jan Michał without delay.

When no admonition or threat against her could make her lift the pen, Walter had Lilka brought in. Then, in a quiet, conversational tone, he told her that Lilka would lose a finger for every day that Anna delayed. He saw to it that the army surgeon was standing by.

"Do not worry for me," Lilka said, her face hard and true.

Despite the housekeeper's bravery, Anna inked the quill and put it to paper.

With the passing of each day, Anna became increasingly fearful of the moment when Jan Michał would be handed over to Walter.

Walter's moods became more and more foul, too, and his temper shorter. His soldiers, like the women servants, trod lightly, lest he fly into a rage. He was still experiencing a great deal of pain and talked about going to Warsaw to consult another doctor.

Three weeks after the letter had been sent, Anna awoke to the sound of carriage wheels in the drive below. Was this the moment she had been dreading? Was Jan Michał in that carriage?

When she called out, a guard unlocked her door.

Hair undone and only her wrap around her, Anna rushed down the stairs.

A lone messenger stood in front of Walter.

No sign of Jan Michał.

"I have a letter for the Countess Berezowska-Grawlinska," the young man said, drawing an envelope from a leather letter folder.

"Where is the child?" Walter demanded.

The man seemed puzzled. "I have only the letter."

"I am the Countess Berezowska-Grawlinska," Anna said, extending her trembling hand to receive the missive. Instead of feeling elation that Jan Michał was not sent, however, Anna was seized with foreboding.

Walter snatched the letter from the man's hand and went into the reception room. Anna quickly followed.

When the letter had been opened and read, Walter looked up at Anna, his face above the black beard ashen.

The messenger had followed them into the room, and Walter turned on him now. "Wait in the hall!" he barked. "And close the doors."

The man made a quick exit.

"What is it?" Anna asked. Her heart was pounding.

He looked at her, his face screwed into folds of fierce anger. He crumpled the parchment now and threw it at her.

Anna quickly retrieved it, unfolding its creases.

My Dearest Cousin Anna,

Merciful God has taken your child, Jan Michał. By accident, the infant swallowed my emerald stickpin. He was buried on Sunday last with the fullest graces of God and His Church.

This note comes with a carriage so that you may be returned to us, who share your loss.

With love and hope,
Zofia

Jan Michał was dead. . . . Anna's throat went dry. She stared mindlessly at the words that blurred before her. Her son was dead. How could that be? God would not allow such a tragedy. "Jan Michał!" she screamed, finding her voice. "My baby Jan! It's not true!" Her body stiffened and she watched her hands tear at the parchment, as if to do so would invalidate its words. "No! No! Not Jan Michał!"

Her continued screaming was suddenly interrupted when she was struck across the shoulder with a blunt object, propelling her across the room where she crashed against the wall.

Anna looked up to see Walter towering above her, sword in his hand. His face above the beard, no longer white, was inflamed now.

Anna cared little if the sword were to slice through her. It might relieve the pain. "You wouldn't let me go to my son," she screamed, "now he's dead at Zofia's hands. Your sister killed Jan Michał!" The tears that she had withheld from Walter all these weeks filled her eyes, but she refused to allow them to fall.

Picking up the letter, Walter crushed it in his fist and pitched it away, fastening his eyes on Anna. "Damn you! And damn your son if he was so stupid. You'll bear me another."

"Never!" Anna spit upon him now.

Walter looked down at the spittle on his shirtsleeve, then at Anna. "When the time comes, you'll pipe a different tune." Throwing down his sword, Walter went out into the hallway to speak to the messenger.

Anna pulled herself up into a kneeling position. She looked at the sword, wishing she had the strength to use it on Walter. Or even on herself.

The gleam of the sword suddenly made her think of the stickpin. What agony her son must have suffered before death claimed his little soul. How could Zofia have been so careless? And how like her to be so terse in her description.

The emerald stickpin. Anna's heart stopped. Zofia did not have the emerald stickpin. Anna had it. It was enfolded in blue velvet and placed in the box with the crystal dove. The box was at that very moment upstairs in her little room, in the bottom of the wardrobe.

The stickpin was upstairs and Jan Michał was alive. *Alive.* Even the word seemed to pulse. *Alive.* The letter was but a ruse to make Walter think his son was dead. The clever Zofia had not killed Jan Michał. She had *saved* him!

There was no stopping a new wave of tears, but now they were tears of relief and joy, and they were shed privately. Her son was alive, and the unsuspecting Walter had been vanquished.

Slowly Anna became aware of the muted voices in the hallway. Walter was dismissing the messenger.

"But I was told," the young man was insisting, "that the countess would be returning to Warsaw. That is why the carriage was sent."

"The countess will not return to Warsaw!" Walter bellowed. "Now, be gone. If you are on this traitor's land but two more minutes, I'll have *you* shot as a traitor."

Anna felt freedom slipping away. She rushed out into the hallway, wiping at her tears. "Walter! Let me return to Warsaw. I beg you to let me go!"

The front door banged shut.

Walter turned to glare at Anna. "Look at yourself, cousin. You're in no condition to travel."

She begged him again, to no avail, and momentarily she could hear the wheels turning in the gravel, moving for the road. She made a move for the front door, but Walter extended his foot, dashing her to the floor.

57

Walter's plans to take Anna to Saint Petersburg had to be delayed. Orders arrived dispatching him to Warsaw, where he was to serve as a Polish-speaking aide to Catherine's ambassador who was en route to negotiate a treaty between Poland and Russia. Walter was taking only half of his men. The others were to stay at the Stelnicki estate.

Anna begged him to take her, but he refused. His resolve to ensconce her as his mistress in Saint Petersburg had not abated even though he thought his son dead. When Anna pleaded with him, he slapped her, then struck her repeatedly until she nearly lost consciousness.

Several weeks passed before the bruises healed. The weeks of winter took those at the estate, the jailers and the jailed, into 1793.

The room was very cold. Wood was being rationed by the soldiers, who evidently had little skill at chopping. A maid brought up an armful in the morning, and with it Anna was expected to keep the fire in her grate. It was an impossible task. The mythical Sisyphus could not have been given one more impossible, she thought, trying to keep the fire alive with such little fuel through the course of a frigid winter. Even with the fire going, the sting of the cold did not lessen.

Anna was allowed no correspondence. She was aware of letters that came to the house, but they were intercepted before reaching her.

Would Walter contact his mother while he was in Warsaw? Would her aunt and cousin be able to keep Jan Michał's existence from him? How *was* her son?

And Jan Stelnicki. Was he safe? If he were alive, he could not know she was being held captive in his home. Were there gods somewhere laughing at the players in this irony?

It was through Lieutenant Szymon Boraviecki, the young Polish mercenary who had been left in charge of the house and a contingent of eight or ten men, that Anna gained knowledge of the momentous events taking place in Poland and elsewhere on the continent.

On the twenty-first of January, King Louis XVI of France climbed the stairs to the *guillotine*. Though by now it came to most as no surprise, the actuality still shocked Anna. Lieutenant Boraviecki augured that Queen Marie Antoinette would follow her husband's steps to the scaffold.

The eyes of every monarch in the world must be on Paris. It was not good news to the patriots, by any means. Anna knew that the execution of the French king would make less secure the crowned heads in countries allied against Poland and its democratic reform. They would not wish their own landless commoners seeking rights and land. And less secure monarchs would use their powers and influence to see that the new order in Poland would be crushed like a flower beneath a boot.

Poland was not faring well, but Walter had been too quick to pronounce the patriots' movement dead. Under the leadership of Prince Józef Poniatowski and Tadeusz Kościuszko, a brave, and for a short time successful, defense was waged. But Poland's two allies, Austria and Prussia, who as recently as 1791 had agreed to defend Poland under attack, proved faithless. Austria's new emperor, Francis II, abandoned his father's policy that supported Poland. Frederick William of Prussia, in flagrant violation of his own promises, declined to protect a constitution that never had his "concurrence."

Anna remembered Jan's warnings of more than a year before when she spoke up for Poland's allies. Reminding her that Prussia and Austria already had shared much booty with Russia subsequent to the Polish Partition in 1772, including the acquisition of Halicz, he pointed out that greed seldom lessens; it only grows.

Thus, Poland's resistance, left to heroic but small and makeshift forces, had been overcome by the great Russian armies. What retribution was to be imposed upon the Polish *Sejm* and King—with Walter's help—remained to be seen.

Kościuszko and his small, battered forces, nobles and peasants alike, withdrew to Leipzig to salve their wounds and regroup. Anna prayed that the men from the Stelnicki and Gronski estates were numbered among the survivors. And Jan, always a prayer for Jan.

* * *

Anna was allowed, under guard, to use the library for an hour each day. Very often, it was Lieutenant Boraviecki himself who sat with her. She was glad for the companionship and the opportunity to share a conversation and point of view.

One day in mid-February they were discussing the future of Poland. The lieutenant was arguing that the changes might not be so great. "And the good to come of it," he said, "is that Catherine's influence will temper the potential for the rising of the peasants. What happened in France must not happen here."

"You think, then, our peasants would rise up?"

"Why not, once they've seen the French king put to death?"

"For the *excesses* of the French aristocracy, Lieutenant. While I have personally witnessed some excesses among the Polish nobility, one cannot compare them to the French. And the democratic reform was exactly the prescription that would satisfy commoners."

"Bones to the dogs?"

"Hardly that. Real reform. Overdue rights, land ownership, self-esteem."

"It's a difficult argument to make."

"Oh, no, it's not! And the irony lies in the fact that the greediest nobles are trying to save every scrap for themselves while turning Poland over to a Catherine who will annex the whole of it to Russia, like some senile woman stitching a new patch to an already unwieldy quilt."

He nodded. "I expect she will want something for her trouble."

"She'll want *Poland*. Don't you care?"

The lieutenant shrugged again.

Anna studied his handsome boyishness, the brown wavy hair, the clean-shaven, angular face. "Are you not interested in politics, Lieutenant Boraviecki? Have you renounced your Polish citizenship to serve Catherine?"

"No, I am a Pole. My parents are landowners."

"Isn't it hard to reconcile your two selves? The Pole and the Russian soldier? Don't you feel a loyalty to Poland?"

"The interests of the two are not so separate."

"Oh, but they are! It is Kościuszko's cause that reflects the true Poland, one that is proud, spirited, and unwilling to be ruled by foreign powers. Weeks ago you told me that it was your sense of adventure that led you to become a mercenary. Lieutenant, Kościuszko heads an adventure close to the heart of every true Pole: freedom." Anna stood and, walking to a shelf nearby, drew down a book. "Have you read this?"

"Plato's *Republic?* Yes, I have."

"In it he writes that he who refuses to rule is liable to be ruled by one who is worse than himself."

"Ah, two parts wisdom, one part wit."

"Then you agree?"

"Lady Grawlinska," he sighed. "You are a woman, and too much of an idealist, I suspect."

"You're implying that I'm missing something."

"It can be pared down to simple terms."

"Then tell me, Lieutenant. Don't patronize me."

"I am a realist. As such, I know that Kościuszko and his followers, no matter how high-minded and patriotic, are doomed. If you only knew the power Catherine has at her command."

"Ah, that does shear the subject down to its basics, doesn't it? Power? You, Lieutenant Boraviecki, are on the side that will triumph. Is that it? You should ask my cousin Walter to introduce you to his sister. You have much in common."

"Ah, but don't they say opposites attract?"

Anna's gaze immediately went to the lieutenant's face. His meaning was clear. Oh, she should not have been surprised. In many little ways she had been picking up on his interest in her. Now he had put it out there on the table, as if playing a card.

He laughed self-consciously. "You didn't think that you could make me into a patriot, did you?"

"No. I would ask something else of you." Anna realized that she was impulsively playing her own card.

"What is it? If it's within my power—"

"Power. There's that word again."

"You're speaking to a man who doesn't have much of it."

"You have the power to let me go." There it was. Just like that. She took in a deep breath.

"Lady Grawlinska," he said, drawing out her name as if his other words would be painful, "that is impossible."

"You have only to be looking the other way. I'll see to the rest. Lieutenant, I want my freedom."

"I can't, my lady."

"I've entertained you with my stories and myths over the past months. I'd like to tell you a true story now . . . about Walter."

Without waiting for his approval, Anna launched into the story of her coming to Halicz, the attack at the pond, and the myriad ways in which it altered her life.

By the time she was finished, he sat quietly stunned. "I see why you hate him."

"Yes, and he continues to plot against me with this plan to place me in Saint Petersburg."

"But if it's against your will?"

"Who will there be in that godforsaken land to stand up for me? No woman has power there but Catherine." Her gaze held his. "Szymon," she said, using his Christian name for the first time, "please . . . please help me."

"Lady Grawlinska, I *have* helped you."

"How?"

"By not telling Walter your baby was here and that you somehow smuggled him out with your aunt."

Anna gasped. "You knew? And didn't tell?"

He nodded. "And I suspect, too, that your son did not die, as Walter believes. Yes?"

Anna nodded.

"Lady Anna, I don't think I have to tell you . . . that I care for you. And if I could do this thing for you, I would." He sighed. "But I am helpless."

Anna stood now. "I thank you for keeping your silence about my son, but you risked nothing with your inaction." The game had reached its conclusion. "If you would see me to my room . . ."

"You must understand—"

"Oh, I do." Anna tried to smile. "Lieutenant Boraviecki, if you should find yourself in Warsaw, I suggest you stay clear of the faro tables. The odds are always with the house."

Later, in her room, she regretted her cutting comment. She had been in the wrong. It was too much to ask of him. She had used his interest in her, the *power* of his interest in her. She knew that had he aided her to escape, Walter would have his commission—if not his life.

58

Walter remained in Warsaw longer than anyone would have thought. The summer of 1793 was hot and dry. Even from her small, airless room on the second floor, Anna could see deep cracks in the earth. Dust would sometimes blow against the house as if the Polish country were a desert. The shrubbery and trees were burnt brown; the springtime grasses were long since dead. It was as if the countryside mourned the Russian invasion.

More than a year had passed since she came with the countess to Halicz, only to find a prison at Uście Zielone.

Anna's heart quaked when news arrived on the twentieth of August that a treaty had been signed on the seventeenth. The document, engineered in 1792, was now official: Russian bayonets had overturned the Third of May Constitution and imposed aristocratic privilege. Under the guise that within Poland were the seeds of another French Revolution, Catherine was overseeing a second dismemberment of Poland, one which could only make Poles nostalgic for the Partition of 1772.

A powerless and miserable King Stanisław signed the treaty and advised the *Sejm* to do likewise, that resistance was useless. It was said that Stanisław wanted to resign, but that Catherine, his lover of years before, insisted he keep his title, meaningless as it had become.

Under duress, the *Sejm* adopted the treaty that gave Russia a huge block of the republic's lands: all the east provinces from Livonia to Moldavia. And when they resisted Prussia's gains of Great Poland, Kujavia, Toruń, and Danzig by remaining silent for many hours, the Russian ambassador claimed that silence meant consent.

Anna could only think that as the interpreter for the ambassador, Walter had played a role, however minimal, in this dismembering of his country. The thought was a bitter one.

Poland was now less than one-third of its original dimensions. Warsaw and what could still be called Poland was occupied, as well. Small towns were being garrisoned; many of the villages were being pillaged. The slightest attempt at self-defense meant Siberia, a godforsaken land of cold under the autocratic control of army officers.

Lieutenant Boraviecki confided in Anna the news that, upon Walter's return, the detachment would leave for Saint Petersburg.

Anna was all but certain that the once-graceful home of the Stelnickis would be destroyed. What would happen to the servant women who had persevered with her? Anna had had no news from anyone in Warsaw, and she knew that if Walter had his way, she would soon be in Saint Petersburg with no hope of ever seeing her home, her child, or other loved ones.

Escape. Voltaire's advice rang in her ears.

Within a week they arrived.

It was during Anna's allotted time in the library. She would think later how seemingly small details may irreversibly alter the course of one's life. Had the men arrived an hour earlier or ten minutes later, she would have been securely locked away in her room.

As it happened, Anna and Lieutenant Boraviecki were quietly reading in the library. In the months since their impasse, they had found less and less to talk about.

At first, Anna thought it was rolling thunder in the distance and gave thanks for the summer storm that would slake the thirst of the landscape. Although the noise moved closer, the sunlight did not diminish. It had not been thunder she heard. She recognized now the rumble of many horses over the hardened earth.

In no time there was a great flurry of movement about the house. Then shouts and swearing. Walter's detachment, much larger now, had arrived. And they were an undisciplined, drunken lot.

"Don't be afraid, my lady," Lieutenant Boraviecki said. "No doubt they've been celebrating the signing of the treaty and their return to Russia." He stood and moved to the door. "Stay here for now. I'll keep them out of the house."

He will not be able to keep them out, Anna thought, throwing down her book as soon as the door closed. There would be no keeping Walter out.

She ran to the door, pausing to give the lieutenant enough time to move away, her hand simultaneously reaching for the door handle. He had not locked the door. Anna pulled it open, peering into the music room. Bolting from the library, she ran from one room to the next, toward the rear of the house and into the kitchen. Two kitchen maids gasped at the sight of her.

Scarcely seconds later, another maid ran into the kitchen through the swinging door off the dining room. She was followed by a Russian soldier, who in one swoop grasped the girl at her slender waist and lifted her atop his shoulder. He carried her off toward the servants' chamber. Anna exchanged quick looks with the two panic-stricken maids. All of them knew the danger.

Old Lilka entered the kitchen and tried to calm the two. They would not listen, however, and fled through the rear.

"They will run right into their hands, there in the back of the house," she told Anna. "Foolish girls."

"It is a chance," Anna said. "I must take it, too!" She started for the door.

"Stop, my lady!" Lilka called.

Something in the woman's cry halted Anna, who turned to see the old woman hurrying toward her.

"It will do you no good to go outside. There are a hundred men out there. They are drunk and crazed."

"But I must get out!"

There came the sound then of heavy boots in the dining room.

Lilka pulled Anna to a pantry in the corner of the kitchen. "Hide here," she hissed, pointing to a pile of large bags of grain stacked against the wall. "Until they leave!"

When Anna hesitated, the woman's work-hardened hands pushed her into a crouching position behind the sacks.

At that moment the door swung open and a soldier shouldered his way through, pushing Lilka aside. "Out of my way, old woman!"

"Are you all right?" Anna asked, after he had gone out through the back.

"Stay hidden," Lilka whispered, her head bobbing to the left and right, like an old eagle. Satisfied they were safe for the moment, she came near to Anna. "My girls do not listen. They run, with no place to hide. You must listen to me, Lady Grawlinska. I have a hiding place. Help me move this sack."

Anna helped the woman slide a huge bag toward the wall, revealing a trap door in the floor where the bag had been. "It's a curing cellar," Lilka said, pulling the door out of its frame. "Sit on the side and jump down. Hurry!"

It was the last thing Anna wanted to do. She was afraid that once inside she would be helpless, that there would be no way out. But Lilka's strong, wiry hands began directing her. "You must hide here until it is safe," she said in her reedy voice. "Otherwise they will kill you; they will rape you and they will kill you."

Anna found herself crouching in the cellar, looking up to find that Lilka was handing her a lighted candle. Then the woman began replacing the door.

"What about your own safety?"

The woman grunted as the door closed over Anna. "What would they want of me?" The door closed with a bang.

Anna could hear Lilka whispering a prayer as she pulled one of the sacks over the trap door.

The cellar was no more than half her size in height. It was a narrow passage that extended far out under the dining room to the outer wall of the foundation. A light glimmered there. An exit?

Anna's candle, which she set down now, lighted her immediate surroundings. Above her head, spiders' webs stirred lazily in the heat and smoke of the candle flame. Sausages and hams, swaddled in white cloth, hung from the joists in the floor.

The floorboards above her creaked and moaned with the weight of many men. Anna could only imagine the chaotic scene above as she listened to people running and screaming, doors slamming, glass breaking. Those Russian oaths she could understand were vile obscenities. She heard, too, what sounded like death cries from some of the women.

"God help us!" she cried out aloud. She fell to the ground, pressing her hands to her ears as though she could shut out what was happening.

By the time she removed her hands, she was uncertain how much time had elapsed. From the yard came sharp commands and the sounds of a bugle. Horses neighed restlessly, their hooves stamping on the hard ground.

The Russians were moving out.

If she were to hold out just a little longer . . .

"Anna Maria!" someone shouted.

Anna held her breath. Walter! He was in the dining room, almost directly above her.

"Anna!" he called. His steps moved away then, and his cries grew more remote. He was checking the upstairs rooms. He would be insane with anger.

Anna looked to the light at the end of the passage. Picking up the candle, she crawled in that direction.

Her dress considerably hindered her progress, and her hands and elbows became scratched and raw. When she had finally moved the twenty or thirty paces, she found only disappointment. The source of light was a small window. Breaking it was of no use because it was barred with a cross-work of iron, allowing no escape.

She turned around and started to crawl back to her point of entry.

"Anna! Anna!" Walter's angry voice was directly overhead again.

Anna stopped, chilled by the sound. She had to bite down on her finger to suppress the despair that welled up within her.

There were fewer movements in the house now, fewer noises. The commotion in the yard increased as the men made ready to ride out.

He doesn't know of this hiding place, she assured herself. He might even assume she had escaped before today. He would leave with his men. *Go!* But he would question Lieutenant Boraviecki and Lilka . . .

Something else then claimed Anna's attention. She smelled something strong and pungent. Holding the candle up, close to the floor of the dining room, she could see thin wisps of smoke seeping through the floorboards.

The house had been set afire!

She had hesitated to get into the cellar out of fear of being trapped. That fear had now become reality. Anna tried to control the panic that rose up within her. Abandoning the candle, she quickly crawled to the spot just below the trap door.

She reached up and pushed, to no avail. The sack that Lilka had placed there held the door secure. She half stood and put her shoulder to the task. The door moved slightly. She pushed at it, again and again, in little fits of energy. The door budged a little more each time until she had it nearly half out of its frame.

She extended her hand then in an effort to push the sack aside, and it was at that moment that someone locked on to her wrist. Sack and door were pushed aside in one stroke and Anna felt herself being pulled up into the kitchen as if she were a rag doll.

"Ah, they say the best fish swim near the bottom!"

It took Anna a moment to take in the voice and face. It was Lieutenant Boraviecki. "Thank God," she breathed, happy that she had been pulled out, and happy that her fisherman was not Walter.

"I think he's given up," the lieutenant said. "He's gone outside."

"You're not going to give me over to him?"

"No, Lady Anna."

"What am I to do, Szymon?"

"If we can get you to the east side of the house, the way should be clear for you to disappear into the garden and then to the wheat fields. You'll have to run like hell because everything on this estate is going to go up like dry tinder. Let's go. I'll get you as far as the door."

They turned and Anna nearly tripped over Lilka's body. She stopped suddenly, then looked at the soldier.

He nodded. "Walter did it. She wouldn't tell. But I sensed she knew something. That's why I came back in here. Come now!"

As they made for the rear exit, they were checked by the appearance of Walter in the doorway.

"Isn't this a pretty sight?" Walter said.

"Let her go, Walter."

"Are you crazy?"

"Just let her go. She's been through enough."

Walter laughed. "Just like that? I think not." He started to move toward them, into the kitchen.

The lieutenant drew his pistol.

Walter stopped, stunned for a moment.

"You've already fired your pistols outside, Walter."

"So I have. But I have my sword."

"That you do." The lieutenant's blue eyes bespoke his determination. "Draw it and you die. Take a step forward and you die."

Walter stood still, uncertainty in his face.

"Now," Lieutenant Boraviecki said, "take three steps to your left so the countess may pass."

"Why are you doing this, Boraviecki?" Walter grudgingly moved to his left. "Has she wormed her way into your heart? A year of imprisonment has made her quite resourceful. Szymon, you're prepared to give up everything?"

"I am. Anna, follow the directions I gave you and Godspeed. Don't look back."

"But—"

"Do it, Anna! I'm the best marksman in the regiment, not that I need to be at this range. The odds are with me. Go, and consider your troubles from Walter finished. Hurry!"

Anna looked from Szymon to Walter, then back to Szymon.

"I'll see you at the faro tables," the lieutenant said. "Now, go!"

"I need something from my room first."

"What?" Szymon cried.

"A box."

"It's that important?"

"Yes."

"Christ! It's useless to argue with you. Take the backstairs. The front have burned. Hurry!"

Anna edged her way past Walter, then ran.

The upstairs hallway was filled with smoke, but she found the room, the wardrobe, the box. In seconds she was once again in the smoke-filled hallway, then flying down the narrow servants' stairs. As she ran past the kitchen for the outside door, she heard Szymon admonish her again to hurry.

She knew, as Walter must have, that Szymon was going to kill him, *had* to kill him.

Outside, Anna faced a wall of heat. All the Stelnicki buildings had been set ablaze. A few men ran while others struggled with their horses among the confusion and smoke. She took her chances and made for the east side of the house.

Heart and head pumping, she ran into the dry and untended garden, toward the wheat field.

Praying all the while she would not be seen. Praying no one would care to come after her if she were seen.

Into the field then. On and on, she ran, breathing in the oppressive heat, coughing from the smoke. She stumbled once and fell. When she pulled herself up, she allowed herself the luxury of looking back.

The house was fully afire now, as if the earth had opened to allow the flames of Tartarus to feast upon it.

Then came the report of a gun. She stared at the house a full minute. Nothing.

The undisciplined regiment was moving out.

The lieutenant had risked his life for her. If only she could go back to assure herself that he was safe and that Walter was indeed dead.

But Anna knew better. Reluctantly she turned around now and moved off in the direction of the Gronski estate.

Szymon Boraviecki *had* gambled.

59

A hot breeze stirred the wheat as Anna ran, the sun beating down. By the time she came to a thicket at the side of the road, she was wet with perspiration. The bodice of her dark dress clung to her. She set down the hand-carved box. Exhausted, she let herself fall into a little gully of soft, tall grasses. Small trees shaded her.

She lay there panting. No one had come after her. No human sound could be heard, only the muffled roar and crackle of the fire that was destroying the Stelnicki estate, buildings, and crops. The men and horses seemed to be gone.

Anna resisted fatigue. She could not rest too long, for the dried fields could very well carry the fire right to her. After she caught her breath, she stood up and climbed atop a tree stump. From this vantage point, she could see that the house had been fully engulfed. Flames shot out of the window of the room in which she had spent the past fifteen months. Tongues of fire were licking at the fields, too, tongues that moved hungrily toward her. The drought had rendered everything fuel for the flames.

Anna jumped down. She set about removing her full underskirts so that she could move less encumbered.

Picking up the box, she started toward the Gronski estate, not knowing what she would find. If it were locked, she had no key. What if it, too, were destroyed?

At first, she attempted to walk through the gully, but the way was so tangled with weeds and briar that she fell twice. She climbed the incline to the road then and hurried along at a quick pace, casting a look back now and then, afraid that she might catch sight of a Russian regiment bearing down on her. She couldn't see the fire any longer, just the funnels of smoke that poisoned the sky, some black, some white.

Anna came to the little bridge spanning a tiny tributary of the River Dniestr, a shallow stream that separated the Gronski and Stelnicki estates. She let herself down the ravine to the beckoning water.

Removing her shoes, she left them with the box at a spot shaded by a willow and waded into the narrow ribbons of water. The muddy bottom was soft, the water cooling. Bending over, she cupped her hands and splashed water on her face, then drank greedily.

Taking all the stays from her hair, she let it fall to her shoulders, bent, and drew up water to run through it.

She sat on a large rock, allowing her feet to dangle into the stream. And for a brief time she was transported back to childhood. Happy if just for moments by the most elementary components of life: the sun, a tree, a rock, water. These were the things that were real, that endured, that gave life. For just a few moments, the reality of what was befalling Poland and its people did not exist.

How is it, she wondered, that men can kill as they do?

Anna drank again before she left that spot.

It seemed an hour before she reached the buildings of the Gronski estate. The doors of the barns and stable stood open, empty. The manor house seemed untouched, the back of it closed and shuttered.

As Anna moved around to the front, an open wagon with a single horse came into view. In it were furniture, statuary, and other items of value from the household.

Then came the screaming.

On the other side of the wagon, two women were striking and kicking one another. As Anna moved closer, she saw that one was a servant girl, the other—older, broader, brightly dressed—a peasant of the coarsest character. The girl was unable to provide a contest and fell, only to be mercilessly kicked in the back, stomach, and groin.

"Stop!" Anna called out. "Stop!" Her voice seemed not to carry.

Even before Anna could pick up her skirts to run toward them, another servant woman came running from the house. Unnoticed by the others, she raced to the wagon and quickly pulled from it a golden candelabra. Lifting it high into the air, she brought it down on the larger woman, striking her in the back of her head.

The woman dropped like a stone, and by the time Anna came upon them, lay still, a dark pool forming at her head.

"What is the meaning of this?" Anna demanded.

"Lady Berezowska!"

Anna looked to the blond and buxom woman whose hazel eyes reflected a delighted amazement. The woman who still held the candelabra was Marta.

"What are you doing here?" Anna asked. "What in God's name is happening here?"

"That's my Marcelina that this one was trying to kill."

At that moment a man's raised voice could be heard calling from within the house.

Marta's face clouded instantly. She looked down at the colorfully clad dead woman.

"Who's in the house, Marta?"

"It's her husband. They're looters, parasites. Oh, Madame, what are we to do?"

"We must hide her, Marta. Come, quickly!"

Anna placed her box near the wagon. Marta spoke as each of them took an arm and dragged the woman's body thirty paces where some shrubbery concealed her from the house. "I don't understand their Russian, Madame, but I know that the woman became furious when her man took notice of my Marcelina. She fought with him in the house and then came out here to kill my daughter. Oh, Madame, I did what any mother would do!"

Anna said nothing as they rushed back to Marcelina. She had not even recognized the bloodied girl who lay unconscious.

Suddenly, the man emerged from the house.

Anna stood tall, her eyes narrowing in assessment even as her heart quickened while he walked toward the wagon with steps that faltered now and again. He had been drinking. His grizzled hair and beard were long and unkempt. He was perhaps forty-five. The expensively tailored clothes were tightly stretched on his thick form. Anna recognized the waistcoat with the gold buttons as belonging to her Uncle Leo.

"I am the Countess Anna Maria Berezowska," she said in Russian when he stood towering before her, close enough for his sour breath to reach her. "In the absence of my cousin, the Countess Zofia Gronska, this estate is in my custody."

He stared blankly through his fog of liquor. "And I am the tsar of Russia," he mocked in a low Russian dialect. He bowed. "The tsaritsa, my wife, is about somewhere. Has the good *Countess* seen her?" His smile revealed gaps between rotting teeth.

"I have not," Anna said, even as she spied the dark pool that had been left behind. "I must ask you to leave these grounds immediately," she said, taking a few steps toward the wagon, as if to examine its contents. She hoped that her dress, though not very full without her underskirts, would hide the bloodstained ground. "You may take what you have here and go."

"May I?" He stepped up to Anna and struck her across the face with such force that she nearly fell. His ring slashed her cheek. "Oh, Countess, there is much more to go in the wagon. See how much room I still have?" He noticed Marcelina now. "What is the matter with the young chicken?"

"She's ill," Anna said, wiping at a small trickle of blood that ran down her cheek.

"Pity. Now you will do her work. I'll save space for her in the wagon."

Realizing that he meant to take Marcelina with him, Anna became indignant. "I am the Countess Anna Berezowska—"

The man struck her again, propelling her to the ground.

"You may not look like a countess in your ragged dress, but you have the gall of the aristocracy, I grant you that. Countess or no, you will do as I bid you!"

Marta helped Anna to stand.

"Nina!" the man called. "Nina!" His eyes surveyed the landscape.

Anna made certain her dress once again covered the stain. "Perhaps she's in the house."

He grunted. "Inside, then!" At that moment, he noticed the box on the ground. "Well, what's this?"

"It's mine!" Anna said.

He held Anna at arm's length while he opened it and held up the crystal dove to the light. "This will fetch a pretty price," he said.

The box fell from his grasp now, and Anna scrambled to retrieve it. "What else is in it?"

"Nothing." Anna had no sooner gotten the word out of her mouth than the opalescent ring flew free of its velvet.

"Nothing?" The man picked it up. "A pretty little nothing it is, too." With some difficulty, he put it on his little finger and admired it. Then, taking the box from Anna, he replaced the dove and positioned the box in the wagon underneath the seat.

He prodded Anna and Marta toward the front door. When Marta tried to stoop to see to Marcelina, he kicked her. "Come, you've work to do."

While Marta did not understand the words, the meaning was clear, and she had to pick herself up, leaving her daughter.

On the way inside, Anna surreptitiously slid the velvet-wrapped emerald stickpin into the bodice of her dress.

Anna took in the first floor. It had already been sacked of anything of value. As they walked, Marta whispered to Anna. "If he says he will spare our lives, don't believe it. He'll leave no witnesses behind. He desires Marcelina, but when he's done with her, he'll kill her, too. You must flee, Lady Anna. I'll detain him somehow, and you must flee."

The man turned about, glowering, as if he understood Polish.

Anna didn't dare answer her.

They followed him upstairs and through several rooms that had already been stripped of most of their furnishings. He touched those things that he wanted them to cart down to the wagon. Anna nodded each time.

Anna and Marta were told to disassemble the mahogany bed in the guest room Anna had used when she came to Hawthorn House. While they did so, Anna watched the man carry past the room armloads of books from the Gronskis' tiny upstairs library. A few seconds later there came a great clatter as he dropped her uncle's most treasured possessions over the railing to the marbled hallway below. To think he treated the cherished Gronski books with such disdain caused Anna's temples to pulse with anger. These were symbols of the family's place in Poland and as valuable as the ancestral weapons that hung on the walls of manor homes all across the nation. Anna was glad that the Countess Gronska had at least removed the family weapons when they went to live at the Praga town house two years earlier. It was a bit puzzling, Anna thought, how these two components—weapons and books—which so defined the nobility were such unlikely bedfellows.

"You must try to escape," Marta pressed. "I can detain him."

Anna and Marta carried the feathered mattress to the top of the stairs, but before they could descend, the man appeared with more books that he threw over the railing. He seized hold of the mattress from them now and hurled it over, too, so that it fell atop the small hill of books.

"There!" he said, laughing stupidly at his antics—until he noticed the women staring at him. "Go back to work!"

"Is he the only one around?" Anna asked, once they were back in the bedroom.

"There were others yesterday, but they left, taking much. Only he and his woman remained."

"What in heaven's name are you and Marcelina doing here?"

"Somehow, Lady Zofia knew that the house would be lost. We were sent to salvage those things that we could carry back to Warsaw. The two men she had hired to assist us were killed by the others. But it was that one," she hissed, nodding toward the hallway, "who killed harmless Stanisław."

"Old Stanisław! Your father-in-law . . . my God!"

"You must run for it, Madame! I can't leave Marcelina. He'll not have her while I'm alive. And it's only a matter of time before he discovers his wife's body."

Anna and Marta carried the bedposts downstairs and out to the wagon. They both could have run, had it not been for Marcelina, who still lay motionless.

"Get on with your work!" the man growled as Anna and Marta came back into the house. He was lounging on the mattress where it had fallen upon the pile of books. In one hand he had a book that was opened to an engraving. In the other, he held a liquor decanter from which he had been drinking. It was this hand he used to gesture above. "And don't forget the eagle," he cautioned.

As Anna and Marta walked up the stairs, he called to his woman. "Nina! Ni-na. Ni-na." He went on calling her name, each time in a different pitch, as if enchanted by the various sounds the name of the dead woman could produce.

At the stairhead, Anna examined the large stone eagle that rested on the newel post. He was thief enough to cart away the symbol of Poland.

The two women quickly found that the statue was too heavy for them to lift. Anna wondered if he had been joking about taking it. He probably had no idea how heavy it was. Anna peered over the railing. She could see him there, mumbling to himself as he turned the pages in search of more engravings.

It was then that it came to her.

Using only her eyes, she motioned for Marta to help slide the eagle along the upper railing. When Marta saw Anna's intent, her eyes waxed like two moons, but she wasted no time in following directions.

They pulled at the eagle. Slowly it moved, a thumb's width at a time. It slipped from the newel post to the railing with a little jolt that made it teeter there for a moment before it was steadied. Then Anna and Marta moved it along the railing while struggling to maintain its delicate balance. Their foreheads beaded with sweat and their fingers on the stone tore and bled with the strain.

At last, Anna saw that it was in position. She looked down to see the Russian ripping an engraving from a gold-edged book.

"Now!" she sharply whispered.

The two released the eagle.

With amazing speed and force the stone bird plummeted to the first floor in search of its prey.

The mattress muffled the bone-crushing sound of the impact.

The man had managed the shortest possible outcry. Had he seen it coming?

Marta galloped down the staircase. "Who is to say that women are helpless?" she sang out in hysterics as she went to kick the lifeless form. "Who says?"

"Yes," Anna said, following her down, "women can kill, too. Let him be, Marta. You can't do anything more to a dead man."

"But I would like to," Marta said. "To kill poor Stanisław! This one's death was too quick."

The looter lay faceup, his open eyes bulging, blood streaming from his mouth. His neck and chest had been crushed like a bunch of red berries.

Anna walked over to him and stooped to pull the ring off his finger. It took some doing.

She hoped that he had had a moment to make his peace with his God. As for the stone eagle that weighted him to the mattress like paper to a desk, it was unscathed.

Anna and Marta hurried out to Marcelina and managed to revive her. Removing a few bulky items from the wagon, they laid her in it, assuring her that the looters were gone.

They made several trips back to the house to rescue the Gronski books. By the time this task was finished, the Gronski fields and out-buildings were afire.

"Let's go," Anna said, making ready to board the wagon.

"Wait, Madame." Marta turned and ran into the house.

Anna waited impatiently for what seemed a long time. "Marta, hurry, or we'll all be roasted like pigs on a spit!" Smoke and ash were flying through the hot winds.

At last the servant appeared at the door, rolling the stone eagle before her.

"What in God's name are you doing, Marta?" Anna screamed, running to her.

"The rear of the house is afire!"

"And we will be, too, if we don't get the wagon moving."

"We must take the eagle." Marta stopped at the top of the short staircase. She looked Anna in the eye. "It is the symbol of Poland and this great house. We cannot leave it to destruction."

"Leave it be, Marta! Do you want to forfeit our lives for a bit of stone?"

"We can't, Madame. Bad fortune will follow us all the days of our lives if we do not take it."

There came the sound of glass exploding as the rear rooms of the house yielded to the fire. Anna looked at the servant, who was not about to give up her task.

"All right, I'll help. Let's lift it together from the porch." Once the eagle was on the ground, they rolled it out to the wagon. It took every effort then to get it lifted and aboard.

Breathless, the two climbed up onto the bench. Anna took the reins and slapped the old horse. The wagon began to rattle slowly forward, down the long drive, toward the river.

"Of course," Marta said, "we'll have to scrub the blood off the eagle before the Countess Gronska sees it."

"I doubt that it will come off, Marta."

Before they reached the road, Anna halted the wagon and turned around. The fire was eating up the rooms of the house that had so impressed her . . . was it only two years ago?

The Gronski house served for the moment as a great lamp to offset imminent twilight. The entire estate was going up in flames as though it were tinder that had been dried for a hundred summers. Anna recalled an old proverb: "The thief takes only something; the flame takes all."

A way of life was dying. Paradoxically, along with the pain of loss and death, the fire held a strange and beautiful power, too. It was both magnificent and terrible to watch.

Anna slapped the horse again, and the heavily laden wagon made for the road that ran along the River Dniestr.

Within the hour, a faint orange glow behind them was all that lighted the moonless night. Anna could not actually see the road in front of them, but the horse's instinct seemed a good compass. They moved slowly. Except for the mournful croaking of frogs near the river, the night was as still as death.

Sensing that the two peasants were afraid of the night's spirits, Anna initiated conversation. Marta told her that Jan Michał was a robust and cheerful child who kept the Gronski household busy and entertained. Anna found it hard to imagine him now; she had not seen him in well over a year.

"Have you heard anything of your husband, Marta?"

"No, Madame. Walek stood with General Kościuszko. We hope for the best. Of course, he cannot write."

"Have there . . . have there been any letters from Count Stelnicki?" In other times, in other circumstances, she would not have dared such a question of a servant.

"Not that I know of, Lady Anna."

"No word whatsoever?"

"No, Madame."

Marta and Marcelina soon fell into a fatigued sleep. In the pitch of night, Anna dared not hurry the horse.

60

At daybreak the travelers came upon a cluster of peasant dwellings. The inhabitants were receptive, recognizing at once the Gronski name.

"Take the candelabra, Marta," Anna said, "and give it to these people. We will need food and water for our journey to Warsaw. And try to bargain for a fresh horse."

The three were received into one of the little cottages where they washed and ate a tasty breakfast of *kasza,* cakes, and chicory. Anna and Marta were pleased to see Marcelina eat a fair amount. She would be fine in a few days.

As they stood thanking their hosts, Anna thought how different these Poles were from the peasants of France. She knew there were some abused and bitter peasants to be found in Poland, but it was hard to imagine these good people, who were saddened by the losses of the Stelnicki and Gronski estates, taking up pitchforks and scythes against the Polish aristocracy. On the contrary, it was people just like these, from border to border, who had taken up their farm implements against the foreign influx, as they had for centuries. Such was the essence of being Polish.

The three had just climbed into the wagon when Anna noticed that the candelabra had been returned to its place behind the seat. "I told you to give them the candelabra, Marta," Anna said.

"They would not take it, Madame."

Before Anna could question further or insist that they accept the payment, a force of Russians arrived in a long caravan of a hundred mounted soldiers, several well-appointed carriages, and assortment of supply vehicles.

The sun played on the gold braiding of the captain's long red coat as he directed his stallion toward the wagon. Neither his demeanor nor that of his mounted men indicated that this regiment was anything other than rigid and disciplined. His face was clean-shaven and sternly set. "Who are you?" he asked. He removed the three-cornered hat but did not introduce himself.

"I am the Countess Anna Berezowska-Grawlinska of Sochaczew." Anna was careful to use the name Zofia had used in writing to her.

"You are of the nobility?"

"I think I just made that clear, Captain. Is it *captain*?"

"Yes, Captain Krestyanov." He eyed her dress and the modest wagon.

Anna told him about the burning of the estates, avoiding mention of Walter's regiment.

"You were fortunate to have escaped, Countess."

Anna nodded. His words rang hollow.

"Tell me, Countess, are you allied with the empress?"

Anna swallowed hard. "My name has been attached to the Confederacy of Targowica."

The captain made a show of calling for a list from his lieutenant. Anna thought he still doubted her nobility.

"The name again, Countess?"

Once she told him, he began searching the list which went on for pages. "And your destination?" he asked even as he looked.

"Warsaw—or rather, Praga."

"Ah, here it is, Countess Anna Maria Berezowska-Grawlinska."

Anna had been right in suspecting Zofia had registered both her surnames with the Confederacy.

"Why is it you do not use your husband's name exclusively?"

"I'm a widow, Captain Krestyanov," she said, pronouncing his name with precision. "I plan to start using my maiden name exclusively."

"Isn't that unusual?"

"My marriage was unusual. Captain, are we to be allowed to continue?"

He held her gaze. "Listed here also is a son, Jan Michał Grawlinski."

"Yes. He was too young to travel. He is in Praga, at the home of my aunt, the Countess Stella Gronska. She, too, is allied, if you would care to look." Anna knew that while something sweet usually catches the fly, here a little condescension and irritability might go a long way toward convincing him of her station.

"That's all right." He would not be manipulated into looking for the name. "You have the sanction of Catherine, Empress of Russia. We, too, are going to Warsaw and we ask the honor of your company along the way. We will afford you protection. I'll see to it that the countess is accommodated in a better vehicle. One of my men will take charge of your wagon."

Anna sensed Marta stiffen. She attempted to refuse his offer, but her objections fell on deaf ears. She soon found herself being helped into a luxurious carriage.

Dr. Kurowski, the owner of the vehicle, was a prosperous Polish physician, a rotund man with a full beard and thinning gray hair. When he grumbled his greeting, Anna assumed he had been given no choice in sharing his capacious coach.

They were soon under way.

As they passed through tiny hamlets, Anna became aware of the slow, mournful tolling of church bells. "Is our country mourning the invasion of the Russians?" she whispered.

"It's more likely funerals," the physician said. "All the Polish patriots who were foolish enough to go against the Russian tide have been slaughtered like deer."

Later, Anna caught sight of a funeral procession, watching as men and women lifted their voices in a sorrowful song for those who had died and for those who were left behind to face the devastation of the country. Anna sighted then a group of peasants following a dung cart laden with a pine box, its crudely drawn coffin portrait a testament to the youth of its inhabitant. For the survivors, masses of peasants—people who knew little, but whose hearts were big—the world had betrayed them. Their lords, their nobility, their king had all failed them. The Prussians, Austrians, and Russians would sit at Polish tables and drink Polish blood.

Anna felt at one with these people. Yet, she was part of the aristocracy Catherine had chosen to spare. At what cost was the aristocracy saved? She felt traitorous toward those faceless thousands gathering in every Polish village, town, and city across the length and breadth of the country.

Anna realized that her nobility itself meant little to her. What truly mattered was the safety and well-being of her loved ones and the plight of the whole nation. She prayed for Aunt Stella and little Jan Michał. She prayed for Jan Stelnicki—where in the flow of blood was he to be found? And, yes, she prayed for Zofia. Jan Michał would be in Walter's hands were it not for her aunt, her cousin, and the emerald stickpin. As for herself, where would she be, sadly, had not Zofia affixed her name to the Confederacy?

At one point, the carriage was halted briefly to allow for another funeral procession. "Why is it," the physician muttered, "*we* must be delayed? These patriots have nothing but time left to them to bury the dead!"

"Then you don't support the cause?"

"I am my own cause. I've learned well at the hands of the nobility."

"That is a sweeping statement, Doctor. In fact, the selfish nobles are those who invited Catherine in. There are so many other nobles worthy of respect."

He grunted.

Anna persisted. "The patriots' cause has united all Poles, whether they are of the aristocracy, the landed gentry, the merchant class, or the peasants."

The physician shrugged. "The cause has failed, nonetheless."

"Do you intend to remain in Poland?"

"I do. Oh, I have an eye to my main chance, Lady Berezowska-Grawlinska. I'll cater to the Russians, if need be. I expect to grow quite rich."

"You can do that? Without a care that Poland is being torn into strips like a sheet?"

"I'll take those strips and make them into bandages and charge the Russians for them!" The thick black brow above his left eye lifted, his forehead furrowing. He smiled, revealing small, yellowed teeth. "What about you, my lady? You, who have been so careful to ally yourself with the *evil* empress? Do *you* care?"

I do! Anna wanted to scream. But she realized that the doctor had removed her line of defense, as surely as if he had removed her heart.

Part Six

Through bravery you may win a war,
and through bravery
you may lose.

—POLISH PROVERB

61

The first sign of the retinue's coming into the city came with the sound of children at play in the streets. Dusk was just starting to settle. The air was stiflingly warm. Anna raised the shade just as the carriage set upon the cobbled streets of Praga.

At Anna's urging, the physician had his coachman halt and relay to the Russian captain that Anna wished to leave the procession at this point.

Turning to the physician before alighting, Anna thanked him for his hospitality.

He nodded perfunctorily. "Good-bye, Lady Grawlinska-Berezowska."

Anna hoped never to see him again.

The captain himself helped Anna from the carriage. "I'll have two soldiers escort your wagon to your aunt's. Which street is hers?"

"It's on that bluff overlooking the river, to our left. But an escort is not at all necessary, Captain."

"Just the same, it will be done. These streets can be dangerous."

"Praga streets? Since when?" Anna suddenly realized that the children she had heard were not playing; they were begging, their voices chanting, "Bread! Bread! We are hungry, please!"

This, in a wealthy section of the city?

The little ones pressed close to Anna as she was escorted to the wagon in which Marta and Marcelina waited. The oldest boy, dark and gaunt, ran ahead of her. "Bread, milady? Coins?" He was no more than seven years old. The others followed, taking up the cry, "Bread, milady?" A tiny girl came last, her blond hair a nest of tangles, her dress torn.

Anna stopped and faced the little band. She was certain that these children had only recently taken to begging. They were not the usual street urchins. "Why is it that you beg?" she asked the boy. He stared wide-eyed, amazed that he was being interviewed. The girl took his hand.

"Is this your sister?"

He nodded.

"You are a very pretty little girl," Anna said, kneeling down. "Look at those dimples!" She could not help but be reminded of Louis and Babette, yet she held her composure. She would do something for these waifs who crowded around her. "Would you like bread for your sister and for yourself?"

"Yes, milady," he politely whispered.

Anna could sense the impatience of the captain, but she persisted. "Tell me, then, why it is you beg?"

The boy looked up in fear at the captain.

"You may tell me," Anna said, "I'm sure he will not understand much of your Polish."

The boy took heart. "Since *they* have come, no one may go to work in the fields. My father is unable to feed us."

"Come, Countess," the Russian pressed. "Ignore these street wretches. They're but homeless bastards." He looked down at them with a reddening face. "Away with you!" he shouted. "Be gone!"

The eyes of the seven or eight little ones became enlarged with fear of the foreign soldier. They knew his meaning, if not his Russian words. But their hunger and their hope kept them stoically huddled together.

"Captain," Anna said, drawing his eyes to her, "your illustrious empress may deny us our homeland and the parents of the *wretches,* as you say, their livelihood—but will she also deny them the miserable crust of bread for which they have been reduced to begging? Is Catherine a woman without a heart?"

The man bristled at Anna's audacity, his face becoming pinched and more purple than red, but he was unwilling to create a scene.

Anna gave her remaining provisions of food to the small, out-stretched hands. "Wait, now," she said to those she had missed. "Don't go yet."

Anna hurried to the wagon, well aware that she was delaying the entire procession. "Marta! Give me anything you and Marcelina have not eaten. Hurry!"

The loyal and wide-eyed servant was quick to obey.

As Anna took their leftover portions and walked back to the children, she could sense the eyes of hundreds—of mounted soldiers, of coachmen, of Polish gentry and nobles, of the physician—all upon her. She held her back straight, her head erect, embarrassed but determined to stand up to the Russians in this one small matter.

The little ones cried with delight when she handed them the partial loaves of bread, sausage, and apple cake. Several of the collecting throng of bystanders called out, "God bless you, milady! God bless you!"

Anna turned to the Russian. "I'm sorry for the inconvenience, Captain. I'd like to go home now."

The street was dark and silent when the wagon pulled to a halt in front of the four-storied Gronski town house. After the women were helped down, Anna dismissed the two-man Russian escort.

She turned to look across the River Vistula, toward Warsaw. It seemed that Fate, like the tide, always returned her to the capital. Zygmunt's Column still rose high in the castle's outer courtyard, and the Royal Castle sat on the tall embankment of the Vistula as it had for centuries, the king no doubt moving through its cavernous rooms; but now it was a foreign power that ruled the city streets. Her eyes moved then to the bridge, where she could see the horses and vehicles of the Russian-led procession as it continued on toward the great walls of the capital.

Anna heard the door of the town house open now and turned to see a large and familiar figure emerge, her head bent humbly but joyously downward and her ruffled white cap fairly glowing in the dark like some alien moon.

"Lutisha!" Anna called.

The bulky servant swooped down the steps and in moments was imposing a great bear hug upon Anna, then upon her daughter and granddaughter. "Thank God. Thank God," she kept repeating.

A flood of feelings stirred, eddied, and rose within Anna. If she could not call the Gronski home her own, it was at the very least a place of protection where she was welcome and certainly a happy alternative to what might have been her fate in Saint Petersburg. Within this home, she thought, *are people whom I love and who love me.* Her heart quickened now at the realization that she was about to see one of the two people who meant life itself to her. "My child?" she managed, choking on emotion. "Jan Michał?"

"Oh, he's fine, Lady Anna!" Lutisha assured. "A beautiful child and as quick as can be," she added, her large hands swiping at the tears that wet her face.

Anna smiled, keeping her own tears at bay. *He will have to be quick, to survive in times such as these.*

As Anna lifted the folds of her tattered and burned black dress to ascend the few steps, she looked up to see Zofia standing in the light of the doorway, like the scarlet vision of a saint. Of the reddest velvet, her gown was trimmed with hundreds of hanging and undulating silver beads that caught the moonlight as she quickly descended the stairs toward Anna. Red velvet ribbon was laced through the high piling of her white powdered wig. Her lips and cheeks were heavily rouged and her eyes shone like polished ebony.

"Anna!" Zofia cried. "Oh, darling Anna!" She seemed genuinely glad to see her cousin, her outstretched arms flying about her like the wings of a falcon.

Despite everything, how could Anna not warm to that welcome? However, her return of her highly perfumed cousin's tight caress was more restrained, more guarded. "I'm so happy to be back, Zofia."

"It's wonderful to have you here and out of harm's way," Zofia said. "You aren't to leave again, do you understand? This is your home!"

Home. For the moment Anna forgot the circumstances of her departure when Zofia had declared that she had affixed the Gronski and Grawlinski names to the Confederacy of Targowica—and when Zofia had implied that *she* loved Jan Stelnicki, warning Anna to forget him. Anna put these things from her mind now, warming to her cousin's af-

fectionate words and expression and the love and security they promised
after so many bleak months of isolation. Knowing, too, that her cousin
had kept Jan Michał from Walter, she acquiesced, welcoming the hot,
happy tears that collected in her eyes.

Zofia's mouth moved to Anna's ear, though, and her voice was immediately transformed. "The Russians are here," she hissed through
clenched teeth. "We welcome them with celebration, or we die. Make
no mistake about it, Ania!"

Even while her cousin spoke, Anna's eyes moved up to the doorway where, in the flickering yellow light spilling out from the house
onto the portico, there stood a tall figure in the red uniform of a Russian
soldier. Anna could discern, too, the noises of partying within the
house. Her exquisite delight at being back in Praga vanished. Her heart
dropped with the weight of a stone, for she became overwhelmed with
the certainty that this doorstep offered only some new despair.

Zofia stepped back, holding her at arm's length, her face stern as a
midwife's, her dark eyes wordlessly begging her to submit to the circumstances in which she found herself. Then, as her gaze turned toward the house and she began to guide Anna to the steps, Zofia
underwent still another metamorphosis.

Her intent face was effortlessly changed into one that radiated a lu-
minous—and false-faced—gaiety. She bubbled over in exclamations of delight as she guided Anna up the stairs and past the soldier who eyed
them coolly, into the house, and to the main staircase. "It's so unfortunate that you must rest, cousin, and cannot meet my friends tonight,"
she said loudly and with all the aplomb of a seasoned actress. "However, I shall see you early in the day tomorrow. Sleep well, darling." She
kissed Anna on both cheeks.

And then she was gone, like the shapeshifter she was.

Anna started up the staircase. She could hear Lutisha behind her
and turned, whispering, "Where is my son?"

"He sleeps in the attic room, Madame, so that he is removed from
the noises below."

"In the attic?"

"Yes, Katarzyna sleeps there also so that someone is near should he
become frightened."

At the landing of the second level, where Anna had her rooms,

Lutisha turned to her, barring the way to the third level and attic. "The boy is in fine health," she assured Anna, "but we should let him sleep while the frolicking below is not yet too loud."

Anna's first reaction was to overrule the servant, but her own maternal instinct made her concur, reluctantly. Besides, her nerves were shattered, and every muscle and bone in her body attested to the long journey and the ordeal before that. It would be heaven to yield to the temptation of her soft, feathered bed. She doubted that even the sounds of the lost souls in Tartarus could bother her this night.

"Lady Anna?"

"Yes, Lutisha?"

"How is old Stanisław? Has he stayed at Hawthorn House?"

Anna turned around. Before she could rest, she had to console Lutisha on the death of Marta's father-in-law. She imagined that downstairs Marta was telling Katarzyna and Tomasz about the murder of their grandfather.

It was already a bright and warm midmorning when Anna awoke to whispers in the room. She sat up abruptly and looked to the open door, pulling her hair back from her eyes.

There, just inside the doorway, stood Aunt Stella and Lutisha, both displaying subtle smiles. Anna's eyes moved downward, and when they stopped, she let out a little gasp.

Standing there, too, his tiny arms stretched upward for the steadying grips of the countess and Lutisha, was Jan Michał. Anna thought him a vision in his red short pants held by suspenders. His half-sleeved shirt and little shoes were white, spotlessly so. Blond curls fell around his round face with its perfect features and velvet red cheeks.

"Come along, my little man," Aunt Stella said as they guided him closer to Anna.

Delighted at the attention, he laughed, emitting a stream of high-pitched gurgles.

Anna stared in disbelief. Of course, she expected him to have grown, but to see the tiny babe she had slipped into her aunt's embroidery satchel so many months before—to see him taking his small steps, his expressive mouth turned up in laughter—filled her with amazement. In the interim of their separation, Jan Michał had been transformed from a red-faced infant, indistinguishable from a thousand others, into a toddling human being with his own unique and vibrant personality.

And what did it matter that those warmly flashing eyes were the brown of Walter's? She thought back to that defining moment in the Gronski kitchen when little Tomasz noticed that the infant's blue eyes were giving way to brown. She had been horrified to think that her son was Walter's legacy.

But Walter was gone, no more a threat to either mother or child. And if Anna had Jan Michał as a result of Walter, so be it. He was a child to be thankful for.

Removing herself from the bed, Anna slipped to the floor and knelt, stretching out her arms, beckoning her son. "Come here," she whispered. "Come to your mother, Jan Michał."

The countess and the servant relinquished their holds, so that the child stood alone. Anna's words had prompted him to focus solely on her for the first time. His little steps stopped and his forehead wrinkled in sudden surprise, then panic. He turned to stare up with enormous eyes at Lutisha and reached out to her, desperately clinging to her skirts.

He had not been two months old at the time of his separation from Anna, and he seemed to hold no memory of her at all.

"Come, Jan Michał," she pleaded softly, her heart tearing, "come to me."

He whimpered now, a tiny fist thrust partially into his mouth and tears forming in the wide eyes that were fastened on Anna with uncertainty.

Fighting back her own tears and the searing disappointment that cut through her, Anna continued to speak to him in soft, soothing tones. She moved toward him on her knees by almost imperceptible degrees.

In time, the fear and shyness began to dissipate, and slowly, slowly, the corners of his mouth turned upward again until he was coaxed by Anna's cooing sounds and silly faces into laughing, lightly at first, then very merrily. Did he remember her?

"Come, Jan Michał," Anna persisted, moving still closer, her arms outstretched. "Walk to Mother."

Doubt clouded his face once again, but he vacillated only briefly. Breaking into a smile and warbling some mirthful exclamation, he toddled the three or four steps into Anna's arms.

She held her son to her, lightly, as if he were a baby bird she might crush.

"I'm holding my son at last," she murmured, looking up at her aunt and Lutisha. "You two shall be my witnesses. I ask you both to hear my vow never again to be separated from my son."

Aunt Stella and Lutisha gave in to their tears.

Anna breathed deeply. She did not want to cry in front of the child. He would not understand tears of joy.

After a few minutes, she realized that she had yet to properly greet her aunt. Lifting herself from the floor, she kissed the countess, who was wiping her eyes.

"Welcome home, Ania!" Countess Gronska exclaimed.

It was only later, when Anna went to see the countess in her anteroom where she sat sewing, that Anna more fully assessed her. Countess Gronska was like some delicate old Dresden figurine, her health almost visibly failing. She was ill, seriously so.

Paradoxically, however, with failing health came a healing of the countess' attitude, which had brightened considerably. Her mind seemed lucid. Any trace of peculiarity had vanished.

And the black that the countess had worn since the death of her husband was gone. Now Anna found herself staring at the lovely dark green dress her aunt wore so elegantly. She had given up her mourning. Young widows were allowed a year and a day to grieve, but sometimes, older women who had lost lifetime mates were expected to wear the black for the rest of their lives.

"Come in. Come in, child!" the countess said. "Why do you hesitate so?"

"Your dress, Aunt Stella—it is so beautiful!"

"Too beautiful for an old widow?"

"No, no. I was just . . . surprised."

"I've realized some things, Anna Maria." The countess set aside her embroidery. "I've realized how dear life is. And how fragile. I still have some life and some fight left in me. Oh, I was so focused on the death of my Leo that I could not remember the wonderful days and years of our marriage. I only remembered the day of his death, obsessing about one day of loss when there had been so many full, happy days. I was doing both him and myself an injustice. On the day I realized this, I put away the black dress. In fact, I had it burned."

"I see."

"Do you disapprove?"

"Oh, no! Oh, Aunt Stella, you've come back to life."

The countess smiled. "I think perhaps it was little Jan Michał who did it. I realized after we came back to Praga without you that this little life was for a time my responsibility. I had to live, if only for him."

"I thank you for that, Aunt Stella."

"And there is Poland, too, my other distraction."

"Are things as bad as they seem? What with Russians in Warsaw, Russians in this house?"

"No, Anna, Poland has not fallen. Not yet! Our resistance is still to be fully tested."

"Then you still maintain hope?"

"As long as Kościuszko lives and breathes, there is hope."

"And he does live?"

"By God, Anna, he is Poland's living symbol of liberty. He spent some months in self-exile in Paris, but even now he is bringing together a force of nobles and gentry and peasants, biding his time. One day he will show Catherine that Poland is not the easy prey she thinks."

Is Jan with him? Anna wondered. He had most certainly taken part in the early actions against the Russians. Had he survived? Had anyone heard from him? Anna would not allow herself to think the worst.

"Aunt Stella, I came to speak to you about Walter."

The woman pitched in her chair, and the focus of her dark eyes clouded.

"You know," Anna said softly, "that Walter is the father of Jan Michał."

"Oh, I know," she replied, her voice a monotone. Her eyes cleared again and fastened on Anna. "I know. May God forgive him. He told me so last summer at the Stelnicki home, spitting out the details without a shred of shame."

"And you bravely managed to steal Jan Michał away from his influence. For that, Aunt Stella, I will be eternally grateful."

"Oh, believe me, dearest, I fought for you to leave with us, too, but he turned a deaf ear to me. What can bring a man to such maddened behavior? And what he did to you . . ." The countess' voice trembled with emotion. "Oh, Anna, what this past year has been like for you, I cannot imagine."

"It was not so terrible," Anna lied. "Anyway, it's past now and I'm home."

"Anna, you know that Walter was an adopted child?"

"Yes, Zofia told me."

"Oh. Don't think that I put down his failings to that, though. Look at Zofia. She's of my blood, but you'd never know it."

Adopted or not, Anna thought, how was the countess to take the news of her only son's death? Clearing her throat, Anna tried to dispel the sick apprehension within her. "Aunt . . ." she started.

The countess gave Anna her full attention.

Anna's mind had traveled back, however, to that moment in the burning Stelnicki home when she had left Walter with only a sword to protect himself from Lieutenant Boraviecki, who held him covered with a pistol at close range. Out in the field, she had heard the shot, seen the building being consumed by fire.

"What is it, Anna?" the countess was saying. "You've lost all your color."

Anna was brought forward to the present. "Aunt Stella," she said, her hand reaching out to one that was frail and blue-veined, "Walter is dead."

The realization moved like an eclipse across the woman's face. She sat motionless many moments, her body still as a corpse, the knuckles of her other hand whitened by the tightness of her grip on the arm of the chair. Then her head fell forward onto her chest.

"Aunt Stella!" Anna pressed. Had her aunt suffered a heart attack? Anna would never forgive herself for bringing it on.

But the woman's hand remained warm, and when the countess lifted her head, there were tears glistening in her eyes, though none had spilled. She tilted her head toward Anna. "I have no desire to know the details, Anna. Not now." She exhaled deeply, a long audible sigh, and when she spoke next, it was with a bitter resignation. "Oh, he came to the house once while he was in Warsaw doing the empress-whore's dirty work. He had turned against his family, against his motherland. What was there to do but to follow Leo's example and disown him? And let me tell you, Anna, that to do so hurt no less because he was adopted. Well, he can bring no further shame down upon this house or his good father's name . . . not any longer."

Anna had no idea what to say or how she could comfort her aunt. She felt foolish in her silence.

The countess spoke again: "Somehow Leo and I failed in our parentage. We produced a man with the soul of a barbarian and a woman with the spirit of a wanton she-dog." Her eyes sought out Anna's. "How I envy my dead sister to have a daughter like you. And to think we said at the time she was making a poor match! I'd like to think of you as my own daughter, Anna Maria, because I have no children, not really." Then, like water from a newly opened sluice gate, the pent-up tears were released, rushing down her aged cheeks.

Anna squeezed her hand. "You are my mother now, Aunt Stella."

The countess smiled and her face seemed to glow. "Only you, my little Ania, have taken all the seeds of the beautiful swamp lily and flourished." She wiped at her tears. "But the wetlands are now being drained and the hoards of weeds are spreading their own hearty seed. You, dearest, must learn to be a lily who can adapt, who can live despite the weeds. Though they sprout up all around you and threaten to choke the very breath from you, you must survive."

Anna found herself staring at her aunt.

"I speak in parable, Ania, but do you understand?"

"I . . . I think so."

"I am old. It matters little for me. But you are young and have the time to change. To adapt to the maelstrom that Poland has become." Countess Gronska studied Anna's expression and seemed to read it like words on a page. "Oh, you needn't become like Zofia to change, Anna. Don't think I mean that."

"How am I to change then, Aunt Stella? And, more importantly, how is Jan Michał going to survive what is happening and what yet might come?"

"You must marry, child. It's the only thing you can do, for yourself and for your son. God help us, but perhaps Zofia can be helpful in this way. But this time you must be certain that the man you marry wants you only for your own sake."

"I desire only one man, Aunt."

"Lord Stelnicki?"

"Yes."

"Listen to me, Anna. Life isn't often as one imagines or dreams. My own marriage was arranged. It was not my choice . . . oh, there was another young man I loved desperately! But it was not to be. I have no regrets. My marriage to Leo was a good one even if our children have not lived up to our expectations."

"I intend to wait for Jan."

"Is he still with Kościuszko?"

"I don't know. I thought perhaps he has sent some word here."

"To my knowledge, he has not." The countess sighed. "So we don't know whether he has survived. You know, if the Russians maintain their grip, and if Jan returns home alive, he will come back a poor and title-less man, Anna. He would have little to offer a wealthy woman of the aristocracy as you."

It was not Anna's aunt's suggestion that she consider marriage or her reminder that Jan would be stripped of title and possessions that cut her like a blade; rather, it was the genuine doubt in her voice when she said "if Jan returns home alive."

"Marriage to another," the countess continued, "one who hasn't so openly supported the patriots' cause, will assure you of your rightful place in the aristocracy."

"You've changed in the past year, Aunt. I remember the outrage you displayed when Zofia informed us she had affixed our names to the Confederacy of Targowica. And at our last meeting with Jan you showed great admiration for him because he had the courage of his convictions."

"My loyalties haven't changed. Don't think less of me, Anna Maria. Of course, I still support Kościuszko and his forces. God knows, I've helped to fund him with money and even jewelry. But I worry for your future and for that of Jan Michał. I wouldn't presume to pressure you into marriage—"

"No, Aunt Stella," Anna interrupted, "you will not pressure me. Let's not forget what my marriage to Antoni led to. Jan is *alive,* I know he is. And whether he comes back as a nobleman or merely a citizen, I would stand by a *Count* Stelnicki just as I would a *Citizen* Stelnicki."

The countess sat stunned into silence, as if she had been slapped. Tears brimmed again in the suddenly vulnerable eyes.

Anna immediately regretted her words. To hurt her aunt was to break a butterfly on the wheel. "Oh, Aunt, I'm so sorry. I—"

"No, Anna," the countess said, giving a little wave of a hand mottled with age spots, "your words ring true. If only you could know the remorse I feel over imposing upon you your marriage to Antoni Grawlinski."

"You didn't impose it."

"Oh, I most certainly did! I was a crazed woman for months after Leo's death, but I make no excuses for myself and will not shirk from my responsibility in the matter."

Anna assured the countess that she held nothing against her, but even as she spoke she realized she *had* held closeted feelings against her, feelings that, once aired, vanished like sour vapors freed from a long-sealed jar. "One must settle with the past, Aunt Stella, settle and then let go."

The countess looked with love on Anna. "I thought," she said, "it was *my* place to give advice to the young. Come here and give me a hug. Wiser the egg than the hen!"

Anna knelt at her aunt's chair and embraced her, holding her quietly.

"Since we are settling with the past, may I ask about my home at Halicz? Is Hawthorn House completely gone?"

Anna looked up at her aunt, but her words failed her. She could only nod.

"I see," said the countess with resignation.

"We'll build another!" Zofia exclaimed.

Anna stood up quickly. Her cousin still had that way about her of appearing unannounced.

"We'll build one more magnificent than any mere *szlachta* manor house," Zofia continued. "We'll build a palace! I'm becoming wealthy enough to build both here in the city and in the country. Once this threat of war dissolves."

Anna sat down. "Then you plan to build even if the Russians control us?"

"If the Russians are victorious, I shall build. If the Poles are successful, I shall build."

"Zofia," the countess said, exercising deliberate control, "if you think that erecting magnificent buildings is establishing something of worth and substance, you are wrong. Our families do not live on in splendid buildings, as so many magnates might think. Our ancestors live on, we will live on, Jan Michał and those who come after us live on

through what is *in* our houses, no matter how humble. The many portraits that overflow our dining hall into the library filled with ancestral
books do honor to those of our house who have passed. The cutlasses,
swords, sabers, and guns arranged about our family coat of arms on the
walls of our reception room celebrate the courage of the house. And the
icons found in both servants' and master's rooms reflect not only a faith
bred in blood and bone that salvation awaits us, but also a faith that
Poland will be freed of its oppressors, no matter how long it takes."

The three sat in silence.

After a little while, however, Zofia made her own little speech. "Oh,
I know you both criticize me with your silence. You don't or won't understand. Mother, our estate at Halicz has been destroyed. And I ask
you both: What is there to ensure the safety of *this* roof above our
heads? We're surrounded by the Russian serpent who can lower his
conquered women into his pit at his slightest whim. The only way to
keep him from devouring us is to dance before him so that he can spit
gold at us, rather than his venom. It is clear to me that you are united in
your disapproval of my dance."

Zofia stood now and studied her mother's face, then Anna's. "But if
I were to stop my dancing, so too would our breathing. And Mother,
you would die quickly because you are set in your ways and your manners and customs are what they are. If I dance, our safety will be assured, and we will be able to rebuild at Halicz, making it a grand place
to bring your paintings and swords and books and icons of the Virgin.
A place peaceful and pleasurable for your last years, Mother."

When the countess did not respond, Zofia turned pleading eyes to
Anna. "Can you at least understand me, cousin?"

"I understand that your dance is but a euphemism."

"Oh, I suppose you think I speak the words of a whore, but I can
see where my fortune lies, and I would rather ride the whirlwind and direct the storm than lead a long life."

Zofia's words reminded Anna of her conversation with Doctor
Kurowski, the physician in whose carriage she had arrived in Praga. He,
too, saw the Russians as his main chance.

"Anna," Zofia said, coming to stand before her cousin's chair, "the
time will come when you must assist me in my dance."

Anna stared at her cousin as if she had started speaking Dutch. She
was spared from formulating some response when her aunt, who

seemed not to have heard her daughter's last comment, broke her silence with a brittle voice. "Zofia, your brother Walter is dead."

Zofia stood motionless. The countess' words seemed to hang in the air.

Slowly Zofia turned to her mother, then back to Anna, her face blanching, her eyes becoming remote. She was genuinely startled.

But the moment was a brief one. Zofia regained her composure, squaring her shoulders and fastening her gaze on Anna. "I'm sure that you can't overly mourn my brother, cousin, considering what costs he has exacted from you. Perhaps if you remember he's given you little Jan Michał, whom you love so dearly, your hatred will not follow him to the grave." Without waiting for a reply, she turned to the countess. "You, Mother, must mourn for both of us, as I have no such energies to spend on the dead and the past. I must see to our future."

Turning on her heel, Zofia whisked from the room, never even inquiring as to the circumstances of her brother's death.

At the first opportunity, Anna asked Zofia whether any word had come from Jan. Anna thought her cousin stiffened slightly, but her demeanor remained cool, her face a mask. "No, darling, he hasn't written a word."

62

In the music room at the Gronski town house, Anna was reunited with many of her patriot friends. For appearance' sake, they were there for a recital and Anna did play the piano for a short while, but the latest news to reach Warsaw, if not completely surprising, was nonetheless shocking.

The Queen of France was dead, and as many opinions of her were voiced in Anna's political group as there were people. She was described as a woman of many faces: a heroine, a vixen, a martyr. No one could deny, however, that she was a victim. Only ten days before, on the sixteenth of October, she followed her husband's steps to the *guillotine*. Reports had it that she went to her death nobly, head held high, much to the consternation of her detractors who had hoped to see her stooped and cowering on the bloody scaffold.

Anna had initiated the meeting of patriots. Several of her friends were absent, like Baron Michał Kolbi, who had followed Kościuszko, but there were new additions to the little collection of gentry, bankers, artisans, men of business, wives, and simple townsmen. With Michał gone, however, Anna was the only member of the *szlachta;* at one time the distinction of her title among the untitled might have made her uncomfortable. Now, nothing mattered, other than the cause.

It was not only France's fate that confounded the group that day. Conversation moved inexorably to recent events in Poland. For appearances, the king was said to rule, but policy was now created at the Russian embassy. Russian garrisons policed the entire country. And, on the fifth of the month, as a result of a new treaty, what little territory Stanisław and the *Sejm* had not already conceded to the aggressors the previous August fell into Russian hands.

"Do you know," Anna asked the group, "that this may be to our advantage?"

"Our advantage, my lady?" a merchant asked.

"Yes," Anna said, "perhaps it's the motivation we need to demonstrate to those Polish fence-sitters that appeasement will only lead to slavery."

"And to inspire a groundswell of support for Kościuszko," the merchant added.

"Exactly!" Anna said.

"Another advantage Catherine might not have counted on," one townsman said, "lies in the thirty thousand Polish soldiers she has discharged. These restless men have gravitated toward Kraków and Warsaw and are the kind of men who hunger for revolution. No Russian dares walk the streets of Warsaw alone without fear of being beaten bloody."

"But unless our magnates take decisive action and risk losing the silks they sit upon," another predicted, "our fate is sealed."

"Those who have turned traitor by signing the Confederacy of Targowica will not lift a finger," the townsman said. "They are a lost cause. Living high off the hog, they are, accepting graft from the Russians while landless *szlachta* and idle peasants swarm hungry in the streets."

However varied were the opinions of the group members toward Marie Antoinette, their assessment of Catherine was spoken with one clear voice of hatred. She had seen to it that Poland was reduced to a loaf of bread over which Russia, Austria, and Prussia vied like hungry animals. But the group also held to the hope that the concerted effort of the Polish people, noble and non-noble alike, could still stage a successful campaign for liberty.

Anna's friends assured her that theirs was but a small patch on a quilt that covered Praga and Warsaw, that there were many other such groups—drawn together by their desire to be free—who held other such secret meetings. With prayers and hope, they watched and waited, waited and watched.

While the weeks slipped into winter, Anna came to know her child and a bond was formed as Jan Michał learned to accept her as the most important person in his little sphere of experience. Anna often gladly did things for him a servant routinely did in such households, and he took to calling her "*Mat-ka*" after his own fashion. He was a happy and healthy child, forever curious, always moving, touching, tasting, listening.

On Christmas Day of 1793, however, Jan Michał lay gravely ill. Anna had had his little bed moved down to her room, so that she could watch his progress moment to moment. He hadn't eaten for four revolutions of the clock; everything that was fed to him was immediately expelled. His bedclothes were continuously wet with perspiration and his forehead raged with fever. He cried very little, and this worried Anna as much as if he cried perpetually. She fought off sleep in order to stay at his side. Mysterious fevers like this were not uncommon, and they were often fatal. Would he pass away at some quiet moment when her exhaustion had overcome her? Would she wake to find her son dead? Was their happy reunion to end in tragedy?

On the first day of his illness, Anna had gone to Countess Gronska to ask about a doctor. The family doctor, however, was not in Warsaw; he had, like so many good men of every profession, followed Kościuszko. He was using his talents to tend to the wounds of the patriots.

When the child's condition only worsened, a tearful Anna went in to see her aunt again.

Countess Gronska was preparing to go to Mass at the cathedral. "Is he no better?"

Anna shook her head. "Oh, Aunt Stella, what can we do?"

"I don't know, Anna, although there is one person who may have an answer."

"Who?"

The countess seemed to hesitate.

"Aunt, tell me! Who is it that might help?"

The countess sighed in resignation. "Zofia."

"The physician has arrived," Marta announced in a whisper.

"Thank God!" Anna cried, leaping up from her place at her son's side. "Stay with Jan Michał, Marta, until I bring the doctor upstairs."

Anna hurried down the staircase. Somehow, Zofia *had* been able to secure a physician—and on Christmas Day of all days. God bless her, Anna thought, and God bless the doctor!

The physician stood in the hallway, his wide back toward Anna as she reached the bottom stair. He had removed his heavy cloak and was shaking it free of a smattering of snowflakes.

"It's so good of you to come across to Praga, Doctor," Anna said. She was buoyed by his very presence. "And in such inclement weather. I'm so relieved. . . ."

Anna's words trailed off as he turned around to face her. She stood staring in surprise. It was Doctor Kurowski, the physician who had reluctantly shared his coach with her.

The doctor could not help but notice Anna's reaction, and his little dark eyes, set under fleshy folds and bushy eyebrows, studied her for a few moments.

"Ah!" he sighed in recognition, his eyes twinkling. "It is the countess who worries over street children."

Anna's distaste for the man was still fresh. "It's my own child that worries me now," she said, assuming the felicity of an actress who must disguise her personal dislike for a fellow player. "Will you see him?"

The large man harrumphed. "It is the reason Zofia—Lady Gronska— sent for me," he said, picking up his brown satchel. "Take me to him."

He asked only one question as he followed Anna up the stairs. "How old is the child?"

Anna had to think for a moment. "Nearly twenty months."

Both Marta and Lutisha were with Jan Michał when Anna and Doctor Kurowski entered the room.

The doctor, huffing from the stairs, approached the bed, drew back the covers.

Anna stood to his side, her eyes intent on his expression. His grizzled beard, however, seemed to cloak any reaction.

"This room is not nearly warm enough," he announced brusquely.

Anna sent Marta for more wood for the ceramic stove. The chamber had a fireplace, as well, dating from the days previous to tiled stoves and the doctor insisted that both be lighted.

The physician removed the child's damp nightclothes and prodded with chubby fingers until Jan Michał's face became red and pinched in pain, his screams reaching an ear-piercing level. His little limbs flailed wildly. Anna could only helplessly watch.

The doctor turned to her. "I think it would be best if you wait downstairs. Have your maid bring me some oil of fat, honey, hot water, and fresh bedclothes."

Anna sent Lutisha for the things he requested. She hesitated, however, to leave the room herself.

The doctor's eyes fastened on her. "Don't question me," he said. "You've requested my services, so do exactly as I say."

Anna could only obey. Outside the room, she encountered Marta returning with firewood. "Marta, please arrange for you or your mother to remain in that room at all times, unless he should object. Do you understand?"

"Yes, Madame."

Later, when Anna heard Lutisha come down again on some errand, she followed the servant into the kitchen.

"He's ordered hot coals for the bed warmer," the servant told Anna. "He's going to roast that child alive. I've never seen a little one in such agony." The woman's face, wet with perspiration, fixed on Anna's. "Dear God, Madame," she wailed, "I don't think Jan Michał will live out the day."

Left alone in the kitchen, Anna sank into a chair. How thoughtless the servant had been in what she said. But her raw emotions had spoken the truth as she saw it. Soon came the sound of the sickroom door opening and closing. Jan Michał's screams ran through Anna like little knives. It was all she could do to keep despair at bay. She put her head down at the kitchen table and prayed to the Black Madonna.

Eventually, Marta came down to take up kitchen duties. She had little news and her face was grim. When Marcelina and Katarzyna came in to help with the Christmas meal, Anna retreated to the reception room, taking a seat not far from the freestanding clock. The countess arrived home from Christmas services, and when Anna could provide no real news of Jan Michał, she went to her room.

Anna sat alone. An hour passed as if it were twelve, the chimes of the clock sounding oddly discordant. Occasionally, she could hear Jan Michał's cries piercing the walls, but during the second hour, Anna did not hear a single sound from him. She could not fathom what his silence portended. The ticking of the clock was about to drive her mad. She could scarcely restrain herself from rushing upstairs.

At last, she heard the door open upstairs and the sounds of the doctor's voice as he left Lutisha with instructions.

Anna was waiting for him at the bottom of the stairs.

His inscrutable face did not invite hope.

"Is he . . ."

Doctor Kurowski cast her an impatient glance and moved past her toward the hook that held his coat. "The fever is breaking," he said as he walked. "The child will recover."

"Thank God," Anna said, taking in and expelling a breath as if it meant life itself to her.

"Keep the room warm, unbearably so. Apply the oil to his entire body four times a day and keep him heavily blanketed. He's taken and retained a water-honey solution. See that he's given this regularly for nourishment until he's able to digest something more substantial. You might try a light broth with a touch of absinthe."

The physician stood now with his fur hat and coat on, ready to depart.

"Yes, Doctor." Anna felt dizzy with relief. "Thank you so much."

Lutisha hurried down the stairs and moved toward the kitchen. Her hands swiped at the heavy perspiration on her face. "Thank God," she was muttering. "Thank God and the white eagle."

"Ah, yes, the eagle," Doctor Kurowski said. "Tell me, now that all of the Commonwealth is in Russian hands, do you still harbor notions of the eagle repelling the Russian bear?"

Anna felt her lips tighten, but she managed a smile. "As long as Polish hearts and minds are set on liberty, Doctor, I will share that dream."

"A dream is all it is, my dear girl, and it is all you will be left with in the end." He picked up his satchel. "And now there is the matter of my fee."

"The fee? Oh, yes! How much is it?"

"Fifty ducats."

Anna's first thought was that he was not serious, that he was toying with her. She found herself playing Echo to his Narcissus. "Fifty ducats."

"That is what I said, my lady. My time is valuable. And this is a holiday."

"Yes, it is. Christmas Day." Anna was certain her irony would be lost on him. "But I don't keep such sums here at the house. My money is invested. May I send you the money on Monday next?"

"I am afraid that I must insist on some assurance—"

"*I'll* see to your payment!" It was Zofia's voice that suddenly rang out. She had entered the hallway from the rear of the house. Her flamboyant but ruffled manner of dress indicated that she was only now arriving home from her round of Christmas Eve festivities. "How much is your fee, Doctor Kurowski?"

"Fifty ducats."

Zofia paused, blinking only once at the enormity of the sum. "The child is well?"

"I don't provide guarantees, but I think he will recover."

"Good. Wait a moment. I'll get your money." Zofia turned, moving toward the library, where Anna knew the Gronskis kept a wall safe behind the portrait of an ancestor.

Without a further word to the physician, Anna turned on her heel and hurried up the stairs to Jan Michał.

In the evening Anna went to Zofia's room. Her cousin had slept most of the day, missing Christmas dinner. She was now preparing to receive guests.

"How is the boy?" Zofia asked.

"The fever has broken and he's sleeping soundly."

"Good! I'm so glad, Anna. Truly. I'm not having so very many guests in tonight. Not more than fifteen or twenty, so there shouldn't be too much noise to disturb him."

"I'll move him back up to the attic room."

"And you must get some rest, too, Anna. You look so very tired."

"Zofia, how did you happen to learn of Doctor Kurowski?"

"Oh, he's well known among my friends. A Russian lieutenant highly recommended him."

"I see."

"Though my friend didn't intimate in any way that his rates were so impossible. Fifty ducats!"

"I think that he adjusts his rates to his patients."

"Whatever do you mean?"

"Only that I think he took a dislike to me."

"To you, Anna? I doubt that."

"I'll go to the Lubickis tomorrow for the money."

"You will not! Those funds represent your future security and should be left untouched."

"I'll not allow you to pay such an outrageous bill."

"What does it matter to me?" Zofia laughed, casting a look at Anna through the mirror on her vanity. "I wouldn't be surprised if, within a week or a month, the very same fifty ducats were back in my wall compartment. Now, put it out of your mind. The important thing is that your child received good care."

The cousins chatted a while longer, Anna sitting behind Zofia, who was applying makeup to her face. Then, thanking Zofia again, Anna rose to leave.

Zofia, however, spun around on her stool and stood, catching Anna's arm. "Anna, darling," she said, her black eyes boring into Anna's, "I am only one woman. You have your sick child to think of now, but when he is well I will ask you to assist me in the entertainments I provide for our Russian interlopers. It is this that keeps this household safe and what will maintain our security in this quickly dying country. You must face the fact that the Commonwealth is not likely to rise again."

"What . . . what can I do?"

"You're a beautiful woman, Anna, a desirable woman. You turn more heads than you might think. I've seen it. You know the Russian language better than I, and with your charm and intelligence, you could develop the sort of wit that would be expected of you. Charlotte Sic and I think that you would make a splendid hostess."

Anna was struck speechless at first. She gently pulled free of Zofia's grasp. "I'm afraid," she said, "that I have no talents for such an occupation."

"Nonsense! You let me be the judge of that when the time comes." Zofia released her cousin. "Now run along. I must get ready."

Anna went up to Jan Michał, purging her mind of all thoughts of Zofia's proposal.

Early the next morning, Anna went to the Lubickis for the fifty ducats.

The new year 1794 seemed to bring with it assurance of Jan Michał's full recovery. Anna exulted in watching her son return to the same curious and carefree child he had been before the sickness struck.

She could not help but wonder when Zofia would approach her again about entertaining the Russians. A day did not go by that she didn't rehearse her refusal.

What was Zofia's motive in suggesting such a thing? It was unfathomable. Was she so concerned about the physical well-being of the household? Or did she think, as Anna suspected, that such behavior on Anna's part would ultimately scuttle any hope of happiness with Jan? Was it possible Zofia still had hopes of marrying Jan?

It was a mystery.

"It's coming!" the Jewish baker cried as he burst into the music room, a late arrival.

Anna was just finishing her piece at the piano—one of the few she remembered from childhood—but the man could not wait for the last note to resound, much less the applause. "It's coming!"

"When?" came the chorus.

"Next month. February it's to be."

"How do you know?" a shopkeeper asked. "I've heard April."

"Wait, wait, wait!" complained a seamstress. "Why must we always wait?"

The baker smiled. "The winds move at their own speed."

"That's a fine maxim," the woman countered, "but I tell you all here today that if Kościuszko does not make his move soon, the Commonwealth will be so tightly locked in Catherine's claws that any struggle will be futile."

Anna remained at the piano, listening with no little interest. Her patriot friends had been assembling every other week at the Gronski town house since the initial meeting the previous September. Anna arranged the meetings for a day Zofia routinely spent at her dressmaker in the Market Square, and at midmorning, a time when the Countess Gronska kept to her room reading the Bible and her political publications. Anna was certain neither her cousin nor her aunt would approve of the meetings. Zofia would think them hazardous to her standing among the Russians, while the countess would think it scandalous that Anna was socializing with men and women of no rank. Because the Gronski home was itself sometimes a den of Russians, it was the least suspicious of the available meeting places. Lately, however, such meetings had become extremely dangerous, should they be found out. Catherine had ordered the arrest of all subversives.

Still, Anna hid nothing from the servants. She trusted them implicitly. She had come to realize that while the flame of patriotism sometimes sputtered among the nobility, especially certain magnates, among the peasant class it burned with the steadiness and reliability of the best beeswax candle.

The first gatherings at the town house had yielded little news. It was the simple camaraderie the members felt that served to bolster their spirits and keep hope for the Commonwealth alive.

Lately, however, the rumor mill had been turning at full tilt. It did seem certain that Kościuszko was about to embark on some definitive course of action.

A cluster of four or five friends stood around the piano in front of Anna, thereby blocking her view when the door opened and someone entered. Anna assumed it was merely Lutisha or Marta seeing to the refreshments.

But it was not long before she realized that the spirited conversation in the room lagged, normal tones becoming whispers before waning to a tense silence. One man in front of Anna turned around and bowed.

Anna stood. She could feel the blood draining from her face.

The motionless figure in green at the door was Countess Stella Gronska. She wore a smile, but it was one Anna, in her distracted state, could not read.

How would she react to Anna's secret meetings in the Gronski home, the danger in which she had placed all of its inhabitants?

Everyone's eyes were on the countess, then turned to Anna as she slowly walked toward her aunt. The walk seemed interminable. Inside Anna was trembling, her heart beating against her chest like a caged bird.

"Hello, Aunt Stella," Anna heard herself say. The greeting sounded so insipid and hollow.

"Hello, Anna Maria," the countess rejoined.

Anna tried to take her hand and guide her out into the reception room, but her aunt would have none of it.

"Did we disturb you? I thought you were reading or napping."

"Did you?"

"I . . . I've just been entertaining some friends." Anna still could not decipher the countess' lingering smile.

"I see," she said. And then the smile vanished. "Anna, when I came in, the entire room seemed to be abuzz with some news. What is it?"

"Only rumors, Aunt Stella."

"What is it?" she pressed.

"Nothing definite, but the word about the capital is that Kościuszko is about to launch his campaign."

"Praise God!"

"Aunt Stella," Anna whispered, "I didn't want you to learn of these meetings."

The countess' brown eyes studied Anna, surveyed the silent group, returned to Anna. She gave out with an abrupt little laugh then. "My dear, this may be more Zofia's house than mine now, but don't you think I know everything that goes on?"

"You knew?"

"Of course! You have these meetings every other week. On Thursdays, when Zofia has gone on her shopping tour. Am I right, or is my mind failing?"

"You are right. It was unforgivable of me to impose on your hospitality. I assumed too much. In the future—"

"Anna Maria!" the countess interrupted.

"Aunt?"

"May I join your little company of friends?"

Struck silent, Anna gaped in astonishment.

"Oh, I know," the countess said with a little wave of her hand, "what customs I've held to hard and fast. But these are perilous times, Anna, and I'll not be left in the past."

"I . . . should be glad to introduce you, Aunt Stella."

"And I look at it this way," the countess continued in a voice strong enough for all to hear, "why should I settle for stale news of the patriots' movement in old publications when I live across from the capital and the cognoscenti meet in my own house!"

"She calls us the cognoscenti," blurted out a shoemaker, his hand quickly moving to his mouth in embarrassment at voicing his thoughts. Everyone laughed at him now, and the tension in the room evaporated.

Anna took her aunt by the hand and proceeded to introduce her to everyone in the room, each person bowing courteously before her.

After the introductions, the countess fell into a lively conversation with a banker, whose bank was one of Warsaw's six largest, all of which had declared insolvency the year before.

After everyone had gone, the countess seemed exhausted, but happily so. "Anna," she said, "don't ever forget that you are as a daughter to me and that my home is your home."

"Thank you, Aunt Stella. But Zofia mustn't know about this."

"Oh, Zofia," the countess cried, giving a little wave of her hand. "A pox on Zofia!"

63

The Market Square in Kraków was not unfamiliar to Lieutenant Jan Stelnicki; his family city town house was here in the old capital, and he had played here, knew all the streets that led to it. It was only now, however, after having visited dozens of towns and cities with General Tadeusz Kościuszko, that he realized how large this square was. Even Warsaw's square couldn't compete.

Today he was thankful the square was so huge, for it teemed with humanity. The rows of three- and four-storied buildings were bursting with people hanging from the roofs and windows. All about, one could sense History in the air. This day, the twenty-fourth of March would live forever, and—God willing—would mark the beginning of the end of foreign influences in the Commonwealth. Just as the white storks were returning now to their Polish roofs after a long winter, so too, Jan prayed, would Polish patriots, peasant and noble, soon return to their homes.

Like everyone else, he stood in the sunny but cool morning, awaiting the appearance of Kościuszko. With the little commander, he had seen more than town squares. He had seen battle and blood, bravery and death. He had seen, as he saw today in the press of the crowd, the love of liberty in nobles, in gentry, in townsmen, in Jews, in peasants. How could such a cause fail? he wondered, feeling the emotions of the crowd rushing about and through him like a river.

Before the partition in '92, he had experienced victory and defeat. At Dubienka he had taken a sword wound to his right shoulder, but the victory there was so sweet he seemed not to notice the pain. The real sorrow of that campaign came when Frederick William of Prussia broke his promise to protect Poland's independence. And it came when Prince Ludwig marched his Lithuanian troops away from battle.

But the campaign truly fell to pieces when certain magnates convinced the king he had no choice but to join the Confederacy of Targowica. The king's own nephew, General Józef Poniatowski, who had overseen a fine victory at Zieleńce, resigned his commission in protest, along with General Kościuszko. Jan was glad his wound had kept him from Warsaw for that black day. Kościuszko had come back bowed, but not broken. Never broken, Jan thought, not Kościuszko.

Jan had spent much of '93 in Paris with Kościuszko, who harbored hopes of enlisting the French in the Polish cause. The little general was a man who persevered. In time, however, word came that a new revolutionary spirit was afoot in Poland and they returned. Kraków was free because on the twelfth of the month General Madaliński took it back from the Russians.

General Kościuszko entered the square now and the crowd erupted in cheers, chants, and shouting. The pandemonium went on many minutes. Madaliński stood with him, and if he resented the fact that Kościuszko was stealing his thunder after only arriving the previous day, he didn't show it.

Kościuszko walked to the middle of the square, not far from where Jan stood with his contingent. He wore his white striped long coat, white breeches, white shirt, red vest, and over the ruff at his neck lay the ribbon that held his Polish military cross. On his head he wore, as did Jan now, the four-cornered hat of the peasant, red with a black sheepskin rim at its base.

Why *not* take the hat of the peasant? Jan thought as he looked about at the masses. After all, the cause would be nothing without the peasants. There were thousands here with their scythes, ready to follow the little general.

The crowd grew hushed and the general spoke to their hearts, vowing to fight for the liberty, the integrity, the independence of his native land. He issued manifestoes to every class of man—for they were all here today—calling them forward to give unselfishly to the Commonwealth of Poland and Lithuania. It was his intention to "unite the hearts, hands, and endeavors of the whole land."

Kościuszko then proclaimed the Act of Insurrection, taking on dictatorial powers and establishing a provisional constitution that granted freedom to the peasants and land to anyone who took up arms for the Commonwealth.

"Feel at last your strength," he called, as if to the nation at large. "Put it wholly forth. Set your will on being free and independent. By unity and courage you shall reach this honored end. Prepare your soul for victories and defeats. In both, the spirit of true patriotism should maintain its strength and energy. All that remains to me is to praise your Rising, and to serve you so long as Heaven permits me to live!"

The little general raised his peasant cap in the air and the crowd roared wildly, lifting him aloft and carrying him away.

Jan twisted his own red four-cornered cap in his hand. His heart felt as if it would burst with pride.

If only Anna were here to see this, he thought. Anna, with her eyes like emerald lightning. And then the tears came.

64

Anna walked into the reception room and was surprised to find Count Paweł Potecki.

He stood immediately. "I'm waiting for Zofia," he said.

"I should be glad to keep you company while you wait." Anna sat. She sensed he was on a mission of some sort. He was dressed rather austerely in dark clothes, and there was a nervous tension in his manner. He was a handsome man just the same, and he bore himself nobly. She still felt grateful to him for his concern for her in the aftermath of Zofia's party at which the drunken Princess Sic had ridiculed her.

"Congratulations, Lady Anna. You've become a mother since last we met."

"Thank you."

"It was a boy?"

"Yes. A strong one, too."

"Ha!" he laughed. "You remember our conversation. Had it been a girl, I'm certain she would have been strong, too."

"No doubt," Anna laughed.

As if on cue, Jan Michał burst into the room, a piece of rye bread clutched in his little hand. "*Mat-ka*, look!" he cried. "Bread!" He stopped at his mother's chair and held it up.

"Ah, the crust!" Anna crooned. "Is it good, Jan Michał?"

"Oh, yes. Luteesha says it is best!"

"Is Luteesha baking today?" the count asked Jan.

The boy turned to the stranger and nodded uncertainly.

"Aren't you quite the little man?" the count asked.

"Oh, yes!" the child said.

The count laughed and scooped the boy up onto his knee.

A breathless Marta appeared at the door in pursuit of Jan Michał. "Oh, I'm sorry, Madame," she said. "I didn't know you had a guest."

"Lord Potecki is waiting for Lady Zofia."

Marta was blushing. "I turned my back on the child for one moment and he was down off his chair and gone."

"Another few minutes," the count joked, "and he would've had a sword and some of this armor off the wall and been on his way to Kraków."

Marta's hands went to her mouth in horror.

"It's all right, Marta." Anna laughed. "It'll be some time before he can manage any of these weapons. And, God willing, he won't have to."

Jan Michał climbed down and ran to the servant.

"Marta," Anna said, "be certain Jan doesn't eat anything more before the noon meal."

"Yes, Madame," she whispered and curtsied before closing the door behind her and Jan Michał.

"He's such a bright child," the count said as he stood. "You must be very proud of him."

"I am. Must you leave so soon? Zofia should be home at any minute."

"I'm afraid I dare not wait any longer. Zofia is unpredictable."

"Untamable, isn't that what you called her, Lord Potecki?"

He laughed. "An untamable bird, as I recall. Well, she's unpredictable, as well."

Anna could not help but laugh, too.

"Will you say good-bye to her for me?"

Anna read the tension again in his face. "Good-bye?"

"Yes. You've no doubt heard of Kościuszko's call to arms?"

"Of course. It's a great hope." Then Anna realized what he was saying. "You're off to Kraków!"

He nodded.

"God bless you, Paweł!" His first name came out on the crest of Anna's emotion.

"Too many nobles have lent deaf ears to the call," he said. "They're afraid of what the little general promises the peasants. But, by God, our outside aggressors should be our first concern."

"You'll be put to good use, I'm certain." Anna's hand touched the count's elbow. "I'm proud of you."

"I would have thought you'd despise the very notion of war, Anna."

"I expect I do. But I'm in full support of the patriots' cause, as is my aunt."

"Do you have someone in the war effort, Anna?"

"Yes, with Kościuszko . . . Lieutenant Jan Stelnicki."

"I'll be sure to look him up. Thanks for your confidence. I doubt Zofia will be so approving." He smiled sadly.

"No, I doubt that she will."

"She'll be livid."

"You love her, don't you, Paweł?"

"Yes," he said. His face was coloring.

"She told me you asked her to marry you." Anna was shocked at her own audacity.

"Yes. Too many times to count. Our relationship is one of convenience, not convention. Zofia's convenience, to be sure. Anna, you're her cousin. Tell me, does she love another?"

Anna was taken aback by the question. "I . . . I don't know." She was saved from any further questioning by the opening of the door.

"My, what a serious tête-à-tête!" Zofia intoned. "Hello, Paweł. Hello, Anna."

Anna quickly excused herself, bidding the count good-bye and wishing him well.

"One would think Anna was seeing you off to war, Paweł," Zofia said before Anna could effect an exit.

Anna climbed the stairs to her room, her mind reeling. Why had Zofia refused such a fine man? Was it because no single man could satisfy her? Or did she still have her sights on one man?

For a half hour, Anna could hear Zofia loudly carrying on in the reception room, no doubt railing against the count's plans. His voice could be heard, too, but it maintained a leavening quality of reason.

Not long after the voices had gone silent, Anna heard the front door close. She went downstairs and found Zofia still in the reception room.

"Obviously," Zofia said, "you know exactly what he plans to do."

"I do."

"And I suppose you approve?"

"Yes."

"He's a fool," Zofia scoffed.

"Zofia, it's not for you or me to approve or disapprove. He is his own man and must do as his conscience dictates. Would you want it any other way?"

Zofia looked up at her cousin, as if digesting the meaning of the words. She drew in a long breath, then expelled it slowly. "Conscience, indeed!"

"Zofia," Anna pressed, her hand reaching out to grasp her cousin's arm. "Paweł loves you! Do send for him, or let me send for him!"

"Oh, Anna," Zofia said, pulling away and moving toward the door.

"Zofia, don't let him go to war in this manner, with his spirit clouded. He may not return!"

Zofia turned around, her dark, almond-shaped eyes fastening on Anna's. "What is it that they say? 'For every fool there are two more.' Well, cousin, I beg you not to include me."

Anna was at the Lubicki mansion in Warsaw when the news came. She had only just finished discussing financial matters with Lord Lubicki when Helena's twelve-year-old brother arrived home from the outer courtyard of the Royal Castle.

"Kościuszko has met the enemy," Mundek cried in his piping voice, "and the battle is ours! Long live the republic!" The huge house came alive with excitement as family, friends, and servants cried out joyfully: "Long live the Republic! Long live the white eagle! Long live the little general!"

Over the next few days, details trickled into Warsaw. Kościuszko's manifestoes had not been in vain. Hundreds and thousands of peasants armed only with scythes and other makeshift weapons, as well as a host of nobles and their retainers, joined the Polish standard of the white eagle flying against a red background.

Kościuszko had not waited for Russians to march on Kraków. He moved north with his four thousand regulars and two thousand scythe-armed peasants. On the fourth of April, near Racławice, Russian Generals Tormasov and Pustovalov staged simultaneous attacks on Kościuszko from separate directions. But before a third Russian force led by Denisov could take part, the Polish military, bolstered by the wild and daredevilish scythemen, staged frontal assaults that routed the Russians.

Catherine lost a thousand men while Poland gained hope. Anna wondered what the Russians who held Warsaw prisoner were thinking. They had cause for worry.

* * *

Anna was playing with Jan Michał in his attic room when Lutisha, standing at the door on the third level, called, "Madame, the Countess Stella begs that you come down to the music room. Your guests are here."

"Good heavens, Lutisha, I've lost all sense of time! I'll be down directly. Please send up Marcelina or Katarzyna to look after Jan."

It was only a few days after Kościuszko's great victory, and as Anna hurried down the steps, she imagined the jubilant faces of her patriot friends.

But she opened the door to restrained, even dour, faces.

The men rose as she entered. "Good day, Lady Berezowska," came an unsynchronized chorus.

"Good day," Anna said, her eyes surveying the group of twenty or twenty-five. "Why are we not celebrating?"

She was soon to find out. She seated herself next to her aunt, who seemed just as curious. While everyone else remained silent, Citizen Donakevi, the banker, started to explain the situation to her, beginning with a question: "Lady Anna, do you know Kiliński the shoemaker?"

Anna shook her head.

"I've heard of him," Countess Stella said. "He's a good patriot, is he not?"

"He is a patriot, Lady Gronska," the banker said, "but perhaps to the extreme."

"Don't patriots often have to go to extremes out of necessity?" Anna asked.

"Yes, of course, Lady Berezowska. You're quite right. But let me explain. Jan Kiliński and others are inciting a great number of Warsaw citizens to rebel and wrest control of the capital without waiting for Kościuszko to come up from the south."

"But if it can be done . . ." the countess said.

"Oh, it might be possible, Lady Gronska, but it will take a man like Kościuszko, with his even-tempered leadership, to take the city with a minimum of bloodletting and loss of life."

"And this band of rebels?" Anna asked.

"It's a motley collection of angry citizens, unemployed soldiers, and the inevitable rabble of the city. If fully agitated, they will become ungoverned and bloodthirsty."

"A mob," Anna said.

"Exactly. Warsaw could become another Paris."

"And Catherine . . ." Anna mused.

Countess Gronska let out a long sigh. "Her wrath will flare white-hot and it will rain down on Praga and the capital like dragon's fire."

"Dear God, can nothing be done?" Anna canvassed the group of anxious faces, slowly coming to realize there was an odd expectancy in their expressions. What is it? she asked herself. What do these people want of me? She turned to Citizen Donakevi, her question on her face.

"Lady Berezowska," he said, haltingly, "we wish to ask you . . . that is, we are hopeful that you might be able to do something."

"Me?" The little word reflected her astonishment. "What could *I* possibly do?"

"You could get in to see King Stanisław," the banker said, his words flowing smoother now. "You are the only one of us who might gain his ear. My lady, you would be speaking for many more than the men and women assembled here. You would be speaking for thousands of citizens who do not wish to see anarchy in the streets. We *must* wait for the little general to liberate Warsaw."

"The king doesn't know me," Anna said, shaking her head.

The banker seemed disappointed.

Anna forced a laugh. "Did you think because I'm noble, I know the king?"

"I didn't know, my lady, but . . ."

"Yes?"

"Lady Gronska knows the king."

Anna caught her breath. She immediately knew he wasn't referring to her aunt, who sat there as silent as a stone. "My cousin?"

His hesitant nod attested to his discretion.

Anna could only imagine what gossip followed in the wake of Zofia's stylish shoes.

The banker continued: "The Countess Zofia Gronska has access to the king, and you, as her cousin and a member of the nobility, will be granted an audience. We feel certain that you will."

"It's unthinkable." Anna's head pounded at the thought. "What could *I* say to the king?"

"You must carry our message to him," said the banker's wife in an emotional plea. "My dear, something must be done at once to terminate this premature insurrection. There are human lives that depend upon it!"

Anna grew dizzy as her eyes moved around the room. How had this test come to her? Of what did these hopeful and trusting people think her capable? She had never been so unsure of herself.

Then she remembered Michał Kolbi's words two years before when she had asked him what help she could ever be to his little group of patriots. He had assured her that one day she might be of invaluable service. He would remind her of that himself—were he not with Kościuszko providing his own invaluable service.

"Lady Berezowska?" the banker whispered, calling her back to the moment.

Anna looked to her aunt. The Countess Gronska seemed about to nod her approval, but held back. Anna knew she was letting her decide for herself.

Swallowing hard, Anna said, "I'll go to the Royal Castle this afternoon."

Zofia arrived home from the Market Square at one in the afternoon. Anna wasted no time in going in to see her while her cousin began preparations for some afternoon event. She breathlessly explained the threat of Kiliński and his band of rebels.

Zofia's face registered surprise. "How do *you* know of such things?"

"I have friends, reliable sources."

"Still meeting with that ragtag group of yours? I trust you're not doing so in my home."

"You must believe me, Zofia. The city is at risk!"

"Oh, I believe you, darling. It's just that such matters are so tiring. I'm surprised at your interest. But what will happen, will happen."

"You speak as if this has no impact on our lives. Well, it does, and just as people make things happen, so too can they prevent them from happening. I've got to do something."

"What?" Zofia snapped. "What is it that you think *you* can possibly do?"

Anna paused, taking a breath. "Will you take me this afternoon to see the king? I'm to tell him of the plot. If anyone can do something to prevent it, he can."

"The king?" Zofia laughed, turning on Anna. "Are you out of your mind?"

"Zofia, people are depending on me."

"What's come over you, Anna? Will you ever lose your country naiveté? There's nothing you can do. Leave the political intrigue to the men. What do you imagine yourself—a Joan of Arc?"

"No, it's just that I believe—"

"Enough!" Zofia interrupted. "I can't go with you today. I have other plans."

"Zofia, please—"

"No, Anna! The whole notion is absurd. I'll have no part of it, and I won't hear any more of it."

Anna turned and started to leave when she noticed a letter on Zofia's writing desk. It was partially hidden by other papers, but a small part of the red seal was showing. Anna immediately thought it might be the Stelnicki seal.

Anna stopped and turned back. "Would you at least write a letter of introduction to the king?" She made a little gesture toward the secretary.

"No, now I have very little time to get ready." Zofia advanced and closed the secretary. She was wearing her stage smile. "Good-bye, Anna."

Anna dressed hurriedly, allowing no time for thought out of fear she would lose her nerve. She donned an afternoon dress of white Indian cotton and fashioned her hair in an upward style, setting off the auburn nicely with her amber barrettes. She wore no cosmetics or jewelry.

Once in the hired carriage, she had time to think. Might that letter in Zofia's secretary have been a letter from Jan? Was Zofia trying to hide it? Or was she imagining things? And if it were from Jan, was it addressed to Anna? Was her cousin up to her old tricks of intercepting mail? Or was it possible Jan had written to Zofia?

It had been so very long since Anna had seen or heard from Jan; she could only wonder if he still cared about her, if he had forgotten Zofia. Anna struggled to put this doubt from her mind.

Why couldn't she fully trust in someone? Jan still loved her, he must. Her concerns turned then to the matter of his safety. God protect and keep him, she prayed.

Presently Anna realized she was in the Royal Castle's outer courtyard when from her window she saw the column with the statue of Zygmunt atop it. She suddenly remembered her first trip to the capital on a search for a doll. She had fallen in love with a crystal dove instead.

The tall clock tower on the castle came into view. Is that truly where the king lives? she had asked her father. What would he think to know his daughter was going to *see* the king? And on such a mission? Somehow, his memory gave her strength as she alighted from the carriage in the inner courtyard.

Russian guards were in evidence everywhere. Anna's heart tightened. Would it even be possible for her to speak to him away from Russian ears?

The King's Apartment was on the first floor. Anna was shown up the Great Stairs and into the white Officer's Hall. Two guards stood at the door through which she entered, another two at the door at the far end. She was relieved to see that these, at least, wore the red and yellow uniform of the Polish Royal Guards. A long stretch of green and white marble squares moved beneath her as she nervously approached the King's Deputy who sat at an ornate desk of French design. No one else was present waiting to see the king. She noted a tall white-and-gold clock that was chiming three o'clock. Supposedly, he held audiences until five. Anna could only pray he was here today.

She presented herself. "I am the Countess Anna Maria Berezowska. I am seeking an audience with the king."

Anna's heart beat rapidly as she surveyed the man. Everything about him was large: his girth, his features, his moustache. His cordiality, however, was as lacking as the hairs upon his head. "You are expected, Lady Berezowska?" he inquired, unsmiling.

"No," Anna said, the veneer of her confidence already cracking.

"Hmmm," he murmured, opening a leather binder. Officiously he began running his stubby finger up and down its pages, humming as he did so.

It was not long before both the finger and the humming stopped. The fat official's milky blue eyes rose to stare at Anna, as if in accusation. "Your name, Lady Berezowska, does not appear on the list of those who have access to his Royal Highness. The king knows you?"

"Yes."

The eyes narrowed underneath their fleshy folds. He was openly contentious.

"It is *not* my first time at the Royal Castle."

"And the other occasion?" he asked impertinently, as if she had been there only once before.

Anna bristled at the boorish official. That he was correct irked her. "I attended a concert and supper reception. It was some time ago."

"And if I were to send your name into the king, would he recognize it?"

"Perhaps not," Anna conceded. "Please, Officer, it is imperative that I see him."

"I'm afraid that's not possible, my lady. For an audience, you must state your business in writing. On the letter's merit, your request will be granted or denied. It may take a week."

"A week! I don't have a week. This matter is urgent!"

The chubby fingers of both hands interlocked now, and he leaned forward. "What is the nature of your business?"

"I'll not discuss it with anyone other than King Stanisław."

"Then I can help you no further. Good day to you."

The man had the effrontery to dismiss her. Anna felt blood running hotly into her face. She turned from the desk, not to retrace her steps, but to rush the entrance of the next room.

She heard the fat man bellow behind her, but the two guards at the doors were so startled they failed to react in time. She ran right past them.

Anna met with immediate disappointment, however. She found herself in a huge anteroom, massive paintings lining its walls and people sitting on uncomfortable-looking French couches. The men and women here were all waiting to see the king.

The official and his guards were in quick pursuit. Anna had little to lose now, so she ran for the two doors that surely led into the king's audience chamber. "Stop that woman!" the official shouted.

The two guards in front of these doors were quicker to react. They stepped together in front of the doors, effectively barring her from entering. "I must see the king!" she cried. "I must!"

The other two guards came from behind now. Though Anna still fumed with anger and embarrassment, she knew she had lost. She turned to see the deputy bustling over to her, his face inflamed, his taut lips thinned in a taut smile. "You two," he said to the guards who had let her slip by, "escort the countess to her carriage without delay. See if you can do something right! And it would be best," he said, addressing Anna, "if you do not return, Lady Berezowska."

For once Anna spoke before filtering her words. "And your nose would not be so red if your capacity for vodka were as spare as your good manners."

She watched him blink in dumb surprise. Then she swept out of the room so quickly the soldiers had to step in double time.

Inside her moving carriage, Anna laughed at the image of the deputy's face. She could not imagine what had come over her.

But the sweet taste of her little victory quickly dissipated as the carriage wheels rumbled over the bridge to Praga. What was she to do? She could not meet her friends a failure. She prayed for some direction, some plan.

By the time she stepped out at the Gronski town house, the scheme had come to her. She had less than two hours.

Anna stared at her reflection in disbelief.

Zofia had gone out and the countess had taken to her bed. She was having one of her bad days—these seemed to come more frequently now. Anna was free then to bribe Babette into helping with her scheme.

The servant dressed her in Zofia's breathtaking red velvet gown with its wide skirt, puffed sleeves, and trim of hundreds of undulating silver beads. Then she fitted to Anna's head one of Zofia's towering wigs, weaving through it red ribbons tied in many bows. She painted Anna's face as if it were a canvas: the red lips were heart-shaped, her cheeks well rouged against the whitest powder, and her upper right cheek was home to a black beauty patch in the shape of a crescent moon. A Renaissance poet would have dedicated a sonnet sequence to her, she thought to herself, a smile pulling up the corners of her mouth.

The array of jewelry was impressive, too. But it was her neckline that gave her pause. The dress was scandalously cut, leaving little of her breasts covered. She thought of changing, but there was no time.

"Oh, Madame," Babette cried, "you are exquisite!"

"Am I? Tell me, Babette, do you think that, for today at least, I might equal Zofia's allure?"

"*Oui*, Madame. Today you surpass your cousin."

Anna knew she was going to need that little confidence.

"Is it a big party you're going to, Lady Anna?"

"It's more of a masquerade, Babette."

"Oh, Madame! What fun!"

The hands of the tall white-and-gold clock in the alcove read 4:45 when Anna reentered the Officers' Hall. Her heart leapt at the small miracle she found there: the fat officer had been replaced by another soldier!

Anna could not believe her luck. She presented herself, leaning forward and saying confidently, "I wish to see the king without delay."

The old man's forehead wrinkled in nervous amazement at the vision before him. "Yes, yes, milady," he stuttered, the wide eyes beneath wiry gray brows moving down, lingering over Anna's breasts. "And you are . . . ?"

Anna stiffened at the man's forward gaze, but was quick enough to assign her involuntary reaction a motive other than modesty. "You don't know?" she asked in mock astonishment. "You truly don't?"

"Why, why, why, no, milady, I–"

"I am," Anna intoned, mustering her mother's confectionery smile, "the Countess Zofia Gronska of Halicz." Anna could only pray that he didn't know her cousin by sight.

"Oh, yes, yes, the Countess Gronska, of course! Do forgive me, milady." Bending so low over the leather binder that his nose nearly touched its pages, the intense little man quickly located Zofia's name. He stood immediately. "If you'll excuse me but a minute, Lady Gronska, I'll see if the king will receive you. Will you be seated?"

"Thank you." Anna allowed the man to seat her, then watched as he quickly shuffled into the next room.

The minutes were insufferably long. Anna was only too well aware that the four soldiers in the room were the same that had helped abort her earlier visit. To disguise her nervousness as impatience, she tapped her polished fingernails on the desk.

Anna knew of at least one reason why Zofia was so disinclined to help her get to the king. She was deathly afraid that he would say something to her about his intrigues with her. But what did that matter, after all? It didn't compare with the importance of her message. And what if

Zofia knew Anna had read her diary long ago? Anna chuckled to herself. What if Zofia could see her naive little country cousin now?

At long last the old man returned. "You are to see the king directly," he announced.

Anna's condescending smile was her answer. She stood, but before she could pass through into the next room, several citizens were escorted out. Their dour faces made her suspect her arrival had cut short or superseded others' visits. *So be it,* she thought, *my business is the business of all the people.*

Anna advanced now, her head held high, her eyes straight before her, every inch aware of the stir she was creating. Every eye was upon her. All was proceeding as planned.

Anna passed into the large anteroom, its walls lined with a series of panoramas of Warsaw. She felt dwarfed and somehow intimidated by the paintings. How was she to help save the capital and the Commonwealth?

Just as she was nearing the entrance to the king's audience chamber, the door opened and he stood there—the fat official she had hoped to avoid at all costs. He stood aside to allow Anna to pass, and, bowing slightly—what his girth would allow—he smiled, his lusty eyes taking her in, from head to toe.

The veins at Anna's temple pulsed more with fear than indignation. Praying that Babette's makeup hid her emotions, she forced a smile of greeting, nodded, and walked past him. Her affability may have been a mistake, she immediately realized. Zofia wouldn't have given him a sideward glance.

As she passed him, she saw his smile fade. The lackluster blue eyes stared intently, and Anna could almost see his mind at work, challenging his power of recall.

Then she was past him and in the audience chamber, wondering if she had been recognized. She could imagine him checking with the old man to see under what name she had been admitted. If he knew Zofia by sight, Anna would be undone.

She was startled now when a guard she had passed announced, "The Countess Zofia Gronska of Halicz!"

The room was all red, gold, and white. The king sat on his audience chair under its elaborate canopy. His hand lifted slightly, a finger motioning her forward.

Anna's confidence waned. She became dizzy. Aside from a single guard, she was alone in the room with the King of the Commonwealth of Poland and Lithuania. She doubted her ability to speak. What crazed derring-do had led her here?

Anna pushed herself forward.

"Why, Zofia," the king exclaimed, "this is a surprise, but then you are always full of surprises!"

Anna slowly advanced.

It was not long before the king's eyes were squinting. "You seem different," he said.

Although he appeared a slight figure in the huge gilded chair, Anna thought he seemed less old and decrepit than he had at the supper. She knew he was into his sixth decade. His own gray hair was drawn and tied behind his head. Though his bearing was noble, his plain face bespoke gentleness. Anna could have imagined him more as a tailor or a barber than a king.

Anna came to stand just before the dais.

"Why, you're not Zofia!" he cried.

"No, I'm not, Sire."

"Well, then, just *who* are you?"

"I am Zofia's cousin, the Countess Anna Maria Berezowska of Sochaczew. Forgive me, Your Majesty, but it was the only way I could get in to see you."

"Let me get a look at you." The king leaned forward. "My, you certainly are no less beautiful than my wicked Zofia."

Anna felt her face flushing. "I'm afraid it took some doing."

The king laughed loudly. "A masquerade, is it?"

"Yes, exactly, Sire." Anna could scarcely believe she had the king laughing. "Actually this pretense involves a very grave matter."

"You are far too young to be thinking about the grave," the king quipped. "As for myself—"

A voice boomed out now from behind Anna. "Your Majesty," the fat official cried, "this woman is not the Countess Gronska. She is an imposter!" He had already taken several steps into the room and was bearing down on Anna.

Anna's heart stopped. She had needed only a few more minutes.

"Do you think that I don't know that, you fool?" the king snapped, halting the official in his tracks. "Do you think I've lost my sight and hearing? Of course, she is not Zofia."

"But, Your Majesty—"

"But nothing! Be gone! I intend to receive this lovely creature."

Anna could not resist turning to see him lumbering away like a wounded bear.

"An altogether impossible man," the king muttered.

"I'm afraid he's especially angry with me."

"Whatever for?"

Anna related the earlier encounter that had ended with her comment about his red nose and the consumption of vodka.

King Stanisław laughed again, more vigorously than before, and Anna could not help but join in.

"Now, my dear, what is it that has prompted your little enterprise?"

Anna whispered because the guard was within earshot. "It is rather confidential, Your Majesty."

"Ah, I see. Secret, is it? Well, come with me to my little portrait chamber. There we can talk in front of all the heads of Europe, as well as the Pope, but they'll not repeat a thing, I promise!"

The king stood and stepped down from the dais. He was no taller than Anna. He escorted her then through several other rooms and into a small chamber behind his new Throne Room. This gold chamber was dedicated to his contemporaries. Anna took in the seven monarchs' portraits, noticing that Catherine's hung over the fireplace, as if in the place of honor.

The room had a grand intimacy about it, and Anna was certain that this was where the king took celebrated guests for confidential talks and decision making.

As the king directed her to a chair, she could not help but notice the intricately inlaid floor.

"Thirteen kinds of wood," the king said, noticing her gaze. "And look at the porcelain painting on this tabletop," the king continued with increasing enthusiasm. He directed her to an exquisite table in the middle of the small room. "It depicts an adventure of Telemachus. Do you know him?"

Anna smiled. "Telemachus was the son of Odysseus, was he not?"

"Oh, excellent," the king crooned. "Excellent, my dear!" They sat across from each other. Anna had the impression the king would chat at length about Telemachus if given the opportunity, so she came right to the point. "Your Majesty, do you know of a man, a shoemaker by the name of Jan Kiliński?"

"I can't say that I do. All my shoes are foreign made, you know."

Anna didn't know whether he was serious or whether it was a little joke. She plunged ahead. At length, she set about explaining everything she knew about the rebel plot. Her friends had armed her with a store of information detailing the insurrection. She stressed especially the reaction that would come from Catherine should it be a bloody purge.

"Oh, you needn't tell me of Catherine's temperament. I know it well." His beadlike eyes moved to the portrait over the fireplace, lost focus momentarily. Anna suspected he was thinking about his long-ago liaison with the woman who had schemed to put him on the throne. "But you, Lady Berezowska," the king said, once again in the present, "you are a very courageous woman. Your love of your homeland is quite apparent."

"What can be done?" Anna pressed.

The king slowly shook his head. "It is indeed a volatile situation. If only they would wait for Kościuszko. Oh, what a great man that little general is. It is a sad day when a king can do nothing for his people."

"Nothing? But, Sire, surely something can be done to stifle this—"

"My dear Anna," he interrupted. "May I call you Anna?"

"Of course. You're the King!"

"Oh! And you do make me laugh. My God, I need to laugh these days. Anna, whom did you see when you came into the courtyard?"

"Soldiers."

"Russian soldiers. Why, even the loyalty of my own guard may be in question. The Russians are famous for their bribes. I may be the King of the Commonwealth, but I am a pawn to Russia's empress. Nothing is decided in this room anymore. And you'll see only grim faces leaving the audience chamber. The power is in the Russian embassy."

"If you speak, your citizens will listen."

"Citizens like you and your marvelous little group of patriots will listen, but those who are at the core of the threat—the rebels and the rabble who, mind you, have just concerns—will not. I lost their respect long ago. And perhaps rightly so. I'm caught now in an ever-tightening vise between my people whom I love and Catherine whom I once loved."

"I see." Disappointment coursed like a tide through Anna.

"But please don't think that my love for Poland is any less than yours. Oh, I could tell the Russians downstairs what you've told me, and they would undoubtedly scuttle the insurrection. But it would be at the cost of much Polish blood, and my own self-respect. Sadly, ours is a history of invasions. The Swedes, the Turks, the Tartars, the list goes on; I'm sure you know your history. Do weapons from the past hang upon the wall of your manor house?"

Anna nodded.

"Of course. It is a Pole's right, Anna—indeed, it is his *inheritance* to fight for liberty. I don't know Jan Kiliński, but I respect him." The king managed a sad smile. "Do you understand?"

"Yes," Anna whispered, holding her tears at bay.

The two conversed a while longer, and Anna came away with a great sense of empathy for the man. It was sad to see someone so helpless and weak. He would have been a happier man if Fate had led him somewhere other than to the throne.

"I am deeply touched by you, Anna Berezowska," he told her before she left. "You are as brave as you are beautiful, and I shall not soon forget it."

65

Anna was awakened on the morning of April 17th by a great commotion across the river. She hurried up to Jan Michał's room, where she would have the best view of the capital. Her son had already awakened, it seemed, and been taken down into the kitchen.

Anna looked across to Warsaw. The revolt had come. Cobbler Jan Kiliński and his rebels had not waited for Kościuszko. The streets and outer courtyard of the Royal Castle raged and reverberated in chaos. The sharp reports of gunfire were matched by war cries and screams of pain. Anna could not see the Market Square from the town house, but there came such pulsating cries from that direction that she could only imagine the horror.

"My God," cried the Countess Gronska, coming up to the window, quite breathless from the stairs, "why couldn't they wait for Kościuszko? Why?"

Anna had no answer. Her heart was torn. She was thrilled to see the Polish flag flying from the tower of the city walls. She was proud of the citizenry who had risked everything to join the rebels. And she would be thankful if the effort succeeded in gaining independence. But she knew in her heart that they should have waited.

"This violence is so unnecessary," Countess Gronska said.

The revolt raged all day and into the night. The Gronski shutters facing the river were closed, but the shrill noise could not be shut out. The household could only wait. There were no men to send across the bridge to aid the cause.

Countess Gronska took to her bed. Her health ebbed to its lowest point in weeks. Anna sat with her through the night.

The prolonged contest lasted into the early morning hours, but at last the Prussian and Russian forces in the city—those still alive—started to withdraw. All through the night and into the next day, sounds of boots and horses' hooves could be heard on the bridge as the foreigners left Warsaw.

The countess lay restless, listening.

"Do try to sleep," Anna urged. "We have won."

"Thanks be to God, Anna. But we may rue this day should Catherine send them back."

By the end of the second day, Anna stood at Jan Michał's window again. One of her patriot friends had provided her with the news. Some seven thousand Russian and Prussian forces were gone. The frenzied mob had hanged a good many Polish traitors; however, their king was their king, and the people forgave him for his weakness. Stanisław, in turn, provided food, medical care, and shelter to the rebels.

As the sun set, an orange globe sinking into the Vistula, Anna turned her gaze across to the Royal Castle, high on the embankment. Though the gutters of the city street flowed with foreign and Polish blood, that building, which had withstood greater attacks since its creation by Mazovian dukes in the thirteenth century, stood unscathed.

Somewhere, Anna thought, behind one of those many windows, sat a sad man, a man who had not asked to be king.

* * *

In those first weeks following the revolt, Anna's group met often. Anna made no effort to hide the meetings. If Zofia knew of them, she didn't seem to care; her Russian friends were gone.

When the Countess Gronska was well enough, she would attend the gatherings, often voicing her opinions. "We as members of the *szlachta* must lead the way," she told Anna one day after the others had left. "But where are the others? We are still the only titled members of our group."

"There are other groups, Aunt."

"But you know as well as I that many of the *szlachta*, not to mention the magnates who joined the Confederacy, are holding back, too cautious and afraid that they will lose their peasants who have joined the insurrection with the promise of freedom and their own land."

One day, Anna's estate manager made a surprise visit. Jacob Szraber assured Anna that her estate at Sochaczew was in good order, but informed her, while nervously shifting from one foot to the other, that he was joining a special Jewish regiment under the command of Colonel Berek Joselewicz. "It is," he said proudly, "the first Jewish regiment since biblical times."

What was Anna to say? She gave him her blessing, kissing him on either cheek.

It is a sad irony, she thought, after he had left. Many of the Polish nobles were being too cautious, yet the peaceful Jewish community of Praga and Warsaw had risen to fight for the land that had welcomed them. God bless them!

The Third of May celebration in Warsaw was wildly jubilant. The Constitution still lived. Citizens gathered in the outer courtyard of the castle and in Market Square to celebrate and talk of how next year at this time the provinces of the entire Commonwealth would be free. After all, news had come that insurrections were occurring all over Poland. The city of Wilno had rid itself of the Russians. Danzig and Courland were attempting to do the same.

Zofia hired an open carriage and took Anna and Jan Michał across the river to observe the celebration. It was Jan Michał's second birth day.

"It's not safe to get out of the coach in these swarms of peasants," Zofia said, as they came into the outer courtyard of the Royal Castle. "The view from our seats here will have to suffice."

Anna held Jan Michał on her lap pointing out Zygmunt's Column, just as her father had done for her. She prayed that in centuries to come other parents would do the same for their children. Atop the granite structure stood the bronze figure of the former king, a sword in one hand, a huge cross in the other. The juxtaposition of these two symbols made for a paradoxical proverb Anna was coming to understand: "He that brandishes a sword will maintain the peace."

The carriage slowly made its way down a narrow and crowded street toward Market Square. Jan Michał had never seen so many sights, so many people, so much activity. He began to rock forward and backward on his mother's lap, his brown eyes glittering with delight.

Zofia laughed. "Anna, your son thinks that all this is for his birthday!"

"And so it is, cousin!"

Zofia looked at her strangely at first. Then the black eyes caught Anna's meaning. "The future and all that, you mean?"

Anna smiled.

The carriage managed to enter the square, but then the crush of the crowd brought it to a standstill.

"Maybe we should get out," Anna suggested.

"Not on your life," Zofia said. "We'd be stamped to powder. And, besides, some of these people haven't bathed since Christmas. Where do they all come from?" She feigned a shudder. "Like pigs in a potato patch! It seems like they're waiting for something."

"Kościuszko is going to speak."

"What?" Zofia cried, her face flashing annoyance and suspicion. "You knew this!"

"Yes," Anna said softly.

"And you knew not to tell me. You knew that the last place I want to be is at some political demonstration."

"It's a celebration, Zofia."

"Not my kind. If I thought we could get out of here . . ."

But at that moment a great cheer went up in front of the Town Hall, which sat in the middle of the square. General Tadeusz Kościuszko was being carried up the hall's steps on the shoulders of two men.

The little man in the white, long-tailed coat tried to settle the crowd by nodding in all directions of the square while waving his red four-cornered peasant's cap in the air. He seemed so unassuming, Anna thought. In that, he was like the king.

When he spoke, however, not a hint of weakness could be detected. With great enthusiasm, he addressed the citizens of Warsaw, congratulating them on their great victory. He cautioned them on their excesses, for a tide of hatred had been rising against certain magnates suspected of treason. And as he had done in Kraków, he proclaimed liberty for peasants who had left their serfdom to take up arms.

At this point in the speech, Anna heard Zofia snarl in disapproval. She was not surprised by her cousin's reaction. No noble who had willingly signed the Confederacy of Targowica was likely to be pleased by such news.

Zofia remained quiet once Kościuszko had been hustled away from the masses, and the street began to clear enough for the carriage to make its way back.

Jan Michał had fallen asleep in Anna's arms; it was past his nap time.

Anna's eyes still swept the faces of the Polish soldiers. She had come hoping that Jan Stelnicki would be there, that he still rode with the little general. But he was not present today.

As the carriage moved onto the bridge to Praga, her eyes moved to her extreme right, to the ramshackle tavern, the Queen's Head, where Jan had spent so much time.

No, he wasn't there, just as he had not been in the square. Jan Stelnicki was not in Warsaw, she was certain. Had he been there, he would have stood with the little general. And he would have contacted her.

But where was he?

Zofia sat in the coach, quietly seething. Anna was getting a bit too clever for her own good.

Even though Zofia herself had offered to hire the carriage and spend the afternoon in the capital, she considered herself duped by her cousin. Anna had known all along Kościuszko was going to be there. Somehow, she managed to have her thumb on all the politics. Oh, Anna had wanted to hear the silly little general, that was certain, but she was really there to look for Jan Stelnicki. Zofia would bet every jewel she owned on it. Her cousin's eyes never stopped darting about.

But it was all too clear Stelnicki was not in Warsaw. For all Anna knows, she thought, he is dead. So many have died. It's best that she think him dead.

The carriage arrived at the town house. As soon as the three entered the reception room, Marta came running. "A letter!" she cried.

"So?" Zofia's mood had not improved.

Marta stopped suddenly. "It's from the king!" Her face glowed with wonder.

"Give it here," Zofia demanded.

"Oh, Mademoiselle Zofia," the woman cried softly, "the letter is for Lady Anna."

Zofia felt her stomach tighten. "What?"

It was true! Marta handed the letter over to Anna.

Anna seemed as surprised as anyone.

"Well, open it up!" Zofia sighed. "That will be all, Marta."

Anna's fingers fumbled with the seal. At last, she pulled the letter open. She read the dozen or more words, looked up at Zofia, then read them again.

"Well, what is it, Anna, for pity's sake? It looks like an invitation."

"It is. To a royal reception!"

Zofia snatched the invitation away from Anna, looking immediately to the addressee. She was certain there was some mistake. It was an invitation no doubt meant for *her*.

But, no. The invitation was addressed to "Countess Anna Maria Berezowska, Patriot."

"But your name is included inside the invitation, Zofia."

That was some consolation, Zofia thought, more confused than ever.

"And your mother is invited also."

"What?" Zofia's eyes took in the whole invitation then. It was true: the three of them were invited to the Royal Castle. "Perhaps it's merely a mistake by the king's secretary. In the addressing, your name was somehow substituted for mine." Zofia was becoming confident she had struck the answer to the little mystery. "After all," she said, "King Stanisław doesn't know *you*."

Zofia could not help but notice Anna's green eyes widen slightly. "Or *does* he? Anna?"

Anna's face was flushing apple red.

"Anna!"

Zofia found the story that now spilled out of her cousin incredible. Was it possible? Anna had impersonated her and managed to get in to see the king. What nerve she had! How did she dare? And when Zofia started to believe it, she became incensed to think her name was used for such a stunt.

Yet, as the story went on, and the details unfolded, Zofia's anger dissipated. She knew the fat deputy and laughed to herself to think her cousin had beaten him at his own game. And, after all, if Anna's story were accurate, the king had not been put off by her trickery. What anger Zofia retained by the time Anna concluded her account she would later take out on Babette for aiding Anna in her subterfuge. "I must admit," Zofia said, "I've underestimated your enterprise, Anna."

Anna smiled, as if she knew Zofia would be impressed.

Instead, Anna's smug reaction irked Zofia. "So you favorably impressed the king?"

"Oh, yes, I'm certain of it."

"Well, that's the answer, then."

"The answer to what?"

"The invitation! The old king was caught by your charms. Congratulations! You've made a conquest. And this is no romp in the field; you've reached for the summit of the highest mountain."

"What do you mean?"

"I mean," Zofia said, her tone deepening to a sultry effect, "that at the royal reception, the King of Poland will undoubtedly ask you for an assignation."

Zofia watched with amusement as Anna blinked at the word.

"An assignation?"

"Yes, darling," Zofia replied with mock impatience, "an appointment to meet. Oh, the whole thing reminds me of that story about Zeus and some girl Cupid had smitten him with. Zeus transformed himself into a bull in order to carry her off. What was *her* name?"

"Europa. And I'm not about to be carried off by some bull."

"No, darling, *your* meeting is to take place in plain sight. How clever of Stanisław."

"You think that the king . . ."

"Of course, you goose! Why, it's a great compliment. I should be jealous, but I've had my own tryst with Stanisław. I suppose he implied as much. Ah, I can see by your reaction that he did. Well, this is a great opportunity for you, dearest. After all, Europa gave Zeus great sons and achieved no little glory for herself. You may firmly establish yourself at court. Oh, he may not be an ardent lover, not like the bull that Zeus became, but I shouldn't give everything away. Why, Ania, you look a bit pale."

That night, Zofia sat at her vanity removing her makeup, but it was the reflection of Anna's stricken face that the mirror returned. She could not help but laugh aloud. In a few moments, though, with the makeup removed, it was her own serious face that stared back at her. What *did* the king see in Anna?

Anna had thought of not attending the royal reception, of pleading some illness, but she knew Zofia would see through such a guise. She thought of telling Aunt Stella what the king's intent might be in hopes that her aunt would empathize with her—and provide advice. Yet, she couldn't bring herself to speak of it. And there was always the chance that Zofia was wrong; perhaps the king was not seeking an assignation. Then again, Anna knew only too well that her cousin was well versed in court intrigue and might very well be correct in her assumption.

By the night before the event, Anna lay in bed, sleepless, convinced that King Stanisław had singled her out as his newest mistress.

Anna's plan was to go to the supper as plainly made up and attired as possible. She would do all she could to discourage any fervor on his part.

On the day of the supper, however, Zofia took over all aspects of the preparations, behaving like an overly fastidious mother orchestrating her daughter's initial bow into court society. This seemed a momentous event for Zofia. For Anna it became a descent into the unknown, as in her worst nightmares. When she objected to some detail of her dress, she was outnumbered, for even Aunt Stella sided with her daughter, saying she probably knew best in the matter of these royal functions.

And so, Anna was prepared like a prize fish for the master's plate. Zofia and the French maids stuffed her into a white silk gown that Zofia had ordered for her on short notice. The bodice, the puffy sleeves, and the trim at the hem were of a silver material that shimmered magnificently. It would have made a lovely wedding dress, Anna thought, suddenly realizing that Zofia, in her perverseness, may have meant it as such. Was she being offered to the king? Her fear intensified.

Clarice coerced Anna's reluctant feet into buckled silver slippers while Babette attached to her head a great white wig fitted out with crystal pins and silver bows. It was even more elaborate than the one she had worn on her masquerade to the Royal Castle.

Anna watched her reflection as Zofia doused her in diamonds, clasping about her neck a two-tiered necklace that drew the eye in the direction of her breasts.

"Why, Anna," Zofia said, "you are more bosomy than one might ever have expected. Oh, don't blush, for pity's sake. While love enters a woman through her ears, it enters a man through his eyes!" She then fastened a three-stranded bracelet to Anna's right wrist and teardrop earrings to her ears.

Babette took over with makeup while Zofia went off to get herself ready. Although at Zofia's orders Babette did persist in making her wear on her cheek a little beauty patch in the shape of Cupid, Anna refused to allow her face to be made up as flamboyantly as it had been when she impersonated her cousin. The red of her lips, the rouge on her cheeks, the whiteness of her face were more subtle now.

Fully dressed and made up, Anna stood alone facing the mirror, transfixed by her own reflection. She drew in her breath. Yes, one *would* think it was her wedding day, she mused. Despite her fears for what the day held in store, she knew she was beautiful. She had to admit it, marveling at her reflection.

"Anna!" Zofia called from below. "The carriage is ready. Hurry down. Mother and I are waiting. It's nearly two o'clock!"

"Just a moment!" Anna called back, continuing to study herself. There was something not to her liking. Tearing off the beauty mark, she dashed a little powder in its place. Satisfied then, she picked up the silver-lined white silk wrap and hastened downstairs.

"What kept you?" Zofia asked.

"Oh, I'm sorry to have kept you waiting, but the little cupid just would not adhere."

"Where is it?"

"I shall have to do without it." Anna knew very well it was too late now to remedy the situation. They were due at the Royal Castle in less than half an hour.

"Anna, you are lovely," Aunt Stella whispered.

"She is a bird about to try her wings," Zofia told her mother.

Anna's aunt was dressed beautifully herself in a beaded gown of dark blue. A blue mantilla lay over her own hair, framing her face. Anna was taken aback slightly to see the faintest hints of color on her lips and in her cheeks. Observing the interest her aunt had taken in the occasion, she felt a twinge of guilt when she remembered that her fears for the evening had made her half-hope that her aunt wouldn't feel quite well enough to attend. But this was one of her good days, and whatever its outcome Anna was glad for it.

In the carriage, Anna's gown of silk was so full she had to sit alone on one side, facing her aunt and cousin.

"It has been many years since I have been to the Royal Castle," the countess said, once they were under way. "I am glad to have the chance to see it once before . . ." Her voice trailed off, and before long her lips were moving in silent prayer.

Anna wondered how her aunt would react to finding out that the king was about to ask for an assignation with her niece? Of course, she would not condone it, even if it put the whole household in good stead with the king and his court. Or would she?

Anna watched Zofia now, radiant in her green-and-white gown, emerald necklace and earrings. She was calm; she seemed to gloat, like some sly serpent coiled comfortably on a warm rock. Anna suspected that Zofia saw this as the beginning of a new life for her cousin, the kind of life *she* liked, the kind that would preclude any room for Jan Stelnicki.

As the wheels rumbled over the wooden planks of the bridge, their repetitive clacking seemed to fall into syncopation with Anna's thoughts: *Where is my love? Where is my love? Where is my love?*

The carriage moved off the bridge, heading for the city gates. Not even he could save her now, Anna brooded. If she were to consent to an assignation, her life would be reduced to nothing. She would lose her own self-esteem and Jan's love. And what if she denied the king? What then? Of what was a king's injured pride capable? The very security of everyone in the Gronski household might be imperiled.

Anna was sick with trepidation by the time she stepped out of the carriage into the Great Courtyard of the Royal Castle.

The Russian soldiers were gone. There was that to be thankful for, at least. The three women were helped to alight from the carriage and were escorted into the castle wing on the Vistula side. Servants took their wraps and a functionary directed them up the circular marble stairs. There they found themselves in the Antechamber to the Great Assembly Hall. The supper would take place in the Assembly Hall, but there was first to be a ceremony in the Throne Room, so the three followed other guests through the Marble Room, where there hung portraits of more than twenty past Polish kings. They entered the National Hall now, a kind of Pantheon of Polish history, its huge canvasses displaying scenes from the interconnected past of Poland and Lithuania. A line taken from the *Aeneid* praising outstanding citizens ran along the top of the walls. Anna found it striking that all of these motifs and decorations at the Royal Castle had come in recent years from King Stanisław himself. They reflected such a depth of culture in the man, and yet he could be so ineffectual in governing.

The Throne Room was actually smaller than the National Hall, so the guests here, some two hundred, had to stand while waiting for the king's entrance. The three women stood near the rear, where the windows faced the Vistula. "Look!" the Countess Gronska whispered. "Why, if this room were cleared, the king could see our town house from his throne."

"Cleared or not," Zofia sang, "I think Stanisław may have his eyes on it just the same."

Anna took her meaning, but her aunt did not.

More people were crushing into the room. Anna was becoming overwhelmed by the lack of space and the heavy scents of powder and perfume. She was soon dizzy with claustrophobia.

Before she could voice a complaint and try to effect an exit, however, the French princess Charlotte Sic sidled over to them. She was as overly dressed, made-up, and perfumed as Anna remembered.

Zofia gave her a light embrace. "You do remember my cousin Anna, Charlotte?"

"*Oui.* Oh, my dear!" she squealed. "Is this the same cousin? From the country? Oh, you will forgive me, about that time you were on the stairs during Zofia's party? I don't know what came over me. It was unforgivable, but you will forgive me, won't you?"

"Yes, of course."

"How charming of you. And you are breathtaking today. The king's eyes are not so bad—"

"Charlotte," Zofia interrupted, with a stilted cordiality, "I wish you to meet my mother." Zofia took Charlotte by the arm to turn her in the direction of Countess Gronska, and when Anna saw the French princess wince in pain, she knew that Zofia had pinched her to shut her up.

It was painfully clear to Anna that Zofia had discussed the matter of the assignation with her friend. Who else knew about it? Anna's anxiety increased.

Anna looked at her aunt, who was staring wide-eyed and dumb at the bizarre plump creature before her, a jeweler's shop on legs.

When Zofia and Charlotte fell into a quiet conversation in French, Aunt Stella leaned over to Anna. "If this is typical of a French princess," she whispered, "I have no mercy for the fate of their aristocracy."

Anna had to put her fan to her face and turn to the window in order to hide her amusement.

Her light-hearted feeling did not last, for everyone started to bow and curtsy—there was no room to kneel—at the entrance of King Stanisław.

He swept through the entrance near to Anna. She kept her head low as he passed by so as not to draw his attention.

"My good and loyal subjects," he began, once he was on the dais, "it is my happy duty today to publicly acknowledge some of our most deserving men who have been as responsible as anyone in seeing that the white eagle continues to fly. These are men who . . ."

His dry voice droned on while he slowly moved through the ceremony. The room was so crowded and airless that an hour passed with the heaviness of three. Anna thought that the formalities would drag on forever, but because she dreaded what might come later, she almost wished that they would. She looked at Zofia, so smugly expectant. Did she think Anna's prestige at court would somehow benefit *her*?

When would the king speak to her? Anna wondered. Would he do so privately? What would he say? And if Zofia were right, if he did wish an assignation, what would *she* say? The Countess Gronska took hold of Anna's arm, jolting her from her thoughts. "Anna," she whispered, "the king spoke your name. He asked if you are present."

Anna's heart seemed to stop, though blood rushed to her head. The room was perfectly still. From their place at the foot of the chamber, Anna could see his gentle, birdlike eyes moving through the crowd of elegant ladies and gentlemen, pausing but briefly now and again, and moving on.

"Speak up!" Zofia hissed. "He's looking for *you*."

Anna could not speak. She held her breath until the king's gaze fell on her and when it did, she froze in terror. People turned to stare at her. A few dared to whisper.

Anna wished to be anywhere but there in that room, the subject of everyone's attention. She thought of dashing for the door.

"There is a woman here today," the king proclaimed, his eyes fastened on Anna, "who has touched my heart. She is a woman who is as great a Polish patriot as any of our men."

The chamber was as a tomb; there wasn't a movement or rustle of silk.

King Stanisław's hand beckoned to her, as it had done not so many days before.

Anna's feet would not move. He nodded, motioning again. She heard the whispers of her aunt and the princess at her ears, urging her on.

Swallowing hard, she picked up her skirts and moved slowly, as through a dream, toward the throne with the little man standing there, a hundred carved eagles flying against the red velvet backing of the canopy.

The hushed nobles cleared an aisle for her, as they had done for the king. Though Anna couldn't fasten her gaze on any one thing, she sensed the eyes of everyone on her. She trembled as she moved forward, yet for every step she took, the room seemed to expand and take the king that much farther away from her.

At last, she stood before the dais and knelt, her gown spreading about her like a white flower.

Anna stared at the floor. The king's voice resonated loud and strong now, almost youthful. "Although it was through Catherine and the Polish *Sejm* which elected me, it was also through Almighty God that I became King of Poland. And it is through Almighty God, ultimate Bestower of all things, and through Russia's Catherine that I create for you, Anna Maria Berezowska, Countess of Sochaczew, the title of Princess."

If Anna herself did not gasp, she heard others around her do so.

Suddenly, she felt the king's cold sword touch one bare shoulder, then the other.

"Princess Anna Maria Berezowska of Sochaczew," the king said now, "the title of Princess is yours for as long as you may live and will pass to your descendants on into eternity. . . . You may rise now."

The ceremonies were over and people began moving toward the Great Assembly Hall, where the supper would commence.

The king stepped down from the dais and helped Anna to stand. "You see, child, I told you I would not soon forget your deed."

Anna could only smile her appreciation.

"Go now," the king urged. "I'm sure your family is eager to congratulate you."

Too stunned to speak, Anna bowed and fell into the flow of the crowd. For more than a century, the Republic's *Sejm* had denied Polish kings the right to confer titles, so for King Stanisław to do so, he had to call upon the auspices of a foreign power such as Russia. That it was Catherine was no little irony. Yet it seemed of little consequence to those who congratulated her and wished her well as she slowly wended her way through the dense throng, smiling and nodding. She was dazed and happy. The king's interest in her had been a fatherly one. There would be no assignation!

Aunt Stella was crying as Anna approached her. "Oh, Ania, if only your parents had lived to see this day. I thank God that *I* have!"

Anna hugged her, holding her trembling, frail form.

"My dear, my dear!" Charlotte Sic blurted. "We are both princesses! Who would have thought?"

Anna looked to Zofia, whose smile seemed oddly enigmatic.

"Though if I were to place a monetary value on a title, dear," Charlotte chattered on, "I should have to say yours would have more purchasing power than mine." Her double chin trembled as she laughed. "After all, if I were to return to Paris, it's likely my head would be used as a doorstop!"

"Congratulations, Anna," Zofia said at last. Turning abruptly, she fell into the line of people moving toward the Great Assembly Hall.

Anna stared after her. "Isn't she happy for me?"

"Hmmm," Charlotte hummed, placing her hand on Anna's arm in a confidential gesture. "Zofia had expectations for you, Anna, and I think you may have *outdone* them. Therein lies the problem. Ah, Zofia is lovely tonight, isn't she? The green of the dress, the green of the emeralds, so appropriate. Excuse me, my dear," she said, removing her hand and moving away, "I'll go see what I can do to settle the ruffled feathers."

"Doorstop, indeed," mumbled Countess Gronska as she watched the princess disappear into the crush. "At least there is some *purpose* to a doorstop!"

At the supper table, Zofia exhibited a restrained affability but, uncharacteristically, didn't take an active role in the conversation. She left the Royal Castle early, accompanying Charlotte Sic in her carriage.

"It's been like a fairy tale, Anna," the countess said as they made ready to leave.

Anna could not disagree. The whole event had seemed dreamlike.

In the carriage, she studied the countess' serene expression, suspecting that her aunt was relishing the notion that her niece had become one of the most eligible women in Poland, one who might even marry a magnate. Her status as a princess would place her sons within the sphere of the elected monarchy. Jan Michał, she suddenly realized, might some day be elected king.

But did her aunt think that she would be able to forget Jan Stelnicki? She smiled to herself at *that* notion.

They hadn't even alighted from the carriage when they heard noise and music coming from the Gronski town house. Outside, a retinue of carriages, coachmen, and footmen was assembled.

"I'm afraid that Zofia is entertaining, Aunt Stella."

"Sweet Jesus," the countess cried, "there is no need to placate the Russians now. They're dead or exiled. And yet she insists on these revelries."

Anna thought that Zofia would hold her parties no matter what power controlled Poland, but she would not say as much to the countess.

They entered through the rear of the house and used the servants' stairs to reach their rooms unnoticed. Anna kissed her aunt good night. The woman's mood had soured.

An hour later, a knock came at Anna's door.

It was Clarice. "Lady Zofia wishes you to come downstairs, Madame."

"Tell my cousin that I have already retired, Clarice."

"Very well," the servant said, giving a curtsy, something she didn't always do. "Oh, Madame, I overheard the news. Congratulations!"

"Thank you, Clarice."

A few minutes later, Clarice reappeared. "I'm very sorry, Madame, but Lady Zofia says that if you don't come down, she'll bring all of her guests up to you. Please allow me to prepare you to greet them."

Anna couldn't believe it, but she would not chance having those people come upstairs. Clarice helped her put her gown on again, and once her face and wig were made presentable, she went downstairs.

She hurried to the reception room where many of the party were assembled. She stood in the doorway. No one noticed her at first.

Some thirty guests, mostly Poles, were drinking, talking, and laughing. Anna could see into the adjoining music room where couples were dancing to the Bulgarian rhythms of hired musicians. None of these people had been to the royal supper. This was Zofia's court, Anna thought. These were her subjects.

Anna's attention was drawn then to the corner of the reception room, where a clothespress stood. Standing upon it was Zofia, who seemed to be making a toast to someone.

Zofia's glazed eyes noticed Anna. "Ah, the guest of honor!" she cried drunkenly. "Come, toast my cousin!" Holding her wineglass high in the air, she called out even louder: "Come toast Princess Anna Maria Berezowska! To the Princess!"

Those in the reception room were already quiet; others streamed out of the music room. Most raised their glasses toward Anna. "To the Princess!" they cried in a clumsy chorus.

Almost immediately a handsome man appeared before Anna, and taking her hand, kissed it. "But the Princess does not have a drink," he said, handing her a glass.

Anna accepted it, attempting to smile even though she was aware of a wetness he had left on the back of her hand. She sensed the handsome face was merely a mask for the devil himself. A chill ran through her.

Anna studied the glass of dark liquid, wondering if it were whiskey.

She was certain Charlotte Sic was around somewhere and thought it might be a mean joke of hers to have her choke on whiskey again, as she had done that day long ago at the Royal Castle. She sipped at it and found it had a sweet taste.

"I am Albin Brazow, Princess," he declared, pressing himself closer. His breath was sour.

Anna nodded uncertainly, taking a step back while he turned to pick up another glass from the table. He was extremely handsome, extremely vain, and extremely drunk.

He called out a second toast: "To the beautiful Princess!"

Nearly everyone joined in. Except Zofia. "Albin Brazow!" she sang out now. "You and your ruby ring will see me to my room tonight, but only one will leave it!"

Everyone laughed.

Albin bowed dramatically in Zofia's direction. "Which of your desires is the greater, my lady?" he called. "Your desire for jewels, or for men?"

"That will depend on the caliber of the jewel and the caliber of the man!" She laughed at her own comedy, while motioning Albin over to help her down. "But jewels tend to last longer, don't you think?" She fell now into his open arms and they both toppled giggling and wrestling to the floor.

Setting down her glass, Anna used the commotion to make an exit.

Zofia's voice rang out before Anna could make it to the stairs. "Why do you leave, Princess Anna?" she called.

Anna hurried along, but was only part way up to the first landing when Zofia came from behind and stood at the bottom of the stairs.

"Anna!"

Anna turned around to face Zofia. Albin stood just behind her cousin.

"Why do you leave?" Zofia's eyes were wild. "Albin is interested in you."

"I'm tired and I'm going to bed."

"Ah, but if Albin were Stelnicki, you would not run so fast! Don't delude yourself. If Stelnicki were here, he would not choose you, Princess or not!"

Anna could only stare at her cousin.

"Don't retire so early, Princess," Albin pleaded.

"Albin is better than any man here tonight, Anna." Zofia was shouting now. "If Stelnicki is even alive, you're a fool to think a man like that would wish to spend the rest of his nights with you!"

Anna turned and hurried up the stairs to her room. No one followed her.

66

What should have been one of the most memorable days of Anna's life had been tarnished. Zofia never apologized, avoiding her cousin for a full week. Anna struggled to shake off her bitterness, and as the days passed, it was only the growing political and military concerns that allowed the incident to fade into the background.

In her wrath against Poland's insurrection, Catherine enlisted the aid of both Prussia and Austria, no doubt promising them part of the Polish map, as she had done twice previously. Anna wondered how long the Commonwealth could hold out against three militaristic empires. She wondered, too, how King Stanisław could keep Catherine's portrait in its place of honor in that little gold chamber.

The Prussians wasted no time in responding to the empress's bribe. Kościuszko had moved out to meet the Prussian army led by King William himself, who had once promised to defend Poland's independence and whose picture also hung in that gold room. The Polish forces had sufficient cannon and fields of peasants wielding scythes, but too few rifles; no Polish rifle manufacturer could meet the demand. The Kościuszko forces stood a mere thirteen thousand to the forty thousand well-armed Prussians. They were overrun and forced to retreat on the sixth of May at Szczekociny. Worse yet, on the fifteenth of June the Prussians went on to take Kraków.

When the news of the setbacks reached Warsaw, certain Poles instigated a pogrom against those suspected of being Russian sympathizers, summarily executing a number of them. Anna heard that Doctor

Kurowski was one of those hanged in the Market Square. Though Anna held no affection for the man, she knew that he had probably saved Jan Michał's life, and so said a prayer for the repose of his soul. The wrongs of war know no sides.

Kościuszko returned to Warsaw and immediately punished those who had initiated the pogrom.

In July, a combined force of Russian and Prussian troops moved against Warsaw. The Kościuszko forces dug in outside of Warsaw and applied artillery and earthworks in such a way that they managed to thwart the greater enemy armies.

At noon one day, Anna sat in Jan Michał's attic room, absently watching him amuse himself with a small wooden soldier. Her mind was on the expected siege of the capital. She would take and use a gun herself to protect the Commonwealth for her loved ones, but she dared to think of how much better the world would be if every mother, Polish or foreign, saw to the destruction of every gun and cannon.

Carrying a tray, Lutisha climbed up the narrow stairway and placed a cup of coffee before Anna, then proceeded to feed Jan Michał his lunch.

Anna drank. "What kind of coffee is this, Lutisha? It has an under-taste."

"Coffee has become scarce, Madame. We have added a bit of chicory to it."

"I can taste the chicory," Anna said, sipping at it again, "but it still seems a bit strange." She drank it down, however, hoping she could dispel the listlessness she felt.

What if the city is taken, she worried. Would the lives of citizens be in danger?

Anna soon realized that she couldn't focus her mind to any one thought. A lethargy settled over her, and she lay back against the settee. She could no longer lift her limbs. Her eyelids became weighted, too, but she refused to close them, certain that Lutisha had given her a poison. This must be what the River Lethe in the underworld is like, she thought, the river of forgetfulness.

Against her will, her eyes closed. Anna felt her legs being lifted onto the settee, then whispers nearby indicated someone else had come up to the attic. Who was it? Zofia? Aunt Stella? She wanted to call out, to ask why this was being done to her, but her throat had closed upon the words.

When Anna heard her son's name, she managed to force open her eyes. Jan Michał's face came slowly into half-focus. His face was being lowered to hers. She felt his lips on her cheek. She wanted to reach up for him, but her arms would not respond. Her eyes closed involuntarily.

Soon she heard the receding sound of feet moving down the stairs. She could hear her little son saying, "Out? Out?"

Much later Anna awoke to find the countess sitting next to her.

"You must forgive me, Anna," her aunt whispered. "There was no other way. We placed a harmless drug in your coffee so that Jan Michał could be taken without delay and without a struggle."

"Taken?" Anna managed to say.

"Listen to me, Ania. Warsaw has become a very dangerous place. Perhaps death is approaching for all of us. Who can say?"

"But where?"

"Walek returned. He is taking all of his family to your estate at Sochaczew. All except for Lutisha, who has insisted on remaining with us. Jan Michał's presence among a band of peasants will not be questioned. The presence of all of us would only encumber them. Things are fast becoming unsafe, and even though, God forgive her, Zofia has affixed our names to the Confederacy . . . well, one never knows with the Russians. And we must face the fact that my traveling days are over."

"Aunt Stella, why didn't you just tell me of this plan?"

The countess sighed, fixing her sad, brown eyes on Anna. "Because you had vowed never to be parted from your son. Lutisha and I both heard you."

Anna couldn't respond. She knew her aunt was right.

"You're not to worry, Anna Maria. I've given them money which I'm certain they'll use wisely."

"Jan Michał," Anna whispered. She felt her lower lip trembling and hot tears beading in her eyes.

Countess Gronska took her hand. "You must be strong, Ania. You must think of the well-being and future of your son. If Poland somehow survives this onslaught, Jan Michał, as one of its princes, might one day be elected king."

The countess kissed Anna and left.

Anna lay for a long time staring at the ceiling. They had done the right thing, she told herself. She hoped she would have made the same decision. As it was, it was done. Jan Michał was gone.

Countess Gronska took to her bed. If Zofia did not, Anna realized just how ill she was.

Warsaw was spared for the moment. The tide turned when a brave band of Polish peasants, led by a patriot named Minewsky, captured a large Prussian convoy with artillery and supplies enough for an extended campaign as it ascended the River Vistula. Without this support, Prussia's Frederick William lost thousands of men and withdrew after two months, retreating to Poznań. The immediate threat to the capital went with him. For every Polish victory, though, news came of some defeat.

When good news came, the countess seemed to rally a little, but not for long. Anna started to sleep in her aunt's room, tending to her every need.

Wilno fell to the Russians in mid-August. A week later, a Polish force led by General Dąbrowski set out for Wielkopolska to support a Polish uprising; buoyed by his success in this venture, Dąbrowski pushed on into Prussia.

And so it went. Hope faded, however, when the Austrians joined Russia and Prussia in taking apart Poland, like children pulling at the petals of a flower.

Anna wished she had been born a man. How she would have liked to take her ancestors' armor and weapons from the wall at Sochaczew and set out against the Commonwealth's aggressors! She remembered Zofia sarcastically asking if she thought she were Joan of Arc. How she wished she had such a calling.

But, like every citizen of Warsaw, she could only pray when word came that Catherine had sent her most bloodthirsty leader, General Suvorov, to attack Poland from the southeast. Kościuszko immediately moved against the Russians, engaging them at Maciejowice.

And then came worst possible news: when the Russians managed to separate Kościuszko from his supporting column, he was badly wounded and captured.

What was to become of Poland without the little general? Was Jan with him? Anna wondered. Was her beloved in the hands of the Russians?

With no one to fend him off, Suvorov turned now, like a starving tiger, and moved against Warsaw. Coming from the southeast, he would reach Praga first before crossing to Warsaw. Anna, her tiny group of patriots, and every citizen of the capital waited for the full brunt of Catherine's anger. Stanisław's former lover had sworn to see the city reduced to flame and ash. No one doubted her resolve. Patriot reinforcements gathered in the city, but they were a motley coalescence of survivors from campaigns in all the provinces. Anna knew in her heart that these brave men, taking a stand as their forefathers had done so many times before, were as men sculpted out of sand, as compared to the high tide of men and cannon that were flowing swiftly toward the city.

67

On the first of November, All Saints Day, Anna realized that just as the Russians were moving toward Warsaw, so too was death coming for the Countess Stella. Her eyes were like saucers in her drawn and ashen face, her body frail and shrunken.

Anna was just leaving her aunt's room to go down to the kitchen. Lutisha had not yet brought the morning meal, and Anna wondered what was keeping her.

It was a white-faced Zofia she met, hurrying up the stairs toward her. "Anna," she cried, "we must leave this house immediately. Even now Suvorov is camped before the glacis of Praga. We must cross the river. The capital will be safer."

Anna's heart leapt in fear. The Russian general's reputation for the cruelest inhumanity was well known. No citizen, noble nor commoner, would be safe. "The capital? But where? Where in the capital?"

"To Lord Potecki's town house. Before Paweł left on his silly patriotic quest, he gave his staff instructions that his house was at my disposal. I've already sent Lutisha there with many of our valuables. There are only the three of us remaining, and we mustn't tarry!"

The three of us, Anna thought, remembering the countess. "But, Zofia . . ."

"What? What is it?"

"Your mother . . . she will not last the trip."

"Is she so ill?"

"Zofia, she's dying."

Zofia's almond-shaped eyes grew round, the pupils darker. "Oh, Anna, this is terrible! Unless we flee, we'll all die. These wooden houses will ignite like tinderboxes."

"The countess can't be moved," Anna said, her voice and resolve thickening. "You aren't suggesting that we abandon her?"

"No, of course not. Do you think she will rebound? Perhaps tomorrow we can move her."

Anna offered no such hope.

The two went in to see the countess, who lay motionless under the quilt. They stood on either side of the large bed. The rise and fall of the countess' breast came with such long moments between that Anna sometimes thought she had already succumbed.

Zofia said nothing. Her face was bereft of emotion as she stared at her mother. In time, she reached her hand toward her mother's, which lay palm up at her side, but Zofia withdrew hers before establishing contact.

During the night Anna and Zofia took turns at the countess' bedside. Toward dawn, occasional blasts could be heard in the distance.

It was during Anna's vigil that the countess awoke. "Anna? Is that you?"

"Yes, Aunt Stella, I'm here."

Her voice was a rattling whisper punctuated with pauses. "What is . . . that noise?"

Anna paused for a moment while she lighted a candle. She knew it would do no good to lie. Her aunt was too shrewd. "It's the sound of cannon," she said, sitting again in the chair at the side of the bed.

"The . . . Russians?"

"Yes, Aunt."

"Outside Praga?"

"Yes, Aunt."

"Dear God," she sighed. "It's so sad . . . to be defeated, Anna. At least I'll not live . . . to see Poland bow . . . to the likes of Catherine."

"You'll get well, Aunt Stella. You must! You shouldn't say such things."

"No, Anna, I'm too old . . . and set in my ways for such changes . . . I couldn't live when there is no Poland. . . . I wouldn't want to. And my life has been lived. But you are young . . . you have resiliency and strength, like Poland herself."

"Aunt Stella, you mustn't tire yourself. You must rest."

"Listen to me, Ania. Marry Stelnicki if you love him. If you both somehow survive this cataclysm . . . let nothing stand in your way. . . . Nothing!"

"Lie back now, Aunt, and sleep."

"Anna," the countess persisted, her voice becoming more urgent while she tried to lift herself. "Make certain that your children and your children's children keep our Polish ways. . . . Make them proud of our heritage and Poland will not die." She attempted now a brave smile. "We will outwit that Russian she-wolf, after all."

Anna returned the smile and squeezed the countess' hand. "Poland will not die, Aunt Stella. It will never die. You told me so yourself. Not even if Russia were to hold it for a hundred years."

The countess seemed satisfied, falling back into her pillows and a light sleep.

By morning Countess Gronska could neither move of her own power nor draw breath to speak.

Zofia and Anna were both present when she stirred slightly and began tapping her finger on the crucifix of her rosary.

"What is it, Aunt Stella? What do you wish?"

"She wants a priest," Zofia said. "Isn't that it, Mother? You wish to have a priest?"

The countess did not respond.

"Aunt," Anna whispered, bending over the small form in the bed, "close your eyes twice if a priest is what you wish."

Anna and Zofia stared in silence. Only the sound of distant cannon could be heard. Anna reached for her aunt's hand.

The wide brown eyes stared vacantly, and Anna thought she hadn't understood, that her mind had already been taken.

But then the delicately wrinkled flesh that were her eyelids quivered, widened and closed, once, then twice.

"I sent for a priest during the night, Mother," Zofia said, taking the countess' other hand. "He came while you slept and gave you the last rites. Do you understand?"

Tears were beading in her eyes, tears of thanksgiving, and the two slow, painful winks released them. The countess looked to her daughter, then to Anna. Peace settled over her. Her body seemed to slacken. Anna thought she looked angelic.

Just then the frail body tightened and convulsed as a paroxysm caused the countess' once-lovely eyes to nearly burst from their sockets.

She fell back now and lay still, dead, the brown eyes still staring.

A long minute passed in silence.

" 'The golden bowl is broken,' " Zofia said at last, reaching up to close her mother's eyes.

Anna was stunned to hear Zofia allude to the Bible.

" 'Then shall the dust return to the earth as it was,' " Zofia continued, " 'and the spirit shall return unto God who gave it.' " Heavy tears glistened in the black eyes. "She was a good woman, Anna. She deserved better than Walter and me."

"It was a beautiful death, Zofia. If there is beauty in death. She was so happy to die in the state of grace. Why, I must have slept so soundly I didn't hear the priest's coming or going."

"There was no priest, Anna."

"What?"

"There was no priest. Oh, I sent for one, but there wasn't one to be found in all of Warsaw. They're with our wounded and dying men—or fighting and dying themselves."

"But Zofia . . ."

"You're shocked that I could lie to her? It was a happy death. That lie made it so. And, besides, you know as well as I that Mother was in the state of grace. It is God's will and a blessing that she die now."

"It was her will, as well," Anna said. "She didn't wish to live to see the Russians take Poland."

Anna's statement and a loud volley of cannon fire seemed to jar Zofia onto another line of thought. "But *we* must, cousin," she urged. "We must live. And you must move quickly if you are to survive. By the sound of it, they may have already entered Praga. Go get ready immediately, Anna. Wear only the simplest dress and no petticoats to encumber you."

"But your mother, Zofia, she must be buried."

"There's no time!"

"I'll not leave her." Anna took a quilt, unfolded it, and placed it on the bed parallel to the body.

"Anna, what are you doing?"

"I'm taking her body downstairs. You yourself said these houses would go up like tinderboxes. And there's liable to be Russians and looters."

"Anna, we must leave," Zofia pleaded. "This is no Greek drama about burial rites and you are no Antigone. Go upstairs to the attic window and look out over Praga to the east. Death is approaching for us. My mother would not wish you to risk your life—"

"You may go, Zofia," Anna said sharply as she struggled to tuck the quilt under her aunt's body. "But I will not!" Their eyes clashed now in a contest of wills.

"Sweet Jesus," Zofia said at last, mimicking an expression of her mother's. "You are stubborn. It's the Gronska coming out in you. Very well, we'll stay long enough to store her body in the cellar so she can be buried later. Will that suit you?"

"Yes."

"Good. But just remember how badly it ended for Antigone. Let's just get this done." Zofia pulled her mother's body to her while Anna tucked in the quilt.

It was as they rolled the body back that the pillows were dislodged and something else, something foreign and heavy, fell from the bed to the floor with a metallic clatter.

Anna could only stare at what she saw there on her side of the bed.

"What was that?" Zofia came around to Anna's side before her cousin could reply.

They both stared blankly at the pistol that lay there.

"I guess it shouldn't surprise us," Anna said. "She wasn't about to yield peacefully to the Russians."

"Even in death," Zofia laughed, "Mother is full of surprises. Pick it up, Anna, and put it in your skirts. We may need it in the carriage."

"But I—"

"Just do it, damn it!"

Anna obeyed.

The two cousins then lifted the body from the bed. Zofia led the way, out into the hall and down the stairs. Working together, they quickly made their descent to the first floor, then to the cellar, where they laid down their burden.

"You go on up and change as I told you. Hurry, now."

"What are you going to do?" Anna asked.

"I'm going to cover her in another blanket or two and drench the body in water. If the house does burn, she will be spared for burial."

"I want to say a prayer."

"Antigone to the last!" Zofia scoffed. "There's no time for that now. Go and change quickly. When I'm finished here, I'll see to the carriage. Go!"

Anna climbed the steep stairs that led to the kitchen. She quickly ran through the swinging door and into the hallway. She was on the stairway and nearly to the second floor when she heard the front door open.

Some instinct stopped her at once, her heart catching in fear. She turned around to see the door swinging wide and the boots and trousers of a soldier in the door frame. The trousers were those of one who wore a red uniform, a Russian uniform.

Anna felt a great panic rise within her. Zofia had been right. Time was short and theirs had run out. Anna took a deep breath, squared her shoulders, and started to descend the stairs. She fought for calm. She had faced looters before. She had faced the King's Guard. She had faced the king himself. She and her cousin would somehow brave this out.

With each of her descending steps, more of the Russian came into view: his sash, his saber, the gold buttons and embellishments on the coat. It was an officer's coat, Anna realized. Was this a bit of hope? Perhaps an officer would treat two noblewomen with respect. Then she remembered General Suvorov's reputation and hope vanished.

As she came to the landing midway down the stairs, the officer came into full view. He had taken two steps into the vestibule and seemed to be waiting for her to descend. He was dark-haired and wore no hat. Beneath a heavy moustache, he was smiling strangely. The eyes were reddish brown.

"Hello, Anna," he said.

Anna could feel the blood draining from her face. Her heart thundered in her chest. Her surroundings began to lift and swirl around her.

She found herself reaching out to the railing to keep from falling. Was this happening? Everything whipped around her as in a whirlpool. Was this possible?

He seemed to wait silently, complacently, while she tried to think. The motion within her head slowed. Her focus cleared. He was still smiling.

Her voice sounded small as she dared to speak, as frail as her aunt's had been. "Walter?"

"In the flesh, cousin."

"Dear God," Anna breathed.

Walter laughed. "Is that all you can say?"

Anna could not speak.

"Thought me dead, did you? *Left* me for dead, I should say. You thought your making a conquest of Lieutenant Boraviecki would solve your problems. It didn't quite work out that way."

"Szymon?"

"Dead. Not without managing to get a shot into me, I grant you. But before he could get off a second shot, I ran him through to the heart."

Anna winced. A man had died to keep her from Walter's control. But she could not think of that now. "What do you want?"

"Ah, straight to the point, cousin! I like that. I came to see that you are not left to die in a burning building, as I had been left."

"You don't think I wish to go with you?"

"You have no choice. Only I can save you now from the slaughter coming this way. Only I—as a Russian officer."

"As a Polish traitor!"

Walter's face darkened. "I'm a realist, Anna. Poland is no match for Russia."

"And you've helped see to that!"

Walter shrugged. He took a step forward. "Aren't you going to welcome me with at least a cousin's innocent kiss?"

Anna's heart tightened and she drew back and up a step. The scene at the pond flashed like a knife through Anna's mind. Her right hand moved to her skirts, where the pistol was hidden. She had fired her father's pistol once. Her father was teaching her how to aim, but her mother put an end to her lessons once she found out. Anna feared she would not even recall how to hold it. And, no matter what Walter had done, she knew she could not bring herself to shoot him.

"Don't worry, Anna," Walter said contemptuously. "I haven't come for you."

"What, then?"

"I've come for my son."

Anna could not move, could not think. What did he know? "Your son is dead. There is no child here."

"I will look for myself. And if he is not here, you will tell me where he is."

As Walter moved forward, Zofia stepped out of the shadows of the reception room and came to within a few paces of her brother. Anna suspected she had been listening to the exchange.

"You have no business here, Walter. Anna has told you: her child is dead. Go to the cemetery if you wish to see him, but leave us alone. We will manage our own escape."

"Ah, Zofia. I have every confidence you will. But I know different about my son. I was just about to tell our cousin here that I ran into our farm manager, Walek, two months ago. He pretended otherwise, but I knew he was one of those foolish legions of peasants who carried scythes into war. He assured me that the child had swallowed no emerald stickpin, that there was no sad funeral, and that my son still lives! I was grateful enough to him that I didn't turn him in to be executed."

"What of it?" Zofia cried. "You have no claim on the child."

"I'm his father! And if he is not here, one of you will tell me where he is." His gaze moved up to Anna. "Anna?"

"He does live," Anna said. "Since I came back to Warsaw, I have not tried to hide the child. But I have not named you as the father. As far as anyone knows, he is Antoni's child. It's *his* name he bears. So you see, Walter, you have no claim, as Zofia says."

"Ah, *as Zofia says*," Walter spat. "The clever Zofia. What a lucky brother I am to have such a clever sister, one who has done me out of my inheritance. You should be proud of her, too, Anna. Coming up with that scheme about the stickpin. Worked like a charm, didn't it? Oh, my sister's full of schemes. Strange, isn't it, how our father fell into the swamp at such an opportune time for her? *She* was at least saved from a marriage to Grawlinski. And I can think of another scheme that makes you terribly beholden to her."

"Walter," Zofia interrupted, "I want you to leave this house."

"Not without my son, and not without telling our sweet cousin here how she came to be a widow."

"What are you talking about?" Anna asked.

"He's talking gibberish, Anna, and I'm going to put him out."

Zofia moved toward her brother.

Anna could not imagine what Zofia had a mind to do, for she surely could not overpower him.

Zofia pushed Walter back toward the door. But this was no helpless servant, easily frightened and bullied. This was a soldier who had seen war. With one arm, Walter threw her to the floor. "You cunning bitch!"

Anna stood helpless on the stairs.

Zofia lifted her head from the floor and threw back her dark hair, which had come undone. "You are an orphan my parents plucked from the gutter only to get grief in the bargain!"

"Your parents' grief came from within their own bloodlines. Who was it who held me back from trying to pull your father out of the quagmire? Who?"

Zofia, flushed with anger, pulled herself to her feet now and began to rush toward her brother.

Anna watched in horror as Walter drew his saber and fixed his eye on Zofia. In that split second, Anna saw the intent in those brutish eyes that had haunted her dreams, the reddish eyes of a devil. He meant to run her through just as he had done to Szymon Boraviecki.

No other thought entered Anna's head until the pistol had been drawn and fired.

Walter stumbled backward, grasping his reddening chest and staring up at Anna, dumbfounded. His eyes closed then, and he fell like a stone to the marble vestibule floor.

"Sweet Jesus," Zofia cried, looking from Walter to Anna and back again. "You killed him. Anna, you killed him."

"I thought he meant to kill you." Anna dropped the pistol and took hold of the railing for support. "I was certain—"

"Oh, he did. You can be sure he did." Zofia ran to the front window in the reception room. "I just pray he had no other soldiers with him," she called.

Anna started down the stairs, moving closer and closer to the man she killed.

"We're lucky, I think he was alone," Zofia said, coming back into the vestibule. "There, there, Anna." She gave her cousin a hug. "Don't look so glum. You saved my life!"

"What did Walter mean, Zofia, when he said you helped make me a widow?"

"I'm sure I don't know."

"You do, I can see it." Anna held her cousin at arm's length. "Walter was the one that day, the sniper who killed Antoni. Wasn't he? And he could only have known about the duel between Antoni and Jan through you. You engineered my husband's death! Isn't that right? Isn't it?"

Zofia pulled free. "I did it for you, darling. I took responsibility for matching you up with Antoni. I didn't know just how despicable he was."

"So you used Walter's . . . attraction to me to free me of a hellish marriage?"

"Yes, exactly. You should be thanking me."

"For doing murder? And in the bargain, didn't you wish to keep Jan from harm, too?"

Zofia shrugged. "It's the old adage about two birds and one stone. You know that one, Anna. But Walter didn't keep the bargain entirely; he allowed Antoni to have his shot. Jan was lucky your husband had such a poor aim."

"Zofia," Anna said, her gaze catching and holding her cousin's, "for whom did you wish to keep Jan from harm? For me, or for you?"

Zofia smiled. "For the one clever enough to win him."

In her second-floor room, Anna quickly changed into a simple brown dress, wearing no underskirts as Zofia had urged. She resecured the combs in her hair that held it atop her head.

She didn't need to question Zofia about Uncle Leo's death. Walter had said enough for Anna to fill in the details. Zofia and Walter had found their father that day he had gone to determine whether it was Jan who had attacked Anna. They had found him in the swamp struggling for his life, and Zofia, who was about to be forced into a marriage she didn't want, had held back her brother, who had his own grudge against his father. They had watched their father die a hideous death. To think they might have rescued him . . . Anna thought she would be ill.

She suddenly became aware of a great cacophony of noise from outside and sprang into movement. There was no time to think about Uncle Leo. And let Zofia wait, Anna thought, impulsively running up to the attic room to look out the window. As soon as she pushed open the door, memories of her son overtook her. "Let Jan Michał be safe," she prayed aloud. "Let him be safe."

Anna was not prepared for what she saw from the window.

Praga was in chaos, its streets filling with peasants, as well as with nobles, many of whom were carrying some treasured furnishing or item of value. Some of the wealthy seemed to be trying to bribe others to help them with their heavily laden carriages, but most of those in flight took no time to listen. They were too concerned with escaping the terrible onslaught.

The streets within Anna's view bulged with people rushing—at least to the extent the crowding allowed—toward the Bridge Vistula that would take them across to the capital. Anna thought it a network of human ants scrambling from some predator to the safety of their community anthill and underground chambers. She could not guess whether the city afforded any real protection from the Russians, but she knew that she and Zofia would have to join that crush of people. And they must do so *soon*.

Praga was afire now. Anna could see two separate columns of black smoke moving with the wind toward the riverfront. As yet, no Russians were in view.

"Anna!" Zofia screamed from downstairs. "What's keeping you?"

"Coming!" Anna flew down the stairs to the second level and ran back to her room to collect her own treasures. She placed the wooden box that contained the crystal dove into a hatbox, adding to it the emerald stickpin, and the opalescent ring—all wrapped in velvet. Lastly, she placed in the box her diary, the record of her years since her parents' deaths.

"Anna!"

Downstairs, Anna found that Zofia had bargained with a hulk of a man to drive the carriage. He grumbled his greeting and offered no assistance. Anna saw that he had only one good eye.

Anna and Zofia climbed into the open carriage and the driver goaded the two nervous horses into the street that would take them down to the bridge. The street was thickening by the moment with persons on foot and an occasional wagon or carriage. Pungent smoke and ash filled the air now, and the booming explosions of artillery were closer, much closer.

"Damn Russian scum!" the driver bellowed.

Anna realized what that simple exclamation meant: Praga had fallen. Death might be imminent. Everyone around them knew that Suvorov was merciless. Anna's left hand clung to the side of the carriage to hold her in her seat. To her right, Zofia knelt on her cushion so as to survey the scene from a higher angle. "Sweet Jesus," she would mutter occasionally, her head turning and eyes darting.

Anna thought of Walter. She and Zofia had dragged him to the cellar and placed him next to his mother. How ironic it was that he had not been told that his mother had died less than an hour before his arrival, and now he lay next to her in death.

The Gronski town house was on the riverfront and not so very far from the bridge, but all of Praga had turned out, it seemed, so that traffic moved at an exceedingly slow rate.

Suddenly there came frenzied, fearful cries from the west moving down toward the river, like waves. "The Russians!" the people screamed in terror. "The Russians!"

And then they were upon the crowd. Anna and Zofia saw them at a distance first, few in number. Anna watched numbly as the swords, sabers, and cutlasses were lifted, catching the dull sunlight before coming down to be reddened with the blood of innocent Polish citizens.

The cool November day had turned hot with the glowing orange wall of fire that moved, like the Russians, in the direction of the Vistula.

The carriage came nearer the bridge now, where several roads converged at its access. Traffic came to a near standstill as all the arteries filled with screaming, crying people. The masses seemed to Anna as the numberless blades of grass on a thick lawn.

"Press on, you idiot!" Zofia shouted at the driver. "These people are like rats running to a mill! Give the whip to the horses, do you hear?"

Although their own lives were in danger, a few peasants in the street turned to watch Zofia rant and rage at the driver.

The carriage picked up speed.

The press of the crowd increased and the carriage rolled over a growing number of unfortunates who had fallen in the street. Anna held her hands to her ears in an attempt to shut out the shrieks of the dying and the gut-wrenching screams of those who clawed their way, panic-stricken, toward the bridge. She could not block out the sounds, however, nor could she close her eyes to the blood upon their carriage wheels. It was more than she could bear.

"Slow down!" Anna screamed, trying to rise from her seat. "Zofia, make him slow!"

"Quiet, you fool!" Zofia cried, pulling her back into her seat. "Do you want to die?"

"No, but I don't want to kill, either."

Zofia fixed her gaze on Anna. "Too late for that, cousin!"

They were but a short distance from the approach to the bridge and in a still tighter crush when several desperate men and women attempted to board the carriage.

"Get out, you filthy swine!" Zofia shouted. The brutish driver cursed the interlopers, too, lashing them with his whip. They fell back into the surging crowd with bleeding faces and torn eyes.

At last, the carriage reached the approach. Here, where each street was depositing its human cargo, traffic all but stopped. "What now, milady?" the driver asked. "There are too many to drive over and it looks like the bridge supports have been torched."

It was true. Anna could see flames licking at the underside of the bridge.

At that moment the mounted Russians seemed to multiply, descending on the heaving, hysterical crowd, slaying everyone about them. The soldiers descended like red locusts, their gold glinting in the sun's glow, mindlessly destroying everything as they moved. Those who couldn't get out of their path were cut down unmercifully. Anna saw a woman rush forth, her baby clutched to her breast. A Russian bore down on her with his curved cutlass, and in an instant she was decapitated, the baby lost to sight.

Anna prayed as she never prayed before. She was convinced now that her own death was imminent. She prayed most for her son and for Jan Stelnicki, hoping that somehow they would survive.

Anna turned her eyes to the left then and found herself staring into the grinning face of a Russian. She caught sight of him just as his massive arm was reaching down into the carriage to lift her out. She struggled to fight him off, calling to Zofia. The more she yelled and pummeled him, the more he laughed.

Zofia demanded that the driver whip him, but he dared not do so.

The soldier had Anna all but lifted out of the carriage when Anna felt Zofia pulling her back.

"Take me, Ivan!" Zofia was crying out in Russian. "Take me!" Anna fell back into her seat, the man's hold released. Her cousin knew this man! She turned to Zofia to find that she had stripped to her waist. The soldier had taken the bait and was now maneuvering his horse to her side of the carriage.

"Take this, Ania," Zofia screamed above the din, thrusting an envelope into her hand. "Go to Paweł's town house on Piwna Street, near Saint Martin's Church! And don't think me so terrible, darling!"

To Anna all of this was unfolding like a nightmare. Her cousin was standing on the carriage seat, her magnificent breasts swaying pendulously for all to see. Had she gone mad?

"Ivan," Zofia cried, "you know that we are allied with Catherine. We must get the carriage to the bridge. You must help us!"

Anna saw his greedy eyes take in Zofia. In a moment he was barking orders to three other soldiers in red who moved in to create an escort. The carriage started to move. How many in their path were run over or slain by the Russians Anna could not guess. She closed her eyes to the horror and prayed the bridge would hold.

When she opened her eyes, it was to see Zofia being lifted up and onto the horse of the bulky Ivan. As her cousin settled herself astride his mount, the paws of the Russian bear moved roughly over her naked breasts. Her blood red skirt fanned out against the horse's white shoulders and belly.

"Zofia!" Anna screamed.

Only her cousin's dark eyes answered her. They seemed to say, *This is how it must be.*

Soon, the wooden planks of the bridge could be heard beneath the carriage wheels. Anna looked to see Zofia and the Russians falling behind the carriage now. "Zofia!" she called again. Her voice was tiny, however, in the roar of the crowd. She realized that Zofia would not be crossing with her. She was remaining with the Russians on the Praga side.

Zofia shouted something Anna could not hear and waved her on.

Anna turned around in her seat, stunned, and certain she would never see her cousin again.

There were hundreds on the bridge so that movement was at a

snail's pace. Intermittently the crowd behind the carriage leaned into it, pushing it forward because they, in turn, were being propelled forward by the myriad souls behind them.

Anna's eyes fell upon the letter Zofia had given her. It was addressed to her. She turned it over to see the red Stelnicki seal. It had been broken.

In the midst of all the horror and death, she opened and read the letter.

It was dated more than two weeks before.

> *My Dearest Anna,*
>
> *Our engagement at Volhynia did not go well. The fears I wrote to you about were not unfounded. I am not far from Warsaw as I write this, but duty forbids me to see you, my love. There is much to be done before the Russian devils come down upon the capital.*
>
> *Keep yourself safe, Anna. My hope is that you have left Warsaw, but if this finds you still there, at least find shelter within the capital itself. Praga will be most unsafe. It is there that the Russian terror will be unbridled and merciless. Seek the protection of the city walls as soon as possible, dearest. And know that I love you more than life itself. Should I survive what is to come—and, God willing, I will survive—I shall make you my bride and Jan Michał my son.*
>
> *All my love,*
> *Jan*

God protect him, Anna prayed. *God protect us all!*

Zofia had been up to her old tricks of intercepting Anna's letters from Jan. How long had she had this one? Why hadn't she heeded his advice? They could have fled Praga long ago.

But there was no time for regrets or contempt for Zofia. Anna's senses were filling with the single-minded conviction that she must survive. The knowledge of Jan's declared love would make her death at that moment an easier one, but she was not about to accept such an end. Her father had often recited the proverb "To believe with certainty, one must begin with doubting." Her doubting days were over. She now knew in her heart that both she and Jan would survive and make a life together.

Anna looked behind her to see the Praga side slowly receding. She caught sight of Zofia's red skirt, a splash of scarlet on a massive painting of unspeakable outrage.

"Help me! Oh, God, please help me!" The cry came from the hysterical mother of two bruised and bleeding boys. While she struggled to carry one and drag the other by the hand, the three were being crushed and mauled by the endless stream of maddened people trying to get past them.

"Here!" Anna shouted, as the carriage began to pass them. "Here, get in! Give me the little one!" Anna took the youngest from the mother's arms. The woman then hoisted the older boy into the carriage, and Anna gave her her hand, helping her aboard.

The driver turned around, whip raised.

"They will ride!" Anna shouted. Her gaze met his single seeing eye.

He looked at her defiantly for a moment, then, with a shrug of his broad shoulders, turned back to the business of driving.

The grateful little family settled into the seat across from Anna.

Anna allowed two old peasant women into the carriage, also. One sat next to Anna and though she made room in her seat for the other, the woman declined, finding space on the floor. Anna wondered whether it was out of deference for the nobility—or that her place on the floor precluded her seeing the unfolding hell about them. In no time their wrinkled, toothless mouths were moving in silent prayer.

Suddenly, there was a great swell of screaming, and the carriage was pushed forward by the masses behind. Anna turned to see the Praga side of the bridge engulfed in a high wall of orange flames. A score of the crowd had caught fire, too, and they were hurling themselves off the bridge into the waters of the Vistula.

Anna's eyes searched for the red of Zofia's skirt. It was not to be found. Had the Russian brute brought her to safety?

The driver whipped the horses, and the carriage moved at a slightly faster rate. Those in front moved to the side or were run down. Those who tried to cling to the carriage suffered the sting of the lash.

Anna stood now and while the driver's hand was in midmotion, she pulled the whip from his grasp. "You're not to kill these people!" she screamed. Without a thought, she threw the whip off to her right and into the river below.

The man's eye widened in shock and anger. Indecision flashed across his face. He had not expected this of Anna.

He dropped the reins. "Well, then, milady," he shouted above the din, "I gather the driving's up to you."

He turned now and jumped from the right side of the carriage into the crowd and was immediately lost from sight.

Anna sat frozen in terror. The carriage ceased any forward movement while the crowds around it continued in their slow surge forward, moving around and past the stalled vehicle.

Above the roar of the panicking mob came the cracking sound of splintering timbers. Anna knew that the fire and the awesome weight of the fleeing hundreds would quickly put the bridge into the river. They would never make it to the Warsaw side. All rational thought deserted her now, giving her over to a palsy of fear.

Anna's hands instinctively went to her hair. The old childhood habit of thrusting her extended fingers through her hair in moments of distress had returned. Years before, her father's understanding and gentle reminders had helped to break her of the habit.

Later, she would swear that at that moment she had heard her father's voice in her ear, the words were so distinct, his tone—at once warm and firm—unobscured by the years: *"Sometimes you must place yourself in the way of destiny."*

The two boys had become hysterical. Collecting herself, Anna stood now and tried to comfort them, assuring the mother they would make it to safety.

Turning, she lifted the peasant woman from the floor and seated her next to the other in her own vacated place. With great difficulty, she climbed down the left side of the carriage, holding tight to it all the while so as not to be pulled free from it amid all the jostling. Slowly, slowly, she made her way to the front and with a Herculean effort, pulled herself up into the driver's seat.

Anna picked up the reins and, miraculously, the frightened and confused horses responded to her signal. The carriage began to move forward. Anna had no time to exult in her success.

Suddenly, the bridge rumbled, cracked, and swayed not more than a few dozen paces behind them. Anna could not help but turn around. The bridge was moving slightly side to side, wriggling like a lazy snake. It was at that moment that part of the structure nearest the Praga side collapsed, sending those closest to the break tumbling from the jagged timbers and into the turbid waters.

Anna turned back. Setting her sights on the city's walls, she urged the horses forward.

The hysteria of the mob, too, seemed to push the carriage farther toward the capital. A few jumped from the imperiled bridge, but most continued to push in one maddened forward heave. The structure swayed precariously, ready at any moment to give way beneath the strain.

The carriage was but a hair's breadth from Warsaw when the bridge gave forth with a great dying groan of splitting timbers and trembled in the balance. The high-pitched cries of a thousand pierced the air.

There swelled then a final, violent wave of people pushing, rushing madly forward, and the carriage was carried with the tide, rolling off the bridge and onto Warsaw soil.

"We're safe," Anna called out joyfully to her passengers. "We're safe!"

Polish soldiers and citizens were waiting to help Anna and the others alight from the carriage.

"Here, take this," Anna said to the mother before they took their leave. She pressed the opalescent ring into the stunned woman's hand. "This will help you start afresh."

The woman started to refuse, but Anna quickly sent her and her children on their way. She gave the emerald stickpin to the old peasant women, who were equally reluctant at first and had to be coerced into accepting.

The crystal bird and her diary remained in the box.

An ear-splitting clamor cleaved the air then, and Anna turned to witness the length of the bridge, with its burden of nobility and peasants, collapse, crashing loudly into the Vistula. The crescendo of heart-tearing screams subsided as hundreds were carried away by the waters.

And yet, there came continued shouts and cries from the Praga side.

Anna stared, her mind unable to process the horror unfolding before her. Though the bridge was gone, Suvorov's Russians on horseback descended in fiercely dense legions, continuing to herd Praga's citizens onto what was left of it and into the cold water below. People tumbled off that broken bridge like so many drops of water from a waterfall.

No story or historical account Anna had ever read prepared her for such a sight.

It was then that Anna spied Zofia in the crowd near the broken bridge on the Praga side. The red skirt atop the white horse was unmistakable. Was she allowing herself to stay with the Russian while he steered good Polish men and women to their deaths? Was she so evil?

No, Anna realized now, Zofia and Ivan themselves had gotten caught up in the inexorable flow of the crowd. The white horse rose up in a great panic as the myriads were pushed toward destruction by the Russian legions descending toward the river.

"May the Madonna help us," Anna prayed aloud, her heart leaping in her chest as she saw the horse, the Russian, and Zofia come to the shore side of the broken bridge and go tumbling in a blur of white and red, red and white, through the air and into the Vistula. Almost immediately they disappeared from view as the waters swallowed them.

"Zofia!" Anna screamed. "Zofia!" She called until her voice gave out. Her cries were lost amid the pandemonium. Zofia had told her once that she would rather ride the whirlwind than lead a long life. Well, she had done that.

And Anna knew that *she* was alive at that moment because of Zofia.

From her days as a child, when her mother had threatened to deny her the crystal dove, Anna had not allowed herself to cry in public.

Now, as all of Poland seemed to dissolve before her eyes, the tears began to roll, slowly, steadily, down her cheeks, splashing onto the simple, brown muslin of her dress.

Epilogue

Life is like the moon—
now dark,
now full.

–POLISH·PROVERB

25 November 1794

Few blank pages remain in my diary now. This will be my last entry.

On the day of the Praga massacre, I managed to take shelter at the town house of Count Potecki, where Lutisha tearfully welcomed me.

Few Polish citizens left on the Praga side of the River Vistula were allowed to live. The burning of the bridge was fortuitous, however, for the Russians were held at bay, allowing the night to cool their red rage. In the morning, the English ambassador to Poland and the papal nuncio crossed the river and secured from Suvorov assurance that the capital would be taken peacefully.

And so it was that Warsaw capitulated without a whimper, and nothing remained of Poland to partition further.

Citizens still cry openly in the streets, for loved ones lost and for Poland, effectively erased from the map of Europe. I have not ventured out, not out of fear or my old aversion to public crying, but because I will not allow my tears to join the people's river of tears. I do not believe that my country can be waved away because someone wills it so. Aunt Stella once said that should Poland be held by a foreign power for a hundred years, her people, her language, her customs, her faith would allow her to endure—and one day live again, like a flower long dormant.

Word has come that my son Jan Michał is safe at Sochaczew. Although my home there still stands, the Gronski Praga town house has been destroyed. I have seen to the burial of the Countess Gronska and her son, Walter. Aunt Stella had not wanted to live to see Warsaw fall; her prayer was answered.

No news has come of Zofia. I can only assume that the River Vistula has taken her.

Count Potecki has arrived home, bringing with him a note from Jan Stelnicki. My love has survived! He writes that he has been wounded, and tells me that I'm not to worry. I do worry. He and my son await my arrival at Sochaczew. His brief note is signed Citizen Stelnicki. *Citizen* Stelnicki? I refuse to believe that his title and nobility can be taken summarily from him for his patriotism. Our nobility, like the Polish spirit of all our people, resides in our souls.

I dreamt of the mythical Jurata last night. I remember how I admired the goddess for daring to break with tradition by marrying a nonmagical being—a man. Perhaps I have more in common with Jurata than my green eyes. I am to marry a man whose nobility has been taken from him. But I do not truly imagine myself another Jurata because my love for Jan is such that it will take no great courage for me to follow my heart.

My crystal dove sleeps once again in its scratched but sturdy box from the Tatras. It has survived so much. I take it now to Sochaczew, where I will live with and for life—with and for the man whom I love.

Anna Maria Berezowska